THE
SHINING
CITY

DAW Fantasy Novels by
FIONA PATTON

The Warriors of Estavia:

THE SILVER LAKE (Book One)
THE GOLDEN TOWER (Book Two)
THE SHINING CITY (Book Three)

The Novels of the Branion Realm:

THE STONE PRINCE
THE PAINTER KNIGHT
THE GRANITE SHIELD
THE GOLDEN SWORD

THE SHINING CITY

Book Three of
The Warriors of Estavia

FIONA PATTON

DAW BOOKS, INC.

DONALD A. WOLLHEIM, FOUNDER
375 Hudson Street, New York, NY 10014
ELIZABETH R. WOLLHEIM
SHEILA E. GILBERT
PUBLISHERS
www.dawbooks.com

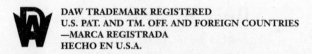

To my little brother Alexander Bernard Potter
for flying pirate ships.
And to my great-nephew Alexander Brian Schauer
for flying pirate ships to come.

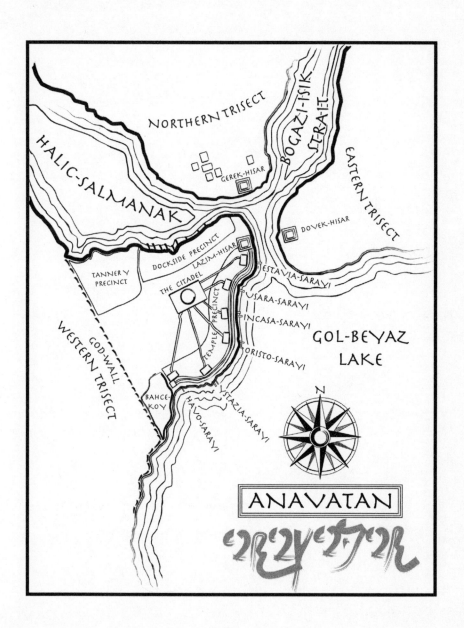

NORTHERN TRISECT

HALIC-SALMANAK

BOGAZI-ISIK STRAIT

EASTERN TRISECT

GEREK-HISAR

DOVEK-HISAR

DOCKSIDE PRECINCT

LAZIM-HISAR

TANNERY PRECINCT

THE CITADEL

ESTA-VIA-SARAYI

USARA-SARAYI

INCASA-SARAYI

TEMPLE PRECINCT

ORISTO-SARAYI

GOL-BEYAZ LAKE

GOD-WALL WESTERN TRISECT

BAHCE-KOY

HAVO-SARAYI

STAZIA-SARAYI

N

ANAVATAN

Estavia-Sarayi

"The first of the Gods to rise, fully realized from the waters of Gol-Beyaz, was Incasa, God of Prophecy, created by the earliest needs of the people to know: will our harvest be bountiful, will our children grown up strong, and will our labors be successful.

"Under Incasa's care the needs of the people changed to: make the harvest bountiful, keep our children strong, and bless our labors with success. Havo, God of the Seasons, Oristo, God of the Hearth, Usara, God of Healing, and Ystazia, God of the Arts, arose with this change.

"When the Gods built the shining city of Anavatan for the people, Estavia, God of Battles, came into being as their needs changed once again to: protect our bounteous harvest, our strong children, and our successful labors.

"The God of Creation and Destruction was formed in answer to new changes, but in the early days of Its being no one knew for certain what those changes were, not even the young God Itself. Those days were fraught with tension and confusion."

—The Chronicles of Anavatan: City of the Gods. Book twenty-eight: The Age of Creation and Destruction. By: Ihsan, First Scribe to Ystazia, God of the Arts

"Feed them, clothe them, and teach them, but don't expect them to go where you want them to once they're grown. Children are more stubborn than donkeys. That's why you need a lot of them to make sure there's someone left behind to tend the bar.

"Gods are no different."

—Niklon, owner of the Kedi-Meyhane Inn and Tavern,
Western Dockside Precinct

GOL-BEYAZ LAKE SHIMMERED in the moonlight. As its silvery glow reflected in the hundreds of market fountains, courtyard pools, and tiled reservoirs across Anavatan, the God of Prophecy rose from the waves until He towered above the skyline. His snow-white gaze took note of every unbound spirit flickering in every glittering pool. Alone, each one was no more than a tiny spark of possibility, but together they could destroy a city.

Or create a God.

Six years ago, Incasa had manipulated just such a gathering to bring the God-child, Hisar, into being. Three young street thieves—Brax, Spar, and Graize—caught in the crossfire of Its birth, had become Its protectors and Its teachers, standing by Its side as It took Its first steps toward adulthood. Incasa had manipulated that also. Now, with a new gathering of spirits arising from a cavernous darkness and the enemies of Anavatan massing on every front, it was time for Hisar and Its three companions to take the field in the roles Incasa had prepared for them: as Champions of the Gods' Shining City.

Two of them, Brax and Spar were well on their way. Brax, at twenty-one, was already a fully ordained ghazi-priest of Estavia, and Spar, despite his stubborn refusal to bend to anyone's authority save his own, was carving out his destiny as a powerful seer in the service of Hisar Itself. Only Graize remained unconvinced, but Incasa was not concerned. Long ago, a delicate prophecy of hope and companionship had been born as two figures standing on a snow-capped mountain ridge. It was finally time to bring that prophecy into being—to set their feet on the path that would lead them there at last.

The God of Prophecy turned His pale gaze inward, seeing both rain and fog on the horizon. Rain was the dominion of Havo, wielded by the Harvest God to create growth and life, but fog belonged to Incasa. Opaque and unknowable, it was the most ancient symbol of prophecy. It masked the future, and because of that, it made it malleable; and Incasa was the God of Malleable.

Reaching out, He caught up each and every prophecy that had formed Hisar. Weaving them together with the events that would soon engulf His city, He fashioned them into a single vision of water echoing in a cavernous darkness and cast it into the future where two powerful and subtle prophets would be sure to see it: one willing, the other unwilling, but both unable to resist it. That was the way of prophets, He mused. They were like cats crouched before a tiny hole in the sand. Eventually, they had to stick a paw in it. It's what they were.

Rising up above the waves until He hovered in a shaft of silvery moonlight, Incasa passed one last glance across Anavatan. To His unfathomable gaze, the lines of responsibility and obligation forged between the Gods and their sworn followers crisscrossed the city like bands of fire, but here and there, a new signature was steadily growing. The unsworn were beginning to turn their attention toward the young God of Creation and Destruction, and It was beginning to turn Its attention toward them.

Incasa nodded to Himself. Hisar was almost ready to take the field as well. As a thin tendril of fog whispered along the Bogazi-Isik Strait to the north, and rain clouds began to gather to the south, He returned to the depths of Gol-Beyaz with a satisfied expression.

✦

Across the city, Hisar crouched in the shadows of a dilapidated warehouse, remaining absolutely still until It was certain that Incasa was gone. Then, shaking out the wings of Its dragonfly seeming in a shower of iridescent brilliance, It returned Its own gaze to a crude figure of a tower etched into the base of the wall. Changing to His golden seeming, Hisar traced the outline, feeling the faintest thread of power trickle back to It through His fingertips. The tower. His symbol.

He shivered with pleasure.

The tower figures had been cropping up all over Anavatan in the last few weeks, scratched into the shadowy recesses of the Dockside Precinct wharfs or on the worn sides of the great wooden vats in the Tannery Precinct. Seeking them out had become Hisar's favorite nighttime game. He'd found them on roof tiles and on windowsills, on awning poles and on doorjambs. Many were carved into the undersides of the dozens of loose cobblestones that littered the streets, some tucked right up against the walls of hostels and camis across the city. This night He'd even found one scratched onto a pebble and tossed into the main fountain before the Derneke-Mahalle Citadel itself. Accompanying each one was a tiny seed of power that sparkled against His fingertips like fire. It made Him hungry and a little frantic, driving Him out into the darkness to find them, night after night.

Now He rubbed the side of His face against the carved figure, feeling it tingle against His cheek before an accompanying buzz deep within His chest caused Him to snap His luminescent gaze around to the south. Spar was awake.

Returning to the dragonfly-seeming, It leaped joyously into the air and, with a whirl of wings, headed for Estavia-Sarayi.

✦

Standing on top of the Battle God's armory tower, a blond-haired youth wearing the blue tunic of Cyan Infantry Company stood, staring out past Estavia-Sarayi's temple walls to the sleeping city beyond. A large red dog pressed against his side, and he stroked its ears fondly before returning his attention to the streets below. This was his favorite time of night: after the merchants and artisans had laid down their tools and before the bakers and fishmongers had taken up theirs. When everyone else was wrapped in dreams, he could be alone with his own.

Earlier that night, a dream of a mountain path rising out of the fog and water sparkling in a cavernous darkness had awakened him. He'd lain on his small pallet for several moments, staring out the latticed window, before rising. Then, moving as quietly as possible so as not to awaken his abayon sleeping in the next room, he'd thrown on an old tunic and headed outside, the dog padding silently behind him.

A faint tingling whispered through his body, and he lifted his face to the spring air as a fluttering of wings against his cheek heralded the arrival of Hisar. Words echoed in his mind.

Do the Gods dream, Spar?

The question echoed in his mind and he frowned. "I don't know, Hisar," he answered aloud. "You're nearly a God. Do you dream?"

The fluttering coalesced into a male close to his own age of fifteen, with golden honey-colored skin, almond-shaped gray eyes fashioned to resemble Graize's eyes, blond hair much like Spar's own only streaked with silver, and features modeled on Brax. As the dog woofed a greeting, Hisar hovered in midair for a moment, then, as Spar set a red ceramic bead on a leather cord about His neck, His bare feet touched the battlements with a faint slap of nearly physical flesh against stone.

"Yes," He answered, wrapping power about Himself until He'd fashioned a golden tunic similar to Spar's.

"What do you dream about?"

"Lots of things. A flock of white birds with teeth like knives flying north, a flock of brown birds that spit flaming arrows from their mouths flying south, horses made of grass joined with horses made of mist, and both sweeping east. Water sparkling in darkness and a snow-capped mountain path disappearing into the fog."

Hisar cocked His head to one side. "They're symbols, right?" He asked, His tone pitched to reflect His body's age. "Prophetic symbols?"

Spar nodded. "The birds are probably symbols of our enemies. The white birds are the warships of King Pyrros of Skiros and the brown birds are the warships of Duc Bryv of Volinsk."

"And the horses are the Yuruk nomads of the Berbat-Dunya wild lands and the Petchan hill people of the Gurney-Dag Mountains?"

"Yes."

"Then why couldn't I just see them like that?" Hisar demanded. "Why do I have to waste time with birds that aren't birds and horses that aren't horses?"

Spar gave a dismissive shrug. "Because prophecy is more than just seeing things. It's the odds and probabilities of the future interpreted by our own experiences. Have you ever seen a fleet of foreign warships in full sail?"

"No."

"Then how do you expect to know what they are if they show up in your prophecy? You have seen a flock of white birds. Maybe when you actually see the ships, they'll become ships.

"But I doubt it." Spar turned his gaze to the south before Hisar could voice another protest. "Do you remember the map I showed you? The one in the Citadel?"

"Yes." In the last nine months, Spar and Hisar had visited much of the city's Western Trisect, showing the young God to the people and showing them to Him.

"King Pyrros has taken the islands south of Gol-Beyaz in the Deniz-Hadi Sea."

Hisar nodded. "He's Panos of Amatus' father. She's a powerful seer. I remember watching Panos speak prophecy with Prince Illan at Cvet Tower in Volinsk. Her abilities are very strong."

"Yes. Pyrros is waiting for word from Volinsk to send his fleet of white birds against our southern watchtower of Anahtar-Hisar."

"But you told me that Anahtar-Hisar couldn't be taken."

"It can't. A third of our own fleet's down there to defend it. But that's a third that won't be berthed at Anavatan when the ice on the northern Deniz-Siya Sea melts and the Volinski ships—your brown birds—sail against the city. They're the real threat, but if we bring our entire fleet north, King Pyrros will attack the south. He's there to split our forces and make us weak."

"And the Yuruk and the Petchans?"

"The same. They've made an alliance with Volinsk for trade and livestock and access to the silver lake once Volinsk has defeated us."

"But we have the Gods and Their Wall," Hisar pointed out.

As one, they turned to the western skyline. From this distance, the most ancient and formidable of Anavatan's defenses, cradling the city's landward side, seemed little more than a faint indigo glow, but Spar knew that the God-Wall's ten-foot-thick, thirty-foot-high stones were topped by the power of the Gods. It raised its protection another forty feet, shielding the people from both physical and metaphysical enemies alike. The wall's stone parapets dropped sharply as it left Anavatan, snaking along the western shore of Gol-Beyaz to become little more than an anchor for the Gods' power at its end. This allowed the villagers along its length to reach to the western fields and pasturelands while still maintaining the Gods' formidable protection.

"The God-Wall will not hold."

Spar shook his head. Years ago Illan of Volinsk, a powerful seer and enemy of Anavatan had sent Spar these words to rattle him and make him doubt his own abilities. But Spar had won through, and in the last six years he'd traveled the wall's entire length with his adopted abayon, Kemal and Yashar of Estavia-Sarayi's Cyan Infantry Company. He'd stood on it, slept on it, and dreamed of it, but he'd never taken it for granted. The tiniest of the wild land spirits had worked their way through it once before when he'd been nine years old and living on the streets of the city's Dockside Precinct. They'd become a swarm of destructive power that had sucked out the life of everything in their path. If they could get through, so could other things. Bigger things. He knew the wall was not impregnable. Of all the people of Anavatan, he knew it best. He didn't need some foreign enemy to remind him of it. But the God-Wall was not his problem.

As he returned his attention to the present, he saw Hisar watching him patiently and gave a cynical snort in response to the young God's point.

"The wall's only strong if the Gods are strong," he countered. "And the Gods are only strong if the people are strong."

"But the people are behind the wall and the Gods," Hisar answered, a smug expression on His face. "So they are strong."

"The wall has gates, so the wall is vulnerable. The Gods have distractions and agendas of Their own, so the Gods are vulnerable. And the people are . . ." Spar shrugged again. "People. Physical. We're always vulnerable." He swept an arm toward Gol-Beyaz, glittering with the power of a thousand silver lights in the moonlight. "Anavatan needs free access for travel and trade, so it's vulnerable to the seaward sides. That's why there's two fleets coming from the north and the south."

"But there are three watchtowers to the north, and two to the south," Hisar insisted. "Aren't they enough?"

"They would be if we were fighting one side at a time. There're only so many Warriors to hold the line and so many Gods to stand beside them. That's why you're dreaming of birds and horses. They're going to come at us from all three sides at once."

"But we'll repel them?"

Spar turned a somber expression on the young God. "I don't know."

Hisar's golden brows drew down to meet in a vee at the bridge of His nose, much as He'd seen Spar's draw down in the past. "But you're a seer; can't you see it?"

"No. There's dozens of possible futures forming up right now; hundreds of dozens. The future's like the weather: it changes all the time. No one can see who'll win through yet, not Estavia's Sable Company seers, not even the Oracles of Incasa. Maybe Incasa can, I dunno," Spar added. "He hasn't said."

"The people of Anavatan are sure of it even though they have no prophecy. I've heard them say so in the marketplaces," Hisar countered.

"The people believe in the strength of the Gods and the Warriors of Estavia. It's enough for them, but it's not the same thing."

"So the only thing you people—you seers—do know—the only thing any of you can actually see—is the threat?" Hisar shook His head, His golden hair flying about His face with the movement. "What good is that?"

"It gives us a chance to ready a defense. You saw the sea chain the smiths of Ystazia are making?"

"You know I did; we visited their workshops last week." Hisar cocked His head to one side. "They asked me to send strength to their work and weakness to the Volinski sailors. People ask me that sort of thing a lot, but I don't know how," He added in a petulant tone.

"You will one day," Spar said absently. "When the chain's done," he continued, "they'll stretch it across the mouth of the Halic-Salmanak at the first sign of danger. That'll protect the western wharfs."

"But what'll protect the temple wharfs?"

"Estavia's fleet."

"The fleet that's down by a third in strength?"

Spar gave his familiar one-shouldered shrug. "Ystazia's shipwrights have been hard at work, too. Maybe they'll be done in time."

"Maybe? You haven't seen that either?"

"No."

"So, what *have* you seen?"

"Ants racing around an overturned anthill mostly. But ants going the same way at least."

"More symbols. Very not helpful," Hisar sneered.

"As helpful as birds and horses."

Hisar snorted at him. "The enemy has seers, too, you know," He pointed out. "Petchan sayers, Yuruk wyrdin, Skirosian oracles, and Volinski sorcerers. Isn't it likely that they've already seen all your preparations?"

"Yes. Just like we've seen theirs."

"But they won't break off even though they don't have the . . . what's it called, element of surprise, now?"

Spar shrugged again. "The element of surprise is only one tactic in a battle. They think they have the strength of numbers enough to beat us. They think that'll be tactic enough. They want control of Gol-Beyaz Lake, and they're committed to taking it. Seers aren't commanders; they're scouts gathering intelligence. Incasa and His priests will mask and muddy the waters the enemy draws their prophecy from, like tainting a well. They'll do the same to us. We'll all sift through it looking for droplets of clear truth, making our predictions and giving our advice, but in the end, the enemy commanders'll send their soldiers and sailors against us and our commanders'll send our soldiers and sailors to repel them; offense and defense."

"That's a pretty martial point of view coming from a seer," Hisar pointed out.

"I've been living in a martial temple for six years. It rubs off."

The young God turned away. Glancing out across the city once more, He frowned. "I don't want people attacking my city," He said after a moment.

Spar raised a blond eyebrow. *"Your* city?"

Hisar's gold-flecked gray eyes flashed with a hint of the Gods' more common silver. "Yes, *my* city," He retorted. "I'm supposed to be a God of Anavatan. That makes it mine. But I don't even know how to protect it."

He raised His head. *"A CHILD OF GREAT POTENTIAL STILL UNFORMED STANDING ON THE STREETS OF ANAVATAN; THE TWIN DOGS OF CREATION AND DESTRUCTION CROUCHED AT ITS FEET,"* He intoned, allowing His voice to take on an echoing richness He rarely employed.

Spar nodded as the lien forged by the oaths he'd sworn to the young God nine months ago sent a thrill of power traveling along his spine. "Yes," he agreed. "The child is ringed by silver swords and golden knives, and its eyes are filled with fire. It draws strength from Anavatan's unsworn and was born under the cover of Havo's Dance."

"That was my first prophecy," Hisar observed, His voice returning to normal. "Seer Freyiz of Incasa's own temple said so. I was formed of wild land spirits and birthed by Havo's spring storms six years ago. I was raised by knives and swords in the battles between the Yuruk and the Warriors of Estavia a year later. The God of Creation and Destruction, that's what I am. That's what Incasa saw, and that's what he told His priests."

"That's what Incasa *wants* you to be," Spar corrected. "Is it what you want?"

Hisar shook His head with an irritated gesture. "I don't know. I don't even know what it means. Create what? Destroy what?"

He scowled. "*A CHILD ARMED AND ARMORED, AND A SHIMMERING TOWER, STRONG AND DEFENSIBLE, RAISED TO DEFEND THE CITY OF THE GODS, STANDING BEFORE A SNOW-CLAD MOUNTAIN COVERED IN A CRIMSON MIST OF DANGER AND DEATH.* Another old woman's prophecy about me." He sniffed. "At least that one makes a bit more sense, but how'm I supposed to do it? I can't even send strength to a sea chain. Where am I supposed to stand and who'm I supposed to stand against; they're coming from three sides. If I'm a God, why don't I know this and why can't I do the same things the others can?" He shot Spar a resentful glare. "You're my priest. You're supposed to figure this stuff out for me," He added accusingly.

The thrill of power up Spar's spine became an itch and he pressed his hand against his chest with a scowl. "Stop that," he ordered. "I'm not a priest."

"You swore oaths to me. You were my first. That makes you my First Priest."

Together, they turned to stare out at the night sky to the west. Somewhere out there was the one other person who'd sworn oaths to the immature God, oaths made in a moment of rage and jealousy, but still oaths: Graize, Hisar's first abayos and Spar and Brax's earliest enemy, whose prophetic ability and ties to Hisar rivaled Spar's own. He was hiding out there in the wild lands somewhere, a dangerous and unstable enemy that would have to be turned or destroyed before they could win any kind of lasting security.

"Why are there always mountains?" Hisar wondered out loud. "Have *you* ever seen mountains in prophecy?"

Spar considered sidestepping the question, but, as a chill of foreboding whispered through his mind, he nodded. "Tonight. I saw a mountain path, just like you did."

Hisar straightened eagerly. "What do you think it means?"

Again Spar considered sidestepping the question, and again he chose not to. "I don't know yet," he admitted. "Mountains usually mean challenges—really, really big challenges," he added. "And paths mean choices. Choices create the future. So, a challenging path leading to a . . . challenging future probably," he hazarded.

"And the fog?"

"Fog means the choices are still hidden, still unformed."

"Like me," Hisar grumbled. Kicking at the parapet, He grimaced as His toe passed partially through the stone. "I'm sick of being unformed," He complained.

"Me, too. Be patient."

"Why?"

"Because."

"That's no answer."

"It's the only answer. The future takes its time, and even the Gods can't rush it."

"If I was the God of Time, I could rush it."

"But you aren't the God of Time, are you?" Spar leaned his elbows on the stone parapet with an amused expression. "There is no God of Time. Time holds its own dominion, and even Incasa can't cheat it. Like I said, you'll just have to be patient and wait like the rest of us." With that, he turned toward the tower stairs. "Now I'm going back to bed. Brax wants my help training the new temple delinkon in the morning, and he'll give me more grief than I want to put up with if I'm not rested."

Hisar gave an unsympathetic sniff. "You could always beg off; say you have to go have a vision or something."

"I could. But I don't lie to Brax. He's my kardos. He's family."

A melancholy expression came and went in Hisar's eyes before He turned to peer down at the darkened courtyards below. "He's down there, you know," He said quietly. "Practicing even though it hurts him to do it. I can feel it." He pressed His hand to His chest in unconscious imitation of the sworn—those who had given their oaths to the Gods. Hisar's connection to Brax—created when, driven by hunger, the young God had attacked him on the battlements five years ago—was a touchy subject and not one He and Spar discussed very often. "He keeps going until his whole world is thick with pain," He continued. "He should rest, but he can't; Estavia's lien is burning inside him too brightly."

"She frets," Spar answered. "Ever since he got captured by . . ." He paused, unwilling to speak Graize's name in this regard. ". . . the Petchans last year She can't leave him in peace; She's like a hen afraid a fox will get at her favorite chick."

"The Petchans have the muting effect," Hisar acknowledged. "I faced it, too." His expression darkened. "I hate it," He spat. "It cut me off from Graize. It cut Estavia off from Brax. She's afraid of losing him again, but She'll burn him out if She's not careful."

"Brax is strong. He'll be all right."

"But . . ."

Spar chopped his hand down in a sharp gesture. "It's his choice, Hisar. He swore his oaths to Her; he loves Her. He's Her Champion; her favorite, just like Kaptin Haldin was all those centuries ago."

Hisar's almond-shaped eyes narrowed. "Yes, you've told me those stories, and it sounds to me like Kaptin Haldin was the first one She drew energy from to gain form just like I did with Brax. And if Kaptin Haldin's essence tasted anything like Brax's, which I'll bet it did," He added tactlessly, "then he probably met his end because She sucked him dry and then burned him out."

"Even if She did, he'd have let Her," Spar retorted. "And so would Brax. They're Champions. It's expected of them."

Hisar frowned. "I wouldn't expect that of you," He pointed out.

Despite the seriousness of the conversation, Spar's mouth quirked up in a half-smile. "I'm not a Champion. Apparently I'm a First Priest."

"But . . ."

Spar shook his head. "There's no buts. Besides, Estavia's got thousands of warriors and militia from one end of Gol-Beyaz to the other. That should be enough for Her."

"It isn't," Hisar insisted. His young face drew down in a pout that made Him seem even younger. "And it's not enough for that lot either," He added, waving one arm to take in the entire temple. "They made him a ghazi-warrior at sixteen, and then a ghazi-priest right after that. They named him Ikin-Kaptin and put him in charge of a patrol last year, the youngest officer ever."

Spar shrugged. "People follow him."

"Because he's *Her* Champion?"

Hisar's sarcastic tone was tinged with jealousy and Spar raised an eyebrow at Him in response. "No, because he's him. People are drawn to him because he gives himself fully to whatever he believes in; you know that. The temple commanders are drawn to him too. He's got strength."

"So, what's it going to be this season, then?" Hisar insisted, "a full kaptincy? And after that, what—command of the entire temple?"

"I didn't know Marshal Brayazi was that close to retirement," Spar answered sarcastically.

"Whatever. They still want to pile even more responsibility on him; I've heard them talking about it."

Spar stilled another foreboding chill that worked its way up his spine. "You shouldn't eavesdrop," he said distractedly.

Hisar just snorted at him. "How else am I going to learn things? And don't change the subject. They're putting too much on him all at once; so is *She*."

"He wants it," Spar replied quietly. "He always has."

"He'll crumble under the weight of it. He's already starting to fall."

Spar straightened. "Then we'll just have to help him carry it," he said, his voice firm. "Because he won't put it down."

"But . . ."

"No." Spar chopped one hand down. "War is coming, Hisar. Our enemies are gathering and our defenses are strengthening Estavia's resolve. She won't be put off, and neither will Brax." His expression softened. "Don't start fretting, all right? We won't be put off either. Reaching out, he lifted the bead from around Hisar's neck. "Why don't you go flying or something," he suggested, attempting a lighter tone. "It'll be hours before dawn."

"I could go looking for more tower symbols."

Spar nodded. He and Hisar had found the first one together months ago, carved on the side of a horse trough on Kedi Caddesi. "How many did you find tonight?" he asked.

"Three." Hisar cast him a sideways look. "Or I could go west, into the Berbat-Dunya wild lands," He mused.

Spar maintained an even expression. "You could."

"But you don't want me to."

"It's your choice."

"But you don't *want* me to."

Spar sighed. "I don't want you to get hurt. Graize is crazy."

"He made me. I know where to find him. You've looked; I know you have, the way the seers do when their eyes go white, and through your own way, in the dark place when your eyes go black, but you can't find him."

"The wild land hides his movements," Spar acknowledged.

"Not from me."

Spar shook his head. "He'll reject you, just like he always does."

"He promised that he'd never be gone from me again. I'll make him remember that. We need him," Hisar added in a firm tone. "I need him."

"I know, Hisar."

"It's the only way to keep him and Brax from killing each other."

"I *know*, Hisar."

The force of Spar's reply sent the young God back a step. "Maybe I'll just go looking for those white bird-ships instead," He said, attempting a flippant tone of voice to cover His hurt feelings.

Spar sighed. "Just be careful," he said in a gentler tone.

The young God gave a disdainful sniff. "They can't hurt me," He retorted, His voice dripping with a condescension that matched the age of his seeming.

"Be careful anyway."

"Yes, Aba." Spinning about, Hisar's male form vanished to be replaced by a shimmering metallic dragonfly. It circled Spar's head for a single heartbeat, illuminating his face in a golden light before taking wing over the battlements.

Watching It disappear into the clouds above, Spar draped the red ceramic bead around his own neck.

"He'll crumble under the weight of it."

"No, he won't."

He's already starting to fall."

Spar's eyes narrowed. He'd protected Brax from his self-imposed destiny as a warrior-priest with a huge target on his forehead for six years, and he wasn't about to stop now. Brax would *not* fall.

He turned. "Come, Jaq."

Refusing to glance down at the courtyard below, Spar headed for the armory stairs, the dog padding obediently along behind him. As they disappeared through the doorway, his eyes slowly darkened until the blue was obliterated completely by the black of his own private prophetic seeking. Brax would *not* fall, and he and Graize would *not* kill each other. Spar would see to it as he always had.

Somehow.

✦

Step, strike, strike. Hold. Step, strike. Turn, block, strike. Faster. Faster, strike, step. Breathe, breathe the pain away, breathe. Slowly.

Estavia's lien buzzing through him like a furious swarm of bees, Brax advanced across the darkened training yard. The small shield strapped to his left arm was an encumbrance he'd managed to integrate into his attack months ago, but the residual pain and weakness in his right leg was a constant source of frustration. Now, he paused just long enough to allow the trembling in the thigh to ease.

"You're only twenty-one years old and you're acting like an old man," he berated himself. *"Concentrate."*

"The injury was a deep one. It will take time to heal." Chief Physician Samlin's dry voice retorted in his mind. *"You're lucky. The sword bit deep into the muscle but missed the tendons. You'll walk, you'll fight, but not if you don't rest."*

"I can't rest."

She won't let me.

Unspoken words, barely even thought. Estavia was the God of Battle; the only response She knew to weakness or to danger was to fight. And the danger was growing all around them. He had to be ready to face it. But where? There were too many battlefields. He couldn't hold the line everywhere at once. He had to make a stand somewhere.

Her lien burning through his veins with a renewed sense of urgency, he raised his sword once again, seeking clarity in the familiar motions of attack and defense.

"What did you do?"

"I took them away from you."

The memory of Graize's words spoken nine months ago—the last time they'd crossed swords and Brax had lost—whispered, unwanted, through his mind, burning with an intensity that rivaled Estavia's lien.

As he advanced across the yard, he acknowledged his enemy with a snarl: Graize; the weakness and the danger that drove him onward. Somehow, the stand he took had to be against that weakness and against that danger. Somehow he had to defeat it, defeat Graize, once and for all.

A stab of pain shooting up his leg as his foot twisted on an uneven bit of flagstone pulled him from his thoughts, and he clamped his teeth down on an involuntary hiss. Stretching out the leg, he waited for the pain to ease.

He'd been at Estavia's temple for six years, ever since he'd sworn his oaths on the streets of Anavatan to save Spar and himself from the spirits of the wild lands. He'd seen countless battles since, but the most debilitating injury he'd taken had come from Graize: petty thief, street seer, trickster, liar, and rival from their childhood turned enemy commander.

And it had been nothing compared to Graize's most damaging blow when he'd somehow cut Brax off from Estavia's presence nine months ago, leaving him to face an echoing emptiness alone. Spar and Hisar had saved him, given him back to Estavia, but the memory remained, weakening them both, God and Champion. If it could happen once . . .

He straightened with a savage expression. It would not happen again. Graize would never get the chance again.

Strike, strike, step, block, step. Breathe.

A low line of rosebushes marked the eastern edge of the infantry's central training yard. When his bare foot touched earth, Brax turned and headed south toward the commissary building. Focusing on his breathing, ignoring the pain, he struggled to keep his mind on task, but as the late night breeze brought him the scent of new plantings, his mind wandered again.

Word had come down that Havo's farmers had broken ground four days ago. In less than a week, the Seasonal God's shepherds would be moving their flocks to their summer pastures. Far to the west, the Petchan and Yuruk shepherds would be doing the same. After that, their riders would be free to make raids against the western villages and the Warriors of Estavia would move out to protect them and their livestock as they had every year. Only this year, they would also be going north and south, concentrating their strength wherever Estavia's Sable Company seers believed the threat would be the greatest. And the threat was the greatest everywhere.

Pausing to brush a lock of damp hair from his face, Brax glanced across the courtyard to the temple's main fountain, sparkling brilliant silver in the moonlight and beyond that to the Seer's Shrine. He didn't envy Sable Company. As the months had passed, even the feeblest of the city's street seers had seen the signs of danger looming at every turn. Throughout the winter the people had flocked to their temples demanding answers. The temples had gone to the Gods and finally received a response they hadn't heard for centuries.

"Prepare for invasion."

Anavatan and the villages along Gol-Beyaz Lake had exploded in hysterics, but under the temples' firm leadership, they'd finally calmed down enough to swing into action, building defenses, stockpiling supplies, drilling militia to face the invaders coming by land, building new ships and recruiting sailors to face the invaders coming by water, and training anyone and everyone who might have even the slightest sensitivity to prophecy to overcome the muting effect of the Petchan sayers; throwing their strength behind their Gods, who in turn labored alongside Their followers. If the people were strong, the Gods were strong. If the people were weak; if the people weren't ready . . .

He shook his head, splattering a line of sweat into his eyes. They would be ready, he told himself sternly. The people would be strong, and so the Gods would be strong.

He glanced across the darkened training yard. Since the beginning of winter, the ranks of warrior-delinkon at Estavia-Sarayi had more than doubled as the Battle God had scooped up recruits by the handful. Every senior ghazi had been roped into their education including Estavia's Champion. Brax had thrown himself into their training with a single-minded intensity, sometimes drilling up to five troops a day, driving his body into exhaustion to still the constant, frantic buzzing of Estavia's lien. They would also be ready. They would also be strong. But would he?

Step strike, step strike.

He had to be.

Brax carried on across the yard, feeling Estavia's lien travel through his body and along his arm to spark across his sword She'd returned to him five years ago at the feet of Her temple battlements after he'd lost it in the waters of Gol-Beyaz. The worn leather grip and comforting weight of the weapon calmed him and, by the time he'd finished a complete circuit, passing the commissary, armory tower, and infantry barracks, he was bathed in sweat; the pain in his leg radiated up through his injured elbow to thrum across his forehead, but Her lien had eased enough for him to slow, and finally stop. Gulping air through his mouth, he sheathed the sword with deliberate care, then collapsed against the side of the small training yard fountain.

It was only then that he noticed the figure standing, half hidden, behind a tall cinar tree at the edge of the rose garden. He squinted at it.

"Brin?"

Detaching from the shadows, his bi-gender friend and occasional lover and fellow Cyan Company ghazi-priest, stepped forward with a smirk. "I knew I should have worn a less identifying perfume."

Bending down, Brax struggled to bring his breathing under enough control for speech. "Where's Bazmin?" he asked finally.

"Asleep." Brin nodded toward his sword. "It's coming well. You're moving with a lot more flexibility in the leg."

"Glad it looks that way. Not in the arm, though."

"What does Samlin say?"

"The same thing he always says: be patient." Brax straightened. "Train mindfully."

"You?" Brin scoffed. "You might as well ask the storms of Havo's Dance to wreak havoc mindfully."

"Funny."

✦

"Overdo it and I'll chain you to the bed myself!"

Chief Physician Samlin's warning echoing in his ears, Brax stood in Calmak-Koy's small practice yard, dressed in leathers. His left arm was strapped tightly to his chest and he wove his sword back and forth in a series of awkward, chopping motions, testing the restrictions caused by the bindings. Every pass to the right pulled him off-balance with a streak of pain, but as he shifted his swing to compensate, he kept his expression carefully neutral. This was the first time he'd been allowed out for limited training since coming to the hospital village two months ago, and he'd no intention of giving the physicians hovering nearby the excuse of a little pain to rescind their permission. Estavia's agitated presence had been burning a hole in his chest for days. He needed to train, to move, to do something, anything, to ease the constant, nagging feeling that he should be out on the grasslands fighting the Petchans with Cyan Company.

Before him, his training partner, a retired Indigo Company ghazi-priest turned hospice instructor named Lerek, raised his sword. "Are you ready, Ghazi-Champion?" he asked, acknowledging Estavia's favoritism with somber formality.

Brax nodded sharply. Raising his own sword, he cleared his mind of distractions, both physical and mental, as the man advanced.

Half an hour later, they called a halt by mutual agreement. Both were drenched in sweat and breathing hard. Fighting to keep his hand from shaking, Brax signaled a healer-delinkos to remove the bindings on his arm as Lerek shook his head.

"If ferocity and a downright terrifying expression were all that was needed, you'd sweep the field, Ghazi."

Brax gave a sour half smile in return. "Tell them," he panted, jerking his head at the crowd of physicians hovering outside the circle.

Lerek shrugged. "They're afraid you'll pull your stitches out and undo all their healing."

"I won't."

"You did."

Brax spared a glance at the blood trickling down his leg and swore as the crowd of physicians swarmed about him at once.

They hadn't allowed him to even pick up a sword for another three weeks.

Brin coughed loudly, pulling Brax out of his reverie. "So, have you finished being patient and training mindfully for one night?"

Estavia's lien purring sleepily within him, Brax nodded. "For now," he answered, unstrapping the shield from his left arm. His elbow felt numb and heavy, and he thrust his hand into his belt with a grimace.

Brin watched the movement with a carefully neutral expression. "Ready for bed, then? Dawn comes early, and we have a host of young delinkon eager to catch their ghazon napping tomorrow."

Brax smiled. Training at dawn or not, bed only meant one thing to Brin. "Nearly," he replied, wiping the sweat from his eyes as he glanced at the commissary. "I'm hungry."

Brin's eyes twinkled. "I'll come with you. I'd hate to lose you to some server of Oristo besotted by your beauty or some scholar of Ystazia skulking about wanting to learn what being the Champion of Estavia feels like."

Brax snorted. Six years ago Spar had shown him an illustration of Estavia's first Champion, the legendary Kaptin Haldin, with lines of red-and-golden power streaming from his body. At the time Brax had wondered what that had felt like, and now he knew.

"On a bad day it feels like all the Champion's organs are being slowly torn out of his body in long, thin strands," he answered.

Brin gave him an unimpressed eye roll. "And on a good day?"

Brax grinned. "Like sex, only a thousand times more powerful."

"Now there's a challenge. Still . . ." Brin sighed dramatically. "I think you might be right. Food must come first. I could use a bit of toast and marmalade. I'm famished from just watching you destroy all our enemies."

Brax's expression darkened. "Only one enemy," he corrected.

"Then I only need one piece of toast." Refusing to be drawn into Brax's mood, Brin tucked Brax's good arm in the crook of one elbow and led him firmly toward the commissary, blithely ignoring his attempt not to limp.

Brax was grateful for the other ghazi's tact. Refusing to glance up at a familiar shadow perched high on the top of the armory tower as they passed underneath it, he decided that ignoring things might be the best response tonight. He had enough physical challenges to struggle against without having to remember the pain of Hisar's ethereal claws digging deep into his chest and the weakness and dizziness that had come from Its feeding. Every time the young God came too close, the memory of those sensations whispered across his ribs, reminding him that Hisar was still little more than the merging of a thousand wild and dangerously predictable spirits whose only directive was to feed. And, he told himself firmly as the echo of those sensations traveled across his chest once again, he had plenty of other things to worry about rather than wondering why Hisar was hanging about the Battle God's temple in the middle of the night. If Estavia didn't want the young God in Her territory, She would soon put the boots to It Herself.

Quickening his step until Brin gave a sharp protest in response, he passed under the commissary archway without looking up.

✦

High above, the shadow stretched out Its wings in a shower of metallic brilliance, then settled down to wait for Brax to emerge again. Hisar had time. It was starting to learn patience as well.

Turning Its head, It stared out across the battlements to the still waters of Gol-Beyaz watching as, far out in the center, the God of Battles mirrored Brax's earlier moves in a slow and deliberate dance, twin swords flashing in the moonlight. Step, strike, strike. Hold. Step, strike. Turn, block, strike. Faster, faster, faster, twin swords flashing in a blur of silver light, strike, step, strike step.

A light breeze, whispering of rain and fog, threaded across the city, and She paused, turning Her crimson gaze upon Hisar. The young God gave an involuntary shiver, but remained in view and, after a long moment, Estavia gave the faintest nod of approval in Its direction before returning Her attention to the dance.

Hisar heard a burst of laughter coming from within the commissary and suddenly found Itself torn between the desire to join Estavia in the cool darkness, or join Her followers in the warm candlelight. Realizing that It could do neither, It thrust the accompanying unhappiness away with a violent gesture and leaped from the armory tower in a spray of golden light. It would go looking for more tower symbols, It thought angrily. That, It could do.

The Young God

BUZZING LOW OVER THE city, Hisar swept Its metallic gaze left and right, searching for the faint promise of power that signified the tower symbols. A whisper of potential on the wind drew It north, along a series of narrow cobblestone streets until It fetched up before the iron gate of a Tannery Precinct Brothel. Peering into the tiny garden beyond, It oriented Itself to the symbol's direction then, changing to Its golden seeming, crept inside.

He found it etched into a clay flowerpot tucked up against the back wall and, after collecting a seed of power that almost vibrated with sexual energy, He raised Himself up and peered through a crack in the shutters with a thoughtful expression.

Up until now, the seeds of power He'd received from the tower symbols had felt purely neutral, as if they hadn't been left for Him at all but were instead just a by-product of drawing the symbol itself. But this seed of power had been different. This one had held a hint of supplication. Maybe. And a hint of obligation. Maybe. It was the first time He'd felt as if the person who'd drawn the symbols had actually wanted something from Him. But what? He'd never seen any of the people who'd left these secret markers all over the city. He didn't know who they were or what they wanted. And what could they have possibly wanted from Him in a place like this? From His wandering with Spar, Hisar knew what a brothel was for, but most of them operated under the auspices of Ystazia or Oristo, and They were the Gods most people would appeal to for sexual help, not to a half-formed God of Creation and Destruction.

The sounds of lovemaking filtered out to Him, and He cocked His head to one side. Long before He'd managed even a partially realized physical presence, He'd watched people having sex, struggling to understand their need for it. Sex often invigorated them—it certain invigorated both Brin and Bazmin—but others, like Brax, were more complicated. Brax needed to rest, not be invigorated, but sex often seemed to relax and exhaust him at the same time, helping him rest. Hisar wondered idly what the person inside was looking for tonight; invigoration or rest or just sex.

Glancing down, He studied His male human-seeming's penis with a slight frown. He'd never even had sex. Of course, until six years ago, He'd been nothing more than a thousand wild land spirits; born of wind and lightning and consumed by hunger. Spirits didn't need sex. Like the Gods they needed power. And, more specifically, they needed the power of their worshipers freely given.

Five years ago, Graize had fought and defeated that swarm of spirits, forcing them to a single sentient form that had become Hisar and bending it to his will. He'd treated Hisar's growing consciousness as something to be used like a tool or a weapon until Hisar had rebelled against his control on the grasslands, helping Spar to free Brax. Graize had seen it as a betrayal and had turned his back on Him, spending the last nine months deep in seclusion in the Berbat-Dunya wild lands and driving Hisar away every time the young God had tried to make contact with him.

But it hadn't been a betrayal. It had been a carefully crafted compromise to keep Hisar's newly formed relationships with Spar, Brax, and Graize safe. And it had worked. Hisar had been very proud of that, and one day He would make Graize understand. On the grasslands, Graize had screamed his oaths into the storm; binding him and Hisar together and forging a lien between them that would someday give Hisar access to the vast stores of power at Graize's command. Hisar would not let that lie dormant. He couldn't. When He became fully physical, He would need them. He would need Graize.

And he would need Brax, too.

Calling up the tiny seed of power He'd just received, Hisar poked sullenly at the flowerpot, feeling the rough clay scratch against His fingertips. Last year, Spar had given him the special red bead that anchored Him in the physical world, but even it wasn't enough to grant him access to the stores of power at Brax's command. Nothing but Brax's worship, freely given, could do that.

"People are drawn to him. He's got strength."

Hisar nodded at Spar's words. Everyone was drawn to him, and yet they still continued to send him into danger, putting that strength at risk. It didn't make any sense.

Leaning against the brothel wall in unconscious imitation of His young First Priest, Hisar remembered standing with Spar before the troop of warriors and militia that had fallen on the grasslands where Graize and his band of Petchans had ambushed Brax last season. They'd been laid out on their backs, side by side, with their weapons next to them in a gesture of respect, but the blue cloaks that covered their features were soaked in blood and the smell of death had vied with the sound of flies. There was no power there anymore; their power, like their spirits, had joined with Estavia.

Hisar had stared down at them dispassionately. He'd seen plenty of death in His short life, both on the battlefield and off it, and had learned early on that the physical was far too fragile a vessel to hold that much power in safety. If Brax had been Hisar's, the young God was certain that He would never have risked him that way.

And if Brax was Hisar's, He'd have all the power He needed to protect His city from the flocks of white-and-brown bird enemies He'd seen. He knew He would.

Turning His head, the young God stared across the strait at the dark bulk of Burun-Hisar, the watchtower that guarded the hospital village of Calmak-Koy and the entrance to the eastern shore. He and Spar had spent months there hovering about Brax's bedside as he'd fought fever after fever after his injuries on the grasslands. It was there that they'd first begun to test the limits of Hisar's own small physical experiences, moving from seeming to seeming as the mood took them, learning what they could do and what they couldn't do.

✦

On a cool, autumn night, Hisar had stood on the threshold of the main healing pavilion, wearing the most physical of seemings, that of the Yuruk girl, Rayne, now a grown woman in her own right. The gray flagstones leading to the large, ornate fountain in the center of the hospital's medicinal herb gardens had shimmered in the pale moonlight with all the radiance of a silver river. A nightingale singing in a nearby cinar tree had sent a stream of fluidly perfect notes into the still night air, and the cold caress of stone against Her bare feet had whispered through Her senses in a fluttering of peppermint-and-indigo prophecy.

Ordinarily, Hisar enjoyed experiencing the physical world as a swirling blend of sensory chaos; it seemed more natural to Her growing understanding of the Gods and Their response to the world around Them, but She wanted more; She wanted to feel the world as an actual physical being might, so She'd bent Her attention to each sensation separately, gripping the red bead about Her neck in an effort to maintain Her focus.

The gray flagstones and splashing fountain had reflected the silvery moonlight, almost hurting Her eyes with their brightness. The smooth stone of the threshold had sent shivers of cold seeping through Her bare feet and up, causing the fine hairs along Her arms and legs and the nipples on Her small breasts to rise in response. The night air, smelling of peppermint and clean water from the herb gardens, had tickled Her nostrils and run along the length of Her tongue in an acrid sweetness. And the nightingale, casting a tiny, indigo shadow in the cinar tree's branches had given Her a thrill of purely auditory pleasure with its song.

Taken separately, each sensation meant little beyond itself, but Spar had said that physical beings did more than just react to each sensation separately. They put them all together to interpret their surroundings; this night, a clear, autumn breeze smelling of growing things and a bird singing without fear of cat or owl. A warm night, a safe night, a night where even the slightest hint of danger could be detected at once.

And for a seer, young God or otherwise, a night of the subtlest prophecy only. A faint warning chill and the fluttering of silver wings in the distance casting tiny indigo shadows across the sweet, silvery peppermint song of autumn. Danger might be coming, but it wasn't here yet. They still had time.

✦

Then. Not so much time now, Hisar acknowledged. Taking one last peek through the shutters, He returned to Its dragonfly seeming, and reluctantly took flight in a spray of metallic brilliance. Maybe next time the person in the brothel would be more specific about what they wanted.

Returning to Estavia-Sarayi, the young God spun about the armory tower once or twice, then lit upon a stone windowsill on the eastern side of the Cyan Company dormitory. The latticed shutters were thrown open to the clean, spring air and tucking Its wings across Its back, Hisar peered inside.

Four sleeping figures in two rooms revealed themselves to Its metallic gaze. Only four, Hisar remembered because Brax now had a room of his own on the other side of the dormitory. Two grown men—Kemal and Yashar, Spar and Brax's abayon—warmed by the crimson-and-silver light of Estavia's lien, lay sprawled on the low pallet beneath the window in the main room, the blankets in disarray now that their own lovemaking was done. Kemal, the younger of the two, had one arm pillowed under his cheek and the other draped across Yashar's buttocks while the older man lay half on and half off the pallet, snoring loudly enough to make his heavy, black beard shake. Their sleeping was smooth and unmarred by troubles or uncertainty and, wrapped in the impenetrable armor of Estavia's embrace, their dreams were peaceful.

In the next room, Jaq, deep red fur speckled with a touch of gray at the muzzle, lay stretched out protectively on the small pallet beside Spar, paws twitching as he chased rabbits or some other such prey in his dreams. The youth held the dog as closely as a child might hold a comforting toy, his expression as guarded and intense in sleep as it was awake.

The young God took wing as quietly as It could across the chamber, setting down on the top of the embroidered screen that served as a door between the two rooms and, tipping Its multifaceted head to one side, It stared down at Spar's sleeping features, illuminated by the fine, faint glow of Hisar's own immature lien. The months since they'd returned from the battle on the grasslands had thinned the young seer's cheeks and lengthened the set of his jaw. His nose had grown faster than his face and it had given him a cross-eyed look sometimes when he stared at things close up.

Not that Hisar had ever told him that, the young God admitted silently. Spar had become very sensitive about his looks in the last few weeks. He had a scattering of pimples through the scattering of new beard on his cheeks and it made him scowl to see them reflected in any polished surface.

Hisar gave a soft snort. It didn't know why that bothered him; there were plenty of youths who didn't care about a few pimples. Just last month, two potter-delinkon had taken Spar's virginity in an empty storage room behind a workshop kiln and they'd had as many pimples as he did. But Spar had always been a little . . ." Hisar struggled for the right word and settled on self-absorbed instead of vain.

"Typical seer."

Brax's voice whispered through Hisar's mind, and the young God chuckled to Itself. Just turned twenty-one, beautiful and desirable with his thick black hair and his wide, dark eyes that hinted of strength and vulnerability equally, Brax'd had sex with more people than a bawd of Ystazia. Maybe that was why Spar was feeling so insecure. He had a lot of ground to cover if he was going to catch up to his older kardos.

Hisar frowned. Spar had seen fifteen years pass. In three months he would be an adult as people counted such things. And if what he and everyone else feared came to pass, they would be in the middle of a war in three months. Spar was not a Warrior of Estavia. Technically, he was not even a seer-delinkos of Estavia; he was the First and only Priest of Hisar. But Hisar had no doubt that if the Battle God went to war, Spar's small family would follow and so would Spar.

And so would Hisar. Spar would expect Him to stand beside him, gifting him with such strengths as a Patron God had at Its command. And that was the problem. Hisar had no idea what strengths It had at Its command. It had no temple, no worshipers, no Morning and Evening Invocations. It had two young priests at odds with each other, a delinname given to It by Incasa, who had His own designs on Hisar's destiny, two restrictive prophecies, maybe three, and a title crafted by Incasa's First Oracle. As Hisar had complained to Spar, It didn't even know what that meant.

Clearly, It needed to find out before this war stole one or both of Its new priests away.

And clearly It needed more followers.

Glancing out the window, Hisar remembered the first time He and Spar had talked about this. Sitting on a low stone wall that separated Calmak-Koy from the northern shore, with Brax, only just recently allowed out of bed, and Kemal and Yashar, on leave from the garrison at Orzin-Hisar, they'd watched Oristo's First Day festivities hosted by the priests of Calmak-Koy's small Oristo-Cami.

Hisar had chosen His golden seeming and a golden tunic that be-spoke no single affiliation, but had decided against the red bead. The thought of all those people staring at Him without recourse to the air had frightened the young God more than He'd wanted to admit.

There'd been a lot of staring, and a lot of whispering, but no one had managed to work up the courage to approach them, and so the day had passed without incident. Hisar wasn't sure whether He'd been relieved or disappointed. The young God had felt the unsworn in the crowd and had hungered for them all.

At dusk, they'd watched the sun set over Gol-Beyaz while Jaq had lain at their feet tearing at a piece of dried meat. With the prophetic vision He and Spar shared, they'd watched as the God-wrought colors had turned the sparkling waters from pink to blue and finally to indigo. The faintest silver light shone from the depths and, as the priests of Havo began to sing the first notes of the Evening Invocation, Hisar had glanced over at Spar with a wistful expression.

✦

"When will I have a temple and a festival of my own?" He asked.

Popping the last of a piece of Oristo's Lokum into his mouth, Spar nodded. "Some day," he answered in a neutral tone, twisting the bit of brown ribbon it had come tied with around one finger.

"Why not now?"

"Because you don't have enough people sworn to you to build a temple or host a festival now."

"I don't have anyone sworn to me at all, except you and Graize." Hisar replied. His tone was so sad, that Kemal cast him a sympathetic glance.

"You will, Hisarin-Delin," he said, using the diminutive with a smile. "It just takes time. The other Gods have had centuries; you've only had a few months."

"But, how do I get more Sworn if I don't have a temple for them to come to?"

"Point. I don't know."

Staring out at the great bulk of Lazim-Hisar that anchored the northernmost tip of the Western Trisect, Spar cocked his head to one side. "I may have a few ideas about that," he answered thoughtfully.

Hisar's expression brightened at once. "What ideas?"

"They're still in the planning stage."

"But can't you tell me just a little? Maybe I could help."

"You will help when the time comes," Spar answered primly. "In the meantime, you need to be patient."

"I hate being patient."

"I know." Spar turned. "Aban, what's that land there to the west of Lazim-Hisar?"

Both Kemal and Yashar squinted past the setting sun to the area Spar indicated.

"Docks and storage areas for the care and maintenance of Estavia's fleet," Kemal answered. "And the first line of embarkation and defense for the Western Trisect. The old sea chain couplings are there too."

"Is it part of Estavia-Sarayi?"

"Not really. It's actually civic lands. So is Lazim-Hisar for that matter," Kemal added, "garrisoned by the Warriors of Estavia for the protection of the people. Why?"

"I was just wondering. We never lifted that far south, Brax and me."

Wrapped in a blanket beside him, Brax nodded. "It had too many guards," he agreed.

Turning his attention to the blazing lights of Oristo-Sarayi clearly visible across the water, Spar's expression grew nostalgic. "They'll be hosting huge outdoor feasts at every one of Oristo's camis tonight," he said to Hisar, watching as the Hearth God, bedecked in flowers, rose over the city as the abayos-priests began to sing. "With dancing and revelry that'll go on till nearly midnight. When I was seven, me, Brax, and Cindar ate until we nearly burst, then lifted enough shine from the dockside festival-goers to buy new clothes and boots for all of us for winter. Remember Brax?"

"I remember. I was warm and full, and Cindar got so drunk he nearly fell into the cami's main fountain and set his beard on fire.

"They float these tiny colored-glass lamps in Oristo's fountains," Brax explained to Hisar. "They're supposed to represent hearth fires, but they look like butterflies made of flame.

"We lifted two purses each while the priests pulled him out," he added, returning his attention to Spar. "It was a good night."

"It was. The bounty of Oristo." Spar gave a cynical bark of laughter. "I doubt that's what the priests actually meant, yeah?"

"Yeah."

Yashar cast them both a reproving look. "What it's supposed to mean, Hisaro-Delin, is that the Gods give to Their followers and Their followers give to the Gods," he said sternly.

Spar's expression cleared. "Right. So, what we need to do is figure out what your bounty is, so we know what you have to give to your followers when you get them."

"Exactly," Kemal agreed. "The Gods are just like people. They each have a job to do; to make the harvest plentiful or add clarity and sparkle to a colored-glass lamp. Or heal the sick," he added as the hospice's physician-priests began the Evening Invocation to Usara behind them. "Everyone has to work, Gods as well as Their followers."

Hisar gave an unimpressed sniff. "Why?" He demanded.

Kemal chuckled. "The simplest answer is because everyone needs to eat, so everyone has to work to earn money to buy food."

"Some people grow their own food," Hisar pointed out.

"And they sell their extra food for money to buy a pot to cook their food in. Either way, it's still work," Yashar added in a dry tone.

"Oh." Hisar pondered this for a moment. "Spar and Brax didn't earn money when they were young," He said triumphantly. "They stole it."

"And if you think it didn't take work to steal, you need to watch the lifters who still run on the western docks," Brax retorted. "You can't get away from it. Work is work."

About to answer, Hisar paused as Kemal raised a hand. He, Yashar, and Brax all stood. There was silence all around them for a single moment, and then the first note of the Battle God's Invocation carried across the water. It seemed to swirl about them, gathering strength, so that when all three men responded, Hisar could feel the power almost lift them off the ground. The protection symbols painted on their bodies each morning glowed through their tunics, and He stilled the urge to narrow His eyes in jealousy. One day, His followers would wear the symbols of His patronage on their bodies, too. One day.

The final note faded, and all three men returned to their seats, each one sitting quietly with his own thoughts while first, the priests of Ystazia, and then Incasa began their own song. As the final note of the Evening Invocations faded, Hisar glanced over.

"I can get away from work," He pointed out, returning to their conversation with martial gleam in His eyes. "I don't need money, and I don't need to eat."

"Don't you?" Casually, Spar coaxed a tiny seed of power from the wind, holding its silvery radiance up between finger and thumb.

Hisar frowned at him. "I should never have taught you how to do that." He pouted as both Yashar and Kemal raised a questioning eyebrow at them.

Spar laughed and passed it over. "What does it matter? You can do it yourself. But you can't do this." His eyes went white for a heartbeat as he touched his fingertips to his chest. As the night air brought them the sound of renewed revelry from Oristo-Sarayi, he sang one, low, quiet note of his own invention.

Hisar shuddered, feeling a responding pressure against His chest where Spar's First Vows glittered like fire and ice inside Him. It grew as a thin stream of essence, flowing between them and, for a brief moment, Hisar felt as He imagined the Gods of Gol-Beyaz must feel, before the stream slowly faded, leaving an aching hunger in its wake.

"Is that my Evening Invocation?" He whispered.

Spar lifted his hand away, the fingers shimmering with a metallic glow that only they could see. He reached over and pressed them to Hisar's lips, and the young God shuddered once again as this small bit of physical power was transferred as well.

Spar's eyes returned to their usual blue. "The beginnings of it," he answered. "You can feed on the power of the wind or the water or the land, and the power of the spirits that live there, but what gives you real strength is the power of your people, willingly given. To get that you have to work for it. Just like everyone else."

As Kemal, Yashar, and Brax touched their own chests almost instinctively, Hisar's form shimmered with a restless blur. "Why is it that everything you say always sounds like a lesson these days?" He demanded.

"Because you're serving an apprenticeship," Kemal answered for Spar.

"As what?"

"As a God-delinkon."

"When will it be over?"

"In one hundred days, on the Fifty-Ninth Day of Ystazia," Spar answered for him. "When I turn sixteen."

"Oh." Hisar returned His attention to the silvery glow beneath the waves of Gol-Beyaz. "Will I be an adult then, too?"

"Probably."

"And we'll know what my bounty is?" Hisar continued, the wistful expression on His face once again, "and how I can use it?"

Spar nodded.

"And I'll have a temple with a fountain, and followers, and a full Invocation, and a festival of my own?"

"You will."

"Soon?"

"Soon enough."

"Good." Hisar gave a pleased smile. "Then let's start right now. Who can I have?"

✦

In Spar's bedchamber, a sudden, sharp slap against Its mind knocked the young God from Its perch in a startled spray of gold-and-silver light. It took wing out the window at once and, as the dragonfly seeming disappeared over the rooftops of Anavatan, Estavia rose until She towered silently over Her temple.

Her crimson gaze tracked Hisar's progress with a dark expression. She suffered the young God's presence in Her territory because It was still a delos and because of Its connection to Her Champion's kardos, but there were limits, and planning to increase Its power base in Her temple was one of them. It was time the delos had a temple of Its own somewhere other than in Her Cyan Company dormitory.

She frowned in irritation. Estavia was the God of clean and simple decisions made on the battlefield. The complicated business of raising delon was the responsibility of their abayon, not Hers. And since Spar was one of Hisar's abayon, She would have Spar's own abayon take care of it for Her.

Formed the thought into a directive, She smacked it down into Kemal's sleeping mind with a crack of power.

"FIND A TEMPLE FOR HISAR AND GET IT OUT OF MINE!"

Kemal fell out of bed with a shout of surprise; bleary-eyed confusion shot back along the lien and Estavia resisted the urge to slap him as well. Catching up Marshal Brayazi's mind, She knocked their thoughts together, repeated Her order, sent the image of Hisar's growing need for followers along both their liens, then broke contact with an impatient snap, ignoring the marshal's own spike of confusion. Estavia had figured out what had to be done, now it was up to Her kaptins to figure out how to do it; that's what they had their own intelligence for. With Her annoyance cracking in their ears like thunder, the God of Battles returned to Gol-Beyaz with a great gout of irritated spray.

✦

In his own room, Spar opened his eyes, staring up at the low ceiling with a satisfied expression as he listened to Yashar's sleep-befuddled inquiry and Kemal's equally befuddled answer. Hisar's hurt surprise at Estavia's response echoed along his own lien, and he reached out to soothe Its ruffled feathers with an absent thread of power until It calmed. The plan he'd devised on the wall at Oristo-Cami was well underway. As the bounty of Oristo had served his small family of lifters years ago, so would the bounty of Estavia serve him and his young God now. It would build them a temple, making a place for Hisar's followers to gather. That would keep them both safe and strong. That would keep them *all* safe and strong.

With a satisfied smile, he pulled Jaq a bit closer and went back to sleep.

✦

Rising above Gol-Beyaz, Incasa breathed upon His dice before throwing them into the air, watching as His vision of water echoing in a cavernous darkness became a line of sweeping arches made of stone covered in vines. Water cascaded along its length, stretching out over Anavatan and, as the dice returned to His palm, the God of Prophecy caught sight of a tiny movement in the distance. Two of His most sensitive prophet-cats, Graize and Hisar, were already twitching impatiently by His hole in the sand. The vision merged and shifted until it took a double form that both the young God and the unstable young seer would recognize and, with a nod of approval, Incasa withdrew, satisfied that the future was unfolding just as He'd commanded it to.

3

The Wild Lands

*T*HE AIR FELT HEAVY, *portentous, and smelled of blood and salt. The dawn sun peeking above the wild lands like a great, fiery insect preparing to leap from its den, held nothing but malice in its regard. And far away, water sparkled in a cavernous darkness.*

"Stop it."

Crouched on a low rise, Graize looked down on the winter camp he shared with Danjel of the Rus-Yuruk and Yal of the Chalash Petchans. It lay deep in the midst of the Berbat-Dunya where the spirits, gathering beneath the undulating hills like pockets of low-lying marshlands, were at their strongest and most feral. Their constant ebb and flow hid him from the prying eyes of his enemies, but they also muddied the streams of prophecy, causing his mind to tack back and forth like a leaking boat on the water.

Closing his eyes, he willed himself to calm, using the protective mental cloak he'd fashioned in the Gurney Dag Mountains a year ago as a focus. Rent to pieces on the grasslands, he'd spent the last nine months carefully weaving it back together and, along with it, his fragile sanity.

The cloak held and, when he opened his eyes again, the tableau had steadied.

The air smelled of rain falling on the distant northern sea. The dawn sun cast orange fingers of light across the wild lands, sending the last of the night's creatures scurrying for the safety of their dens. And in the distance, water sparkled in the darkness.

Graize's gray eyes narrowed. He was not on the northern seas, so any blood spilled upon its waves was not his concern, nor was he a night creature, so the sun held no malice toward him. He could sense the distant rain and the change from night to day without the aid of prophecy. And water and darkness were obscure and unconnected.

"Get on with it."

The vision faltered for a heartbeat, drawing the images of an armored child, a golden tower, and a dark-haired man on a snow-capped mountain ridge from deep within his mind to focus on, and Graize growled angrily.

"No."

"I'll never be gone from you again."

His own words spoken to Hisar in a moment of comfort whispered through his mind and he slapped them away angrily.

"You're mine, only mine! My God!"

The oaths he'd shouted into the storm sizzled along Hisar's newly carved lien and he bared his teeth at it. "Hisar will be brought back under my control in due time," he growled. "And I will not look at mountains or towers. Enough."

Thrusting the unwanted memories aside, he reached into the pouch at his belt, drawing out a battered, old stag beetle. Using it as a focus, he forced his mind back to the imagery at hand and, grudgingly, it obeyed.

Rain would come from across the northern sea where Prince Illan Dmitriviz Volinsk was planning the invasion of Anavatan, bringing blood and salt in his wake.

But the morning sun could still reveal his plans to their enemies.

The vision wavered unsteadily and Graize rubbed his temples as his right eye dilated, causing a fine line of icy pain to stitch across his forehead.

"Begin with blood," he growled.

Blood nearly always meant blood spilled, but blood also flowed through the body, keeping it strong. Salt was the sea, an invasion by sea brought salt to poison the land, but salt kept the body strong as well. So, the success or failure of Illan's invasion still hung in the balance whatever the prince might think.

As for the sun . . . Graize glanced at the horizon. The sun brought clarity and heralded the end to hiding and the onset of action for those who moved about by day, but in this vision the sun held nothing but malice in its regard. It could reveal their movements, still hidden from view, to the enemy.

"Still hidden from view," he mused. "Hidden from the malicious regard of our enemies. The malicious regard of Incasa's seer-priests, Estavia's Sable Company seers, and Spar. Illan's enemies and my enemy."

He glared at the east. "I know you've been looking for me, little rat-seer," he sneered into the wind. "I can feel you tickling my dreams like a bedbug in the night. But you can't bite me; you're not strong enough. And one day soon I'll make you pay for trying to steal my Godling away."

And the water in darkness?

He shook his head in a side-to-side, up-and-down, motion until the icy pain in his forehead made him stop.

"*Sparkling* water in darkness," he amended, shaking an admonishing finger at the stag beetle. "Water doesn't sparkle in darkness, does it? But spirits in water sparkle all the time because they have an inner power that lights them up like little fireflies. So . . ." He leaned back on his heels. "There are spirits in a darkness, in a *cavernous* darkness. But there are no caverns here. So where are the caverns?"

Reaching out, he plucked several strands of the thick wild lands grass, twisting them together to make a simple fetish the way Danjel and the Yuruk had taught him. Tossing it high, he watched as the wind caught it, and spun it about his face. For a moment, he half expected Hisar to come swooping down to knock it from the air as the Godling had liked to do in the past. But the sky remained clear of Its distinctive shimmer and he banished the thought with a sharp jerk of his head, bringing his mind back on task as the fetish finally came to rest on the ground to the east.

"The shining, sparkling, glowing, betraying city of Anavatan lies to the east," he said in the singsong cadence he used when his thoughts were elsewhere. "Is that where you are, my spirit-filled caverns?"

He lifted the fetish, tapping it lightly against his lips as he considered the entire vision. The ice on the northern sea would be breaking up soon and Illan's invasion fleet would set sail. All of the Volinski prince's years of plotting and planning like a night creature scuttling along a wall would be complete.

"But they're not complete yet," he mused. "He still needs to be cautious or they'll be discovered."

He gave a disdainful sniff. "Why should discovery matter now?"

he sneered, curling his lip. "If everyone's held to Illan's ambitious time-table, all of Anavatan's enemies from Petchan to Yuruk to Skirosian will be mobilizing soon. Hardly subtle, my beetle; that much movement to a single purpose will have lit up the future streams like a pillar of fire on the water already. Every Anavatanon seer from the lowliest street prophet to Incasa Himself will have felt it in their bones and will be preparing a response. So tell me clearly, my all-knowing little creature, what hidden element hangs in the balance that would make its discovery so dangerous at this late stage?"

The cry of a hunting bird sounding overhead jerked him from his reverie just as the answer started to shimmer into view. A small, red hawk wheeled in the sky, then dropped. When it rose again, a mouse dangled from its talons. For a split second, the sun etched a fine patina of copper fire across the hawk's feathers; then, as its owner arose from the grass almost at his feet, Graize's answer vanished.

He grimaced. "Yal."

The Petchan woman raised an eyebrow at his tone. Of an age and of similar medium height and build, she and Graize could have been mistaken for siblings save for the pale blonde hair, blue eyes, and tanned complexion that marked her as a Petchan compared to the light brown hair and gray eyes that hinted at Graize's possible Volinski ancestry. Like him, she was dressed in the Yuruk style, hair worn long and braided with bits of cloth and feathers, brown sheepskin jacket and fleece cap worn to ward off the winds with heavy woolen pantaloons stuffed into black leather boots. Only the hint of a green felt tunic underneath revealed the colorful preferences of her own people.

As she joined him on the rise, she crossed her arms with an unim-pressed expression. "And good morning to you too, Graize-kardos," she noted, keeping one eye on her hawk as it tore into its breakfast.

He waved a hand at her in annoyance. "It was a good morning to go vision-fishing until your bird-delin became entangled in my net, Hawk-Kardos," he said, using her animal-fetish term that Danjel had gifted her with last winter.

"The nearest river is some miles away," she retorted. "Maybe you should use a vision-bird to hunt in the skies instead of a vision-net; you'd get farther. I could have killed you a dozen times while you stood look-ing for fish where there's no water."

"Had you been an actual danger, I would have sensed you," Graize replied, touching one finger to his temple. "As it was, your appearance and your bird-delin's merely muddied the streams."

"Clouded the sky?" she pressed.

"If you like." He raised his face to the faint light and warmth from the east. "The dawn sun heralds a change from inaction to action. Time to move. Time to see the mouse before the strike."

Used to his ramblings, Yal just frowned at him. "Action on a small scale or on a large?" she asked, ignoring the rest of his words with practiced ease.

"Both."

"And the strike?"

"Also both." He glanced at her quizzically. "Why?"

Shading her eyes with one hand, Yal peered at the distant hills. "Danjel's not back yet."

"Ah." Graize gave her a knowing nod. Her bi-gender lover—his adopted kardos—had been tending a herd of wild ponies all winter, taming them for the spring migration, and had left the day before yesterday to begin rounding them up. They would be leaving the winter camp to join with Danjel's people just as soon as the Yuruk wyrdin returned.

"Has your prophecy shown you any sign of Danjel?" Yal pressed.

Closing his eyes, Graize laid his hands against the ground, feeling the grass scratch against his palms as he pushed his fingers through it. "No whisper of seer-horse-herding lovers or swallow-birth-fetish couriers on the plains, Hawk-kardos. Wait an hour, play again, the game may have changed," he answered, his tone dropping back into the singsong cadence. "But." He opened his eyes. "There will be rain to the north."

"We'll be riding north within the next day or two. Will it catch us up?"

"Not in this next day or two if the future holds to its present course," he answered with unusual clarity. "But that's the real trick, isn't it, holding the fickle future to its course."

"As tricky as changing the course of a waterfall," she agreed. "Easier to just go with it, I'd think."

"Unless it pours you down a crevasse." He shrugged eloquently. "You'd get soaked either way, wouldn't you? But that way you might drown. In a future day or two we'll all get soaked with blood and salt. Only time can tell if we'll get drowned."

"And time will tell when, Graize-kardos?"

"When it pleases."

Yal favored him with a doubtful grimace before returning her gaze to the plains. She'd come to the Berbat-Dunya with Danjel, a powerful seer, or wyrdin as the Yuruk called them, after Danjel had carried Graize, screaming and raving with madness, from the southern grasslands last summer. They'd spent the last nine months tending to his broken mind amidst the concealing wild lands, but every time he'd looked to be recovering, something happened to destroy the fragile stability they'd built up for him. He'd been fairly lucid for the last week and Yal'd had high hopes that the onset of spring would bring him added strength, but Danjel wasn't so sure. The Yuruk wyrdin believed that Graize's mind would never be truly strong until he reconciled with the God-spirit, Hisar, whom he'd driven away on the grasslands.

As her hawk returned to her wrist, its feasting over, Yal shook her head, the protective beads of her people clicking together with the motion. She didn't understand the bond between Graize and the God-spirit. When he'd first come to Chalash, Graize had told her that he controlled Hisar, but that summer the creature had betrayed him, throwing in with his enemies and helping one of them to escape. To her mind, that was not a bond she'd want to maintain. Danjel could not properly explain what to the Yuruk wyrdin was an instinctive relationship, and Graize would not speak of Hisar at all, so Yal had simply put it down to the strange ways of her new foreign family and had left it at that.

Her own people did not consort with the spirits the way the Yuruk did. The mountain spirits were too dangerous, too unpredictable, and always too hungry. There were countless stories told by their own seers, or sayers as they called them, of shepherds falling to their deaths at the urgings of the mountain spirits. Even though there were no cliffs here, only endless stretches of plains and marsh, the spirits lay so thick across the land that, even to her non-prophetic gaze, it shimmered with their power, lying deceptively calm and dormant, waiting for the unwary to move among them. And either drown them as Graize had mentioned or simply devour them.

She'd voiced her concern to Danjel when they'd first arrived, but her lover had just laughed. Giving a high whistle, the wyrdin had called up a dozen spirits, tossing seeds of power to them like Yal might have tossed actual seeds to feed the tamed yellow birds back home. They'd spun about Danjel's face like a swarm of mad fireflies, buzzing and singing in a melodic, high-pitched tone. It had teased a rare smile of pleasure from Graize that had seemed to take years off his age, but Yal had remained unmoved. Everyone knew that the singing of the spirits could drive you mad. She was sure that was what had happened to Graize: he'd spent far too long listening to Hisar sing. But neither Graize nor Danjel had heeded her warning.

Beside her, Graize was now studying her hawk intently. The morning sun illuminated its feathers with fire and his eyes lit up suddenly, echoing their brilliance as a vision danced across his mind. "An answer-fish has finally been caught in my sky-net," he said. "Feathers spotted with blood and painted with power. We're going to have company."

"People company?" Yal hazarded with a worried frown.

"Panos and Hares," he answered.

"Ah, the southern oracle and her teyos, the mapmaker. I remember you speaking of them before."

"Yes." Graize nodded, as the image grew clearer in his eyes. "They are traveling north to reunite with her lover, Prince Illan of Volinsk, when his fleet sails down the Bogazi-Isik Strait, but they must travel overland to avoid the malice of the sun."

"The sun?"

"The seers of Anavatan. They can't take the water-path up Gol-Beyaz because the sharp eyes of the Anavatanon seers will spot them as the enemies they are, so they have to walk the plains-path through the heart of the Berbat-Dunya instead."

"Isn't that dangerous without a sayer born to the wild lands?" Yal asked. "I thought the only reason we were safe was because we were with Danjel."

Graize showed his teeth at her. "Panos is not afraid of spirits, wild or otherwise. To her, they're no more dangerous that a swarm of midges. But she can't eat them, not like I can, poor little golden prophet. And she'd find their singing so much to her taste if she could; as tart and sweet as berries dipped in honey."

He glanced slyly at Yal. "They'll have landed far west of Anahtar-

Hisar and journeyed through the coastal foothills and up into the mountains, stopping at Chalash to bring word from King Pyrros to Haz-Chief and bring away word from Maf, beloved but cranky abia to Yal-Delin, long absent from her home."

"Just the two of them?" Yal asked, refusing to be distracted by mention of her mother.

"They'll be guarded," Graize answered dismissively. "But the number's not important."

"It is if we're expected to feed them," Yal answered dryly.

"Very true. How practical you are, Hawk-kardos. Two, possibly four, then. We'll know more once their footprints carry across the land." Graize glanced at her bird again. The creature stared back at him with a disconcertingly intelligent expression much like Hisar's. "The hawk has flown high and dropped low and now it rests comfortably in between, its belly full and its beak smeared with the blood of prophecy."

He lay back in the grass, arms behind his head. "We'll know how many more mice we'll have to provide before the sun reaches its zenith," he stated.

"And Danjel?" Yal pressed.

Graize gave an explosive sigh. "Tell your nether regions to be patient, Kardos; we'll know of Danjel by then as well."

"You've *seen* this?"

Graize waved a dismissive hand at her and Yal grimaced back at him. "Typical sayer," she muttered, shaking her head. As the movement disturbed the hawk on her wrist, she sent it back into the air. "Mice will not do. Find me a warren of fat rabbits, Delin," she told it. "We're going to have company. Hungry company."

"Yes," Graize agreed with a faint chuckle. "Very hungry company."

✦

Miles away, in the heart of the wild lands, the dawn sun sent streaks of orange power feathering across the landscape. Clinging to each stalk of grass, hundreds of tiny spirits, born of wind and rain, lifted their feral regard to its light, drinking in its strength to fuel their minute allotments of prophecy. A herd of ponies grazing placidly among them swallowed grass and spirits alike, spots of silver power sparkling in their shaggy coats like dew. Now and then, one would send its tail swishing through the hip-high stalks, raising a cloud of spirits and midges to swirl about their heads, tangling in their manes and eyelashes, before settling back down again.

Riding with the easy grace of one born to the saddle, Danjel moved slowly through the animals, his two young herding dogs keeping pace beside him. He carried the white yak's tail standard of the shepherd held loosely in the crook of one arm even though there were no other Yuruk nearby to signal to, and kept his jade-green eyes trained on the horizon even though his prophetic abilities had already told him there was no enemy or predator nearby. As the morning breeze caressed his cheek, he reined up, changing form from male to female in a single, fluid motion.

The strong scent of horseflesh and grass came over her and, she breathed it in with pleasure. It had been as mild a season as could be hoped for on the Berbat-Dunya, and the herd had weathered it well. They were strong and healthy and two of the mares were pregnant, one with twins. Danjel estimated that they would drop within a fortnight, plenty of time to bring them to the Rus-Yuruk encampments before that happened. Fifteen ponies for twelve was a good season's work and would help make up for her long absence from her mother's people.

Raising her face to the wind whispering in from the north, she tasted the messages it carried: vast flocks in motion, shepherds in their midst and sentinels on the hills, all beginning the great trek from winter pastures to summer. The people had weathered the season well, too. They, too, were strong and healthy and eager to move to the summer camps, east and south. From there, they would make raids on the villages that ringed Gol-Beyaz Lake as they'd done for centuries.

But this year would be different, and the underlying excitement that colored Danjel's prophecy sparkled with unborn possibilities. This year, her people had agreed to ally themselves with the traditional enemies of Anavatan in exchange for trade and spoils and free access to the lake of power once their Gods had been defeated. An ambitious agenda, and all because of the mad young seer the Rus-Yuruk had taken in as one of their own six years ago. A mad young shepherd who would drive them south and east as surely as Danjel's ponies were driven. Driving them to war.

Pulling a grass fetish she'd fashioned earlier that morning from her pouch, Danjel changed genders once again as he rubbed it between finger and thumb. The stalks were fine and elastic, heralding change and growth, but twisted under his grip with a restlessness that spoke of random movement and out-of-control actions. Pulling it apart, he tossed it to the breeze to go where it would, then shook his head as the individual grasses spun about his face, catching on his clothes and tangling in his hair.

"So, for all your excitement, you're not yet ready to set out on your own," he noted. "I don't blame you. I'm not ready either. I never am when I come home to my wild lands."

He glanced about with a wistful expression. This was the land where he'd been born and, deep in the Berbat-Dunya, alone with the whispering winds and the singing spirits, his prophecy was clean and clear, like the night sky, bright with stars and shining only for him. In the past he'd returned here every year to gather prophecy for his people, drinking in the peaceful silences, and strengthening his sight. No other wyrdin dared to walk the paths he'd walked.

Until Graize.

Danjel closed his eyes briefly as he called up the image of his adopted kardos. Graize, who'd come screaming into Danjel's world like a comet falling to earth, the storm-enhanced spirits of the wild lands tearing at the young seer's flesh and being torn apart in return. He wielded his destiny like a cyclone, snatching up anyone foolish enough to stray into his path. He'd snatched up Danjel and carried him, first to the vast walls of Anavatan where Graize had brought Hisar into the world in as violent a birth as could be asked for, then later to the Petchan mountains where rock and water had cut the Yuruk wyrdin off from the wild lands' open, peaceful horizon. On the grasslands, he'd carried him into battle with the Warriors of Estavia and Brax, Graize's personal adversary, the dark-haired man that colored all his prophecy with madness and pain. But it had been Danjel who'd finally carried Graize to the wild lands and shepherded him back to a fragile sanity.

Pulling a piece of shredded fetish from his hair, Danjel frowned at it. The problem with prophecy was that it changed as quickly as the weather and a good decision last summer might have become a bad decision by spring. It might have been a mistake to bring Graize and his cyclone into the Berbat-Dunya. Who knew what forces might be snatched up to follow him here.

As if in answer to his question, a faint shimmering to the south caught his attention and shifting genders once again, Danjel raised up in the saddle to regard the horizon intently, then gave a sharp whistle.

A tiny spirit, no bigger than a mayfly, appeared at her elbow. Accepting a seed of power, it read her desire, then spun off to do her bidding. Danjel leaned back in the saddle, waiting patiently as her pony began to crop at the tough grass beneath its hooves.

The spirit returned almost immediately, gyrating in the air like a drunken butterfly, its agitation plain. Soothing it with another seed of power, Danjel dusted the news off its tiny wings with one finger like pollen from a flower petal. In a ring of small hills before the wetlands some three hours distant, a party of six—strangers by their pattern of travel—moved north. Four tasted of leather armor and metal weapons, one of parchment and foreign dyes. As for the sixth, the spirit had managed to glean no more than a single glimpse of white sands and sparkling blue waters before being driven back by a dark, fathomless power that hinted at an insatiable hunger rivaling the spirit's own in its near feral intensity.

Danjel smiled sympathetically. The spirits of the wild lands were not used to being denied. After feeding it a final seed of power, she released it with a thoughtful expression. Graize had spoken to her of Panos of Amatus, the strange, sensual oracle from the southern sea; a woman of great, hidden power who tasted of white sands and sparkling blue waters. As the envoy of the Skirosian king, she was deeply entrenched in Graize's plans against Anavatan. It could only be her. Graize's allies were on the move, and the watchful eyes of Incasa's seer-priests would be scouring the lands around the lake of power, so Panos was taking the land route north.

Danjel frowned suddenly, her concern shifting her gender back and forth until it settled on the male. The land route north led straight into a bog hidden from even the most powerful seer by the wild lands' undulating and unpredictable currents.

Glancing up at the sky, he read its portents on the wind. A bank of clouds was building to the north, promising a summer storm within a day or two. If he pushed the herd just a little harder, they would reach the Rus-Yuruk encampments before it hit, but if he lingered to shepherd an incautious band of strangers who had no real business moving about in his domain, it would catch them all out in the open.

He half turned toward the herd, then sighed resentfully. Panos was Graize's ally and Graize was Danjel's kardos so, whether he liked it or not, it was Danjel's duty to ensure that Panos didn't drown in the wet lands or become hopelessly lost in the wild lands.

Changing genders once again, the Berbat-Dunya wyrdin wheeled her pony about and, whistling to her dogs, began the laborious process of changing the herd's direction to intersect with the forces that Graize's cyclone had dropped into her lap. Again.

✦

Back at camp, Graize suddenly sat up with a laugh as he watched a flock of birds led by a single, purple swallow change direction in the sky.

"Kardos!"

Yal turned from where she was laying out the last of their spring supplies before their tent.

"Yonder birds bring news of your shepherd!" he shouted.

"What news?"

"A change of purpose and direction."

"Meaning?"

"Meaning that Danjel will not be here to take the noon meal with us but should arrive by nightfall."

Flopping onto his stomach, he scattered a handful of power seeds into the grass, watching intently in the Yuruk way as a cloud of spirits rose up to devour them. "Hooves disturb the earth," he murmured. "Ten running freely, two burdened from within, one burdened from without, and seven carrying birds on their backs. They do not move to a single design just yet, but they soon will. The swallow draws them together."

"Danjel's coming home," he shouted to her through the grass. "And brings me a gift: six droplets of the purest prophecy shining as brightly as the morning dew."

Yal made a face at him. "I see more than a dozen dusty black starlings," she stated, shading her eyes with one hand to more clearly make out the distant flock. "How does that make six of anything bright?"

He smiled at her, refusing to relinquish his good humor. "It's very simple if you know how to look, Hawk-kardos," he answered in a tone of mock condescension. "A dozen dusty black starlings? Never. Look closer and you will see within the flock, six juveniles, their feathers speckled with silver light. Six newcomers to the wild lands, shepherded by a wise and . . ." He cocked his head to one side. "More or less willing, swallow."

"The company you spoke of? Panos and Hares with four others?"

"How well you count. Yes. They'll be here by nightfall."

"Hungry?"

"Hungry and tired."

Yal glanced at their supplies. "But mostly hungry," she noted sourly.

✦

Danjel arrived exactly when Graize had predicted, driving the ponies before her just as the sun slipped behind the horizon. Panos of Amatus rode easily beside her with Hares and four Skirosian guards dressed as travelers bringing up the rear.

Graize met them as they came over the rise. Panos dismounted at once, dancing up to him to plant a kiss on both cheeks, her wide, black eyes twinkling.

"You taste of bronze-cast bells and marbled prophecy," she crooned, shaking out her hair in a cascade of golden light.

"And you taste of gilded feathers and honey-sweet intrigue," he replied, matching her mixed imagery with pleasure before turning. "You've met Danjel. This is Yal."

The Petchan woman gave Panos a reserved nod from where she was building up the fire in the center of the camp and Panos returned it with a dazzling smile of her own.

"The terns and gulls of the south greet the plains swallows and mountain hawks of the west," she said with musical formality, then glanced at Graize with a sly smile. "And we are pleased to once again be in the vaulted presence of the shining city's eastern lake gull, who looks down upon his domain from the loftiest of minarets like a monarch on a diamond throne."

Graize snorted at her. "Yal's worried you'll eat up the last of our supplies," he said bluntly, ignoring her metaphors.

Yal gave him a dark look but did not gainsay him.

"Our guide is a great prophet and foresaw this very circumstance," Panos answered easily as both Hares and Danjel came forward, carrying a brace of coneys each. "So you see, we do not come empty-handed.

Plus I bring a jug of the finest arak from Maf-abia to her delin." She gave a guileless smile. "Will they be enough gifts to grant us a place by your fire?"

Yal raised a questioning eyebrow at her, but when Panos continued to smile, she unbent enough to nod. "Of course. You are welcome." She cast a pointed look at Graize and Danjel. "My people will help me prepare the rabbits," she said, "while your people set up camp."

"Pitch tents," Danjel added, gesturing at their packhorse. "The night will be clear of rain, but not of insects, and it may be colder than you're used to."

"All nights here are colder than I'm used to," Panos agreed. As the four guards began unloading the horses, she accepted a heavy, woolen cloak from Hares with another dazzling smile. "But basking in the shining company of my beautiful Anavatanon seer will warm me, even if he does scowl far too much for my liking," she added, stroking his cheek.

Feeling lighter than he had for months, Graize gave her a mock bow. "I will try to smile more if only for your pleasure," he said with unusual gallantry. "At least until after we've drunk Yal's arak."

"And after you've helped with the coneys," Danjel added pointedly.

✦

Night came swiftly, the last of the sun's light leaching away to leave the sky a brilliant swath of black velvet scattered with stars. The company sat around the fire, eating roasted rabbit and passing Maf's jug back and forth. Sitting in the crook of Danjel's arm, Yal glanced over at Panos.

"Graize says that you travel to your lover, Prince Illan of Volinsk?" she asked, tossing each of Danjel's dogs a chunk of meat.

Panos' expression grew wistful. "Officially, I travel as my father, King Pyrros', envoy to join our northern ally in his bid against Anavatan," she answered, setting her usual fluidly moving speech patterns aside for a moment. "But unofficially . . ." She sighed. "My body aches to be with my fiery sorcerer once again, and a dream embrace is a poor substitute regardless of how strongly we may connect mind-to-mind. No doubt I shall forget all my official duties when he's next within the true circle of my arms, and I in his. He soothes the itching in my flesh like a balm of aloe and honey. "

"I know exactly how you feel," Yal agreed. "Graize might have been in danger had Danjel taken much longer, and I'm not even interested in a man's bum . . . I mean balm," she added with a gleam in her eye.

Across the fire, Hares looked up from the sketch he was attempting in the flickering light to cast Panos an embarrassed look as the two women laughed, their joined voices ringing out like silver bells in the still air.

"Hares and my mother would have me settle on a fine Skirosian nobleman's balm," Panos explained, her black eyes sparkling. "A powerful priest's or a mighty admiral's; even a wealthy spice merchant so recently come into his lands and titles that his balm has yet to grow hair would do. But they may have to accept an ambitious Volinski prince's instead. Not a terrible burden for them, I should imagine."

"You will . . . settle on him?" Yal asked, her tongue tripping over the foreign expression. "Does that mean. . . . make a life with him?"

"When I see him, it will mean make love to him," Panos replied, "as fire makes love to a forest. As for an entire life," she shrugged. "Who can say? Life can be painfully short, or painfully long. The future is so delicate as to be easily broken if it's squeezed too hard, like a ripe fruit, ready to be eaten, but oh, be ever so careful how you go about eating it if you don't want its pulp all over the ground instead."

"So, you haven't *seen* a future with him?" Yal pressed, refusing to be any more distracted by Panos' metaphors than she had been by Graize's earlier.

"I have seen many futures, some with him and some without him. Such is the way of prophecy when war looms on the horizon," Panos answered in an uncharacteristically melancholy voice. "Still," she added, throwing off the mood as she might throw off a cloak. "Sometimes knowing the future takes the spice out of the present, and I like a spicy present. Don't you?" She waggled her eyebrows in Danjel's direction, and Yal chuckled.

"Yes," the Petchan woman agreed. "And clearly we both prefer exotic, foreign spices."

Danjel glanced at her with a smile of her own. "Well, this foreign spice is worn out from traveling," she said, kissing Yal on the ear. "And we need to be up early tomorrow if we're going to reach the Rus-Yuruk encampment before the rains come." She stood. "I'm for bed. Will you be long?"

"Not long at all; I'll come with you now."

"Kardos?" Danjel turned to Graize.

He shook his head. "Yal will want your balm all to herself tonight," he replied. "I think I'll linger here beneath the all-knowing stars and get caught up on the news from the south."

"As you like. Just try not to be too late. Remember, the ground is a hard and unforgiving surface if you fall off your pony tomorrow."

"Yes, Abia."

Danjel and Yal left, arm in arm, the dogs trotting obediently behind. After a few moments, Hares rolled his sketch into a cylindrical leather case, put two guards on sentinel duty on either side of the rise, then he and the others retired as well, leaving the fire and the last of the arak to the Anavatanon and Skirosian oracles.

The two seers sat in companionable silence for a long time, Panos staring into the fire with an inscrutable smile on her face. Weaving the prophetic bow the eldest of the Petchan sayers had given him last year, back and forth, Graize sat watching as the spirits lit up like tiny candles as it passed them by.

Finally, Panos glanced over with a speculative expression in her black eyes. "All your streams are finally coming together," she observed, "to create one great raging river of possibility. But there seems to be one individual stream flowing contrary to your design, and its recalcitrant behavior could send your plans to the bottom of Gol-Beyaz, yes?"

He shrugged. "If you mean my Godling," he replied, "It will soon fall into line."

Panos laughed. "Of course I don't mean your golden God-child," she scoffed. "It's following the path of youth exactly as It should do. No, this is something entirely different."

"A hidden element hanging in the balance whose discovery could mean the difference between success and failure," Graize intoned in a bored voice. "I know. I've seen it. But since, as you say, all the streams are coming together to create one raging river, a single element can be swept aside if it gets in the way."

"That depends on the element's identity."

"Which is still shrouded." He touched the side of his nose with one finger.

Panos regarded him with a humorous expression. "It's said among the Skirosian oracles that prophecy is like a broken mirror, showing everything there is to see except oneself. I never thought to witness such a perfect example of the saying."

He scowled at her. "Meaning?"

"Meaning that you are intrinsically tied up with the future, and so the element which hangs in the balance is not shrouded at all, beautiful one. It's you."

When he just stared at her, she laughed. "How easily swept aside do you think it is now?"

He snorted. "You always did have an ironic sense of humor," he noted in a dry tone. "I don't hang in any balance."

"No?" Lifting a twig from the fire, Panos watched as the tip slowly burned down. "A gray-eyed seer and a dark-haired warrior standing together on a snow-capped mountain ridge. From the time I set foot upon these shores, that image has been foremost in my mind."

Graize scowled at her. "That's an ancient stream of possibility long since gone dry," he scoffed, ignoring the pang his words invoked.

"And yet it continues to occur."

"And yet it continues to be ignored."

"And yet." Panos gave him a penetrating look as she wrapped Hares' cloak more tightly about her shoulders. "Denial tastes like ashes and melancholy music played in the shadows," she observed with unusual gravity.

"What does wishful thinking taste like?" he retorted.

As the tip of the twig went dark, emitting a thin stream of smoke, Panos thrust it into the fire once again. "Much the same," she answered, "Only the ashes have tiny, smoldering coals hidden in their midst. Such coals can always be used to rekindle a fire long since believed to be cold. Or they might ignite on their own, burning the whole world up in their misdirected passion." Retrieving the twig, she waved the newly glowing tip at him.

"The dark-haired man is my enemy," he replied. "*Brax* is my enemy, as bent on protecting this world that you speak of as I am on destroying it. We will *not* come together with any kind of passion. Not anymore."

"He haunts your prophecy like a splinter in your eye. You will never be free of him until you find a mirror that shows you his true face. And yours. That's why you've never been able to kill him."

"I *will* kill him."

"Unless you haunt his prophecy in equal measure, he's more likely to kill you."

Graize's lip curled in disdain. "He has no prophecy."

"His God speaks prophecy when Her people are in danger. And his kardos, Spar, the one you speak of when anger clouds your reason, also speaks prophecy."

Graize turned his attention to the fire, unwilling to continue the argument, but her words had hit their mark. If he was going to be free of Brax, he had to be free of Spar as well. He stood.

"I always knew I would have to kill them both," he replied, an inexplicable tightness in his chest leaching the anger from his tone. "Your vision has told me no more than that."

"You will seek him out, then?"

Her tone was no more than curious, but Graize still regarded her suspiciously. "I always seek him out," he answered. Heading up the rise, he glanced at the sky, once again expecting the golden shimmer of wings. Once again the sky remained still, and he shook off the feeling of disappointment with a violent shake of his head. "I will sleep in the open tonight," he said shortly. "Clear dreams, Panos."

"And clear dreams to you, too," she answered. "May you actually pay attention to them if you have them." She watched him go with an ironic expression, then began weaving the twig back and forth as he'd waved his Petchan bow, making lines of red prophecy in the air. Then turning, she stared into the darkness beyond the camp.

"Be patient, little one," she whispered. "Learn from the erroneous ways of your elders and know what you truly desire before you reach for it. In the meantime, sing of life's pleasures while you can."

Allowing the melancholy to return, she smiled sadly. "Fly away now, there's a good little God-child. Take a little golden bird's form and fly away, singing."

✦

Nestled in the grass, surrounded by the spirits of the wild lands, Hisar rose, first with some hesitation, then with more confidence as she made no move toward it. They regarded each other for a long moment, then, taking the seeming of a small, golden sparrow hawk as she'd suggested, It headed south.

Panos lay back in the sweet-smelling grass with a pensive expression. *"So, you haven't seen a future with him?"*

"I have seen many futures. Some with him and some without him."

But many more without him, she admitted silently; so many more that she'd stopped looking. But soon enough she would have to come face-to-face with it. War was indeed looming, and many things could happen in war, both bad and good. There was still a chance if he would take it.

Closing her eyes, she cast her mind north to touch the sleeping mind of Prince Illan Dmitriviz Volinsk.

"I miss you," she whispered across the miles. *"Brook no delays in coming to me. The future grows increasingly uncertain the longer we are apart, and I grow anxious without you."*

4

Distant Lands

ACROSS THE NORTHERN SEA, the dawn sun rose over Kitai, the capital of Volinsk, with a sullen, mist-enshrouded glower. An ancient, densely populated city of wood and stone, Kitai sat at the confluence of three shallow rivers, occupying the only solid ground before the land gave way to a vast marsh that separated the city from its harbor. In the centuries since its inception—as a simple, palisade outpost—thousands of workers had struggled each year to keep the river mouths from silting up altogether.

Standing in a small, wooden pagoda on the shoreline, Prince Illan Dmitriviz Volinsk watched the double line of laborers hauling bucket loads of mud, weeds, and ice chunks from the frigid waters. Volinsk's navy had always been compromised by its shallow harbors and harsh winters. The rivers had only just opened up in the last few days and one late freeze could undo all their efforts in a single night. And late freezes were common.

Illan turned his attention to the dozen elderly weather sorcerers crouched at the marsh edge. Surrounded by a host of attendants and apprentices, they knelt on the cold, mossy ground, ears pressed to a series of sacred holes dug to release the whispering of the earth; listening for the promise of spring. Most of the Volinski sorcerers sought prophecy in the old ways, attending to the natural world around them and observing the controlled behavior of birds and beasts—doves and horses for the most part—to predict the future.

Illan resisted the urge to raise his upper lip in a sneer. It wasn't all that long ago that the court sorcerers had sought their predictions in the animals' entrails instead of their behavior. Illan preferred a more scientific method and had left his teachers and the crowded, bustling capital at age fourteen to pursue his own solitary studies at Cvet Tower where the quiet lapping of the waves and the whistling of the wind were his only natural distractions.

Pressing two slender fingers against the bridge of his nose, he banished each individual component of the capital's sensory bombardment: the odors of fish and dung and smoke, the shouting and singing of drovers, tradespeople, and merchants, the swirling ever-constant flow of swine, poultry, horses, and dogs. And people everywhere, their individual destinies pressing against his vision; each one identifiable for a split second before plunging back into the whole like a vast school of fish. One by one, he regarded them, then discarded them, until he'd fashioned a kind of peace behind the wall of his control for the hundredth time since coming to the capital.

Illan had spent the entire winter at Kitai at his brother, the Duc Bryv's, request, trapped in the palace with a host of courtiers, soldiers, relatives, and sorcerers of two separate nations. Volinsk and their ancient enemy, neighboring Rostov, had forged a peace treaty after the Rostovian duc had died suddenly during a night of drunken revelry. His heir, Tonja Ivaniviz, had surprised everyone by sending an offer of marriage to Bryv rather than the traditional declaration of war. Now with their own child, Prince Mikal Bryviz, safely past his first month's birthday, it looked as if the peace treaty might actually hold for a while.

The perfect time to turn their attention to the invasion of Anavatan.

Across the marsh, the fine, high notes of a sailor's pipe came to him on the breeze and he turned his attention to the distant harbor. Half the combined fleet of Volinsk and Rostov lay at anchor, tucked into the limited space that offered both depth and shelter in the narrow inlet. Illan's sister, Prince Dagn Vanyiviz, would be escorting the rest from Korov and Tunoysev—Volinsk's two major shipbuilding cities upriver—within the week. Outfitting each would take no more than another week after that, so if everything went smoothly at court, the fleet should be ready to set sail within a fortnight.

If everything went smoothly.

He cast his mind back to the night before. Standing in the window of his overly ornate palace suite, Illan had sent his thoughts reaching out toward Panos of Amatus. Although their minds touched nearly every night, he missed the calming influence of her physical presence, her soft singsong conversation, the sleepy-eyed seduction of her smile, and the fiery warmth of her lovemaking.

Closing his eyes, he'd envisioned their bedchamber at Cvet Tower, seeing her reclined across the coverlet or seated by the fire, her golden hair framing her face in a halo of prophetic light.

"I miss you."

"I miss you, too."

"Brook no delays in coming to me."

"I'm on my way."

The future grows increasingly uncertain the longer we're apart, and I grow anxious without you."

Unwillingly, his thoughts had traveled back to when Anavatan's God, Incasa, had sent an unexpected storm to smash the atlas table with which he spoke prophecy. Illan had not wanted to admit the concern that action had caused him, but in the ruins, he had seen a single hidden element, still unformed that had put his doubts to rest. A strength to be wielded or a weakness to be exploited: water sparkling in a cavernous darkness. The future was in flux, not uncertain. Incasa did not hold all the cards, and so He would not win through. Not this time.

"Do not be anxious, my love. We'll be together soon."

He'd turned back to his chambers and the new atlas table he'd commissioned that winter. The ornate wooden pieces stood ready in both offensive and defensive formations with a single uncarved piece representing the hidden element, sitting off to one side.

"Soon, my love," he'd repeated, sending a kiss out on the wind. *"Very, very soon."*

A cough interrupted his reverie, and he turned to regard his sergeant-at-arms, Vyns Ysav, standing at a respectful distance behind him. The older man gestured toward the city gate.

"A palace servant approaches, my lord," he noted.

Illan nodded. "A summons from Bryv."

Together they waited for the green-liveried woman to make her way through the mud and traffic to the pagoda steps, then Illan swept past her without bothering to hear her message, Vyns at his heel. Used to the ways of court sorcerers, the servant dutifully fell into step behind them.

Despite his royal birth, Illan was not well known by sight in this city of two hundred thousand people, but the rich cut of his fur-trimmed and embroidered kaftan, leather gloves and thick, fleece-topped boots marked him as a rich and powerful man, and his inward, arrogant expression marked him as a sorcerer of note. The reed cutters, sheep skinners, launderers, and laborers who inhabited Kitai's crowded Fourth Demesne and the merchants, artisans, and street sorcerers who lived in the Third, made way at once and the guards on the gates saluted briskly.

Illan took the log-paved roads of the more affluent Second De-mesne at a swift pace, past a dozen naked bodies sprinting from a line of steaming bathhouses that smelled of herbs and the equal number of bucket-laden bodies sprinting toward the smoldering ruins of a nearby manor house. Fires were such a common occurrence in this city of tightly packed wooden structures that the wood merchants—peddling precut logs and roof shingles—were often on site before the flames had been brought completely under control. Illan ignored them all, passing through the First Gate without pause.

The central Imperial Demesne was, by contrast to the rest of the city, constructed almost entirely of white sandstone, from the encircling twenty-foot-high fortifications to the labyrinthine palace, which long ago had engulfed the orchards and gardens within its walls. Seeing-stone obelisk towers and wooden-and-stone-clad scrying chapels and shrines from tiny, altar-sized affairs to room-sized temples, dotted the riverbanks and clustered about Kitai's city walls like mushrooms, but in the Imperial Demesne, they were particularly ornate.

This morning, court sorcerers of every ability clustered about a tall, fountainlike obelisk, paying close attention as a black horse, draped in tiny silver-and-golden bells, navigated a series of iron spears laid in an intricate pattern before the palace entrance. Illan paused a moment to note its progress, more out of simple curiosity than belief, then headed up the wide, stone steps that led to the Anise Bell Tower, the main hall of the Imperial Palace.

A hushed peace fell over him at once as he passed into the vaulted antechamber, and he relaxed slightly as the servant ushered him into the throne room and the presence of the Duc Bryv Dmitriviz of Volinsk.

Illan's older brother was a large man of thirty-two years, tall and heavyset with muscular arms and shoulders and a thick mane of light brown hair that often fell into his eyes, mingling with long, dark lashes that were said to be the envy of the court. Beardless, as was the fashion for men in Kitai, he often forgot to shave, sporting a rakish shadow of whiskers across his cheeks that sparkled with a faint bronze glow in the sunlight. A great beauty herself, it was said that Tonja of Rostov had fallen in love with him after a single glance at his portrait. Together, by the sheer force of their charm and beauty, they ruled two fractious nations that had been at each other's throats for centuries.

In private, his sister, Dagn had raised the cynical question of what happened when old age stole these fleeting attributes away, but Illan had shrugged philosophically. Anything that kept Volinsk and Rostov allied, even in the short term, would suit his own ambitions. After that, it wouldn't matter; they had a son, it would be his problem.

Today, Bryv was alone in the throne room, watching the antics of a dozen small dogs who, obedient to a complex series of whistles from their handlers, were doing tricks on the brightly woven carpet before him, leaping and tumbling in the air, then falling down as if exhausted only to leap even higher moments later. Bryv's expression was strained, but he nodded his head with polite appreciation as the handlers bowed at the end of the performance. Catching sight of his younger brother, he tossed the chief handler a small purse before dismissing them, then rose to embrace Illan warmly.

"You look pale; have a drink," he ordered, gesturing at a servant who moved forward at once with a glass of thick red wine. "The winds off the marsh are dangerous this time of year, and you've been away from the capital too long to go without fortification."

Illan accepted the glass absently, one eyebrow raised at the sight of the empty chair next to Bryv's.

Throwing himself back into his own chair, his brother grimaced at him. "You're the mighty sorcerer, you tell me," he grated, attempting to mask the concern in his voice with a snarl.

Illan gave an elegant shrug. "Her Grace, your royal wife, the Duc of Rostov, is closeted with the heir," he said simply. "Who's had the entire palace in an uproar, dancing attendance on the distracted and unpredictable moods of his parents all week, because of a minor cough."

Bryv showed his teeth at him. "Yes, that's what his physicians keep saying—aside from the unpredictable mood comment—but Tonja thinks the spring air off the marsh has affected his chest."

"What does his nurse say?"

Bryv snorted. "Croup."

"Then it's croup. Gleb nursed all three of us in our time, you, Dagn, and me. Gleb is always right."

"That's what I told Tonja. Still . . ." Bryv chewed at his thumbnail, staring into space. "Yes," he said finally. "Croup. Nothing to worry about."

"I'm glad we have that settled. Now, you sent for me, Your Grace," Illan said, putting a mild emphasis on the title. "Was there something else you wanted?"

"What? Oh, yes." Bryv straightened. "The Court Weather Sorcerers say the inlet's finally free of ice."

Illan snorted. "Strangely enough, the sailors aboard your scout ship, the *Anaviz*, which Your Grace sent out only this morning to check on conditions in the inlet, reported the same thing. And they didn't have to rely on the musical pattern caused by a dozen white doves splattering on a dozen silver tea pots to discover it."

Bryv chuckled. "Be kind," he chided. "We can't all suffer from an excess of raw talent like you do.

"The point I'm making," he continued before Illan could offer up another comment, "is that, if the weather continues mild, I could be prepared to order the fleet to depart within a fortnight, maybe sooner."

Illan kept his expression carefully neutral. "And?" he asked politely.

Ignoring the tone of condescension that his brother was unable to mask completely, Bryv leaned forward. "And seven centuries ago," he replied, the expression in his pale gray eyes intense, "the Duc Leold of Volinsk made war against Anavatan and the Warriors of the Battle-God Estavia sent his fleet to the bottom of the sea. Anise of Rostov used that defeat to take his life and take his throne. Since that time, no ruler has ever attempted such a move against Anavatan again."

"Yes," Illan acknowledged. "As we've been discussing all winter, Your Grace, the Anavatanon were a people to be reckoned with. Seven centuries ago."

"But not now."

"No. Now they're distracted and divided and we're allied with raiders and pirates of both ability and power." Illan frowned at his brother.

"I thought you'd closed the debate around the Anavatanon offensive. I've seen a spring of long-lasting storms and heavy fog to the south; so have your Weather Sorcerers. This will be to our advantage and to Anavatan's disadvantage. Has some court sorcerer's dancing bear or prancing pony foretold you otherwise?"

Bryv growled at him. "No," he admitted. "As it happens, all of my people, from my Privy Council on down, agree that Anavatan is ripe for invasion. Although, I suspect it's more because Rostov is now off limits, and they're all bored after a long winter of inactivity, than because of any well-timed storms and foggy conditions."

"We are a militant people," Illan agreed with a mocking smile.

"Yes. The royal family particularly so. Speaking of which, you are to attend me at Council this afternoon."

"As you wish."

"Try to get along with Tonja's uncle, Pyotre, this time, would you please?"

"He's an ass who wouldn't know a prophetic vision if it bit him on the pizzle, but yes, be assured, I'll be at my most gracious."

"Good. We'll be finalizing the chain of command, and that'll be a prickly enough subject all on its own. You'll sail with the fleet."

"Indeed. And bring you such tribute the like of which has never been seen in the Court of Volinsk before; the treasures of the south piled before your child's feet as high as his bald, little head."

Bryv frowned at him. "Tonja's brother, Pieter, will command the fleet and Dagn, the ground troops," he continued, ignoring the remark. "You will advise them of anything of a prophetic nature that they need to be aware of."

"Of course."

Bryv ran a hand through his hair in an irritated gesture, and Illan shook his head in mild exasperation. "You only do that when you have to broach an uncomfortable subject, Brother," he noted. "What is it?"

Bryv grimaced at him. "You know there will be at least one Water Sorcerer on every ship?"

"As always."

"And several court sorcerers from both Volinsk and Rostov aboard the flagship?"

"Yes?"

"And that you will not be allowed to toss any of them overboard, *Brother*."

Illan laughed. "You think so little of my temper?"

"I remember it from when we were children."

"Don't fret. I don't know about Prince Pieter, but Dagn has almost no interest in prophetic warnings, no matter how they've been attained. If it's important, I'm sure all of your sorcerers, including myself, will be united in our struggle to keep from being completely ignored."

"As long as you remember that, despite our blood connections, Rostov is not Volinsk. Their customs are . . ." Bryv paused with a frown.

"Archaic?" Illan finished with a patently false tone of encouragement. "Incongruous? Peculiar?"

"Just different, Brother," Bryv sighed. "Tonja and I are trying to bridge a vast gap here. We could use your assistance."

Illan bowed. "For the sake of my beloved little nephew, you will have my complete cooperation, Your Grace."

"Good." Bryv rose. "Now, we have a few moments before Council. I'm going to see my son and be assured by his nurse that it's indeed only croup and nothing to worry about."

"I'll come with you. Perhaps the word of a *mighty sorcerer* will help assure his mother as well."

Bryv gave him a glum smile. "Perhaps, but don't hold out too much hope. Tonja has less interest in prophecy than Dagn does and a more volatile temper."

"As you say, Rostov is not Volinsk, but the royal family is particularly militant."

"Remember that when she starts throwing things."

Chuckling, the two brothers retired, leaving the throne room to an army of servants who swept in to prepare it for the combined Privy Councils of two very different nations.

✦

Far to the south, Panos brought Illan's kiss, tasting of pears swirling ever faster in a beaker of brandy, to mind with a wistful smile. The small band of travelers had broken camp as soon as the dawn sun had sent fingers of light spilling across the plains with Danjel driving the ponies before them, the dogs keeping pace to either side, and the rest of the company following behind, spread out evenly to keep the dust and flying grasses kicked up by the herd's feet, from choking them. Hares, with his ever-present vellum sketchbook and charcoal, and the other Skirosians rode on the left flank with Graize, Yal, and Panos on the right. For most of the morning, Panos had kept them entertained with songs of the southern seas, her black eyes lost in the memory of her home. Now, she raised her face to the sun, allowing its warmth to dance across her eyelashes.

"The shores of Gol-Bardak Lake to the north of the wild lands are strewn with blue and gray pebbles and the shores of the Gurney-Dag Mountain lakes are dark with deep-green moss," she began. "Even the shores of Anavatan are covered with bits of multicolored marble and lake weeds, but the sandy shores of my own home are white, blindingly white in summer and creamy white in winter. The sky is so blue, it seems as if it might have been the very first radiance to burst forth when the world was born, and the waters glitter like clear green gems, dusted with silver pollen. When you turn to the land, the air vibrates with the scents of olive trees and grapevines. Ribbons fly from every home, fluttering like butterflies. The sentinels who guard my mother's residence, high upon the cliff above the harbor, wear dove-gray tunics, and her servants wear pale green shifts. The marketplace is filled with the cries of sweetmeat sellers and wine merchants. You can buy anything there from marble to music; exotic fruits and shimmering fabrics to spices so pungent and rare that only the Skirosian merchant sailors know where to acquire them.

"There are mountains, too, far inland," she added. "Take the right path and you could lose yourself in such a place and never long to be anywhere else, my tortoise," she said suddenly, turning her intense, dark-eyed stare on Graize.

"Why should I want to be lost?" he shot back.

"Because it's so much more pleasant than being found, if you're lost with the right person."

He gave her his own version of an intense stare. "Wishful thinking tastes like coals in ashes," he reminded her.

"And missed opportunities taste like dust and the bitter, inner peel of citrus fruit. You should take the lover of your dreams and chase a rainbow up a mountain path rather than a storm cloud across the sky while the waves of destiny still lap gently at your feet."

He rolled his eyes. "Even for you, that's a metaphor of truly awesome confusion," he noted. "So here's another one. The game is begun, the pieces are in place, and the dice are rolling. The lapping waves will give over to a raging torrent, and all whom I desire to drown will drown. After that, you may take the lover of your own dreams and chase whatever sky-born symbol you want, up whatever path you wish."

"And what will you do?" she pressed.

"Rest." Driving his heels into his pony's sides, he urged the animal forward, breaking off the conversation abruptly.

Panos waved a dismissive hand as Yal cast her a questioning look. "Oracles are often stubbornly blind," she explained. "They will not see what they don't wish to see unless they're forced to. And even then, they may not heed the warnings," she added more to herself than to Yal as a prescient shiver ran down her spine.

"What doesn't Graize-Sayer wish to see?" the Petchan woman asked, her eyes wide.

"Anything beyond his own ambitions, which, like a narrow strait will not permit much passage. My tortoise moves ever so slowly toward the shore even though he may not wish to." She tipped her head to one side. "I think he may be afraid of hidden shoals ahead," she mused. "And they are there for all of us. But he can be nudged forward as soon as he receives an anchor."

Yal frowned at her. "No offense, Panos-Sayer," she said formally, "but I think Graize may be right. Your words are very confusing. Even for a sayer."

Panos just smiled. "All will be made clear soon enough," she assured the other woman. "Physical events conspire and when that happens, even the most powerful seers are powerless to prevent themselves from being anchored in the world."

At Yal's impatient expression, she laughed again. "Wait until we join the Yuruk, then you will understand."

✦

They camped under the stars that night amid the grazing ponies without bothering to set up the tents. The night had fallen warm and sweet smelling, with a faint breeze that kept the insects at bay without chilling the skin. As the moon rose, Danjel sat with her dogs on a small rise, the smell of her pipe smoke drifting across to them. To Panos' unique sensibilities, it smelled of shipbuilding and rain and, as she fell asleep, her dreams filled with images of her father's port on Skiros.

✦

The southern sea never truly grew cold, but its seasonal storms could wreak havoc with a fleet so, for the two months of winter, the island empire's harbors were crowded with fishing boats, bireme and trireme galleys, and trading vessels. Now, with the onset of spring, most of the fishing and merchant ships had departed, leaving the wharfs to King Pyrros' navy being outfitted for the offensive against Gol-Beyaz.

Standing on the central gangway of the royal trireme, King Pyrros regarded the hive of activity about his main port with a satisfied expression. Of average height and build, Skiros' king was not a particularly imposing man physically, but what he lacked in size he made up for in intensity. Just past his fortieth birthday, his bright golden hair, made brighter by a daily wash of lemon juice, was as thick and shining as it had been at twenty, and worn long and loose with tiny shells and gemstones woven into the plaits so that they flashed in the sun whenever he moved his head. His simple white tunic showed off his breadth of chest and shoulders to their best advantage and his bare arms and legs were well formed and muscular from years spent aboard ship. Although his thoughts were elsewhere, his expression remained both commanding and confident, missing nothing.

Now, he turned the full weight of his regard on the young woman standing by his side.

"So, what do you think of my fleet, Daughter?" he demanded with an indulgent smile. "Is it not vast and formidable?"

Glancing up through a veil of hair so like his own, Panos made a carefully crafted shrug of languid indifference. Dressed in a similar white tunic, she'd been enjoying the way the breeze sang across her skin, playing the fine hairs along her forearms like the strings of a lyre rather than paying much attention to her royal father.

"It's pretty," she answered sleepily, casting her gaze across the lines of warships. "Like a flock of swans upon the water. Except that none of them lift their bottoms into the air to feed," she added.

Pyrros snorted. "I should hope not; they're far too costly to upend themselves in such an undignified fashion."

Accepting a scroll from a hovering servant, he glanced at it briefly before returning his attention to the harbor.

"Our northern allies have wide-sweeping ambitions," he noted. "And the riches of two ducal treasuries to set them in motion. However the doom-seekers on my council are concerned that Anavatan is more than a match for us both even with our advanced weaponry." He waved the scroll at the largest of his vessels being outfitted with a heavy wooden catapult. "They're still advising caution even at this late stage."

"Anavatan does has a fleet of its own," she answered, setting her usual cryptic demeanor aside with a businesslike gesture.

"Lake-sailing penteconters," Pyrros snorted. "With no more than fifty oars apiece to bring them into battle against my lovely triremes with more than twice that number."

"Plus the might of six Gods and six nearly bottomless temple treasuries," she continued. "Without our assistance, Volinsk's ambition would be unreachable."

Pyrros gave a bark of amusement. "Then perhaps I should have negotiated more aggressively with Bryv when he asked for my help."

Panos gave herself over to a bout of musical laughter. "I am sure, my lord-father, that you knew all this when you went into negotiations with the duc, and that your negotiations were as aggressive as they always are." Tucking herself into his side, she nudged him gently until he put his arm around her.

"I'm sending you north," he said simply. "I know you feel that you haven't had enough time with your mother, but I need an envoy to represent my interests with Volinsk. And you miss this prince of yours, don't you?"

Glancing at the pier where Hares, her ever-present guardian, was sketching the hills, villages, and aqueduct beyond the royal port, she shivered as a prescient air raised the air along her arms.

"Yes," she whispered.

"Then it's settled. You'll leave at once." Pyrros tipped his head toward the open sea beyond the harbor mouth. "I don't care who ultimately ends up commanding the waters of Gol-Beyaz, Anavatan or Volinsk," he said, returning his thoughts to business. "I just want them in a weak enough position to accept my terms: free and open trade and

access from the southern sea to the northern. If this conflict weakens
them both equally, so much the better. Go and ensure it."

"Yes, Father."

✦

On the wild lands, Panos frowned thoughtfully in her sleep. She did
not care who ultimately ended up commanding the waters of Gol-Beyaz
either, but she was intrigued by the thought of a future where neither
Anavatan nor Volinsk emerged truly victorious. To her prophetic sight,
it appeared the most stable, so she would obey her father's directive
exactly as he had worded it; she would ensure that both sides weakened
each other equally. Perhaps then her own small fleet might navigate into
calmer waters than those her vision kept returning to.

As she sank deeper into sleep, Panos reached into her dreaming
mind to draw up the first element she needed to accomplish her desire:
a single forerunning memory that had set this possibility into being—an
artist sketching hills and villages and the vast, sweeping arches of Skiros'
royal aqueduct. To that, she added the foreign visions that had followed
her since she'd set foot upon these lands, then reached into the distant
past and found the final element she needed: Estavia's first favorite, a
man of might and myth standing on a rocky promontory overlooking
a vast building site shrouded in fog. She drew the element forward and
laid it gently into the present, watching as the current carried it into the
future toward Estavia's latest favorite standing on his own promontory.

With the future she desired begun, she then turned from her own
seeking and reached out for Illan once again.

✦

Beside her, Graize lay, staring up at the stars for a long time, feeling his
own prophecy ebb and flow like the tide; then he stood with a impatient
grunt. He could sense that Danjel had awakened some time ago and now
sat, smoking and reading prophesy in the sparkle of the stars on the rise
overlooking the encampment. Joining him, Graize pulled out his own
pipe, allowing the calm sensibility of the Yuruk wyrdin's presence to
wash over him. They sat smoking in companionable silence for a long
time until the late night breeze sent a buzzing whirlwind of tiny spirits
to spin about their faces. Brushing them away gently, Danjel stirred.

"We're making good time for all we're burdened by those more suited to sitting in boats than to riding on horseback," he observed. "This shouldn't put us back more than a day at most." He glanced over at his companion, his jade-green eyes bright in the moonlight. "You didn't tell me that your ambitions would be catching us up so quickly, Kardos."

Graize just shrugged. "I'm not all-knowing," he retorted. "The future streams do offer up a surprise catch from time to time."

Danjel gave a snort. "That you would admit to that gives me great hope for your future happiness."

Graize turned a suspicious glare on him. "Does it?" he demanded, his tone somewhat affronted. "And what do you see as my future, *Kardos*?"

Danjel waved a hand at him. "I haven't looked for your future," he replied. "I'm simply pleased that it's now possible that you might actually have one instead of hurling yourself into a mire of madness and revenge."

"Little has changed to alter that course."

"Don't be so sure. That one down there has plans for you, make no mistake."

"The plans of others are easily avoided."

Danjel shrugged, refusing to argue the point any further. Staring up at the moon, his bi-gender features, smooth whatever gender he happened to be wearing at the time, turned pensive. "The spirits sing to me of partings," he said wistfully. "You'll not tarry long among the Rus-Yuruk, will you?"

"No," Graize answered and was surprised that his own tone was equally melancholy. "I will travel north, past Gol-Bardak and the warm welcoming tents of my wild lands family, to Anavatan's Northern Trisect and there deliver the envoy of King Pyrros to her fiery sorcerer and fulfill the destiny I have seen in prophecy."

He glanced over, his expression suddenly closed. "And what destiny has your prophecy shown you?" he asked, his voice now carefully neutral. "Swallows and hawks building nests together from twigs and leaves stolen from the western villages this season?"

Danjel blew a long line of whitish-gray smoke into the darkness before shaking his head. "No. My prophecy has shown me a lithe, young grass snake moving swiftly away from its den in search of prey. I'll be going with you to Anavatan." He sighed. "I will miss my dogs, but Rayne will take good care of them."

"You will go as a grass snake, Swallow-kardos?" Graize asked, striking a dramatically sarcastic pose to mask the sudden lightening of his mood. "Isn't that a bit unwise? Aren't snakes the natural enemies of birds?"

Danjel bared his teeth at him. "I'll be sure to keep them well separated," he replied in a sour voice. "But I just got your wits gathered into something vaguely resembling a proper flock. I'll not have them scattered to the four winds the first time you're let out to pasture on your own."

"Then perhaps you should have seen a herding dog instead of a grass snake."

Danjel's hands dropped down to stroke the two dogs lying quietly at his side. "I did."

"And Yal?"

The wyrdin shrugged. "I haven't asked her yet, but she's come this far. What's a few more miles?"

"A lifetime?"

"That's what I'm hoping for." He gave his adopted kardos a sly look. "My prophecy also showed me a bird's nest lined with exotic feathers this morning; and not my feathers. I think Rayne may have you tarry a little before you go. If she's decided to get a child off you, she won't be easily put off with fancy or confusing words. Destiny and prophecy mean little to her."

Graize felt a brush of heat caress his cheeks and turned his head away in annoyance. "She's always made her ambition plain," he admitted. "But she may have found another."

Danjel snickered. "That hardly matters," he retorted. "Rayne has wider appetites that any one lover could ever sate. Besides, she wants your strength for the Yuruk. She told you that years ago. You can't truly leave us, whether you eventually make your home among the Petchans, the Volinski, Panos' Skirosians, or even the Anavatanon once again. The Rus-Yuruk named you as one of us and our ways flow through your veins, just like they do in mine. When your blood and Rayne's run through the veins of a child, you'll be anchored in our world forever."

"Anchored," Graize whispered.

"Anchored." Turning, Danjel swept his arm out to encompass the land around them. "What do you see, Kardos," he demanded suddenly.

Graize frowned at him. "The wild lands?" he hazarded in an exaggerated tone.

"Yes, the *wild* lands. It's different here, and here you can be different, too."

"Now it's your turn to be confusing, Kardos," Graize accused. "And you aren't very good at it—it takes years of practice—so please speak plainly."

Danjel chuckled. "The streets of Anavatan were laid out by the Gods, yes? So the people, seers and nonseers alike, walk the paths the Gods choose for them?"

When Graize gave him a suspicious nod, Danjel took a satisfied drag on his pipe. "And the Petchan's mountain paths were carved out by centuries of sheep and goats picking out the right path in safety and the people follow those, too, just as obediently. Even the plains are crisscrossed with thin tracks as the herds and ponies of the Yuruk follow the same, time-worn routes to winter pastures and back again, year after year.

"And all of these places have left their mark on you.

"But here, Kardos," Danjel stabbed one finger into the grass at their feet, "where you made your first stand and fought yourself free of the spirits so long ago, here where you bled into the waters that kept you alive before Kursk and Rayne bought you to safety, here in my wild lands where there are no paths because nothing ever walks the same way twice, you can make a second stand against destiny. The swath we cut through the grasses at dawn will close up again by nightfall because we'll never set foot there again. Here there are no paths worn by time, so here you can walk any path, straight or crooked, wide or narrow, as you choose, whatever your anchor."

Graize gave him an impatient frown. "And your point is what?"

"That the ways of the wild lands are in your prophecy as surely as the ways of seer, sayer, or wyrdin, and no matter where you make your home you can never truly leave the Berbat-Dunya either. Its domain is in unpredictable movement and so is yours."

Tapping his pipe clean on a flat rock, Danjel rose, his features flowing smoothly from the male to the female. "Now, I'm going to get some sleep, Kardos," she said. "I'll leave you to sort out what that means for your destiny and your prophecy by yourself."

Heading down the rise, she and her dogs left Graize alone with his own thoughts. As the darkness closed around him like a cloak, the sound of water filled his mind. Deep within it, he could see a thousand tiny, sparkling lights and he licked his lips, suddenly hungry. The cavernous darkness awaited and, suddenly he was impatient to be there.

✦

They reached the plains two days later in a spring downpour that covered everything in a cold, gray mist. Sheep dotted the landscape and, as they urged their ponies forward, a tiny spirit spun about Danjel's head, then shot away into the storm as he gifted it with a seed of power. Moments later, a high whistle sounded on the wind.

"They've recognized us," Danjel said. Standing in the saddle, he looked down on his people's lands with a smile, then began driving the ponies forward at an eager pace. "We've been gone for far too long, Kardos," he called over his shoulder.

Graize found himself smiling as well as the memories of his time with the Rus-Yuruk flooded over him, but as a tall, deeply-tanned woman rode forward to meet them, her pony's hooves splashing through standing puddles of water and the white yak's tail standard of a Yuruk shepherd held loosely in the crook of one arm, he felt his mouth go inexplicably dry. She reined up before them, barely gifting their companions with a haughty glance, before turning her familiar scowl upon him.

He attempted a disarming smile.

"Hello, Rayne."

She cast a jaundiced eye in his direction, then uttered the words both he and Danjel had been expecting.

"It's about time you two shiftless wyrdin got home. There's work to be done."

As Danjel pointed defensively at his herd of ponies, Graize found himself releasing a tension he hadn't realized he'd been carrying for so long. He was home. Whatever stream he might navigate in the future, he could tarry here for just a little while in the safe anchorage of Rayne and the Rus-Yuruk. As the sky above them began to darken with rain, he urged his pony forward.

5

Councils

"*YOU'RE FOR ASSEMBLY, GHAZI.*"
The day had dawned wet, raining steadily through the Morning Invocations. The cobblestone streets of Anavatan were slick and dotted with puddles; by the time, Kemal reached the Derneke-Mahalle Citadel, he was soaked through and grumbling. Stalking down the flagstone path that wound its way through the ornate orchards and gardens that surrounded the Citadel proper, he observed darkly that what had once been an occasional duty had somehow become a title: Proxy-Bey Kemal of Estavia-Sarayi to Anavatan's Governing Assembly.

Yashar had snorted cynically when he'd mentioned this observation over breakfast. Seated at their usual table in the Cyan Company Dining Hall, the older man had added an unsympathetic expression to the snort.

◆

"There'll be nothing but proxy-beys there until the day the enemy attacks; a silver asper on it," he stated, stabbing a dried date at the other man for emphasis. "Because proxy-beys can only give assurances passed down from their superiors. They can't make actual promises or take actual responsibility for anything. If any true beys show up today it'll be because they want something specific. You mark my words."

Kemal nodded glumly. "I counted it last week," he said, tearing a piece of bread from the loaf in front of them and dipping it in a bowl of saffron-scented oil. "If we send every reinforcement to every village, tower, and Trisect, that's demanding them, we'd empty the temple three times over."

He sat back, staring morosely into his coffee cup before draining it in one swallow. "We don't have enough trained warriors to present a powerful enough defense everywhere at once," he observed. "We have to outnumber them somewhere, but I don't think we can."

Yashar gave a dismissive sniff. "The village militia can handle the Yuruk. The Petchans, too, for that matter; their muting effect won't mean much right beside the God-Wall. And the navy can bottleneck the Volinski fleet in the Bogazi-Isik Strait. For my money, what we need to concentrate on is the Skirosians. That king of theirs is ambitious and dangerous. Before you know it, he'll be sailing up Gol-Beyaz. We should've put a stop to his plotting before he landed on Thasos."

"Apparently, the governing council of Thasos requested his presence when they found themselves without a leader," Kemal noted sarcastically, accepting a new cup of coffee from a server.

"Yes, and how did they end up without a leader?" Yashar demanded. "She fell off a cliff while riding. Leaders don't just fall off cliffs, Kem. They're pushed or thrown."

Kemal shrugged.

"You should send Brax to Assembly," Yashar continued, finishing the rest of the bread. "He'd go if you asked him to. He's done it before."

"I would, but he'd draw too much attention right now."

"To what?"

"To his relationship with Hisar."

✦

Handing his wet cloak to a server, Kemal made his way along the Citadel's spiraling marble hallways, adding his own set of wet footprints to those who'd arrived before him. The Assembly had been making demands about Hisar ever since they'd returned from the grasslands. So far, Estavia's temple had managed to put them off, but Anavatan's three Trisect beys were becoming increasingly insistent. Spar had been traipsing the city streets with Brax and the young God in tow all season, and the beys wanted to know why.

The first time Kemal had asked Spar that question directly, the youth had given one of his patented one-shouldered shrugs, his blue eyes staring up at his abayos with a guiless expression.

"Hisar needs to understand Its place among the people, Aba, and they need to understand it, too."

"And what is Its place, Delin?"

"We don't know yet. That's why we go out."

"And Brax?"

"Brax's place is beside us."

"FIND A TEMPLE FOR HISAR AND GET IT OUT OF MINE."

As Kemal made for the huge double doors of the Central Assembly Chamber, the echo of Estavia's words reverberated in his mind. He wasn't sure which was more worrisome, Estavia's words or Spar's.

✦

Roused from sleep by the intensity of Her command, he'd thrown on an old training tunic at once and headed for Estavia-Sarayi's central dormitory wing at a brisk trot. The marshal had met him at the door to her private chambers, giving him a flat, irritated look before jerking her head down the corridor.

"My audience room. Ten minutes."

"Yes, Marshal."

✦

"Find a temple," the marshal growled after a sleepy-eyed server had brought them a carafe of strong, black tea and a hastily piled plate of flatbread smeared with mint-flavored honey. As the late night wind sent a whisper of chilled air through the room's three screened walls, she flicked a braid off one shoulder before accepting a cup of tea from Kemal, and leaning back with a grimace.

He echoed her position with a frown. "Find a temple," he repeated, scrubbing at the short growth of beard at the side of his face. "Does Estavia mean *build* a temple, do you think?" he asked.

"On the eve of invasion?" The marshal jerked one hand up in a frustrated gesture. "If She does, She must have a strategic reason for it. I just wish She'd mentioned the reason," she added, "in the morning." Turning her head, the marshal regarded the small, mosaic-tiled map of the city that adorned the one stone wall of the audience chamber.

"Anavatan didn't just grow on its own," she observed with a grimace. "It was laid out by the Gods, with the walls of all six temples butting up against each other to provide protection for the southeastern shore-line. The most appropriate place for a new temple should be along that shoreline, but there's no room, and we can't banish the creature to some outer area of the city. Much as I'd like to," she added in a dark mutter.

Kemal smiled tiredly. "So whose temple lands do we try to appropriate, Marshal?" he asked.

She glared at him. "None, Ghazi. Each temple controls roughly the same amount of property. No one's going to be willing to give up any of it."

Kemal glanced over at the map thoughtfully, a memory prodding at the back of his mind. "What about the area northwest of Lazim-Hisar?" he asked.

The marshal raised an eyebrow at him. "I'm not sure that Admiral Gulun would appreciate you *appropriating* Estavia's naval dockyards," she said dryly.

"Most of the naval dockyards are on the Eastern Trisect, south of Dovek-Hisar," he answered. "The Western Trisect lands are mostly used for storage."

"That's outside the temple perimeter," she pointed out. "Although only just," she amended. "Hisar's temple would be separated from Estavia-Sarayi by Lazim-Hisar itself."

"Perhaps that's for the best. Many delon are happiest close but not in the pockets of their elders. Why should the Gods be any different?"

"Why, indeed?" Setting her cup down, the marshal stood with a yawn. "The storage buildings would have to be demolished and their goods redistributed, but the area around Lazim-Hisar seems to be the only available location, so, it looks like we're going to build young Hisar a temple. I'll inform the command council in the morning after which you can inform Anavatan's governing council."

"Me?"

"It was your proposal." She smiled triumphantly at him. "You're for Assembly, Ghazi. You'll need to be briefed on the day's agenda. Come and see me after breakfast."

✦

As Kemal reached the end of the hallway, he noted sourly that his proposal seemed to have volunteered him for far more than just the announcement of a new temple. Taking a deep breath, he strode into the room with as confident an air as he could muster.

✦

The Citadel's Central Assembly Chamber was a vast, domed hall wrapped with delicately wrought marble viewing galleries and tall, latticed windows. A study in contrasts, on a sunny day enough natural light flooded into the space to fill the room with a golden brilliance; on an overcast day, it was draped in shadow, prudently lit with an eye to the cost of lamp oil and candles. Today, however, each of the twelve candelabra which ringed the walls and the six hanging lamps which hung over the wide, mahogany council table had been drafted into service to try and chase away the gloom that had affected everyone's mood. As Kemal entered, he wondered how Senior Abayos-Priest Neclan of Oristo-Sarayi would view the added expense; Neclan was notoriously frugal, she did not believe in giving in to *moods*, and the Citadel's Chamberlain had been her own personal delinkos.

Over half the Assembly beys had already arrived before him and, shaking his head to clear the water from his face and beard, he glanced about the room to see if Yashar had won himself a silver asper. A usual Closed Assembly Day could expect to see mostly proxy representatives from the six temples and the three civic Trisects with no more than one or two of the twelve villages along Gol-Beyaz in attendance. Since the threat of invasion, however, the villages had been attending regularly, and it looked as if today would be no exception. Eight seats were already occupied, one of them by a full bey. However, Yashar was in no danger of losing his silver asper.

Across from them, Bey Neclan sat speaking quietly with a junior oracle from Incasa-Sarayi. The older woman's lean features held a stern expression, and Kemal felt a twinge of pity for the young seer. Since Bey Freyiz's death last year, the Prophecy God's temple rarely sent anyone of rank to Assembly. It personified Yashar's cynical theory on ducking responsibility.

As did Oristo-Sarayi, Kemal noted. Bey Neclan always wanted something and never sent a junior to speak for her or for her temple.

Nodding to them both, Kemal crossed the room to the long table of food and drink which dominated the west wall. Proxy-Bey Jemil of Usara-Sarayi and Proxy-Bey Aurad of Ystazia-Sarayi stood nearby and, as Kemal approached, the bi-gender physician raised one fine hand in greeting.

"A squalid day, Ghazi. You looked soaked through."

"I am."

"Have a cup of broth, then. It should warm you up."

As Jemil ladled a cupful from a large, silver tureen in the center of the table, Kemal noted a similar cup in Aurad's hand with amusement.

The master musician chuckled as he spotted Kemal's expression. "I don't argue with physicians," he explained. "It doesn't get you anywhere."

"I'm delighted to hear that you've finally gained some wisdom in your old age," Jemil answered. "Now, how about drinking some of it?"

"In due time when it cools a little." Aurad leaned toward Kemal. "Don't expect to get out of here anytime soon," he warned him. "My delos, Bagh, has been singing at Havo-Sarayi this season and told me this morning that First Cultivar Adrian was definitely coming today. You know what that means?"

"They want more protection on the western fields. I know, the marshal briefed me on their latest concerns."

"Hm." Aurad glanced past him as Anavatan's three civic beys entered, First Cultivar Adrian in their midst. As they took their seats, all four clumping together at the far end of the table, he gave Kemal a sympathetic look. "I think their concerns may have just increased, my old friend," he noted.

The Assembly began a few moments later, with a full twenty-one beys in attendance. The upper galleries were dark and still, but Kemal did not fool himself into thinking that a Closed Assembly Day actually meant that they would have some privacy. A dozen servers of Oristo would be coming and going all morning, filling cups and glasses, fetching supplies for the council scribes, and generally seeing to everyone's needs. It guaranteed that any important information would sweep down Gol-Beyaz with all the speed of a winter storm.

And today it would move particularly swiftly, he observed. Sipping his broth, he schooled his expression to one of polite neutrality as the Citadel's senior scribe called the Assembly to order.

Bey Reese of the Northern Trisect was the first to speak. It was believed that his people had worked the lands north of the Halic-Salmanak since before the Gods had built Anavatan, and he'd been a passionate representative of their interests at Assembly since he'd taken over the position from his oldest kardos at age sixteen. That he'd managed to keep their concerns on the table for the last three years despite being the youngest bey on a Council heavily weighted toward subtle and senior political manipulators said as much about his stamina as about his abilities.

Now, he fixed Kemal with an intense stare.

"We need more people guarding the northern approach," he said bluntly. "Both ghazon and battle-seers."

Kemal gave no reaction as the gathered began to murmur their consternation at this unorthodox approach.

"You have Gerek-Hisar," Bey Pashim of Ekmir-Koy pointed out at once. "A well-fortified sea wall, and half Estavia's navy."

"Yes, *Sayin*," Reese answered, emphasizing the title with an exaggerated formality that caused the elderly potter's eyes to narrow dangerously. "We need no added protections by water; but we're highly vulnerable should the enemy land a force of any size off the coast and move inland."

"That's a very big if, *Bey-Delin*," Pashim sneered back at him, drawing a bark of laughter from Aurad that caused him to cough violently into his cup. One well-placed glare from Neclan cowed the master musician, however, and the Council returned their attention to Pashim.

"No enemy force has ever managed to cross the northern terrain successfully," she continued in a lecturing tone. "It's *mountainous*."

"No enemy force has ever crossed the Deniz-Siya Sea with the numbers Incasa's people are predicting either," Reese replied. "And *we* don't have the God-Wall at our flank to protect us."

"Yes, the Northern Trisect is young for a metropolis as a city counts the years," Aurad agreed in a light tone. "Much younger than the Wall."

"Yes, and old as its people count the food in their bellies," Reese snapped, refusing to be mollified. "We provide most of the meat that feeds the Western Trisect. And we have a small, transient population, mostly farmers bringing their herds to market and no militia to speak of," he continued as Pashim bridled again. "If the Northern Trisect were to be attacked, without help from the Warriors of Estavia, we would soon fall, and that would leave the Western Trisect docks vulnerable with the enemy behind the sea chain."

✦

"It also leaves the northern aqueduct vulnerable," First Cultivar Adrian added in a serious tone that cut through the growing tension between the two rural beys. "Which I'm sure I don't need to remind anyone here provides most of Anavatan west of the Temple Precinct with clean drinking water.

"One of my priests serving at the aqueduct's Havo-Cami has some small prophetic ability and has had a dream of approaching danger. The aqueduct cannot fall into the hands of the enemy. If there's even the slightest possibility of a threat to the north, it must be protected at all cost."

"Can the seers at Incasa-Sarayi speak to this possibility?" Jemil asked.

All eyes turned to the junior oracle who straightened with an attempt at a languid gesture.

"At this time there is no one stream that flows more strongly than any other, Sayin," she answered. "We've seen that Volinsk will move south. We've seen that Skiros will move north, and that the Yuruk and Petchan raiders will move east in some form of concerted support to these two main attacks. However, the details have not yet been made clear. Obviously, our enemies' battle plans are not yet fully realized."

"But there is a stream that speaks to this particular threat against the city's drinking water?" Bey Kahet of the Western Trisect insisted.

"The aqueduct has made a brief, insubstantial appearance in vision as water in darkness," she admitted. "Once."

"Once is good enough for me. Can Estavia-Sarayi speak to its defense *today?*"

All eyes now turned to Kemal, some anxious and some hostile. If Estavia-Sarayi promised a full contingent of reinforcements to the Northern Trisect, everyone knew that they would have to be taken from somewhere else.

Kemal decided to err on the side of bluntness.

"No," he answered.

"Estavia-Sarayi recognizes the importance of the aqueduct and the goods provided by the Northern Trisect," he added as both Reese and Kahet bridled. "And we are prepared to send reinforcements to the garrison at Gerek-Hisar."

"How many?" Reese demanded.

"I don't know, Sayin," Kemal replied, using the title Reese's position merited with no hint of sarcasm. "Our command council met early this morning but they've sent me with assurances, not specifics."

"I have an audience with Marshal Brayazi this afternoon," Reese said stiffly. "Will she have specifics for me by then, or am I just wasting my time?"

"If your audience was called to address this issue, Sayin, likely she will."

"And will we also have specifics," Bey Pashim demanded. "The God-Wall may protect the villages, but it does not protect the western fields and, despite Bay Reese's contention that they provide the bulk of the capital's meat, Ekmir-Koy sends its full share of provisions to the citizens of Anavatan."

"Everyone's needs are being addressed, Sayin," Kemal answered in as patient a tone as he could manage. "We're moving swiftly to provide all the Gods' people with a full defense. The numbers will be in place when and where they'll be needed. The enemy is not yet upon us. We have time.

"And to that end," he continued, "I am charged by Estavia's temple with bringing a new concern before the Assembly which will require the full assistance of everyone here, but most particularly the Western Trisect."

As the gathered turned to him, surprise and suspicion in equal measure in their eyes, he took a deep, inward breath. He and Marshal Brayazi had discussed their strategy regarding this momentous announcement, but talking about it and putting it into practice in front of twenty people with their own personal agendas was another matter entirely.

✦

"Incasa-Sarayi will be particularly oblique," the marshal said as they headed for the gatehouse towers at a brisk walk, "unless they've had a directive from Incasa Himself, in which case they may attempt to steal your thunder. Don't resist it. If they seem to be on our side, don't lead; follow. That way, they'll take the heat for it."

Kemal gave a disbelieving snort. "If there's going to be any heat, I doubt Incasa-Sarayi will lead," he observed. "They'll just stand back and let it hit me full force. While toasting a piece of bread and cheese," he added in a sour tone.

"Very likely," the marshal agreed. When he gave her an unhappy glance, she just shrugged. "The main thing is to get them to agree to pay for it, Ghazi. I know that seems like a petty detail," she continued as they made their way into the dark entrance tunnel, "but right now Hisar has no followers to do the work and no priests to bear the expense. Those beys are tighter than armor on a pig and, since it was Estavia's directive, they're going to expect Estavia-Sarayi to pay for it. Remind them that a new God is clearly the responsibility of every temple, village, and Trisect on Gol-Beyaz."

"Is It?"

The marshal sighed. "I don't know," she answered. "But It ought to be." She passed under the raised portcullis, and, as the two Sable Company sentinels on guard before the gate came to attention, she turned. "Make them understand, if you can, that if we take control of Hisar's new temple, we keep control of Hisar. That should get them thinking and maybe take enough heat off you to keep Incasa-Sarayi from making toast."

His expression doubtful, Kemal saluted, then headed wordlessly across the public parade square as the rain began to fall in earnest. When this was all over, he determined, Brax was definitely going to take on this duty a lot more often.

"Or Spar will," he added in a dark mutter. "That would serve them all right."

✦

The Assembly's reticence to accept any responsibility for Hisar's new temple was much as he'd expected, but with help from Bey Neclan, who'd clearly seen the hidden threat behind Marshal Brayazi's words faster than the rest, he'd been able to squeeze a tentative agreement from them: they would look at plans and budgets. For now. The Western Trisect Bey was not happy but, once he'd been reassured that no part of the public docks was being considered, only the naval, he grudgingly fell into line as well.

As the Assembly broke up, Kemal made his way out as quickly as possible, passing Neclan deep in conversation with the Citadel's Chamberlain. As she stabbed one disapproving finger at the blazing chandeliers, he noted, not for the first time, that he was grateful to be a priest of Estavia and not of Oristo.

As he made his way back through the dripping orchards, a fine shimmer of wings buzzed around the Citadel dome, then sped past him so close it ruffled his hair. It coalesced into Hisar in His golden-seeming hovering just in front of him.

Kemal gestured toward the Assembly Hall with his chin.

"You heard?"

Hisar started slightly at being addressed so directly, but recovered quickly. "I heard."

"Then you should go thank Her."

The young God frowned. "Thank who?"

Kemal favored Him with an expectant expression. "Estavia? For initiating the building of your temple? It's customary when someone does something nice for you."

"Oh." Hisar chewed at His lower lip. "I've never actually talked to Her before," He admitted. "I don't think She likes me very much."

"Well, there's nothing like good manners to change an elder's opinion."

"I suppose." The young God's expression suddenly brightened. "I know. You could thank her for me. You talk to Her all the time."

With a spray of metallic brilliance, It changed back to Its dragonfly-seeming, then changed back almost at once.

"Um. Thank you."

And then It was gone, heading for Its new temple site.

Kemal just shook his head. "You're welcome," he muttered then, turning toward Gol-Beyaz, he placed his hand against his chest.

"Thank you."

✦

A few steps behind, Senior Abayos-Priest Neclan took her own leave of the Assembly Hall after assuring herself that the extra candles in the Assembly Chamber would be snuffed out at once and, striding through the rain, she made for Oristo-Sarayi, purposely ignoring the curious expressions of the local merchants and tradespeople.

Chamberlain Kadar of Oristo-Sarayi met her at the temple's entrance.

"Is it true what they're saying, Sayin? Is Estavia-Sarayi building a temple for the young God?"

Handing her dripping cloak to a delinkos, Neclan pursed her lips in irritation at the speed with which her own people could newsmonger. "It's true that Estavia-Sarayi has *decided* to build a temple for the young God *without* speaking to the rest of us," she allowed. "And it's true that they've chosen a site, again *without* speaking to the rest of us. And furthermore, it's also true that they expect us to help pay for it. Was there anything else you wished to know to be true, Kadar?"

The warning tone would have cowed anyone but her own chamberlain. Kadar merely raised an eyebrow. "*Are* we going to pay for it, Sayin?"

"Oristo-Sarayi will offer an *appropriate* amount of money and labor after we are consulted regarding the actual construction." She turned. "Gul, raki, lemon, and a small bowl of steamed rice in my meditation room in five minutes."

The delinkos bowed. "Yes, Sayin."

"Hisar requires a solid footing on the shores of Gol-Beyaz to bring It into line with the rest of the Gods when It reaches maturity," Neclan continued, returning her attention to Kadar. "And the site chosen may be the only site possible under the circumstances. Its proximity to Estavia-Sarayi, however, is entirely too close. It will bear some direct supervision."

"Will you be calling a Consultation, Sayin?"

Neclan considered it, then shook her head. "No, we all have enough to do as it is. Send messages to each of the chamberlains informing them of the temple's decision. Although they will have received news of the building from a dozen different sources already," she added with a peeved expression. "Tell them we'll be discussing it at the regular Weekly Consultation, so anything else of a pressing nature should be passed along at once."

"Yes, Sayin."

Spinning on her heel, Neclan swept from the hall, leaving Kadar feeling some small sympathy toward the Battle God's people.

✦

Across the city, Hisar joined Spar and Jaq on a wide stone pier jutting into the strait, heedless of the rain that splattered down around them. The young God swiftly outlined all that had transpired at Assembly that morning, smiling as His narrative drew an approving nod from Spar. Then, stretching out on His belly, He ran His fingers along a tower symbol He'd found a week ago etched into the pier, before glancing about with a sleepy expression.

Before them, the ground was rough and strewn with rocks and chips of masonry, sloping steeply down to the water's edge where the ancient stone bollard that had once held the southern end of the sea chain had been refitted with a new iron ring and fastener. The air smelled of fish, lake weeds, rot, and wet dog.

Hisar wrinkled His nose. "This is where my temple's gonna be?" He asked in a disappointed voice. "It's awfully smelly . . . and small."

Resisting the urge to frown at the young God's ungrateful attitude, Spar fished a piece of dried meat from the pouch at his waist. "The site goes all the way back past those buildings there," he answered, gesturing at the collection of small warehouses behind them. Twisting off a bite of meat, he tossed the rest to Jaq. "And maybe we'll take over Lazim-Hisar, too. Would that be big enough for you?"

Hisar craned his neck around to stare up at the great watchtower looming behind them. "It is big," He agreed. "It looks like I look in your dark place."

"It's a good site," Spar continued, tossing a lock of sopping wet hair off his face. "It's right beside the western docks. Since you'll probably get most of your new followers from there and the Tannery Precinct, they won't have far to come."

Dry, despite the red bead about His neck, Hisar raised one golden eyebrow at him. "So, I'm gonna be the God of Lifters and Beggars?" he asked, mirroring Spar's dockside accent.

"Most of them are unsworn. And you couldn't want for any better, besides. We think on our feet. That's important when you're new."

Hisar looked down at the ground where Spar had kicked off his sandals as soon as they'd sat down. "You go barefoot a lot," He noted. "So does Brax, even when he practices. Is that what you mean by thinking on your feet?"

"No. Shoes are just uncomfortable sometimes. We weren't raised to wear them and bare feet are better for climbing. Shoes make your feet soft and weak. If you suddenly had to go without them, that would make you weak."

Hisar gave him a sly grin. "And weak followers make the Gods weak, right?"

Spar cast him a sour look in reply. "Right. For the sworn."

"You're sworn."

"Than I guess if my feet were weak, it would make you weak. Good thing they're not weak."

Hisar nodded, then glanced shyly at the tunic Spar was wearing. The youth had bought it that morning at one of the secondhand clothing stalls in the permanent open air market before Ystazia-Sarayi. Considering and discarding a dozen different colors, he'd finally settled on an oversized mustard-yellow tunic decorated with a pattern of fine, pale green threads. Once they'd arrived on the pier, he'd stripped off his sodden blue tunic, folding it carefully, before pulling the new one on over his head.

"Is that my color?" Hisar asked, trying to hide the eagerness in His voice.

Spar scowled down at it. "For now."

Hisar's face fell. "Don't you like it?"

"Not really. But it'll do. We can't use real gold, can we? Your followers'd starve for the sake of their clothing."

"So why'd you buy it then if you don't like it? I could be a different color." The young God turned red then blue then brown to demonstrate. "Does it really matter?"

"It matters. The Gods have all settled on different colors and their priests wear clothes that match." Spar glanced down at his folded blue tunic with a frown. "Mostly. Even if you change your own color, people have seen you as gold. They like to feel part of something and wearing the same clothes makes it easier for them, so right now this is as close to gold as we can get."

"So you wear a blue tunic to feel part of Kemal and Yashar's family?"

"Yes."

"But not black like Estavia's seers, even though you're a seer?"

"No."

" 'Cause you don't want to be part of them?"

"I'm *not* part of them."

"You're a part of me."

Spar paused a moment, then nodded. "Right. Like you said, I'm your First Priest so when I'm acting as your First Priest—like when we're here—I'll wear a color that turns me sallow and makes me look like I'm dying of drink. For you. At Estavia's temple I'll still wear blue. At least until I turn sixteen," he added. "After that I'm not sure what I'll do. I'll probably still be living there for a while."

Growing bored with the conversation, Hisar rolled off the pier, shaking Himself as he'd seen Jaq do so often once His feet had hit the ground. He prowled about for a bit, circling each one of the warehouses, until He came to a small shed tucked up against Lazim-Hisar.

He cocked His head to one side as a familiar tingle worked its way up His spine.

"Spar?"

"What?"

"There's a tower symbol in here. Feels like a big one."

"Yeah?"

"Yeah, but I can't see a way in; the door's locked and there's shutters on both the windows."

"Check around the back for a hole or a loose board."

The young God did as He was told until He spotted a piece of wood swinging slightly ajar. He prodded at it experimentally and it swung away to reveal a small, dark hole in the wall. He peered through it, feeling the tingle in His chest growing stronger.

"Spar?"

"What?"

"I found a way in."

"And?"

"And it's dark."

"Can't you see in the dark?"

"Well, sure I can," the young God answered peevishly. "But if you came over here with a light, then we could both see in."

"I'm not carrying anything to make a light with."

"Come over anyway. Unless you figure you've forgotten how to break into somebody else's place," He added disdainfully.

Grinning at the blatant attempt to manipulate him, Spar jumped off the pier, joining Hisar a moment later. Waiting until Jaq'd had a good long sniff without showing any signs of alarm, he crouched down and studied the dimensions of the hole with a critical air. "I think I can just make it," he decided. "Just."

Lying on his side, he inched himself through the hole like a snake, twisting a little to allow his new breadth of shoulder to squeeze through. Jaq wriggled in a moment later and then Hisar, in Its mouse-seeming, crept in as well. He changed back at once and the three of them stood quietly together until Spar's eyes could adjust to the dim light filtering in through the shutter slats, then moved apart to explore.

The shed was made up of a single room filled with storage crates and barrels stacked randomly about. Someone had cleared the space around one wall, and as they approached, Hisar gave a sudden gasp. Carved into the wall were dozens of tower symbols, some big, some small, some crude, some incredibly ornate. The young God moved toward them like a sleepwalker and, when His fingertips touched the first of the symbols, His eyes fluttered closed in pleasure.

"There's so many power seeds here," He breathed, running His hands greedily up and down the wall. "What is this place?"

Spar made a quick circuit of the room, Jaq trotting obediently at his heels, until he came upon a small pallet made up of loose straw and a single tattered blanket tucked behind a stack of barrels. Eyes wide, he backed away slowly. "It's a hide," he said in a hushed voice.

"A what?"

"A hide. You know, a place to hide. A safe place." He made for the hole at once. C'mon, we need to get out of here."

"Why?"

"Because it's somebody else's safe place, not ours."

"But . . ." Hisar pointed indignantly at the tower symbols, half of which were still buzzing with unharvested power.

"All the more reason," Spar argued. "This is a private place, Hisar. Maybe even a sacred place."

"Yes." The young God nodded emphatically. "Sacred for me. These are me, Spar, my symbols, and they're all over the place. Why are they all over the place if they aren't for me?"

Spar paused. "I dunno. Do they feel like that one did last night did? Expectant?"

Hisar frowned thoughtfully. "No," He said after a long pause. "Not . . . yet."

"Then it's like I said before, it's somebody else's place, not ours. Not yet, anyway," he added in acknowledgment of the young God's aggrieved expression. "C'mon. We're leaving. Now." He and Jaq worked their way out again with Hisar following very reluctantly behind.

The rain had eased off since they'd been inside, and as a thin shaft of sunlight broke from the clouds, the extra power He'd consumed caused Hisar to glow with an almost incandescent light. He stretched His arms wide, preparing to fly as Spar retrieved his tunic and sandals, but when Jaq gave a soft woof of warning, they both turned.

Three youths in the patched clothes of the dockside lifters stood off to one side watching them with carefully neutral expressions, hands draped loosely over worn knife handles, postures alert but nonthreatening. For now. Spar schooled his own stance to match, and they stood for a long moment, not speaking or moving, until he glanced over in Hisar's direction, his expression bored.

"Getting on time to get goin'," he said casually, his dockside accent thicker than it had been for some years. "You wanna go to the bookmongers?"

Hisar's eyes sparkled, but He carefully mimicked Spar's demeanor, shrugging one shoulder with an expression of complete disinterest. "Sure whatever."

"C'mon Jaq."

The three of them sauntered past the bollard, keeping the youths in their peripheral vision until they passed out of sight. Hisar made to speak, but Spar lifted one finger in warning.

"Not yet."

Once they'd made their way into dockside, merging with the crowds of porters and tradespeople who'd become used to the young God's presence in the last nine months, Spar nodded the all clear, and Hisar gave him a puzzled frown.

"What was that all about?" He demanded.

"Manners. That shed was probably their hide. We were in their territory, so we had to let them see that we weren't any threat."

"Their territory? That's going to be *my* temple site," Hisar pointed out.

"Going to be. Isn't yet. We might have to oust them when we start building, so it pays to stay polite for now."

"Hm."

"What?"

The young God shook His head. "Nothing, it just seems like today's all about being polite and having manners."

Spar shrugged. "Some days are. C'mon, let's go see Alesan."

Hisar grinned at him. "Sure, whatever," He repeated proudly.

Spar just rolled his eyes.

✦

The western dockside market was much as it had always been; a collection of shabby stalls and carts drawn together to form a rough semicircle around the wharfs that serviced the northern trade. The southernmost tip was the most respectable section, built up against Ystazia-Cami. It was here that the small collection of booksellers and bookbinders plied their trade. Spar had been coming here, mostly to stare longingly at the books themselves, since he'd been four years old. They had been the only things he'd never even considered lifting.

Now he breathed in the familiar aroma of old parchment and cheap leather as he ran his hands lovingly over a small volume of pastoral poetry in his favorite stall. Four years ago, the library at Estavia-Sarayi had boasted twelve thin volumes, predominantly involving military tactics. In the last few months, Spar had swelled its ranks by another dozen, choosing them at random as the mood took him. The dockside bookmongers mostly carried works of gory fiction and bawdy romances written in heavily stylized verse, but every now and then they threw up something more delicate, like a piece of fine driftwood found on the pebbled beaches of Gol-Beyaz: the history of Adasi-Koy's glass-making industry, the mythology of the people of the Eastern Degisken-Dag Mountains, a medical treatise on illnesses of the mind, or a dozen architectural drawings from the earliest days of Anavatan bound together with a piece of faded blue ribbon.

Beside him, Hisar lounged bonelessly against the stall's front pole with all the grace of a bored fifteen year old, but His gray eyes tracked greedily across the stacks of books. Spar's old teacher, Ihsan, had taught Hisar to read that winter and the young God often wheedled the first read away from him.

Alesan, the elderly bookmonger who owned the stall, had been watching Spar's progress from grubby underfed street lifter to seerdelinkos to First Priest with all the anxiety of a hen watching a needy chick. Now she gestured at the book as she tossed Jaq a heel of old bread.

"That has a lovely piece about the aqueduct," she said. "Quite the poet's best work."

Hisar straightened at once, and noting His sudden interest, Spar nodded.

"We'll take it."

"I'll carry it," Hisar offered.

The bookmonger smiled. "That's four copper aspers. I'll wrap it up for you in a bit of oilcloth; it looks like it's going to rain again."

She handed it to Hisar. "Word is that the ice is breaking up on the coast of the Deniz-Siya early this year," she noted, watching both of them for a reaction. "Old Hazim says this warm weather means calm seas to the north, and any invasion fleet that sets out within the month could be here in less than a fortnight."

"I've heard that, too," Spar agreed. "But I haven't *seen* it." He emphasized the word "seen," and she nodded sagely.

"My oldest, Estill, says the priests of Ystazia are certain the sea chain will be ready in time."

"We saw them making it a few days ago," Hisar piped up, eager to be part of the conversation. "It looks almost done."

"Good." She regarded the young God seriously. "Send the metal the power of your domain," she said. "The strength of Creation for the chain and the weakness of Destruction for the enemy it defies."

Hisar's golden eyebrows drew down in an anxious frown. "The chainsmiths asked me for that, too," he said. "And I would if I knew how." He slumped. "I think. Maybe." He turned to Spar. "Can I?"

"I don't see why not."

"Even though Ystazia's priests are in charge of it?"

"Ystazia won't mind the help," Alesan assured him. "Of all the Gods, Ystazia shares the best."

She turned and caught Spar's fingers up in her own. "You've done well for yourself, Delin," she said. "We couldn't be more proud of you, every one of us here. We all believe in you. We know you'll do your part to send that filthy northern fleet to the bottom of the strait, you and Hisar both. When you get that temple of yours built, we'll stock it with as fine a library as you could ask for."

Spar ducked his head, suddenly embarrassed. "We have to go," he muttered.

"Give my thoughts to Ihsan."

"I will."

He headed off at once, Hisar's laughter echoing in his ears, but once they were well past the market, the young God glanced over at him.

"She knew about the temple already?" He asked.

Spar snorted. "Everyone knows about the temple already. Next to the invasion, it's the biggest piece of news all season."

He glanced at the book cradled in the crook of Hisar's arm. "The aqueduct?" he asked.

Hisar nodded. "That Priest of Havo saw water in darkness. You've seen it and I've seen it again in a dream. There were lots more details this time."

"Why didn't you tell me about it before?"

"It was too confusing. I had to think about it for a while."

"Fair enough." As it started to rain again, Spar tucked himself into a doorway. Jaq joined him, pressing up against his knees, and he gestured. "So tell me now."

Hisar took up a position in front of them hovering a few inches above the ground. "I saw a long . . . troughlike thing made of stone high up, and I heard running water, but I couldn't see it. Is that an aqueduct?"

"Yes."

"First Cultivar Adrian says it provides most of Anavatan west of the Temple Precinct with clean drinking water. How does it do that?"

"Its trough carries fresh water from the northern hills down to the city."

"Does it have big, sweeping arches made of stone and covered in vines?"

"Probably. I don't know. I've never seen it."

"That's how it looked in my dream. The arches disappeared into a deep, dark place, and when I followed, I found myself in a huge, echoing cavern this full of water." Hisar cut one palm along His upper thighs. "Is that part of the aqueduct?"

Spar shook his head. "That's the cistern that's supposed to be under the western half of the city. Ihsan says it's over a mile long."

"It was cold." Hisar shivered. "So very cold and black, like your dark place only more . . . physical. It had yellow-brown pillars of brick and stone reaching up to a vaulted ceiling so far above me that I could hardly see it. Half-formed spirits swam all around me, sparkling like tiny candles. When I moved, I made rivulets of water and spirits that tried to swirl around and catch me as I moved. But I ate them instead and they tasted like . . ." He frowned. "Copper."

"Copper or blood?"

Hisar considered the question, heedless of Spar's concerned expression. "Copper for now," He said finally. "Maybe blood later. These spirits were a lot less formed than the ones on the wild lands and they were a bit . . . drowned. Waterlogged," He amended after a moment's thought. "They might not become anything at all."

"But they might become as strong as the wild land spirits?" Spar pressed.

"Maybe. I guess. I didn't dream that part." Hisar cocked His head to one side. "It wasn't like my other dream. You said I saw birds because I'd never seen an invasion fleet. So how come I can dream about the cistern and the aqueduct if I've never seen them either?"

"I don't know."

"It was dark. It was hard to see. And so very cold."

Spar frowned. "Physically cold or prophetically cold?"

Hisar shrugged impatiently. "How can you tell one from the other?" He demanded.

"From the inside." Spar laid a hand against his chest. "Did it feel cold on the inside or on the outside?"

Hisar considered the question seriously. "Both I think. Maybe."

"Hm."

"Hm, what?"

"Just hm for now. I have to think about it."

"Well, there was more," Hisar continued in a quieter tone. "I wasn't alone. Graize was with me and Brax and you, too."

Spar grew very still. "Did you actually *see* us there? With your eyes?"

Hisar frowned. "I think so. Sort of. Maybe it was more of a sensing of you close by. I'm not sure. Did you see Graize in your vision in the dark place?"

Now it was Spar's turn to frown. "No," he said reluctantly. "I reached out for a sense of him, but . . ."

"But?"

"But Panos got in my way."

Hisar blinked. "Panos? Of Amatus? My Panos?"

"Graize's Panos anyway. The golden-haired oracle you showed me at Cvet Tower years ago."

"I remember. We vision-traveled together and watched her and Illan having sex." The young God sniffed in amusement. "It didn't interest you very much. You were a lot younger then."

"So were you."

"I suppose." Hisar cocked His head to one side. "So, why would Panos of Amatus block your vision of Graize," He wondered out loud.

Spar shot Him a cold glare. "I didn't say she *blocked* me," he replied stiffly. "I said she *got in my way*."

"Oh. Why would she get in your way?"

"I don't know."

"Oh." Hisar stared inwardly for a moment. "So, where is it?" He asked finally.

"Where is what?"

The young God bared His teeth at him. "The *aqueduct?*"

"Oh. West of here." Spar gave a vague wave. "It starts in the hills past the Northern Trisect and ends up somewhere in the Tannery Precinct, I think."

"Don't you know?"

Spar shook his head. "I've never seen it."

"You've been all the way to the Gurney-Dag foothills, but you've never been past the western docks of your own city?"

Hisar's tone was both exasperated and amused, and Spar glared at Him again. "I never had reason to," he shot back. "No one lifts in the Tannery Precinct unless they're desperate. It's too poor." His expression grew somber. "Even Cindar never fell that far.

"And the garrison guards maintain the watch there, not the Warriors of Estavia," he added, shaking off the mood with a sharp jerk of his head. "But if you've seen us there, I think we need to go there and see it for ourselves," he said, coming to a sudden decision. Glancing up at the sky, his brows drew down thoughtfully. "But not today."

Hisar blinked. "Why not today?"

"It's too far. It would take us the rest of the day just to get there, and then we'd be stuck there overnight. You don't want to be stuck in the Tannery Precinct overnight."

Hisar sniffed at him. "I wouldn't be stuck," He said dismissively. "I can fly."

"Well, then, I don't want to be stuck there overnight. We'll go tomorrow. Besides," he added. "We have to tell Brax about your vision. I don't want Graize coming on him without warning. After last year, Brax'd attack first and not ask questions later."

He stood as Jaq began to paw at him with an anxious whine at the sound of Brax's name. "Come on, Jaq needs to get back to stand guard over Brax this afternoon anyway, and it's getting near his time."

Hisar frowned. "Why?"

Spar shrugged. "I've no idea, he just does. He's been like that lately and I don't argue with him." He glanced down at the animal fondly. "You should never argue with your protectors."

"You argue with Brax?"

Spar gave a faint snort. "He's not my protector, I'm his. Besides," he added, glancing up at the sky with a squint. "The rain's not going to let up any time soon, and we need to get your book indoors, yeah?"

Hisar started, suddenly remembering the package tucked under His arm. With a worried glance to make sure the oilcloth was still keeping it safe and dry, He nodded.

"But we'll go tomorrow?" He pressed.

"Tomorrow."

"Even if it rains?"

"Even if it rains."

"And find out if I saw Graize with us there actually, with my eyes?" Spar nodded.

"'Cause we need Graize to be with us, actually, physically," the young God added in an anxious tone. "'Cause it's the only way to keep him and Brax safe, even if the mountain challenges are . . . mountainous? Remember?"

"I remember."

Hisar's feet touched the ground with obvious reluctance. "All right, then," He said, glancing pensively at the sky. "Tomorrow, then."

"Tomorrow."

Together, they headed back toward Estavia-Sarayi, Spar and Hisar mulling over the future and Jaq purposely aiming for the present.

✦

In Gol-Beyaz, Incasa watched His new prophecy grow with satisfaction. It had branched out nicely, touching a number of sensitive minds at once, including Spar's as it was meant to. With Hisar's help, the young First Priest had waded into the proper stream far enough so that he could be safely left to his own devices for now.

Brax and Graize would be harder to manipulate, but it could be done. The wild Skirosian seer, Panos of Amatus, had already incorporated Incasa's vision into an agenda of her own, following a stream that the God Himself had prepared many, many years ago. Recognizing where it led, she had already sent a seed of awareness toward Brax. It would only take the tiniest nudge to help it take root in the ghazi's mind. He was not as sensitive or as well suited to such imagery as Graize, but because of this, he was not as suspicious or as recalcitrant either. Yes, Incasa mused, just the tiniest nudge would see Brax maneuvered into position. After that, Incasa and Panos could both return their attention to Graize.

Rolling His prophetic dice along the lake bed, the God of Prophecy reached out for Estavia, traveling down through Her earliest memories to Her link with Kaptin Haldin and then out along Her lien to Her latest favorite, Brax. He had to move with great subtlety since Estavia was still very defensive after Her experience on the grasslands and did not take well to what She saw as interference, but Incasa was the God of Subtlety and the God of Battles was not.

Once the link had been established, He wove His prophecy and the image created by Panos together, and nudged them into the strongest of the future streams like a boat pushed out into Gol-Beyaz, and released it. As the current took hold, He tucked His dice away and returned to the depths.

6

The Protector of Anavatan

*H*E STOOD HIGH ON *a rocky promontory watching as, across the strait, the Gods oversaw the vast labor force building the finest metropolis in the world: the shining city of Anavatan. To the northwest, Usara directed the engineers in the erection of the aqueduct that would furnish its people with all the fresh water they would ever need. To the southwest, Ystazia and Her blacksmiths fashioned the double set of intricate sea chains that would protect its vulnerable northern approach. To the west, Estavia and Her ghazi-priests stood guard over the plains while to the north, Her navy stood guard over the strait. And finally to the south, Havo stilled the shining waters of Gol-Beyaz while Oristo oversaw hundreds of stone masons as they drew barge loads of multicolored marble from the depths to fashion Incasa and His seer-priests' greatest vision: the Wall that would protect Their people against their enemies forever.*

And above it all he stood ever vigilant, the Battle God's favorite, Anavatan's Protector, Champion of the newly ordained Warriors of Estavia, and First Defender of the Gods' Wall of Stone and Power.

✦

"The Wall will not stand."

"He'll crumble under the weight of it. He's already starting to fall."

✦

Brax's eyes snapped open. Staring into the shadowy darkness, he knew a moment of sickly panic as his mind snapped back into the cavern where Graize had kept him prisoner last year. He tried to rise, but a single, gentle touch on his shoulder held him immobile until he realized he was in the temple infirmary. Beside him, Jaq began to whine and, with some effort, he made himself calm, if only for the sake of the dog.

After weeks of enforced inactivity, Chief Physician Samlin had finally allowed him to return to Estavia-Sarayi *under care*. At first, under care had meant a healer-warden who'd shadowed him nearly everywhere he went, ensuring that he followed Samlin's orders and didn't overdo it, as well as daily check-ins at the infirmary for more orders. Now it meant twice-weekly visits to a quiet and shadowy chamber where he suffered through the unnerving ministrations of Senior Touch-Healer Jazet of Usara-Sarayi.

In the years he'd served at the Battle God's temple, Brax had undergone more than his fair share of physical rehabilitation. Calling on the power of their God, Usara's physicians had done what they could to heal his shattered elbow, an injury first taken in the battle at Serin-Koy, and both Brax and Estavia had done what they could to stay calm while another God's lien had flowed through his body. But ever since Graize had managed to sever their connection on the grasslands, Estavia had been unwilling to allow anyone else that kind of access.

After the fifth unsuccessful attempt, Chief Physician Samlin had shaken his head in frustration.

"Think of the Gods as master class artisans," he'd explained to Brax. "They work with power, shaping it in such a way as Their individual talents dictate. Usara works with the power that flows within the body. A broken limb can be mended because there's still power flowing to that limb, but a severed limb cannot be reattached because the connection which allows the power to flow from the body to the limb has been severed."

Brax's eyes had flickered down briefly, and Samlin had followed his gaze.

"Your arm's still in place, yes," he'd agreed to Brax's silent comment. "But the elbow, the connection between your upper arm and your forearm, has been badly damaged. That damage is restricting the flow of power, and Estavia is restricting our ability to reach it."

Pressing his fingertips against the bridge of his nose, he'd thought for a moment.

"I'm going to put you under Jazet's care. I think that might be the best course of action. She'll help you strengthen the flow of power without seeking Usara's direct intervention."

"But she is going to work on my elbow?"

Samlin pursed his lips impatiently. "Yes and no. It's better if you experience her treatment firsthand, Ghazi, rather than ask me for an explanation. Jazet's approach is somewhat less . . . orthodox than you've experienced before."

If Brax had realized just how "less orthodox," he might not have shown up in the first place. Unlike the brightly lit, bustling infirmary rooms he was used to, Jazet's treatment chamber was small and quiet and lit by a single oil lamp set in an iron holder on the far wall. A flutist played a simple tune outside the door, and the air was perfumed with a hint of lavender. Jazet herself displayed none of the impatient temper most of the physicians who served at the Battle God's infirmary used to keep their recalcitrant patients obedient. She merely smiled a greeting, then gestured at the table in the center of the room and waited for Brax to comply.

Used to being either forced into uncomfortable positions or made to lie immobile for hours at a time while the power of two separate Gods burned through his veins, Brax had done as he was told with obvious reluctance. But Jazet's treatments had consisted of no more than two fingers from each hand pressed into various parts of his body.

From the beginning, these gentle but firm ministrations had hurtled his mind into a world of images, memories, and partial visions that had overwhelmed his very limited prophetic understanding, mixing with an array of physical and emotional sensations that had left him both frightened and exhausted.

And from the beginning, Jaq had abandoned his usual place beside Spar to plant himself next to Brax, whining whenever Jazet's probing fingers moved to a new location. Once, when Brax had fallen into the throes of a particularly painful memory, Jaq had climbed right up onto the table with him. Unfazed, Jazet had simply turned her intuitive ministrations on the dog until both he and Brax had regained some composure.

Eventually, Jaq had returned to his position on the floor, Jazet had returned to her patient, and Brax had returned unwillingly to the memory, held in place until it had played itself out fully, flowing from his mind like rain pouring down a waterspout. Only then had Jaq truly calmed.

Now, as Jazet placed one fingertip on Brax's forehead and another under his right shoulder blade, the infirmary fell away and his latest vision rose up once again.

"The Wall will not hold."

"He'll crumble under the weight of it. He's already starting to fall."

Brax scowled. He was a soldier not a seer. He didn't go fishing for the fine, intangible symbols of the future the way Spar did. And although Kaptin Liel of Sable Company had insisted that Brax and most of the other senior ghazi took a watered-down version of the training the seers received to become more sensitive to Estavia's prophetic messages, when the Battle God did send him such messages, She sent them in as clear a manner as possible, knowing his limitations. This hadn't come from Estavia.

So where had it come from?

"The Wall . . ."

"I heard you the first time."

"Hm?"

Brax shook his head. "Nothing, Healer. Just a vision being a pain in the arse."

"Mm."

As Jazet moved one hand down to press against his left shoulder, the words continued to echo in his head, but muted as if he was hearing them spoken from a great distance.

"The Wall . . ."

The Wall had held for centuries, protecting the Gods' city until six years ago when a swarm of tiny but deadly spirits had breached its defenses in a wave of rage and hunger. They'd been beaten back and destroyed by Estavia but not before they'd wreaked havoc across the city during the spring storms of Havo's Dance.

Did this mean that the Wall would fall to the attack they all knew was coming? And who would crumble under the weight of it: Spar? Who else would he be having visions about except his kardos?

His right temple began to ache, and he forced himself to relax his jaw before Jazet noticed and extended his treatment. No wonder seers were always so dour, he thought with a grumble, if this was the kind of mental shite they were always forced to deal with.

Jazet shifted position, Jaq began to whine again, and Brax firmly put the vision to one side. He was not a seer; it was not his job to sort this kind of thing out. So he would go and find a seer and drop it in his lap. He would go and find Spar.

As Jazet placed two fingers in the hollows behind his jawline, he made himself breathe deeply, and very, very slowly, he felt the muscles across his back and shoulders relax as a fine trickle of energy began to descend into his injured elbow.

✦

An hour later she released him with the usual advice to rise slowly and not engage in any strenuous activity for the rest of the afternoon. Jaq headed out the door at once, and Brax followed, knowing that this would be the fastest way to locate Spar.

They found him in the armory tower.

One of the oldest structures in Estavia-Sarayi, the armory tower had been built more with an eye to defense than to style, with a series of small, narrow windows that let in a fine trickle of light only. The entire ground floor was made up of a single room, large enough to hold over five hundred warriors if need be and reached by a double set of iron-bound doors on one wall and a small wooden door leading to Marshal Brayazi's private audience chamber on the other. A stone well, covered with an ornate iron grille took up the northeastern corner, and stone steps leading up to several floors of dormitories and storerooms took up the southwest. Within its shadowy recesses were housed centuries of battle trophies displayed on the walls and on daises lit by a series of hanging lamps, their heavy chains disappearing up to the vaulted ceiling above.

Spar stood before one of the marble daises, his hands resting lightly on the large, bejeweled book displayed on a silver base. The side of his mouth quirked up slightly as Jaq pushed past Brax at once, receiving a sour look in response.

As Brax crossed the floor after the dog, he paused by the dais that held the relics of Kaptin Haldin, a hand-and-a-half sword, its hilt wrapped in silver and its pommel encrusted with gemstones, and a long dagger, equally bedecked, lying on a black-and-gold damask cloth. Years before, when he and Spar had first come to the temple, they'd stood in the same positions staring in awe at the riches before them. The sword had tingled under his fingertips then. Now, he resisted the urge to touch it as he filled Spar in on this latest vision-puzzle, cocking his head to one side as Spar frowned suddenly.

"What?" he demanded.

Jaq began to whine again, and Spar's hand dropped down absently to rest between his ears. "You heard those words?" he asked. "Those exact words? The Wall will not stand?"

Brax nodded.

"Did they actually sound in your head, or did you see them?"

"How can you see words?"

Spar rolled his eyes. "You're right; this is you. What was I thinking? What did the words sound like, then—loud, soft, angry maybe, or like a warning?"

"Soft, like I was hearing them from far away. And like a warning, I guess. It sounded serious, anyway."

"In a voice?"

Brax nodded again.

"What kind of voice?"

Brax frowned in concentration. "In a woman's voice," he said after a moment. "But not Estavia's."

"Accented?"

"I'm not sure. Why?"

Spar turned an intense gaze on his kardos. "Years ago, Illan of Volinsk spoke to me in my head. He said, '*The Wall will not stand.*'"

"The same words," Brax mused. "He made a prophecy to you?"

"At the time I thought he was just trying to rattle me. He probably was, but that doesn't mean it wasn't a prophecy, too."

"Illan of Volinsk doesn't have a woman's voice though, does he?" Brax asked with one eyebrow raised humorously.

"No. But Panos of Amatus does, and she's a powerful, political oracle."

"Why would Panos of Amatus send me a prophetic warning? She's a Skirosian, isn't she? An enemy?"

"Yes." Spar shook his head. "I have to think about this."

"What about the rest of it, me watching the city being built and the bit about someone crumbling under a weight?"

Spar stared into space for a long moment.

"Do you remember when we first came together," he asked instead. Brax nodded.

"Tell me about it."

Used to the youth's roundabout way of explaining things, Brax cast his mind back. "I was about eight or nine, on a job, trying to get through a second-story window in a spice warehouse. Remember the one on Mimar-Caddesi right up against Ystazia-Cami?"

"I remember."

"I couldn't make it. I got stuck."

"I'm not surprised. At my youngest, I could barely squeeze through the bars on those windows."

"But you did. It was our first job together."

"Yeah. Ah." Spar nodded his understanding. "That's why Cindar took me on. There was a special shipment, and he wanted a share."

Brax nodded. "Cinnamon and saffron. He sent me in the night it arrived. I almost got caught. He took you on the next day."

"I remember it was dark and I was scared. I had to find my way across the whole of the warehouse and down the stairs to the steward's office to get the key to the side door. It wasn't where Cindar said it would be."

"But you found it anyway."

Spar nodded. "I could see it in my mind. I remember I was hungry an' Cindar said I couldn't eat till after I opened the door for him," he continued, traces of his dockside accent creeping into his voice again from the strength of the memory. "But you gave me a piece of bread when he wasn't lookin.'"

"I remember bein' scared, too," Brax said, his own accent thickening in response to Spar's. "Scared that he was gonna dump me off someplace for good because I couldn't do the work anymore. He was always sayin' things like that in the early days, but he was thinkin' about it for real this time; I could see it in his face."

Spar studied his kardos for a moment, taking note of the strained expression in his dark eyes before nodded carefully. "Yeah, I saw it in his mind, too," he answered. "I saw him thinkin' about it being just him an' me."

"But you had a nightmare that night. You screamed so loud, we thought you'd bring the garrison guards down on us. I finally got you calmed down, but Cindar couldn't even look at you or you'd start up again."

"You held me all the rest of the night. After that, Cindar never thought about splitting us up again."

Spar's voice was triumphant, and Brax gave him a speculative glance.

"You've used that as a dodge before," he noted.

Spar just shrugged. "It was real enough that night. Not so much later. I had a dream about what life was going to be like with just Cindar and me. Some dreams are warnings about what might be," he continued. "Not what will be."

"Sent by Incasa?" Brax teased.

Spar shrugged. "I doubt it." He turned his blue eyes tinged with darkness on Brax's face. "But who knows," he added. "Look at everything that's happened since then. None of it could have happened if Cindar had split us up, yeah? That one moment could have made everything else happen. Sometimes you have to make the future do as you tell it to. That's what visions are for. We act on new discoveries to change the future to one we desire. Kaptin Liel said that to me once. The alternative is to allow the future to run about unsupervised like an undisciplined delos, free to do as it pleases to whomever it pleases."

"You've changed," Brax noted. "Even a few months ago you never would have quoted a seer kaptin or admitted that something else—anything else—might have a say in your destiny."

"Yeah, well, a few months ago I didn't have a God as a delinkos," Spar responded in a sour voice. Pressing his back against the dais, he slid down until he sat on the first step, one arm draped over Jaq's broad shoulders.

"So what does that have to do with my vision?" Brax asked, leaning against his own dais.

Spar jerked his thumb at the book above him. "Do you know what this book is?"

"Recipes?"

"No, stupid. It's a history of Anavatan. There's a picture in it showing the city being built, just as you saw it, only the picture has Kaptin Haldin standing where you were standing in your vision."

"Ah, right, I remember now."

Spar glowered at him. "And do you remember what the picture's called?" he demanded. "It's called the Protector of the Shining City."

"I thought he was the *Champion* of Estavia."

"He was that too." Spar stabbed a finger at him. "You see yourself as the Champion of Estavia. Do you see yourself as the Protector of Anavatan too?"

Brax's brows drew down in thought. "I don't know."

"Bollocks. If you didn't, you wouldn't have seen that exact picture."

"All right, so maybe I do see myself as the Protector of Anavatan, me and ten thousand other Warriors of Estavia."

"It's not that simple."

"Why not?"

Spar gave him a long stare, then shrugged. "Because you'll crumble under the weight of it."

"I'll what?" Brax straightened, a spark of anger darkening his voice.

"Crumble."

"Says who?"

"Hisar."

Brax blinked in confusion. "Hisar?" he repeated.

"Hisar said it to me. Those exact words. He's afraid the temple's piling too much responsibility on you."

"And He think I'm too weak to handle it? What does He know about it?"

"Nothing. But don't get pissy. Hisar's young, but He's a God and prophecy's part of His makeup."

"So you figure He's had a prophecy that I'll crumble? And you believe him?"

"No. I believe you'll accept all the responsibility they'll pile onto you and more. And that *you're* afraid you'll crumble."

Brax closed his eyes, breathing carefully through his mouth until the throbbing in his right temple eased again. "What?"

"You heard the words in a vision. And it's no secret that you're afraid you won't be able to serve Estavia with your injuries. Everyone knows it; just no one except me'll tell you to your face. Are you afraid She'll dump you off someplace?"

Brax just glared at him.

"You know that's a pile of shite, right?" Spar continued, his voice dripping with crafted disdain. "Warriors get injured all the time; that's what happens when you fart around chasing other people with pointy weapons. So, maybe you can't do that so much anymore. Is that all you are? Is that all you figure you are to Her?"

When Brax didn't answer, he snorted. "And I thought all of our abayon taught you better than that."

Brax scowled at him. "What do you mean?" he demanded.

Spar shrugged one shoulder dismissively. "Cindar taught you a dozen ways to lift someone's shine—curbing, cubbing, lifting, marking, whatever worked best. Kemal and Yashar taught you a hundred different tactics and strategies and a half dozen weapons. Even Kaptin Liel's shown you how to use your mind in battle."

"You know," Brax noted dryly, "for someone who never used to talk at all, you sure use a lot of words now."

"Shut up." Spar leaned forward. "You were raised to be a thief, not a fighter, Brax," he continued with an intense expression. "Estavia's got thousands of warriors who could use both arms in battle better than you ever could when they were half your age. She didn't take your oaths for your physical ability. You used to know that."

"She may not have taken my oaths for it, but that's the job," Brax replied tightly. "If I can't do the job, what good am I?"

"You mean what kind of a protector can you be? I don't know, you should ask Her."

Brax just looked away.

"You used to talk to Her all the time," Spar pointed out. "That was your answer to everything, ask Estavia, ask Estavia, until I wanted to drop a chimney on your head just to shut you up."

Rubbing absently at his elbow, Brax just shrugged. "Maybe I will," he hedged. "Later, when I've healed up some more."

"Do it sooner rather than later, yeah?" Spar shook his head in disgust. "I can't believe I have to tell you all this."

Brax forced himself to chuckle. "Looks like I'm not the only one with a new title. I guess you're finally taking this whole First Priest thing seriously."

Spar made a sour face. "Yeah, I'm taking it seriously. My own prophecy's driving me right at it whether I like it or not." He stroked Jaq's ears absently for a moment. "You heard about First Cultivar Adrian's words about the aqueduct at Assembly," he asked.

"I heard."

"Well, I need to go there to see for myself what's going on. And I need you to come with me." He took a deep breath. "To cross Dockside."

Brax gave him a quizzical look and Spar just shrugged. "Confident and like we're meant to be there, yeah? That's what you said to me once. Except you were talking about here at the temple because we aren't meant to be there, not anymore."

"No."

"And I don't want go there at all," Spar continued. "Not that far west anyway, but I have to, so I'm gonna take your advice. An' I'm gonna take you."

"Fair enough."

Spar looked away. "You don't think I'm being stupid?" he asked with a scowl.

"No." Brax straightened. "I think it's a good idea that we both see how far we've come. And how far we didn't fall."

"Well, all right, then." Spar fell silent, one arm wrapped so tightly about Jaq's neck that the dog finally gave a short wriggle of protest. "Confident," he whispered. "And like we weren't meant to be there."

✦

The next day dawned warm and bright. Spar, Brax, and Hisar, with the ever-faithful Jaq trotting along beside them, headed out just after Morning Invocation. Spar was wearing his new mustard-yellow tunic hidden under a blue cloak, and he glowered at Brax when his kardos laughed at him.

"If I show it in here, everyone'll talk," he said stiffly.

"About what, how . . . unique it looks?"

"No dung-head, about how unique it means."

"That you're color-blind? Joking." Brax raised his hands hastily as Spar rounded on him. "I know what it means. It means you're moving on the oaths you swore to Hisar last year."

"Right, and every gossiping tongue in the temple'll be wagging about it within minutes."

"And you don't want that?" Hisar asked. She was wearing Her Rayne-seeming today, with a pair of hide breeches, kidskin boots, and a Yuruk-style sheepskin jacket, all colored in gold. "Why not?"

"I don't like people taking about me. It makes them think they can make decisions about me, too."

"Oh. I guess that makes sense," Hisar agreed.

"Just promise me you'll choose a better color when you start wearing it more openly," Brax asked, unwilling to stop teasing the youth.

Spar's eyes narrowed. "Maybe that'll be what it takes to prove you really want to be part of our temple," he retorted.

"In that case, you'll have a very small number of very dedicated followers."

Hisar looked worried. "Maybe we should get another color," She said anxiously. "I'd kind of like to have lots of followers."

"Maybe we should just toss Brax into the strait," Spar growled in response. "That should be enough to get a flock of followers."

Brax laughed. He'd awakened that morning with the dawn sun bathing his body in warmth and his elbow much less stiff and painful than usual. Painting Estavia's symbols on his body had been easier than it had been for months; the ink had seemed to flow off the brush. That alone had lifted his spirits immensely, and once he'd shifted the day's responsibilities onto Brin, he'd found himself actively looking forward to their outing. Now he returned the salute of the guards on the main gate, and the suggestive smile of a porter carrying a load of vegetables beyond it, and set off across the public square at a swift pace, as much to annoy Spar as to reach their destination. But Spar matched him step for step, and finally it was Hisar who protested, demanding that they slow down so She could take in the sights.

They passed through the residential streets where many of Estavia's retired warriors made their homes, then crossed into the southern part of the western market. The streets there were already crowded with people buying and selling the myriad of goods that came through Anavatan's docks: fish and oil and cloth and spices and furs and sweetmeats and a hundred other wares. Many called out greetings to them as they passed, but as they continued north, the stalls grew smaller and in greater need of repair, and the crowds grew less affluent and less welcoming. However, it wasn't until they passed the heavy, wrought iron gates of Oristo-Cami that Spar realized with a start that they'd crossed into Dockside proper. His steps faltered for just a moment, then he squared his shoulders and carried on, one hand wrapped in Jaq's braided collar. Here and there, he thought he spotted a young lifter or two slipping through the crowd, but the black leather cuirass Brax wore over his blue tunic and the sword at his side meant that most of those who still plied their old trade melted into the shadows at the first sight of them. Nobody lifted from the Warriors of Estavia or anywhere near them. It was a lesson he and Brax had known all too well in the old days.

A moment of unwilling nostalgia for those desperate but simpler times came and went, but always sensitive to his moods, Brax glanced over at once.

"Seem smaller to you?" he asked, watching two men, both holding small jugs of raki like weapons, arguing outside a tavern much like the one where Cindar'd been killed. One of the men glanced his way, and the argument ceased at once. As the two men moved quickly apart, Spar just shook his head, unable to put his feelings into words here where he'd spent so many silent days.

Brax bumped his shoulder gently.

"C'mon. Confident and like we're meant to be someplace else, remember?"

Spar nodded.

✦

They crossed into the Tannery Precinct an hour later. The streets were more narrow and irregular here, with many of the cobblestones broken or missing. The buildings, too, were in greater need of repair and built much closer together than in Dockside. There was no one to be seen, despite the presence of Hisar, who usually drew a host of curious onlookers and, as they passed the first cluttered alleyway, She glanced over at Spar.

"I can feel people watching," She said, the silence making Her drop Her voice instinctively. "Unsworn people like those three youths at the shed."

"A lot of people in the Tannery Precinct are unsworn," he agreed somberly. "They can't see any use in giving their oaths to some God who doesn't seem to care about them."

"*Do* the Gods care about them?"

"I don't know."

"Should I care about them?"

"If You want them, yeah, You should care about them."

"Don't the other Gods want them?"

"Like I said, I don't know. Gods are big. Maybe people have to want Them first before the Gods even notice they're there at all."

Hisar's eyes narrowed. "All They have to do is look," She said in an unconvinced tone. "It's not like they're hidden. They're right here in Their city."

"Yeah, well, maybe They're busy. Look, don't ask me, all right? I'm no priest, I don't know anything about Gods."

"You're my priest."

"So ask me about You. Yes, You should care, yes, You should notice, yes, you should help people if they ask for Your help, maybe even ask first if they want Your help. Happy?"

Spar stomped off, an anxious Jaq at his heels, leaving Hisar and Brax standing in the middle of the street.

The young God turned an aggrieved look on Spar's kardos. "What's wrong with him?" She demanded.

Brax sighed. "He doesn't want to defend people he doesn't like," he said simply.

"Ah. And he's never liked the Gods," She agreed.

"Right. He thinks They don't care."

"Do *you* think They don't care?"

Brax headed up the street behind Spar. "I think Estavia cares," he answered, "And," he added reluctantly, "like Spar, I think You should. The rest aren't my problem. C'mon."

They caught up with Spar and Jaq at the mouth of Duvar Caddessi a few moments later. The street was wider here, with rows of workshops to the east and warehouses to the west. And looming over the warehouses like the colossus it was, stood the God-Wall.

All four rocked to a halt, staring up at it in undisguised awe.

Made of rough-cut marble drawn from Gol-Beyaz, the Wall at its most northerly end reached a full thirty feet in height, with the Power of the Gods, glimmering a pale yellow at this time of day, stretching it another forty until it disappeared into the bright blue sky above.

"It's so huge here," Hisar breathed. "And so . . . sparkly. There's silver lights flickering all over it."

"That's the Power of the Gods," Brax answered.

Hisar turned to look down Her nose at him. "I know," she replied haughtily. "I can feel *that*."

"What does it feel like?" Spar asked, his earlier mood forgotten.

Hisar frowned in concentration. "Tingly. And empty. Like I want to suck power right out of it and pour power right into it at the same time." She turned away. "I don't like it. Can we go now?" She asked almost petulantly. "I thought we came here to see the aqueduct."

As Spar had before, She turned and stomped down the street without waiting to see if the others were coming. After a moment, Spar and Jaq followed, leaving Brax to stare up at the Wall, feeling its symbol on his wrist burning in time with his heartbeat. The warning words of his vision whispered in his mind, and he narrowed his eyes.

"Nothing's falling and no one's crumbling," he snarled inwardly. *"Do your worst. You'll dash yourself to pieces against us both."*

Turning his back on the golden laughter his bravado had invoked, he followed after the others with a dark expression.

Duvar Caddessi opened up at the edge of the Halic-Salmanak, ending at a steep flight of stone stairs that led to a number of small, wooden wharfs on the pebbled ground below. The others were already standing on the bank, staring up at the aqueduct arching across the water and over their heads, and disappearing into the maze of closely packed buildings behind them.

Brax blinked. "I had no idea anything that big could cross the water like that," he said in shock. He twisted his head to stare along its length. "And they're afraid *that* could be in danger? How? How could you possibly damage *that*? It's as big as the God-Wall."

Spar frowned. "Maybe there's a way to block off the water or something."

"Could a force even climb up it to get to the water?"

"Someone has to climb it to service it, don't they?"

"The priests of Havo service it," Hisar stated. "They have a Cami on the northern shore. They said so at Assembly." Dropping the Rayne-seeming suddenly, the young God leaped into the air in a flash of metallic whirling, drawing gasps from a dozen people fishing nearby. It soared up and over the aqueduct, passing back and forth over it several times before streaking across the water toward the Northern Trisect. It returned a few moments later, taking on Its golden-seeming and hovering a few inches off the ground in excitement.

"It comes out from the hills to the north and the water flows all along the top in a huge, deep trough," He said triumphantly. "Just like I dreamed, Spar. You should come and see. Havo-Cami is built right up against it. I'll bet there's stairs going up inside, too, 'cause there's a door. We should go." He twisted His head to one side in a gesture more reminiscent of His dragonfly-seeming to regard the sparkling water with suspicion. "How do you get across?" He demanded.

"People hire boats like that one over there," Brax said, pointing down the bank. "For one or two aspers you can cross over to buy things at the farmer's market and for a couple more you can hire a porter's delinkos to carry your parcels back for you."

"Have you ever been there before?"

Spar snorted. "Not hardly. They say there's good lifting there, but Cindar'd never drop his shine on anything but drink, never mind a boat. But I always wanted to go," he added in an uncharacteristically wistful voice. "They say there's piles of cheese curds so high, you need a step stool to reach the top, and the jars of honey that smell so sweet, they scent the air for miles."

"I served at Gerek-Hisar for a couple of months," Brax added. "But I never went as far as the farmer's market either."

Hisar gave him a questioning look. "Why not?"

"There wasn't any need to. The servers of Oristo brought our supplies to us."

"You lot are so spoiled," Spar muttered.

Brax ignored him. Reaching into his pouch, he drew out a fingerful of small coins. "So, did you want to pay for the boat, then?" he asked pointedly.

Spar just grinned at him. "Nope." He laughed as Hisar began to vibrate up and down, causing Jaq to begin barking excitedly.

"So we're going?" the young God demanded.

Brax nodded. "I guess it's about time, yeah?"

Spar nodded. "Yeah. C'mon Jaq."

Together, the four of them headed down the beach toward the nearest wharf.

7

The Northern Trisect

IT COST THREE SILVER aspers to hire a boat big enough to take them all across, after Brax had charmed the boat-master's price down from five. Even though Hisar could fly, He insisted on accompanying them in His golden-seeming, hanging over the side so far that His nose almost touched the water.

When they reached the northern shore, He and Jaq scrambled out at once, the dog sending up a spray of pebbles in his wake that drew a disgusted glance from a white cat padding about in the shallows. It glared disdainfully at them both, raised one back paw to shake the water droplets away, then returned its attention to the bubbles rising at its feet. Beside it, a small girl dug into the sand where it stared, flinging tiny, burrowing crabs into a bag at her side with an expert flick of her wrist. Both Spar and Brax gave her a respectful nod as they exited the boat behind Jaq and Hisar, and she gave them a nod of her own in reply.

Before them, the farmer's market took up most of the Northern Trisect with livestock pens to the north, dairy and vegetable stalls in the center, and the honey and fish markets lining the shore. They wandered about for over an hour, testing the wares of the many sweetmeat sellers and arguing over which market had the better scallop and shrimp kabobs. High above, dozens of swifts made their acrobatic way past the many stork nests dotting the tops of every domed rooftop in the market. Hisar watched them fly with a wondering expression.

"Ihsan says that when the Northern Trisect was first built, the priests of Havo drove stakes into the domes so the stork nests wouldn't fall off," Spar explained, biting greedily into a piece of honeycomb. "And they've been there ever since; the same storks year after year, and their delon, and their delon after them. He says Havo promised that if the market was ever in danger, the storks would give warning and Havo would come and protect them." He regarded the graceful black-and-white creatures, standing like sentinels on the edges of their nests. "I guess we've got time yet," he observed, tossing the last of the honeycomb to Jaq before wiping his hand on his tunic.

Brax nodded. "No invading army would come this far," he observed, chewing thoughtfully on his own piece. "Not until after they'd secured the Western Trisect, anyway. If they sent a force overland, it'd be to attack Gerek-Hisar from behind to secure the strait. The northern hills are barely passable to sheep, never mind soldiers with big enough armaments to take a watchtower."

"But they could send a small force against the aqueduct," Spar replied. His brows drew down. "If they knew how to access it."

"How would they know how to access it?"

Spar and Hisar exchanged an apprehensive look. After agreeing to tell Brax about the young God's dream, neither of them had been too eager to actually do it. Finally, Hisar gave a soft snort of impatience.

"Graize would know," He said hesitantly.

"Yeah, he probably does," Brax agreed. "There'd have been nothing stopping him from hiring a boat to the Northern Trisect in the old days; he always had enough shine. But why would he bother?"

Hisar and Spar shared another look, then together, they outlined their earlier conversation in as few words as possible.

Brax listened with an increasingly stony expression and, when they were finished, set off for Havo-Cami without a word.

Hisar glanced at Spar. "So, how do you think it went?" He asked in a worried tone.

Spar's eyes narrowed. "It went fine. He's just being pissy because I didn't tell him before."

"Are you sure?"

Spar shrugged. "Sure enough. C'mon."

Primarily a farming community, the Northern Trisect had two subtemples dedicated to the God of Planting and Harvest, both of them large and beautifully decorated. The most northerly Cami was built right up against the aqueduct, its own wall extending southeast along the shore of the Halic-Salmanak, then north in a crescent arch, encompass-

ing the Cami's orchards and formal flower and vegetable gardens. By the
time they caught up to him at the main gate—a wooden trellis covered
in climbing vines—Brax seemed to have shaken off the mood. Spar led
the way around the back, weaving through a line of server-delinkon
bringing in the day's supplies. As the line froze to stare at Hisar with
undisguised curiosity, he caught up a large round of cheese and headed
inside the kitchen door.

Used to visitors, the Cami's chamberlain found them a guide at
once, a young delinkos of Spar's own age who smiled at him in distinct
invitation, much to Brax and Hisar's amusement. Together, they made a
tour of the public chapel and meditation rooms, then fetched up before
a stout, wooden door at the end of a shadowy corridor.

"Them's the stairs leading to the aqueduct, Ghazi-Sayin," the
delinkos explained to Brax respectfully. "It's always kept locked, 'spe-
cially now since Dimas had her vision."

"This was her first?" Spar asked.

"Not exactly, but she's no trained seer. She only gets flashes now and
again. Says they're more trouble'n they're worth, actually."

"I know the feeling."

They shared a swift smile.

"We sent a message off to Havo-Sarayi and they sent back a seer of
Incasa," the delinkos continued. "I don't know what was said, but since
you're here, I'm guessing they took it seriously."

"They took it seriously," Spar agreed.

Brax gestured at the door. "Can we go up?"

The delinkos nodded, handing him a large iron key at once. "If you
don't mind, I won't come up with you, Sayin. I'm no good with heights.
Or small spaces neither. And it might be best if the dog stayed down
here, too. The aqueduct's dangerous and the stairs are really steep."

Spar nodded. "Stay, Jaq."

"If he kicks up a row, feed him something," Brax added.

The delinkos bowed. "Yes, Sayin."

Opening the door, Brax, Spar, and Hisar slipped inside, leaving the
delinkos with one hand wrapped firmly around Jaq's collar. The stairs
were narrow and shallow, ascending in a tight, stone spiral, with a heavy
ship's cable acting as a railing attached to the wall with heavy iron rings.
Spar headed up at once, but Brax found it a very tight squeeze, his sword

and his shoulders banging against the wall and threatening to unbalance him with every step. After his third muttered curse, Spar glanced back with an unsympathetic expression.

"That's what you get for growing so much, so shut up, will you, I'm trying to concentrate."

Brax gestured at him rudely, but clamped his teeth on his next remark as his sword tried to pull him off the stairs again with his very next step.

Behind them, Hisar floated serenely up the stairs in the lithe seeming of a water snake, a smug smile plastered across Its muzzle.

They reached the top a few moments later. Spar gave the door an experimental shove and it opened at once, spilling a wide shaft of sunlight down the stairs. With an explosive sigh of relief, he scrambled out onto the aqueduct itself, Brax and Hisar tight on his heels.

Eyes wide, Brax gave an impressed whistle. This high up, they had an unobstructed view of the aqueduct's entire length; from the northwestern hills—dotted with tiny, blazing white sheep—where it emerged, then southwest along its length and across the strait to its stone reservoir nestled deep in the crowded streets of the Tannery Precinct. He looked east down the shores of the Halic-Salmanak to the watchtowers of Lazim- and Gerek-Hisars squatting on their opposite banks, then northwest through the farmer's market and past to the high mountains which guarded the Northern Trisect from the coast. Planting both feet on a length of stone stretching across the aqueduct's main trough like a bridge, he leaned over the edge, regarding the gardens behind the shore wall with a critical eye.

"This would make a great sentinel position," he observed. "I wonder why we don't have one here."

"Oh, I dunno, maybe 'cause this is a *Havo*-Cami, not an Estavia-Cami," Spar answered caustically, watching as Hisar took wing in Its dragonfly-seeming. It spun about their heads until he swatted irritably at It, then shot away to buzz the stork nest built around Havo-Cami's stout minaret instead.

Brax glanced over. "Yeah, I guess," he said reluctantly. "But a force, even a small one could come through that narrow pass there," he gestured to the north with his chin, "or down the Halic here and catch the whole area unawares."

Taking hold of an iron ring set in the wall by the door, Spar leaned out to peer in the direction Brax pointed. "Those lands are controlled by the Yuruk," he replied. "They don't use boats."

"Doesn't mean they can't. And besides, Graize does. Still . . ." Brax sighted down the length of the aqueduct. "Seems like a pretty big target, even for him." Leaning against the cami wall, he glanced over at Spar with a dark expression.

"So, Hisar saw me and Graize together in vison and you didn't think to mention it?"

Spar just shrugged. "It wasn't my vision to tell, it was Hisar's. Now He's told you, so get over it. But that's not what's got me thinking," he added. "It's this water sparkling in a cavernous darkness. That's gotta be the cistern."

"How would they get there?"

"From the hills, carried in by the aqueduct. There're spirits in the Gurney-Dag Mountain streams. There must be spirits in the northern hill streams, too."

"But carried into the cistern?" Brax pressed. "That would mean that there'd be spirits behind the God-Wall, right under Anavatan itself. Right now." He shook his head. "They'd have had to have been carried in from the beginning all the way back hundreds of years ago from when they first built the aqueduct. What keeps them from swarming out?"

Spar shrugged. "Hisar said they felt waterlogged. Maybe the darkness keeps them weak."

"Or maybe the darkness *kept* them weak," Brax corrected. "Until there was enough of them to make a swarm. Just like last time," he added quietly.

The two of them fell silent, remembering.

"Seems to me like the aqueduct's more *the* danger than *in* danger," Brax pointed out after a moment. "Or the cistern is, at any rate."

"Maybe." Spar shrugged. "Either way, we're gonna find out. We're going in, me and Hisar. We could use you with us. He saw you there, anyway."

Brax gave an unimpressed snort. "If what He saw comes true, we won't be the only ones; Graize'll have seen it, too. And that brings us back to the question I had before you dropped all this in my lap. Why would Graize bother to attack the aqueduct?"

Spar stared across the Halic with a pensive expression. "Maybe he's not gonna attack it," he hazarded. "Maybe he's gonna use the spirits that traveled along it and down into the cistern to attack Anavatan. Maybe he's gonna make them swarm."

Brax's dark eyes narrowed. "That makes a lot more sense," he agreed. He followed Spar's gaze, a thought growing in his mind. "All right," he said at last. "So, we know Hisar saw Graize in vision. So we go forward figuring Graize is planning some kind of an attack. And we move to stop him."

Spar gave him an amused look. "How?"

"We play him like any mark in the old days. We make him be where we want him to be, when we want him to be, and we lay a trap for him. We plan a defense in a way he won't be able to resist."

Spar nodded suddenly understanding where Brax was going. "*You* command the defense. He sees you in vision and he comes after you."

"With me there, here, actually. He'll make his way into Anavatan from the Northern Trisect where there's no God-Wall and no gate guards sworn to Estavia to get in his way. Graize could scale this wall in his sleep. He'll come here."

"I don't like it. For him to take the bait, you'd have to stay really vulnerable since he'd see any trap strong enough to catch him."

"Right. So, we let him see that, too. We show him the whole game, set, gear and shine at the end. We show him you lying in wait for him, too, with Hisar beside you just like in His vision. Graize'll hate that. It should cloud his judgment if not his vision."

Spar shook his head. "If Hisar's gonna play a part in this, it has to be a willing part," he cautioned, watching the young God balance on the very tip of the cami's minaret, iridescent wings buzzing furiously to keep Its balance. "And Hisar won't go along with anything that might get Graize killed now any more than He was willing to go along with anything that would get you killed last year."

Brax grimaced. "Point," he acknowledged reluctantly. "Too bad. Killing Graize'd be a lot easier."

"I know. But Hisar's seen you both standing together and He means to make it happen."

A muscle in Brax's jaw jumped. "Graize said he saw that, too, a long time ago, but that's a load of shite; you know that. He could never really go along with it, not in a thousand years."

"You saw it, too," Spar pointed out bluntly. "Could *you* go along with it?"

The two met each other's gaze.

"I don't know," Brax said honestly. "Probably not. But even if I could, could *you*?"

"If it keeps you from getting killed, I could go along with just about anything these days. I'm sick of worrying about you."

"Well, I can't be everywhere at once, even if I wanted to be. You said it yourself, I'll crumble under the weight."

"So, you were listening to me."

Brax grimaced at him. "Just because I don't like hearing that others are better warriors than me doesn't make it any less true. I have to make a stand somewhere, and like you said before, Graize is our problem; he always has been. And we need Hisar, so we'd better get Hisar, whatever it takes. You need to talk to Him."

Spar showed his teeth at his kardos. "Forget it," he said bluntly. "This is your plan, Ikin-Kaptin. You want troops, you figure out how to recruit 'em." He stared pensively down at the fresh, clean water spilling along the trough at their feet. "It doesn't look like there're spirits in there," he mused. "But maybe you can't see them in the sunlight."

"Why don't we just jump in and find out?" Brax offered with a grin.

Spar cast him a flat, impatient glance. "Because it'll be freezing cold, even with the sun on it, dung-head. And it's moving so fast, and the sides are so smooth, that you'd drown before you could even shout for help. That's probably why they have these iron rings in the wall: to tie themselves off when they work up here."

Crouching down, Brax plunged his fingers into the water. "You're right," he said with a chuckle. "It is cold." He brought a palmful up to his mouth. "But it tastes good." As Hisar set down beside him with a curious air, he turned. "Can you see spirits sparkling in the water along here?" he asked It.

Hisar gave a sideways turn of Its head, pleased that Brax was asking It for information. "Yes," It answered without bothering to open Its mouth, a feral gleam glowing in Its metallic eyes.

"Are they dangerous?"

"Not to me." With a blur of wings, Hisar plunged into the trough, rising to the surface a moment later with Its body covered in a faint, silvery mist. It splashed about for a time, dipping Its head into the water like a feeding swan, then emerged in a spray of water that splattered both men equally.

Wiping his face with the hem of his cloak, Spar turned for the door. "I have to think about this plan of yours," he said. "I'll meet you both downstairs."

Hisar waggled Its tail at him, balancing on the smooth rim of the trough, Its wings outstretched to catch the light, then leaped into the air. With a shriek that sounded both pleasurable and challenging, It spiraled down to the ground as gracefully as any bird.

From his vantage point, the silver patina still clinging to the young God's body seemed to writhe almost menacingly, and Brax watched It land in the cami's flower garden with a frown, then followed Spar down the stairs, carefully closing the door behind him.

✦

Some time later, they sat in the garden, Brax and Spar sharing a large helping of fried mussels provided by the cami's chamberlain and tossing every second one to Jaq. Hisar lay nearby, delicately licking the spirits from Its flanks like a huge, overfed housecat. When they finished, Spar threw the edge of his cloak over his head to block the afternoon sun and, as Jaq laid his head on his ankles with a heavy sigh, he purposely closed his eyes.

Brax regarded them both for a moment; then, when it seemed obvious that neither of them were planning on moving any time soon, he pulled a stone and a soft cloth from the pouch at his belt and began to hone his sword.

Hisar glanced over, watching Brax's arm move back and forth, the painted symbols on his biceps winking out from beneath his tunic sleeves. Following the young God's gaze, Brax set the sword across his knees. He might as well start recruiting now, he thought. He lifted the left sleeve.

"Anavatan on the shield arm," he explained, his tone similar to one he used to train the newest delinkon at the temple. He lifted the right sleeve. "And Cyan Company on the sword arm. Every one of Estavia's warriors paints these two protections on their arms every morning to remember the oaths they swore when they first became warriors; oaths to protect and honor where they were born and the temple company they serve in."

"Spar paints them, too, and he's not a warrior," Hisar noted, changing to His golden-seeming.

"Spar's abayon are warriors and he lives at Estavia's temple, so he paints them out of respect for them and for Her."

"So what's that symbol?" Hisar asked, pointing at Brax's wrist.

"The God-Wall." Brax twisted his arm so that Hisar could see it more clearly. "Estavia gave me that one Herself when I promised Her I would defend the Wall and keep Anavatan safe."

"But nothing big," Spar muttered from under his cloak, his muffled tone dripping with sarcasm.

"You have other symbols, other protections, on your chest," Hisar added, glancing from one kardos to the other. "You both do."

Brax nodded. "We paint the symbols of our family near the center of Estavia's lien, in honor of those we love and those She loves." He laid his open hand against his cuirass and Hisar shuddered slightly, His expression flickering with barely disguised hunger. "Four people," Brax continued, deliberately ignoring the look. "Because you're expected to include yourself." He made a face. "And one dog. That was Estavia's idea."

"Dogs are beloved of the Gods," Spar said in a smug tone. "And Jaq is especially beloved of Estavia."

Hisar frowned. "But you've got six symbols on your chest, Spar. I saw them when you changed tunics yesterday. Four people, a dog, and a block or a building or something . . . oh." The young God stopped in sudden understanding. "Oh," He repeated. "It's a tower, isn't it? Is that for Me?"

Spar gave no answer, obviously embarrassed, and Brax laughed.

"Who else would it be for?" he asked. "He swore his oaths to You, didn't he?"

"Well, yeah. But you swore to Estavia and you don't wear Her as a symbol."

"That's because Estavia's temple doesn't require it. Every temple's different."

"It looks just like the tower symbols we're finding all over the city." Hisar's golden brows drew down. "You didn't tell Me," He said to Spar, His tone tinged with accusation.

Spar gave his one-shouldered shrug. "Don't get too excited about it. I'm just trying it out."

"How long have you been trying it out for?"

"A while."

"Nine months, maybe?" Brax hazarded.

"Maybe. Who asked you?"

"No one."

"Then shut up."

Brax returned his attention to his weapon with a chuckle, and Hisar glanced at him curiously.

"There's a silver glow along the blade," the young God observed. "I can see it all the time, but it goes all the way up your arm and into your body when you use it."

Brax nodded. "The sword's a part of me," he answered. "And it's part of Estavia; consecrated to Her service. When I use it, I'm using the physical representative of Her own weapons in the field and so Her power travels from Her swords to mine along our lien."

He lifted the sword, allowing the sun to catch the blade in a flash of light. "A Warrior's sword—my sword— is more than a weapon, more than just an extension of my arm, it's an extensions of my oaths and their lien going straight to Estavia. It knows if I'm not being honest with it, or with myself, and it'll turn against my hand if I don't treat it with the highest respect; as I would treat Her weapons themselves."

He held the sword straight out, sighting along the blade, the muscles of his forearm standing out with the effort. "But it's also a physical tool. It's used for attack, not for defense. I don't parry or block with it if I can help it. That's what a shield is for: to keep the sword free to attack. But, with the right move, a warrior could disarm an enemy, or even break their weapon with a shield if they had to. But that takes years of practice." He lowered it.

Hisar stared at him, His gray eyes wide. "Could you do it?" he asked as Brax began to hone the blade once more.

Brax grimaced. "No. The injury to my left elbow throws me off-balance and I have to compensate for it. I don't have the luxury of adding fancy moves on the battlefield. I have to concentrate on the simple ones: to attack with the sword and protect with the shield. But even that's compromised. I don't have the strength in the joint to hold a shield properly. I have to have it strapped on. Thanks to Graize," he added.

"Do you hate him for that?" Hisar asked in a quiet voice.

Brax regarded the young God with a serious expression, recognizing an opening but a little unsure of how to proceed. "I could say no," he replied. "I could say that he got lucky or that it's the risk every warrior takes and pretend that I'm fine with it." He paused, and Spar opened his eyes to watch him silently from the shadows of his cloak. "But yeah," Brax said, opting for honesty. "I hate him for it."

"Will you kill him for it?"

Brax returned his attention to his weapon, considering and discarding a number of answers. "No," he said after a moment. "Not for that." He regarded the young God seriously. "I could say that there are more reasons not to kill him than to kill him, but I'm not sure that's true. Your love for him may be one reason, but I don't know if that's reason enough. It might be. You stopped him from killing me on the grasslands last year, and I owe You. That might be reason enough, too. I know You'll try to stop me from killing him if I try." His dark eyes narrowed. "That's not really a reason, but it is a consideration.

"Now that's a lot of reasons," he continued. "But they don't add up to the single reason there is to kill him: he's committed to the downfall of Anavatan. If You want him to stay alive, You'll have to convince him, if not to change sides, then at least to lay down his arms."

"Me?" Hisar demanded.

Brax just shrugged. "He swore oaths to You. If he'll listen to anyone, it might be You. I'll give You the chance anyway. I'm going to get him here, regardless, because I can't have him running around loose plotting against the city; and we both know he'll come if I give him an opening. After that, it'll be up to You to save his life."

Hisar's gray eyes widened again at Brax's uncharacteristic speech and, as the warrior sighted along the length of the sword blade, it was the young God's turn to regard him seriously.

"Have you killed a lot of people with that weapon?" He asked, changing the subject for now.

"Some."

"Is it heavy?"

"Yes."

"Do you think that maybe, I could . . . try it?"

Spar sat up with a slight frown, but as Brax held the weapon out with a carefully blank expression, he lifted the red bead from his neck and placed it about Hisar's. The young God's form grew more substantial, but it took a concerted effort on Spar's part to send power to Hisar, and on Hisar's part to accept it, for His fingers to finally grip the hilt with any degree of strength. As the young God drew it from Brax's hand, His expression changed to one of surprise.

"It is heavy," He breathed, holding it gingerly as if He were afraid He might break it.

"It's metal," Brax agreed.

"It tingles against My hand."

"That's because it's sworn to another God's service." Brax's lip quirked up in a reluctant smile. "So, if You were to use it, You'd have to use it in Estavia's name."

Hisar's golden brows drew down once again. "Not in My own?"

"Not with that weapon, no. Another weapon, maybe. If You had weapons sworn to Your service," he added, accepting it back.

Both Hisar and Spar slumped slightly in fatigue.

"Do any of the other Gods have weapons sworn to their service?" Hisar asked, staring at His palm.

"I don't think so. Ystazia's artisans probably consecrate their tools to Her; brushes and hammers; that sort of thing. Most of Havo's people are farmers, so they'd have sacred flails and hoes maybe, and Usara's would probably consecrate their medical tools."

"What about Oristo's?"

"Sacred knives and forks," Spar said dryly, pulling a small bottle of cold tea from the depths of his cloak.

They all chuckled, relieved that the tension had eased.

"And Incasa?" Hisar asked.

The others grew serious once again. Brax glanced over at Spar who just shrugged. "I don't know if the Oracles of Incasa use tools in their augury," he said honestly. He took a long pull from the bottle before recorking it and tossing it to Brax.

"The street seers use dice," Brax observed, catching it one-handed.

"So do the street *tricksters* and half of the first are the second."

"Incasa uses dice," Hisar pointed out.

"That's 'cause He's the God of street tricksters," Spar answered, his upper lip curled in disdain.

"And you gave me a pair of dice that He gave to you."

"That *Yashar* gave to me," Spar corrected. "I lost them, and Incasa got them back to me."

"Why?"

"I don't know. I didn't ask Him."

"Why not?"

"Because I wouldn't have trusted His answer."

"Gods are big, and They'll do you if you let Them," Brax intoned after emptying the bottle in one swallow.

"I wouldn't," Hisar protested indignantly.

"Glad to hear it."

"Do you think Estavia would?"

"Not on purpose."

"Graize uses dice. He's a seer. Is he a street trickster, too?"

"He was. Now he's an enemy commander." Standing, Brax sheathed his sword in a single, smooth motion. "It's getting late," he said. "We should get back." Without waiting for an answer, he headed for the main gate.

Hisar glanced over at Spar. "Is he being pissy again?" He asked.

Spar snickered. "No," he answered, pushing Jaq off his ankles as he stood up. "Now he's just being bossy. C'mon." Accepting the red bead back, he followed after Brax with a shake of his head.

✦

They hired another boat to take them back to the Western Trisect, but this time Brax directed the boat-master to take them down the Halic-Salmanak, all the way past the Dockside Precinct to Estavia-Sarayi's temple wharfs on the southern shore of Gol-Beyaz. A school of dolphins caught up to them from the Bogazi-Isik Strait, and Hisar watched them enviously, noting how the silver shimmer of the Gods' Power sparkled along their dorsal fins with a much stronger light that the spirits' power in the aqueduct had done to Him. As they passed Its new temple site, dark and still in the growing twilight, She returned to Her Rayne-seeming.

"Why would anyone walk if they could take a boat," She wondered out loud, running her fingers along the tiny tower symbol carved into the side.

"An excellent question, God-Delin," the boat-master laughed. "And one we keep asking the good citizens of Anavatan."

Brax shrugged. "It doesn't cost anything to walk," he answered.

"Except time," Hisar pointed out.

"Yeah, except time."

The boat put in at Estavia's kitchen wharf a few moments later, and Brax vaulted over the side immediately after Jaq. Spar followed, and as Hisar rose gracefully into the air behind them, the boat-master waved at Her cheerfully.

"Mention it to yonder priests up there, anyway, God-Delin," she said with a wink. "And while You're at it, You could send our trade the power of Your domain; the strength of Creation to our vessels and the weakness of Destruction to the tightness of their purses."

Hisar gave her a startled look, and then smiled shyly as a trickle of unbound power feathered willingly from the boat-master to Herself. "I will," She promised. Changing to the dragonfly-seeming, It flew after the others, soaring into the air, past Estavia's statue, to alight upon the top of the armory tower as they disappeared inside the door. As the setting sun cast a metallic shine across Its flanks, the boat-master waved cheerfully again before heading back out into Gol-Beyaz.

✦

Later that night, Hisar took wing over the city, flying along the length of the aqueduct. The moonlight reflected off the spirits in the water, casting a faint white sparkle over the silver of their natural essence. Alighting on the edge of the reservoir, the young God stared intently into its depths. Somehow, down there, the water and the spirits within it traveled into the deep place It had envisioned; the great cistern.

The spirits were changing down there, It could feel it, their silvery taste turning to copper. Silver was the taste of the Gods; copper was the taste of the people, of their blood and of their power. It was the taste of the physical. And if the spirits in the deep place were becoming physical, then they would be growing as hungry for power as It had been; as hungry as It still was.

Its eyes flashed angrily. There wasn't enough power available to sate Hisar's own hunger, never mind anything else's; therefore the spirits in the cistern would have to be destroyed.

Settling back down again, It tucked Its wings tightly against Its body. Although Graize probably didn't know that yet, It admitted reluctantly. Right now Graize would be coming after Brax just like he always did. And if Brax set a trap for him like he planned to, Graize would fall right into it. Brax was right; he wouldn't be able to help himself.

Hisar shuddered, remembering the tingling feeling of Brax's consecrated sword against Its hand. Brax had said he would give Hisar a chance to save Graize's life, to make him lay down his arms. But if It couldn't convince him to do that, could the young God physically stop Brax from using the representation of Estavia's weapons against Graize? Was It strong enough to do that?

As the lien tingled through Its body in response, It realized It had to be. Hisar and Graize were tied together by bonds of power and obligation; God and follower. Ihsan had said so, Kemal had said so, and Hisar felt it to be true. The young God would not allow Brax to kill Graize. Again, the lien would not permit it. Again, it would break them both if It tried.

Shaking out Its feathers in a disgruntled gesture, Hisar stared morosely into the dark water. They had all seen Brax and Graize standing together; even Spar had seen it. Why couldn't the two of them just accept it and do it for the good of everyone involved? Why did Hisar have to do all the work? In the wild lands, Panos had said to be patient. Spar had said the same thing, but It was tired of being patient. Nobody else had to be patient. What It needed, It grumbled to Itself, was more followers then just two seers who didn't like each other, tied together by a soldier sworn to a different God. That's what It needed.

The young God shot the water lapping against the reservoir's sides a belligerent glare. That and to go down into that cistern and eat every last spirit that dared to try and be physical in Its city, It added. The water sparkled a challenge in return, daring Hisar to dive in, to follow its path down into the darkness. Hisar was tempted, very tempted, but It could feel that it wasn't time. It didn't have the strength, not yet. But soon.

Stretching out Its wings until they brushed against the buildings to either side of the reservoir, It leaped into the air, then turned and headed out across the Tannery Precinct and the western market toward Its own new temple site. It would have the strength soon, but for now, It still had to be patient.

8

Abayon and Delon

OUT IN THE BERBAT-DUNYA wild lands, the days passed swiftly. Danjel and Graize joined their family in driving the last of the flocks and herds to their summer pastures while Panos and her entourage took their ease in the encampments as honored guests.

On their last night among the Rus-Yuruk, Rayne threw herself down beside Graize at the fireside. Passing him a goat's meat skewer, she chewed on one of her own with a reflective expression.

"Danjel tells me that last mare finally foaled this afternoon," she said in a conversational tone.

Sitting comfortably with his back against a rock covered in sheepskins, Graize nodded. These few days with the Yuruk had finally solidified the nine months of mental and emotional stability that Danjel had labored to create for him. His mind still tipped back and forth like a boat listing in the waves, but at least it was no longer taking on water. For now. He felt warm and sleepy and gazed at Rayne with a contented expression, seeing her intent before she spoke it.

"Yes, twins," he answered easily. "Both female."

"Strong?"

"Very." He waved his Petchan bow in the air. "A cloud of spirits rose up around the smaller of the two and were driven back by the larger."

"A good sign. That kind of bond will bring strength to the herd." Stretching her feet toward the fire, she gave him a speculative glance. "Years ago we talked about strength. Do you remember?"

Graize nodded. "And Danjel talked about strength just this very morning," he replied with an innocent air.

She made a wry face in the direction of her kardos seated across from them. "Danjel's chosen to find strength with Yal. Whether that strengthens the Rus-Yuruk in the future will depend on whether Yal chooses to keep it among us. It'll do us little good if she whisks Danjel's seed off to strengthen the Petchans."

"It's not Danjel's seed that she's interested in," Graize pointed out.

"Maybe not now. But if she wants a child one day, she'll have the option of choosing Danjel's seed if she wants it. I've chosen yours."

Graize pulled a piece of meat from his skewer with a discerning air. "Danjel warned me you were planning to line your nest with my exotic feathers this season," he observed in a dry tone.

"That's all my nest is waiting for," she agreed. "You came home in good time. My body's ready; the child will be born in midwinter. It won't be a burden during this year's raiding season and it'll be old enough to leave with my abia during next year's."

"You have it all planned out, then? Down to the very day?"

"Yes."

"So, are we going to start now, or do I have time to finish my food?"

She laughed. "By all means finish. I want you strong and well rested." She leaned back, hands behind her head. "Caleb owes me a lamb," she said with some satisfaction. "He bet you'd play coy with me and make me work for it."

Graize just shrugged. "There isn't time," he answered, dispensing with his usual banter. "We ride out tomorrow, and the future's covered in mist and spray."

"You told Kursk once that the future was covered in blood and gold."

"It still is, except now the blood and gold are covered in mist and spray."

"You also told Kursk that he wouldn't live to see it. It was the first prophecy you ever made among us."

"I remember. His death became more clear the longer I remained with the Rus-Yuruk."

"Is mine?" she asked bluntly.

He gave her a neutral look. "No."

"Would you tell me if it was?"

He stared into the fire, watching its many, ever-changing prophecies merge and shift with the movement of the flames as his eyes struggled to maintain their focus on the present. "Maybe," he allowed. "If you demanded it."

"When we have a child together, I will demand it. I'll need to know how long I have to protect it."

"Place your shine, place your shine," Graize whispered. "What's the game, what's the prize?"

"What?"

He just shook his head. "If I see your death, I'll tell you."

"Good." Rayne stood. "Then let's go make a baby."

He glanced up at her in some amusement as the Yuruk seated around them laughed out loud. "I thought you said I had time to finish my food," he complained.

She scowled down at him. "I changed my mind. Like you said, there isn't time; the future's covered in mist and spray, and I want mine locked down by the time the skies clear."

"And what if the skies never clear?"

"Then we'll waterproof the tent."

"Very practical."

"Yes. So, are you coming or not?" She thrust her hand out to him. He stared at it for a long moment, watching the shadows play across her palm, merging and shifting in time with the firelight. She wanted a child, not a mate; the future was still malleable. He took it.

✦

They broke camp the next morning with Rayne and Caleb leading the Yuruk raiding party that was to accompany them to the edge of their lands. Keeping an eye on the weather, they followed the southern shore of the Halic-Salmanak, riding single file with the Skirosian party tucked safely in the middle.

On the last night they were to be together, in a driving rain sweeping down from the north, Graize dreamed.

✦

He was twelve years old, his youthful abilities at full strength, and the future shining as brightly as the sun. He and Drove had made the crossing to the Northern Trisect early on Oristo's First Day to join the autumn festivities and fleece the hundreds of revelers that crowded into the farmer's market. Throughout the morning, they'd woven past fruit carts overflowing with peaches, plums, and pomegranates, and fish carts overflowing with tchiros, sardines, and herrings. They'd made their way through narrow walls of wine barrels and oil jars with their clay sides glistening in the sunlight, and slid carefully between swaying towers of flatbread and pyramids of green-and-orange melons. They'd sampled the wares of every cart, stall, and table they passed, even paying for some of it as the mood took them. They'd watched bare-armed delinkon ladling out great splashing helpings of black-and-green olives from huge vats of brine, and wizened old spice merchants carefully measuring out minute quantities of saffron and pepper from tiny burlap bags. All around them, people crowded into every available space, as fire-eaters, jugglers, stilt-walkers, and street musicians moved gracefully among them, plying their trades beside sweetmeat sellers, kabob vendors, and raki merchants. The market's militia—doubled for Harvest—patrolled the crowd, but they couldn't be everywhere, and everywhere some sight or sound or odor drew the attention of the people away from their shine. By noon, both Graize and Drove had lifted half a dozen fat purses each.

Dropping a copper asper into the wooden offerings box at Havo-Cami's gate, Graize laughed out loud as he led Drove deep into its well-cultivated grounds. Tucking themselves into the farthest corner of the gardens, they sat with their backs against the cami's northern wall and greedily polished off a fat lamb kebob and a piece of flatbread stuffed with hazelnuts and cheese curds each, washing them down with a jug of raki passed between them. Then, using the bulk of the larger boy to shield his movements, Graize carefully counted out their newly acquired wealth, splitting it between them, then tucked the empty purses into his tunic with a satisfied expression. Most lifters would be afraid to carry the evidence of their trade that way, but they would go for an asper apiece back at the western dockside market and Graize wasn't afraid of anything, least of all catching the attention of some ham-fisted militia-farmer. It was a good afternoon's work.

Beside him, Drove shoved a huge piece of lokum into his mouth before leaning back to stare up at the aqueduct towering above their heads with a wide-eyed expression.

"'S big," he noted in a muffled voice, tying the brown ribbon about his finger.

Graize shrugged.

"Can't see us?"

"No one's up there lookin'."

"You sure?"

Graize gave a derisive snort. "Aqueduct's run by Havo's lot, an' all they care about's food an' weather." When Drove continued to look worried, he shook his head, turning to stare up at the aqueduct himself. The structure stood solidly at his back, blank with complacent disregard, and he waved a dismissive hand in Drove's face. "Like I said, nothin'," he declared as the sound of running water filled his mind. "Same as what's in your head." Wiping the grease from his fingers onto his tunic front, he stood. "C'mon," he said, gesturing at the market. "We can still get in a bit more liftin' 'fore we gotta get back."

Stung by the other boy's remark, Drove bit into an overripe peach, allowing the juice to trickle down his chin, before standing as well. A shadow passed over his face, but Graize was already turning away and he paid it no heed.

✦

Now, as his mind slid from the memory, Graize studied it dispassionately. The shadow that had covered Drove's face in death less than a year later had played no part in the afternoon's events, and the aqueduct had played no part in Drove's death.

He frowned as the other boy, his body ravaged by the spirit attack which had killed him, appeared before him.

"*'S big,*" Drove echoed.

Graize raised an eyebrow at him, but otherwise remained silent.

"*Can't see us?*"

"Like I said then, there's no one up there looking."

Drove's ghostly visage raised its eyes to the great stone arch above their heads. "*Maybe not then,*" he noted.

"Even if there is now, what's it to me?"

"*Nothin', 'cept maybe who's doin' the lookin' now.*"

Graize sent his mind out into the future streams. On a high tower in the middle of the streams, a dark-haired man stared down at him. He bared teeth at him.

"Brax."

Drove nodded. *"The priests of Havo've seen their aqueduct in danger an'
Brax's gone to guard it."*

"Has he now?"

"Spar, too. He's there to help Brax see the danger afore it gets to them."

"And what is the danger?"

"You."

Graize snorted. "Why would I bother to attack the aqueduct?"

"'Cause they're guardin' it, so you'll wanna attack it."

"Will I?"

"Yep." Drove leaned back, arms crossed in triumph.

"That's a pretty twisted prophecy, even for me."

"Yep."

"And what if I don't? What if I just carry on south with Panos and
join up with Illan's fleet like I planned to?"

*"Then you won't defeat Brax there, an' you won't take Hisar away from
Spar there neither."*

"Hisar."

"Hisar's with 'em." Drove made a sour face. *"What? D'you figure It'd
just wait for you to call It back like a dog you're ready to play with again?
There's some kinda danger in that water in darkness you saw, an' It's gonna go
down there an' fight it. Maybe It'll come out, maybe It won't."*

"Maybe I don't care."

Drove gave an elegant gesture incongruent with Graize's memory of
him. *"Maybe Spar does. Maybe Spar'll fight beside It. Maybe Brax will, too.
An' maybe they'll come up stronger. You want 'em fightin' side by side? Maybe
against you? Stronger?"*

Graize glared at him, and Drove just raised his misty shoulders in
another shrug. *"Hey, I'm dead; this is your prophecy not mine,"* he reminded
him. *"You do whatever you want. You always did, anyway."*

He vanished and, beneath a shallow escarpment on the shores of the
Halic-Salmanak, Graize awoke to the sound of rain.

"That's right," he grumbled as he worked his way out from between
Danjel and Rayne. "Go off an' ghost-sulk." Sliding carefully down the
darkened bank, he landed on the shore in a spray of wet pebbles, then
stood, staring down the length of dark water stretching out before him.
They were too far north to see Anavatan's great aqueduct, but it loomed
as solidly now as it had then, only now it was no longer blank with any

kind of disregard. Now Brax stared back at him from its heights, daring him to approach.

Graize's brows drew down in a scowl.

"And what if I don't?" he repeated.

"What if?" he whispered. "What if? Place your shine. Place your shine."

Pulling his stag beetle from his pouch, he stared into the place where its eyes had been. "Holes, my little one," he said to it solemnly, "twisty little holes where twisty little beetles creep. Priests who aren't prophets see danger, and champions who aren't militia rush to protect something that needs no protection against an enemy with no interest in attacking it. It smacks of manipulation. It smacks of a trap. If my own mind hadn't told it to me, I'd call it a liar. And maybe it is a liar, anyway."

He stroked the stag beetle's battered carapace. "And yet," he whispered. "Brax has gone to the aqueduct and Spar's gone with him. Did Spar lay this trap?"

He shook his head. "We don't really think so, do we, little beetle? The baby-seer's not that subtle. He's still a ratty little street lifter hiding behind Brax's fists. But he knows about the trap, and He's brought Hisar in to sweeten the bait."

He crouched down, pressing his fingers into the cold, wet earth. "Danger to my Godling, and do I care?" he whispered in a singsong voice. The tiny spirits bobbing at the water's edge stretched their minute claws toward him in response, and he dipped one finger in, allowing them to nibble at it like little fish, then sat back on his heels, sucking up the tiny spirit that still clung to one fingertip. His prophecy was often chaotic, but it was never subtle. It threw up the images he needed in whatever form it chose to. So what were its images this time?

The aqueduct.

Graize narrowed his eyes as the right pupil struggled to stay dilated against his vision, forcing his conscious mind to do the work. The aqueduct brought fresh, clean, spirit-laden water from the northern mountains to disappear into the great cistern beneath the Western Trisect.

He stared into the darkness, reliving another memory: a child in a ragged, yellow tunic standing on the top of the Tannery Precinct's Oristo-Cami. The aqueduct and its reservoir built up against the God-Wall had been nothing more to him than a solid presence to the north, just visible from the subtemple's windows. The retired priest whose duty it had been to teach the orphans who'd fallen into his care had simply told them that it ended in their precinct and had pointed out the high walls that guarded the entrance to the cistern. But the high walls of Oristo-Cami itself had been of greater interest to Graize, and once he'd vaulted over them and disappeared into the larger world beyond, both they and the aqueduct had been forgotten. Until now.

He stood, allowing the rain to pour down his face. There were spirits in the cistern and they were growing stronger, just as the spirits that had pooled about the city streets had once grown strong. And Hisar was going down into the cistern to fight them.

"Because Hisar will not suffer any other of Its kind to grow in strength," he said with a tinge of pride in his voice. "But the real question is, will I?"

Sighting along the Halic's dark water, he reluctantly allowed the lien created by jealousy and rage on the grasslands to tingle against his chest as he came to a decision. "No," he said. "I will not."

✦

Perched atop Estavia-Sarayi's armory tower in the seeming of a golden eagle, Hisar jerked in surprise as a familiar ripple of power passed across Its consciousness.

Graize.

It turned at once, then checked, Its luminescent eyes narrowing. The lien held no sense of urgency, just intensity. Graize was thinking about It, nothing more. Still, it was a beginning . . .

It made to rise, then sat back. No, It decided, just thinking, even intense thinking, wasn't enough. It hunkered back down in a petulant ruffle of metaphysical feathers. Even when his mind had cleared and he'd returned to come kind of shaky sanity, Graize refused to speak to It. So, if Graize wanted something from It now, he could come to It. Hisar was tired of hovering outside his mind like some kind of half-tamed hawk banging on the shutters to be let indoors.

Shaking out Its wings, dry regardless of the light rain now beginning to fall, It rose fluidly into the air and, ignoring the growing insistence of Graize's thoughts, headed off across the city's rooftops.

The young God maintained a regular nightly patrol of the Western

Trisect now, flitting about in the form of an immature owl, seeking Its tower symbols and the ones who carved them. Peeking through the latticed windows of homes and shops, feeling for the lives within; most of them sworn to one God or another, and a few, tantalizingly free of oaths. Ensuring that all was still well in Its city. When the faintest orange glow to the east heralded the coming of dawn, It would transform to the seeming of a golden swift, passing over the sentinels on the God-Wall close enough to ruffle the edge of their cloaks, before swooping along the length of the aqueduct to alight upon the reservoir once again. Then neatly tucking Its wings against Its sides, It would study the water intently, listening as the priests of Havo began the Morning Invocation and trying to discern if the spirits were stirring in response to the call of the sworn.

Tonight, as always, the water flowing into the reservoir made no answer and, wheeling about, It headed for the site of Its own growing power, Its unfinished temple.

✦

Alighting upon the sea chain's newly repaired stone-and-iron bollard a few minutes later, It cast Its gaze across the work site. Once the other six temples had come onboard, the work had begun in earnest. Piles of building materials showed themselves to Its metaphysical sight: lines of square-cut marble and limestone blocks, stacks of timbers, and piles of slate roof and ceramic floor tiles surrounded by wooden troughs for mixing mortar and strange-looking rope and wooden devices for lifting the heavy stones into place. The foundations had been excavated, and the outer walls begun, and in the very center, Hisar could just make out the small, rectangular pit dug for Its central shrine nearly ten feet below that.

Ihsan had explained its purpose.

✦

"A central shrine is both traditional and essential, symbolizing as it does, the heart of the Gods' community of worshipers. Each and every temple and cami has one, and each and every shrine is individually designed and adorned to represent the sensibility and dominion of its God. Ystazia's for example is extremely ornate, whereas I understand that Estavia's is more practically built with an eye to defense."

✦

Flying across the site, Hisar alit upon the roof of the shed where he and Spar had found all the tower symbols. As, one by one, the storage buildings had been demolished to make way for the temple's foundation, Spar had been adamant that this small structure be left strictly alone out of respect for those who had already consecrated it to Hisar.

The young God twisted Its head back and forth, studying both the shed and the pit. It had a feeling that It had neither an ornate nor a practical heart but rather a ragged, weather-beaten one with a hole in the back wall. But It also had a feeling that neither the six temples nor the master builder would be willing to accept that.

It was going to have to make them. Once It had more actual followers, It amended, to support Its position.

Still, It considered, craning Its head to take in the entire temple site, It may not have many worshipers . . . yet, but It did have a growing host of well-wishers. Although most of the building materials and money for labor and equipment had been donated by the temples, the city's masons had promised marble to line Its entrance hall, the glaziers had offered glass for its meditation room windows, the carpenters were working on a dozen latticed shutters, and the blacksmiths had promised proper iron door handles for the exterior and bronze ones for the interior. Lines of farmers and fishers brought food and drink for the workers' noontime meal every day, and a physician and healer-delinkos were always on site in case of accidents. Spar's bookmonger friends were donating books for a library and Zondar, one of Kemal's kardon, a gardener at Havo-Sarayi, had promised seeds and fruit trees for the gardens she'd insisted be included in the plans.

As the work had progressed, Hisar Itself had become a familiar sight. Perched on the bollard, half in and half out of the physical world, It had watched over the work and silently accepted the offerings, feeling the bindings of power and obligation grow as the workers had become used to Its presence and begun to ask for the power of Its domain: the strength of Creation to their labor and the weakness of Destruction to the rock which blunted their tools and bruised their hands. Every day, Hisar had the growing feeling that It was, maddeningly, on the very brink of being able to grant those requests.

But not yet. The illusive figures who left It seeds of unbound power every night in the symbols they carved were growing in number. They had yet to come face-to-face with their young God, but Hisar was sure that time was coming soon. One night, as It had sat silently upon the bollard, a youth carrying no oaths to any God, had vaulted over the wooden palisade which surrounded the site and left a new offering behind: a single, smooth piece of marble with a simple rectangular form etched on one end. She'd departed just as swiftly, asking nothing in return, but the power inherent in the gift had fed Hisar as nothing had before, and the young God'd had to hold Itself firmly in place to keep from racing after her. But Spar had taught It about patience and It had actually listened, so It had waited to see if she'd return.

She hadn't, but since then, a steady stream of unsworn youths had offered up small bits of stone or tile to the site each night. And each morning, the master builder would set them to one side to be accepted by Spar and Hisar before including them in the building plans. With each offering, Hisar had felt Itself growing stronger and more substantial, feeling for the first time, what it might be like to be a God of Gol-Beyaz.

Now, It turned to consider the silver lake shining in the moonlight. The home of the Gods was barely disturbed by the rain, its surface rippled and pitted, glowing with a bright, almost blinding light to Its sensitive gaze.

Hisar frowned. Since the work had begun, It had sensed the growing interest of the Gods, feeling Their regard as a dull ache deep within the center of Its being. The ache changed in character and timber depending on the God, and Hisar had become adept at telling one from another.

Ystazia viewed the building with a professional scrutiny that tasted of silk and rainbows, and Hisar found Itself wanting to dance when She noticed It. Oristo watched over the workers with a proprietary eye, bringing images of overprotective chickens to Hisar's mind. That made It feel restless and a little confined. Usara cast a blue light across the site whenever He turned His regard that way, watching over the workers' health and well-being, and Hisar found Itself mesmerized by the thought of just how fragile the physical world really was. Havo filled the air with the sound of leaves rustling on the branches of trees still unplanted, reminding everyone that time marched swiftly on. That caused Hisar to shiver like the breeze was blowing right through It. And Estavia's regard smelled of iron and copper and blood that made It want to keen unhappily as if Its own followers were going into battle to risk injury and death.

Only Incasa held Himself apart, and Hisar found Itself unwillingly reaching out, seeking the senior Deity's attention as It had once sought Graize's. But the God of Prophecy remained aloof. Just like Graize. That always put Hisar in a hurt and angry mood, souring Its visits and cutting them short. But the young God always returned and It always, eventually, reached out for Incasa again.

Now, a scuttling sound brought Its attention snapping back to the present, and It watched as a lithe figure appeared on the top of the palisade. It paused to gather its bearings, then leaped to the puddled ground with a light splash, and Hisar felt a thrill of excitement race through It as It recognized the youth who'd been first to leave an offering behind.

The youth bent, set a small piece of stone by the western foundation wall, then backed away slowly.

"You could . . . you know, help some," she said into the darkness, her voice both guarded and suspicious, and Hisar recognized the tone from hundreds of conversations It'd had with Spar. "I don't promise nuthin' back," she continued, "No oaths nor vows nor none a that, but you've had two bits of stone from me now, so a bit of help from you'd be . . . kinda . . . helpful."

Changing to Its Rayne-seeming, the young God stepped off the shed roof at once, then froze as the youth whirled about. "Yeah, I could help some," She said clearly, pushing Her words and Her image more fully into the physical world and matching the youth's dockside accent and cautious stance with eerie perfection. "Whadda ya need?"

The youth squinted suspiciously at Her. "Shine, bread, a new jacket," she said with a snort. "But Gods don't help with that kinda useful shite, do they?"

Hisar gave one of Spar's one-shouldered shrugs. "Not so much," She agreed. "But you musta thought of something else or you wouldn't a asked."

The youth snickered. "Guess so." She folded her arms almost belligerently across her wet tunic. "So how do some say it, the strength of

Creation for somethin' and the weakness of Destruction for somethin' else?"

"Yeah, that's how some say it."

"All right then, I want the strength of Creation for my crew to find a new safe and the weakness of Destruction for the piss-faced factor that turfed us out to fall in the strait an' drown."

Hisar cocked Her head to one side trying to sort out the youth's street talk from what She had learned from Spar.

"I don't know too much about safes," She admitted, "'Cept this one," She amended, indicating the shed with a jerk of Her chin. "Why can't your crew stay here?"

The youth rolled her eyes. "'Cause it ain't that kinda safe. It's a coming by for thinkin' and sittin' quiet kinda safe." She leaned one shoulder against the wall in a proprietary way. "Open for all crews, not just mine. No fights here, no liftin', no hidin' lifted goods. Just bein' safe. But no eatin' or sleepin' neither."

"There was someone sleepin' here before," Hisar pointed out.

"Yeah, that was Zeno. He was in my crew. He took a fall, so we all figured he could rest here till he got better. He got pinched for trespass. That's why nobody's slept here since."

Hisar felt Her body stiffen. "Who says it was trespass?" She demanded in a dangerous growl.

The youth shrugged. "Garrison guards what patrol the docks at night, I guess." She tipped her head to one side. "Say, could you help with that?" she asked.

Hisar nodded. "Oh, yeah, I'll help with that," She promised with an angry expression. "This is *my* temple site. *Mine.* Nobody says who's trespassin' here 'cept me."

"So you can get him free?"

"Yes."

"How?"

"I'll go to my First Priest. He's smart an' he knows stuff." Hisar frowned. "I should probably wait till morning though. He's in vision an' he hates bein' interrupted. He gets right pissy."

The youth cocked her head to one side again. "That be Spar?"

Hisar blinked in surprise. "Yeah."

"'S it true he used to be a lifter on the western docks?"

"Yeah."

The youth relaxed her shoulders. "Well, that's all right, then. I can figure a priest with that kinda training might have somethin' half useful to say. You go talk to him. In the mornin'. I reckon Zeno can wait that long." She turned away, then paused. "An' if it works out I might, you know, *think* about oaths," she said without turning around. "Not like Spar's a course, but some kind. Maybe. If it works out."

As she disappeared over the palisade again, Hisar felt a newly formed thread of obligation follow her into the night and bounced up and down excitedly. Crossing to the youth's offering, She bent and ran Her fingers over the smooth surface, recognizing another piece of etched marble, and feeling the strength inherent in the gifting of it. "Maybe," She whispered. "Maybe's good."

Changing to Its familiar dragonfly-seeming, It lifted into the air, then passed over the youth with the faintest whisper of metallic wings, before heading out across the city, excitement causing It to flip through a series of barrel rolls in midair. It would help her and she would swear to It, and that might just give It enough strength to face the spirits growing in the darkness. It would talk to Spar in the morning, but It wanted to start helping Its potential new worshiper now. Not in the morning, now.

It snapped Its teeth at a nearby gull in annoyance. Spar should be willing to leave his visioning for this, It thought resentfully. After all, he was Hisar's First Priest, and Hisar needed his advice. But Spar had spent the last day and half the night in Estavia's Seer's Shrine with Sable Company and he was always "pissy" after spending that much time with temple seers. It had better wait.

Pausing over the western docks, Hisar wondered what the other Gods did when They wanted to speak to one of Their First Priests in the middle of the night. It bet They wouldn't wait until morning. Not by half, They wouldn't. They'd probably just slam into their prophecy with a bang.

It almost turned toward Estavia-Sarayi, then checked as a thought occurred to It. Spar was busy, but Brax wasn't. Brax was standing on top of his newly built trap for Graize; he'd been there all week.

Banking sharply, the young God shot across the Halic-Salmanak, heading for the North Trisect at a dizzying speed, ignoring the restless stirring beneath It, for now.

✦

Far below, in the great stone cistern, the newly arriving spirits swirled about in vast, silver schools just below the surface, feeding off the tiny flakes of power that sparkled in the darkness. Their constant motion agitated the water, disturbing the slumber of the larger, heavier spirits lying on the bottom. The power was darker there and harder to find, but no less hungry, but these spirits were more patient, waiting—sometimes for years—for those upper spirits to slowly sink under the pressure of their own feeding. The largest of the bottom dwellers would then rise up just a little and devour them. Their tiny allotments of prophecy would fill their dreams and they would sink into slumber once again.

But lately, these heavier spirits had begun to sense the presence of another creature, one so bright with power that their blind hunger for it had driven them to nearly full awakening. If they could reach this new power, they could feast until even the most famished of their number would be satisfied.

If they could reach it.

✦

Standing on the entrance to the reservoir, Incasa felt this growing agitation as a tingle through His own ties of obligation to Anavatan. In the past these spirits had required little tending. Most were destroyed in the reservoir itself by the cool breeze and the warm sun, the rest by the bottom feeders in the cistern. When those became too powerful, Incasa would direct the God of the Seasons to flood the cistern during Havo's Dance, driving them back toward the bottom or spilling them out through the overflow into Gol-Beyaz itself where the Gods could devour them at leisure. But as Hisar had grown, It had sensed the hunger growing within the cistern, and as indignant as a young cat whose territory was suddenly under threat, It now crouched, poised and bristling above the entrance. It wouldn't be long before impatience caused It to thrust a paw inside. But these spirits were stronger than the young cat realized. They had sharp teeth and, once in, It might find it difficult to get out again because they had sensed It, too, and they were as hungry as It was. The young cat would need some help.

Floating slowly down to street level, Incasa passed His snow-white gaze across the buildings to either side. The God of Prophecy rarely left the center of Gol-Beyaz. The calming sense of waves and wind lent themselves to visioning far more than dust and wood and stone. However, now and again, it was necessary to actually see the place where the future was unfolding.

A tiny spark of unbound power drew His attention to a crude rectangular figure carved in the crumbling corner of a nearby doorway. Bending down, He breathed in the trace of the one who'd left it there: a young male, poor, hungry, and most importantly . . . unsworn, but with the finest thread of worship and obligation between himself and the new God of Creation and Destruction already in place.

The seed of power housed in the center of the tower symbol sparkled in the moonlight and He resisted the urge to harvest it Himself. As the eldest of the Gods, Incasa preferred the smooth stream of worship that flowed like a river from His temple and the many camis across Anavatan. The unsworn, especially among Anavatan's youth, were a swirling vortex of unstable potential better suited to a young God. They would be the foundations upon which Hisar would build His new power base and just in time, for battle was imminent and every one of the Gods would need all the followers they could muster.

Rising above the rooftops, Incasa watched as an iridescent figure flitted across the moon, then turned His gaze to the north before returning to the calm stability of Gol-Beyaz with a satisfied expression.

9

The Aqueduct

*H*E STOOD HIGH ON *a rocky promontory watching the construction of Anavatan coming to a close for another day. Below, Marshal Nurcan and the rest of the Battle God's Commanders waited to take their supper with him, but he lingered for a few moments longer, unwilling to break the silence of his own thoughts.*

His gaze swept across the vast building site. Although the Gods' six temples and most of the civic buildings were complete, great, empty gaps still marred the city's skyline with most of Anavatan's future citizens still living in tents and makeshift wooden barracks. They would be properly housed come winter— the Gods had promised it—but with the warm, summer breeze off Gol-Beyaz freshening the air, many chose to take their meals outdoors. The mingled odors of woodsmoke and roasting meat wafted up to him from the hundreds of cooking fires below while, along the banks of the Halic-Salmanak, the navy's twelve new pentecomters stood guard over the western wharfs, already crowded with trade ships; all eager to supply the many markets which had sprung up almost overnight. Whatever the season, whatever the circumstances, he mused, trade always followed hard on the heels of either construction or destruction, often overtaking them both.

The cries of Estavia's sentries on the newly built God-Wall sounding the all clear drew his attention to the northwest. Just within the protection of the Wall, the wide stretch of greenery, set aside to ensure the city's meat supply, was already dotted with sheep, grazing peacefully beneath the reservoir and the wide, sweeping arches of the great aqueduct, built to ensure its water supply. Beyond the Wall, the grasslands merged with the wild lands, then disappeared in a swath of gray-green mist, colored orange by the setting sun. Empty of any threat.

For now.

The wide, twisting scar on his right thigh—a souvenir from the fighting against the Yuruk last season—twinged as he began to pick his way down the narrow trail. He rubbed at it with a thoughtful expression. Soon there would be little need for fighting. The God-Wall would protect them from the Yuruk and the navy would protect them from Volinsk. There would be peace and prosperity, just as the Gods had promised. He wondered absently what he'd do with himself then.

✦

"The Wall will not stand."

✦

On the sentinel platform he'd had constructed at Havo-Cami, Brax dismissed the words with a growl. Beside him, Ghazi-Warrior Feridun made a questioning noise, then returned his attention to the northern hills when his Ikin-Kaptin just shook his head. Staring across the glittering waters of the Halic-Salmanak, Brax's brows drew down in an impatient frown.

He'd had this second vision just this afternoon, caused, once again, by the subversive ministrations of Senior Touch-Healer Jazet, but this vision had been far more tactile than the first. He remembered the smell of woodsmoke and roasting meat and the twinge of pain in his right thigh. Its timing was suspect. He'd sketched it out for Spar but had otherwise kept it to himself. He didn't know where these visions were coming from, and until he did, he wasn't going to give Kaptin Liel any excuse to extend his training in *cultivating stillness*. He'd had more than enough of that during his convalescence.

Leaning against the cami's outer wall, he turned to face the light rain that had just begun to fall, allowing it to cool his cheeks as he studied the vision as dispassionately as he was able.

He was used to being compared to Kaptin Haldin. Ever since Estavia had brought him and Spar to Her temple—practically forcing the command council to take them on as delinkon—his fellow warriors had drawn parallels between himself and Her legendary Champion. Everyone wanted to be part of a new story full of heroism and romance. Brax had grown used to both the favoritism and the responsibility that came with it, but what he wasn't used to was being caught up in visions that slapped him down into Kaptin Haldin's actual memories. That was new. And he didn't like it. He was no seer, and feeling other people's feelings and thinking other people's thoughts—especially people who'd been dead for centuries, was for seers.

"Do you know what this book is about?"

He chuckled. Of course he'd known what the book was about. He knew about nearly every book that contained anything on Kaptin Haldin; Ihsan had seen to that. But he wasn't about to admit that to Spar. It was way too much fun taking the piss on him. And he'd seen that particular picture many times. In the early days, when the heady buzz of Estavia's lien had kept him from sleeping, he would sometimes slip quietly from the bed he shared with Spar and Jaq and make his way to the armory tower. There, standing alone in the shadowy lamplight, he would run his fingers over the brightly painted figure, wondering about Kaptin Haldin's life, what he had felt and what he'd thought. How he'd died.

On the sentinel platform, Brax grimaced. *"Be careful what you wish for, idiot,"* he told himself. *"It just might come back to bite you on the arse."*

"The Wall will not stand."

"I heard you the first time."

"Ikin?" Feridun turned again.

"Nothing, Ghazi, just thinking out loud."

The older man snorted. "A bad habit for young commanders to get into," he admonished in a gruff tone. "It makes their subordinates doubt their ability to lead."

"Hm." Brax's first real command had ended in disaster with six of his troop dead and himself a prisoner of the Yuruk. If Feridun—himself badly injured—hadn't doubted Brax's ability to lead then, it was unlikely that a little thinking out loud would cause it now.

Deep within him, Estavia's lien tingled, disturbed by the memory, and he laid his palm against his chest until it eased.

"Don't think about any of that right now," he told himself sternly. *"Think about the job at hand. Think about the trap. Thinking about the trap will anchor it in the physical world and that will bring Graize right to it."*

Straightening, he stared into the darkness beyond the city wall. Somewhere out there, Graize crept ever closer; Brax didn't need a seer's abilities to know it.

He leaned against the side of the cami once again. He and Spar had taken his proposal to Kemal and Yashar, and then to the command council the very next morning after their visit to the Northern Trisect. It was the first time they'd stood together in that vaulted, windowless chamber in six years, and he'd found himself feeling just as belligerent as he had the first time.

And Kaptin Omal of Indigo Company had been just as unconvinced.

✦

"And you know this man, this Graize, is going to attack the aqueduct? *You've seen* it?" The heavyset ghazi-commander leaned forward, fixing Brax with an intense stare.

Brax just shook his head. "No, I haven't *seen* it, Kaptin; I'm no seer. But the aqueduct's in danger, that much *has* been seen."

"By those who service the aqueduct and by the Oracles of Incasa themselves," Kemal added.

"The Oracles of Incasa have seen a *single* stream that speaks to the possibility of danger," Kaptin Liel corrected mildly, "not to any actual danger as of yet."

"I know Graize," Brax interrupted firmly. "I know how his mind works and I know what drives him. I know that as long as he remains at large with his movements untracked, he's a danger to Anavatan. He orchestrated the surprise attack on Serin-Koy five years ago and he bartered an alliance between Volinsk and the Petchans that will see the hill people enter this season's fighting on their side. He has to be stopped. I can stop him."

"The Northern Trisect's demanding more troops," Yashar added. "This'd have the added benefit of shutting them up for a while."

Kaptin Julide of their own Cyan Company shot him a dark expression, shot with reluctant amusement. "We don't assign extra troops just to shut people up, Ghazi," she admonished.

Beside her, Kaptin Alesar of Azure Infantry gave a bark of cynical laughter. "Because if we did, then no one ever would."

Most of the council chuckled their agreement.

"We're going to be facing attacks on multiple fronts this season," Brax continued. "And you'll be assigning everyone a place in Estavia's defense. Make this my place. If I stand in that stream of prophetic possibility, Graize'll see me, and he'll come for me; he won't be able to stop himself. He'll set any other plans he may have aside for it and we'll have the advantage of knowing it. We can lay a trap he can't help but fall into. We can eliminate any possible danger to the aqueduct and the danger he poses at the same time. Prophecy fulfilled."

Kaptin Nateen of Turquoise Company rubbed at her temples with an irritated expression as his words brought on a murmured conversation across the command table. "Discussions about prophecy give me cluster headaches," she complained. "Let's just assign Estavia's Champion to the aqueduct and have done with it. I have four dozen archery delinkon to train who don't know their arseholes from their target centers and if I don't get them trained up soon, I won't know it either."

Marshal Brayazi raised an eyebrow at her as Kaptin Alesar burst out laughing. "We don't assign troops because of the young's anatomical confusion either, Kaptin," she said dryly. "Or because of their commanders' confusion."

"Then do it because of a young God's confusion."

The gathered immediately silenced as Spar fixed the entire council with his infamous dockside glare.

"Graize is key to Hisar's alliance," he said bluntly. "He was Its first abayos and he swore his oaths to It on the grasslands just as I did. Graize'll come to kill Brax and to take Hisar away from me. And if he calls to It, Hisar just might go to him."

"Oracle Freyiz said you were the key to Hisar's heart," Kaptin Liel pointed out.

"I am, but Graize is the key to Its bollocks."

Kaptin Alesar burst out laughing again. "Meaning what, young one?"

"Meaning you want Hisar to join with the Gods of Gol-Beyaz when It gets old enough to take Its version of Its adult vows. With Graize at large, there's too great a risk that It won't."

"And with this Graize neutralized, do you have enough influence over Hisar to convince It to join with the Gods?" Kaptin Nateen asked gently with a just hint of indulgent condescension in her voice. "Do you truly command the new God of Creation and Destruction to so great an extent, Sparin-Delin?"

Spar gave his familiar one-shouldered shrug. "No. But then, I'm not trying to. I want It to make Its own decision."

"I'm not so sure I feel any more confident about that," she replied.
Spar just shrugged again.

Marshal Brayazi leaded back in her chair. "Returning to the salient point, which is that Graize is a danger to Anavatan," she said firmly. "With which I agree. How many people do you think your trap will require, Ikin-Kaptin Brax?"

"One Infantry troop on guard at the aqueduct," Brax answered at once. "With myself to lead them and Spar to guide us. He'll come by night, so we lay the trap by night."

"And where will Hisar be when the trap is sprung?" Kaptin Omal demanded. "If you can't count on Its alliance where Graize is concerned, how will you keep It from entering the conflict on his side?"

"Because I will give It a choice," Spar answered. "And so It will choose not to."

"You've *seen* this?"

"I have *built* this."

"But you haven't *seen* it."

"Enough." Marshal Brayazi raised her hand. "Brax's troop is assigned to the aqueduct for now. As Yashar says, it will have the added benefit of satisfying the demands of the Northern Trisect," she added in a wry tone. "In the meantime, Spar-Delin, you will discuss a proper strategy regarding Hisar with Kaptin Liel and will report back to me before you take up any position on the aqueduct." When Spar frowned at her, she gave him a stern expression in reply. "You're still a delos. Your safety is the responsibility of this temple and I will not allow you to take part in any form of combat until I know that responsibility has been addressed." She returned her attention to Brax. "You have your assignment, Ikin-Kaptin. You are dismissed."

✦

On the sentinel platform, Brax felt the now-familiar buzz of metallic wings across his cheek as Hisar whizzed by him. They hadn't spoken since Brax had charged Hisar with the mission of saving Graize, but the young God had visited Havo-Cami at least once every night since they'd taken position. It hadn't actually manifested, not yet, but Brax knew that eventually It would overcome whatever was keeping It at bay. Something was on Its mind; probably Graize.

He turned. "Feridun, go and get yourself a hot cup of tea. It's going to be a cold and wet night."

"Yes, Ikin."

Once his fellow ghazi had descended the stairs, Brax lifted his face to the rain once again and waited. It was only a few moments before he felt another buzz of wings, then suddenly Hisar appeared before him in His golden-seeming in what felt like a pop of displaced air.

"That's new."

Brax studied the young God dispassionately. His hair and the golden tunic shot with green threads that He'd chosen to wear in this form was disheveled, and His face was sheened with a thin layer of silver light, almost like sweat. If He'd been a physical being, He would have thrown Himself down, panting with excitement. As it was, He hovered, vibrating, in midair for several minutes before He was able to speak.

"I have a worshiper," He blurted out, then grimaced sourly at Brax's surprised expression. "All right, not a real worshiper, but almost, maybe, she said she might, maybe, if it worked out, so I want it to work out, but I don't quite know how to make it work out, and I would've asked Spar 'cause I told her I would, and I will, but I can't right now 'cause he's doing seer work that he won't talk about yet, he say not yet, but he will soon, he promised, but I need help now."

Brax narrowed his eyes, trying to sort out this unusually fast flow of words.

"You want what to work out?" he asked finally.

"What she wants help with."

"Who?"

"My worshiper; weren't you listening?" Hisar asked impatiently.

"I was, but none of it made a lot of sense."

"I've met someone."

Brax blinked. "That makes less sense."

Hisar blinked back. "Why?"

Brax shook his head. "No reason, never mind. You've met someone. Where?"

"At my temple site. She brought me a piece of marble. She brought me one before. She was actually the first person ever to bring me something like that," Hisar explained somewhat more slowly.

"Ah. She brought you an offering," Brax said, understanding begin-ing to dawn.

"Yes. And she said she needed my help. And I want to help her, but I don't know how."

"What does she need your help with?"

Hisar spelled out what the youth had asked for and Brax frowned.

"Well, first off, I wouldn't try using destruction to influence anyone to fall into the strait. Most people are sworn to one God or another and They take offense at losing their followers that way."

Hisar nodded. "Everyone phrases it like that," He said with a frown. "They need to stop."

"As for Zeno; that's easy enough. Have Yashar speak to the garrison guard kaptin in the morning; they're old friends."

"And they'll let him go?"

"They should. Like you said, it's your temple site. It's not trespassing unless you say it is."

"What about the safe?"

Brax leaned against the wall, more or less out of the weather. "That's trickier. The Gods don't usually find actual homes for people; that's generally the job of Their priests like the Abayos-Priests of Oristo. I suppose you could ask them."

"But if I ask them, then Oristo'll get all the credit," Hisar replied in a petulant tone. "And besides, she asked for *my* help, not the Hearth God's."

Brax shrugged. "Then I guess you better figure out what you can do that the Hearth God can't."

He rubbed the back of his neck with a grimace. "So, why are you all bent out of shape about helping this one person out, anyway," he asked curiously. "The boat-master asked for— what was it—the strength of Creation for her boat and the weakness of Destruction for something else, didn't she?"

"Purses," Hisar answered absently. "That was different. The boat-master was just talking, making conversation. She wasn't really asking. This person was. She left an offering and she offered oaths back. Maybe. If it worked out."

"So that was the difference, then, oaths?"

Hisar frowned at him. "No, I told you, the difference was that she actually *asked. For real.*"

"But you'd like her to make oaths?"

"Well, sure I would, stupid, I'm a *God*. If someone offered you a . . . meal, or sex, or something like that, wouldn't you want them to follow through?"

Hisar looked so indignant that Brax couldn't help but chuckle. "Yeah, I guess I would," he admitted.

"Well, so would I. But it's more than just that." Hisar stilled. "She made me want to help her," He continued in a quieter voice. "She made me feel like I should help her. Like it was . . ." He fell silent, unsure of how to put these new feelings into words.

"Like it's what you do," Brax supplied.

Hisar nodded.

"That's because it is what you do. Like you said, you're a God. That's what the Gods do, They help when They're asked to. Maybe she needs for you to just be there, listening. That's also what the Gods do. They let you know you're not alone; that They've got your back; that They've always got your back."

"What did you do?"

"I took them away from you."

A shiver ran through Brax as he remembered the terrible, aching sense of emptiness and loss he'd felt on the grasslands and, deep within him, the Battle God's lien responded, echoing his pain back to him, equally damaged, equally frightened that it could happen again.

"They're not all-powerful," he said quietly, more to himself than to Hisar.

The young God gave him a disbelieving look. "This coming from you?" he retorted.

Brax gave one of Spar's one-shouldered shrugs. "I never thought Estavia was all-powerful," he replied. "The Gods have limits just like people do. I always knew that." He stared along the dark, rain-pocked waters of the Halic-Salmanak, feeling rather than seeing the silver glow of Gol-Beyaz in the distance. "But I guess I forgot."

He returned his attention to Hisar. "The Gods probably forget, too. They probably want to forget; so do Their worshipers. But we can't forget, and you better not either. So go help your new worshiper however you can, but just remember that you're not perfect. You're going to make mistakes sometimes."

"But how?" Hisar repeated. "I can hardly do anything physical." He sounded so much like an unhappy child that Brax pulled himself out of his own thoughts with a deliberate shake.

"Well, you have some kind of seer abilities, don't you? Sort of like Estavia does?" he asked gently.

"Sort of. I have visions sometimes, like Spar does. And they are getting stronger."

"Then keep an eye on the future streams like Spar does. If it looks like this person or her crew need help, go get help, and don't worry about who gets the credit. Just be there. That's what most important, yeah?"

"Yeah."

They fell silent for a long time with Brax leaning against the wall and Hisar hovering in midair a few feet away. Finally, the young God cocked His own head to one side.

"Graize thinks you had his back," he said. "All those years ago."

"I know," Brax sighed. Spar had told him Hisar's story of Graize's memory, of their supposed first meeting in the dockside doorway, but he couldn't remember it. If truth be told, he actually had very little memory of his early childhood. He remembered being cold and hungry in winter and hot and hungry in summer. He remembered fearing the garrison guards of Estavia and the abayos-priests of Oristo and fearing the spirits that whispered over the streets like mist, seeking the unsworn. He remembered being caught out on those streets as the sun went down more than once and running for shelter, his heart beating so fast and so hard that it drowned out the pounding of his feet on the wet cobblestones. He remembered the cold, biting rain on his face, and the faint scratch of ethereal claws against his ankles. But he had no memory of leading a priest to another boy crouched in a doorway on Havo's Dance. His first memory of Graize had been of a sneering, cocksure little street thief, standing beside another boy, Drove, too big and too able with his fists for Brax take on.

It bothered him that he couldn't remember what had obviously been so important to Graize.

Spar had shrugged it off. *"It's his memory, not yours. It means something to him, not to you. We use it or we ignore it. That's all."*

Brax wasn't so sure.

"So go to a Priest of Oristo and have them dredge it up for you."

"No."

He could no more let an abayos-priest scrape around in his head than Spar could. It would have to be as his kardos had said, they would have to use it or ignore it.

"No, what?" Hisar asked, pulling him from the memory.

"No, nothing, I was just thinking."

"Me, too."

"Yeah? What were you thinking about?"

"That if it's hard for me to be there for one worshiper, it must be really hard for the older Gods to be there for all of Theirs."

"Yeah."

"But I still want as many as They have," Hisar added, a gleam in His eye.

Brax gave an amused snort. "Of course you do," he agreed. "That's also what the Gods do: They collect people." He turned as Feridun's footsteps sounded on the stairs behind them. "Looks like a fog's coming in," he said in a more conversational tone. "Why don't you go check on this potential worshiper, then go talk to Spar. He knows more about this sort of thing than I do. Better yet, go talk to Kemal and Yashar. They've been around longer than both of us. If I come up with anything else, I'll, I dunno, shout for you or something."

"All right."

Hisar flowed reluctantly into Its dragonfly-seeming, and as Feridun stepped carefully onto the rain-slicked platform, It took wing over the Halic. Watching until It disappeared behind the rooflines of the Dockside Precinct, Brax just shrugged at the older man's questioning glance, then returned his attention to the dark shoreline below.

✦

To the west, Hisar headed across the water, feeling for the line of obligation that linked It with Its new, potential worshiper. As It reached the opposite bank, the restless stirring of the spirits in the cistern beneath It made It check in midflight, but It made Itself carry on. Not yet, It told Itself sternly. Soon, but not yet. It needed more strength.

It found the line, so fine that It hardly dared touch it for fear it would vanish, on the edge of the Western Dockside market and followed it, on silent wings, until It hovered above a crumbling three-story dwelling in the Tannery Precinct. Then, changing to Its golden-seeming, It fluttered down, catching hold of the worn wooden shutters with its tiny claws and peered inside. A dozen lives besides the youth's own lit up Its vision; all young, all unsworn, with no ties of obligation except the line she'd extended toward Hisar and the tower symbols that splashed across the entire building like a spray of stars.

It stayed there, watching, "being there" as Brax had put it, as tendrils of fog wove their way inland from the Bogazi-Isik Strait, driving the rain before it and covering everything, physical and metaphysical in a thick, concealing mist.

10

Seers

A S THE MORNING SUN bathed the horizon in light, Panos knew she dreamed. She stood balanced precariously on the edge of a sand-colored cliff, thick with wild grapevines. Behind her lay the island of Thasos; below her, its main harbor bustling with activity, a fleet of warships, their sails a brilliant white against the water's blue, preparing to make way. The light, spring breeze lifted the fine hairs along her arms, and she raised them to its embrace. Too often her dreams were peopled with sight and sounds of a purely symbolic nature, but this dream, with its scratch of bracken against her feet and the taste of salt and anticipation on her lips, held a worldliness that only came from the present.

Her father was preparing to set sail.

Changing to the form of a white seagull, she took wing off the cliff, racing the wind to the waves. The royal trireme rose up before her and she circled it once before alighting upon the mast. Below, King Pyrros struck a dramatic pose for the benefit of his sailors, his feet planted solidly on the polished wooden gangway, a map in one fist, his sword pommel gripped in the other.

Behind him, the court oracles clustered about like a flock of self-important geese. This was an auspicious day to begin the move against Gol-Beyaz. In concert with the Sorcerers of Volinsk, they had planned it to be so. As the strongest of their number raised his head to look into her eyes, she gave a single cry before taking wing for the north.

The wind whistled through her feathers. A tall tower rose up before her, then vanished. The gray-green grasslands rushed past her in a blur. The rain-quenched brilliance of the Halic-Salmanak glowed beneath her and she paused to kiss herself on the brow before continuing on her way.

Graize sat upon the bank nearby, oblivious to the rain falling all around him. Staring into the dawn, making plans. She sent him the image of the Skirosian fleet, then shot out across the water and over the northern hills. They grew steeper, became mountains, became cliffs, and then she was free of the fog and the rain and flying over the icy waves of the Deniz-Siya. As the brown hills of Volinsk appeared in the distance, She reached out for Illan. He, too, stood aboard a royal ship preparing to sail. He, too, was surrounded by oracles for whom this was an auspicious day to mount an attack.

She touched his mind, felt his response, and then her dream changed as the symbols of her prophecy rose up, demanding her attention. The landscape grew fluid, and then stiffened to become one of Hares' beautiful maps, the cream-colored vellum splashed with colored ink. Gol-Beyaz flattened to a strip of silvery-blue, dotted with pale towers, and flanked by lines of cowled crows.

Hovering above the painted outlines of Anavatan, she turned her beak and plucked two feathers from her breast and let them fall. They became a white-clad king and a prince with eyes as fathomless as the sea. They spiraled downward, unhindered by wind or rain, and as Panos watched them go, the melancholy expression returned to her features. There were many fluid possibilities in war, but the blind ambition of kings and princes might as well be etched in stone. The time was coming when she was going to have to decide which feather to fall beside, the king or the prince, but she feared the future was soon going to make that decision for her whatever she might have chosen. With a sigh, she returned her attention to the prophetic map below her.

In Skirosian prophecy, towers symbolized either stability or rigidity, but in this case, both Pyrros and Illan would meet purely physical obstacles; the outcome determined by purely physical combat. There was little she could do to change their fate. Only Graize would face a symbolic tower and, rigid where he might be stable, her shortsighted little tortoise was not going to want her help, but he was going to need it.

She shook her head at the image of a shortsighted seer before bringing her thoughts back to the present.

Most of the crow-seers of Anavatan had their mist-covered eyes

trained on the west, believing that their physical towers could keep watch
to the north and south. All but one: the young seer Hisar had brought to
spy upon her lovemaking so long ago. He was also rigid where he should
be stable and needed help but did not want it. And like Graize, his fate was
not so firmly fixed by physical obstacles that it could not be influenced.

Weary of the ambitions of kings and princes, she decided that it
would be. As the twin feathers of her prophecy reached the outstretched
fingers of Spar's abilities, she formed them into a question, then wheeled
about and headed back to the small camp on the banks of the Halic-
Salmanak with a keening cry.

✦

In the seer's shrine at Estavia-Sarayi, Spar's eyes snapped open. All
around him, he could feel Sable Company beginning their slow journey
up from prophecy as the sun began its own climb toward the horizon.
They moved calmly and sedately like a school of fish rising in the water
with no hint of any unexpected vision to mar their progress.

He frowned.

Driven by the threat of High Spring storms that might conceal the
movement of their enemies, Estavia's seers had spent the last three days
in almost constant visioning, patrolling the streams, ever watchful for
the faintest sign that would signal an attack. However, now that it had
come, they seemed oblivious.

He knew Sable Company was as well trained and disciplined as the
temple ghazon. If anything, they were too disciplined, only reacting
quickly on the battlefield when Estavia Herself was giving the orders. At
all other times, rather than a school of fish, they acted more like a line
of turtles heading for the water, studying and analyzing every symbol's
every meaning, until he wanted to scream at them in frustration.

A white-clad king and a prince with eyes as fathomless as the sea.

Had none of the others seen it?

Were none of the others meant to see it?

Closing his eyes, he reached out, tracing the line of possibility the
image had created as it fell. It rose on rungs of confused sensation and
he followed, feeling honey, tasting sand, and breathing in the soft odor
of lips against his cheek, until finally he heard a woman's face, felt her
black eyes filled with prophecy, and saw her voice.

"Spar."

The word scattered against his vision like a handful of diamonds, bright and sharp. He stared at them, mesmerized until a tiny inconsistency broke the surface of his concentration: words did not scatter and spoken words did not look like physical things. Not in *his* prophecy.

Under his control, the vision steadied to become a simple question: *"Who will you bring to stand against the white king and the fathomless prince, Spar?"*

"Spar?"

The word tickled against his physical senses, and he opened his eyes again to see Kaptin Liel bending over him. The shrine was empty.

"What time is it?" he croaked.

"Nearly dawn."

"The others?"

"Have gone to prepare for Morning Invocation. Will you be joining us?"

Spar shook his head. "I can feel you all from here," he said, matching the kaptin's neutral tone.

"Fair enough. Eat and get some rest if you can, but don't be surprised if your mind refuses to allow it. You went deep, and your prophecy will have a lot to sort through. Sable Company will be reconvening in one hour to analyze what we've seen. You're welcome to join us as always, but if you want a private consultation, come find me when you're ready to talk about your visions."

"You'll be here?"

The kaptin's bi-gender features showed a moment of weariness. "Until the attack comes, I might as well have a cot and a chamber pot brought over."

Spar smiled faintly to acknowledge the humor, then glanced out one narrow window for a moment before turning back. "What did *you* see?" he asked, an uncharacteristically tentative note in his voice.

"Rain and fog," the seer-kaptin answered in a disgusted voice. "Growing ever thicker, concealing movement on all fronts, just as before."

"Nothing specific, then?"

The seer-kaptin raised a questioning eyebrow. "Not yet, Delin. Why, did you?"

"I'm not sure. But you're right; I need to sort it out first. There might be more to it and there might not. Somehow it feels . . . more personal."

"That's a common feeling among young seers." Kaptin Liel raised one hand before Spar could voice an indignant protest. "As I said, come and see me when you're ready." Rising fluidly, the kaptin withdrew, leaving Spar to his own thoughts.

In the shadowy darkness of the now-empty shrine, he puzzled over his vision.

A king and a prince, at least that imagery was simple enough to understand. The king was Pyrros of Skiros and the prince was Illan of Volinsk: the attacks from the south and the north had begun. But . . . behind the king and the prince was the presence of Panos of Amatus, a powerful oracle that felt like honey and tasted of sand. Everything Panos did was subtle, and he had no idea what she was trying to make him do or how to avoid it. That she seemed to have spoken to Brax as well made this vision even more suspect.

"Who will you bring . . . ?"

His brows drew down into a deep vee. Why did he need to bring anyone? Wasn't it up to Marshal Brayazi and Kaptin Liel to stand against the leaders of their enemies?

But the question persisted, niggling at his mind until he found the simplest of answers. Who would he bring to stand against Panos' mighty family?

He would bring his own.

Once decided, he allowed himself to drift into a light doze as the first note of the Morning Invocations sounded in the distance. He felt the Gods emerge from Gol-Beyaz, one by one, Their presence causing a deep, ringing pressure in his chest to thrum along his lien with Hisar; he heard Estavia's people call out to Her, felt Her response catch in his throat, then fade into stillness. Only then did he give in to the pressure and sing one quiet note into the darkness.

Hisar responded at once, with all the excited exuberance of a half-grown puppy. The young God could not manifest in Estavia's shrine, and Spar felt a sudden stab of both annoyance and impatience shooting down the lien. Its thoughts were a whirl of imagery, and as It struggled to bring Itself under control, Spar reached out to calm It as he might have done to Jaq.

The night's events crashed over him like a hurricane.

✦

He came back to himself, slumped against the shrine's outside wall with rain pouring down his face and Hisar nowhere to be seen. Gulping in the cool dawn air, he waited until his head stopped pounding, then cautiously opened one eye. The temple grounds were shrouded in shadow with a bank of heavy storm clouds above, and a thin layer of fog stretching out across the courtyard. Thunder rumbled in the distance.

"That hurt," he complained to the empty air, pushing a lock of sopping wet hair off his face. "Next time get your mind to use its voice instead of its fists, yeah?"

There was no response and, straightening with a grimace, he wiped his hands on his tunic before splashing his way across the main courtyard with a disgusted expression.

✦

The bustling warmth of the commissary wrapped around him like a blanket and, suddenly voraciously hungry, he kicked off his wet sandals just inside the door, and headed for the central table, leaving a line of wet footprints in his wake. He filled a large bowl with rice boiled in mullet fat, smoked fish, stuffed mussels, and olives then, with the bowl tucked under one arm, a slice of melon in one hand, and a huge piece of goat's cheese and a strip of tripe balanced precariously on a glass of cold tea in the other, he made for the Cyan Company dining hall.

✦

A loud, welcoming bark told him that his family had already arrived and, a moment later, he joined Kemal and Yashar at their usual table. He tossed the tripe to the dog at once, ignoring his older abayon's stern expression.

"He's already had his breakfast."

As Jaq dropped onto Spar's feet, growling and chewing in equal measure, the youth just shrugged. "It's a bribe for being away from him all night."

"In that case you should bribe us, too," Kemal replied. "It took him forever to settle and his toenails are very sharp."

Wordlessly, Spar held out the melon slice.

Kemal just snorted. "Keep it. It looks like you need it." He cocked his head to one side as Spar immediately stripped the flesh from the rind with his teeth and swallowed it whole. "You look pale," he noted. "You need more sleep."

"Hungry, not sleepy," Spar answered, shoveling rice into his mouth as soon as he'd swallowed the melon.

"Ah, yes, fifteen," Yashar observed with a nostalgic expression. "I remember it well. There wasn't a table safe from my appetite."

"There still isn't," Kemal retorted.

"I'm sure I've slowed down some." Yashar pushed his empty plate to one side before leaning his elbows on the table. "When you've finished polishing the pattern off your bowl, Delin, we have some news."

Taking a great bite of cheese, Spar washed it down with half his tea before glancing from one man to the other. "News?"

"Our troop's being deployed to Iskele-Hisar."

"When?"

"The day after tomorrow."

Lifting a piece of smoked meat with two fingers, Spar studied it with a scowl before stuffing it into his mouth. "And you want me to come with you," he said in a muffled voice.

"Yes," Kemal replied bluntly. "Ordinarily you'd be safer here, but with the threat of attack by the Volinski Fleet . . ."

"And your determination to station yourself outside the Western Trisect walls . . ." Yashar added.

"We think you'd be safer with us."

"Where we could keep an eye on you."

Spar stopped eating long enough to give both men a somber look. "Brax needs me," he said simply, catching up a handful of stuffed mussels. "And I'll have Jaq. He'll keep me safe."

"One dog against an army of Volinski soldiers?" Kemal asked.

"No. One dog against a small raiding force." He took a bite of cheese, then flipped the rest at Jaq, watching as the dog caught and swallowed it in one motion. "But I do need your help," he added before stuffing the entire handful of mussels into his mouth. Washing them down with the last of his tea, he outlined all that had happened since they'd stood together before the command council.

"Can you get reassigned, Aban?" he asked with a serious expression. "Here, like you were the night Brax called to Estavia on Liman Caddesi. I think Brax and I are going to need you here to counter the presence of Skiros and Volinsk in prophecy."

Kemal and Yashar exchanged a glance. "I'm sure we can be, Delin," Kemal assured him. "But you do know that on that night we were directed to the seer's shrine by Estavia Herself, and we . . ."

"Destroyed it," Yashar finished for him. "Or rather, Estavia destroyed it in Her zeal to respond to Kem's Invocation. I don't know that Sable Company will welcome our presence with open arms again."

"No, not in the seer's shrine," Spar answered, feeling the certainty of his words as he said them. "In the central shrine, in Kaptin Haldin's Shrine."

"Ah." The older man sat back. "That seems more appropriate."

"What about the rest of Cyan Company? They were with us that night," Kemal pointed out. "Will you be needing them as well?"

"No. We just need you, Aban."

Both men smiled warmly at him in response. "When?" Kemal asked.

"I'm not sure." Spar stared into his empty glass as if it could reveal the answer to him. "Soon."

"Seer soon?" Yashar asked with a twinkle in his eye. "Absolutely and maybe? Hurry up and wait?"

"Be warned and be ready," Kemal admonished him in a gentle voice.

"Ah, that kind of soon."

Spar snorted. "Yes, Aba, that kind of soon."

"Well, then, there's time for a second helping of breakfast, isn't there? Extra bread and olives for you, Delin, and Kem . . . ?" Yashar asked, catching up their plates.

"Just coffee, Yash. On second thought, let me." Kemal held his hand out with a stern expression. "You'll take too much and spend the day breaking wind."

Yashar handed the plates over with a laugh. As his arkados headed for the central table, he glanced over at Spar, but when his delos continued to stare into his glass, he leaned back, scratching Jaq gently with one foot. "Asper for your thoughts," he offered, setting a small copper coin on the table with a smile.

Spar glanced at it for a moment, then slowly put it into his pouch. "There's more that I need your help with," he said reluctantly.

"Ask away, it's what we're here for."

"Actually, it's something Hisar needs your help with."

"Hisar?"

"Yeah. But I think He needs to ask you Himself; it's kinda specific. Can you come up to the armory tower? It's easier for Him to manifest there."

"Can it wait until after breakfast?"

Spar glanced up as Kemal returned with a heaping plateful of food, setting it down before him with a flourish.

"Yeah."

✦

He and Jaq took a boat across the mouth of the Halic an hour later, meeting up with Brax at Gerek-Hisar just as his kardos came through the main gate with the rest of his troop. The rain was falling more heavily now and, as they splashed their way toward the tower dormitories, Spar fell into step beside him, ignoring his surprised expression.

"Tired?" he asked.

Dark hair plastered to his skull, Brax just shrugged. "Some," he allowed. "It was a long night. Why?"

"I need you to go out again. With me."

"Right away?"

"No, not right, right away."

"Good, 'cause I need a warm bath and a couple hours' sleep. I sang the Morning Invocation on the aqueduct and nearly fell in."

"Weren't you tied off?"

"I forgot. Like I said, it was a long night." One foot poised above the steps to the tower bathhouse, Brax paused. "Do I want to know where we're going?" he asked, blinking the rain from his eyes with a weary gesture.

"The Bibliotheca."

"Why?"

"It's complicated."

Brax sighed. "It's always complicated."

"I'll explain on the way."

✦

The temple of Ystazia-Sarayi contained the largest collection of books, scrolls, and manuscripts in the known world, housed in one of the world's most beautiful libraries, the Bibliotheca. Brax and Spar had come here only once, three years ago, accompanied by Ihsan. Awed into uncomfortable silence by the wealth of stained glass, polished marble, and silk tapestries all around him, Brax had been relieved when they'd left. Now he handed his wet cloak to an awestruck temple delinkos, tugging irritably at the sleeve of his formal tunic as they stepped into the huge, mosaic antechamber.

"And we're here because . . . why?" he asked in a strained whisper.

"Because Ihsan's here."

"And this couldn't wait until he came to the temple?"

"No. I told you on the way over here, we've set the trap, but there's more to it than that. I saw what Hisar's going to fight, what He's been scratching around the entrance to night after night. And I need to know more about it." Spar glanced down at Jaq. "Stay." The dog gave him a reproachful look in response, then curled up in a corner of the anteroom as Spar headed for the main staircase.

Brax followed, his own countenance as reproachful as the dog's.

✦

They found their old teacher deep in the bowels of the research section, scrolls held open by velvet-covered paperweights and sheets of vellum piled all around him.

Glancing up, he smiled broadly as they approached. "Come to help me write my treatise on First Day rituals?" he asked Spar with a wink at Brax.

Spar just shook his head. "Not today, Sayin. We need to ask you about the aqueduct and the cistern."

"Ah." Ihsan set his manuscript to one side. "I had heard there was some veiled prophecy or another floating about. What do you need to know?"

"How to get in."

✦

"The belief that the main cistern services the entire city is actually a myth."

Sitting on a pile of cushions in one of the smaller reading rooms, Ihsan passed them a large, vellum map. "It's vast, yes, but, as you can see, the Temple Precinct has its own system of wells and cisterns, as does the Citadel."

"So any spirits growing in the main cistern can't reach the temples?" Spar asked.

"Spirits don't usually grow in the main cistern, Spar-Delin. They're nullified in the reservoir."

"But if they weren't?"

Ihsan rubbed thoughtfully at a streak of dried ink on his forearm. "Ordinarily, the temple cisterns are separate, fed through rainwater spouts and underground springs, but they are connected to the main cistern through a series of closed-off pipes and tunnels. In times of drought they can be opened to accept water from the main cistern or used to empty water into Gol-Beyaz during times of flooding." He bent over the map. "The main cistern does, however, feed hundreds of smaller cisterns across the city, especially in the Tannery and Western Dockside Precincts where the need for water by various trades and business is that much greater. It's even said that some homes and shops in the western market can draw fish through wells connected to the main cistern in their cellars. But you'd know all about that," he added with an expectant look.

Brax just shook his head. "We always lived on the upper floors, Sayin," he explained. "We never had access to the private wells, only the public fountains. And I never saw a fish in a public fountain. If there had been, every cat in the city would have been camped out around the rims," he added.

Ihsan sighed. "A pity."

"So water from the main cistern travels under most of the city most of the time," Spar pressed, drawing their attention back to the map.

"Yes," his old teacher replied.

"So if there were spirits growing in the main cistern, they could get to almost any place in Anavatan."

"Yes, *if* there were spirits growing in the main cistern. And I know what you're thinking, Sparin-Delin, if there were, then presumably, they could pose as great a danger as the spirits which breached the God-Wall six years ago."

"Yes."

Ihsan shook his head. "Most spirits are creatures of the air, formed by storms, and only dangerous in vast numbers. They haven't the natural strength to swarm in water."

"But if they managed the strength somehow?"

"Then there wouldn't be enough of them."

Spar scowled at the map, his expression clearly unconvinced. "Hisar thinks there are," he said. "It's had a vision of entering the cistern and being . . . pressed by spirits.

"Forgive me, Delin, I know this isn't my area of expertise, but shouldn't you be consulting with a senior seer before acting on such a limited prophecy?"

Spar shook his head. "This prophecy's already too crowded with seers, Sayin. I need to get in physically and see what's happening down there for myself."

Ihsan sat back with a pensive expression. "Well, the system does need servicing on a regular basis," he allowed. "Bricks and mortar can crumble and pipes can crack and split, so there are a number of entrances throughout the city. The most easily accessible one is in the Tannery Precinct." He pressed a finger to the map. "It leads directly to the reservoir and the main cistern. Elsewhere, there are entrances in each Precinct here, here, and here," he added, indicating each one. "Including one quite close to the site of Hisar's new temple. However, I should warn you that this system is very old and very complex. Most of it was laid out when Anavatan was first constructed. It's too easy to lose one's bearing and get lost, or even drowned in the case of a sudden influx of water. If you're going in, you'll need to go cautiously and with a guide."

"I'll have a guide, Sayin. I'll have Hisar."

"*We'll* have Hisar," Brax corrected firmly.

Spar nodded. "We'll have Hisar."

"I was thinking more in the line of a maintenance worker," Ihsan admonished gently.

"Hisar will do fine."

✦

The young God met them as they exited the building. It swirled about them for a moment in Its dragonfly-seeming, raising the hairs along Jaq's spine with one ethereal wingtip, then, as they headed out across Ystazia-Sarayi's open air market, He changed to His golden-seeming with a snap of displaced air.

"Yashar and I went to the garrison guards," He stated proudly. "I went in and everything."

"Yeah?" Spar asked distractedly.

"Yeah. And I told them that was My temple site and Zeno wasn't trespassing and they better let him go."

He paused to stare at the riot of colored threads displayed before a carpet seller and, after a moment, Brax coughed loudly. "And?"

"And? Oh, right. They let him go of course. Yashar didn't think we should just let him head back to lifting or whatever, so we took him for breakfast."

"Another breakfast?" Spar noted with a raised eyebrow.

Hisar frowned at him. "Well, I didn't eat and neither did Yashar. Zeno ate, stupid," He said, rolling his eyes. "He ate a lot, and stuffed a lot into his pockets.

And Yashar talked a lot," he added.

"What about?"

The young God just shrugged. "Good choices, bad choices, the future, what Zeno needed to get in with a proper trade, who was there to help him, who'll take advantage. You know, the same sort of things he's been talking to you about for so long."

"Ah," Brax noted with a grin. "That talk. That's a fun talk."

"A fun talk to take the piss on, you mean," Spar corrected.

"Sometimes."

"He talked a lot about it with Me, too," Hisar added, tipping His head to one side as He remembered the walk back to Estavia-Sarayi.

They had made their way in silence for a while, Yashar splashing through the puddles like a delos and Hisar floating along beside him, flush with victory. After a moment, Yashar had glanced at Him.

✦

"Did you understand what I was saying to Zeno, Hisarin-Delin?" he asked with a serious expression.

The young God gave him a complacent look in return. "Sure," He answered carelessly.

"Sure?"

"Uh-huh."

"And how it might relate to You?"

"Me? I'm not a lifter."

"No, but You are a youth poised on the brink of adulthood. You're going to have to make some difficult choices in the future. You're a God, so some of Your decisions are going to have wide-sweeping consequences."

He paused, wiping a spray of raindrops from his beard with one hand. "Not everyone who's going to ask You for help will be a half-starved little street thief," he pointed out. "There'll be people who'll try to take advantage of Your inexperience and Your desire for followers to ask You to do things that might not be the right thing to do."

Hisar lounged against a tent pole with an interested expression. "Like what?"

"Any number of things," Yashar hedged. "The point is that You re-member that You can always come to Kemal and me for advice as well as to Spar and Brax. Or even," he added, "to the elder Gods. They're used to negotiating with Their followers. They don't grant everything we ask for, you know. And They shouldn't besides. People need to sort out our own problems or we grow weak."

"And that makes the Gods weak," Hisar answered promptly.

"Yes."

"So how'm I to know when to help and when not to," Hisar de-manded. "I thought We were *supposed* to help, and now you say We're not to."

"No, You are, just not all the time and not always in the way people ask for. You have to assess each request. And ask for advice," he repeated.

"From the elder Gods?" Hisar said with a deeply skeptical expression.

"Yes."

"They don't like me," Hisar countered. "I told Kemal that before."

"I'm sure They like you just fine," Yashar answered, watching an elderly man arguing gently with a boy of five beside a sweetmeat stall. "They're just old. And the old get impatient with the young sometimes."

"Why?"

"Because they've forgotten how long it took for them to get old. And how hard it was sometimes."

"That doesn't make any sense."

"That's because You're young."

"So, what are you, then?"

"Me?" Yashar chuckled as he watched the old man and the young boy amble away with equally large simit rings clutched in their fists. "It depends. I started out old today, but I think I want to be young for a while." He headed for the sweetmeat seller with a determined expression, and after a moment, Hisar followed him.

✦

"That was quite the lecture," Brax noted, glancing about for a sweetmeat seller with little hope of finding one on this particular street.

"Yeah. I mostly listened. It made him happy," Hisar answered. "But we got Zeno sorted out, and now he and the rest of the crew can go back to their shed and have a safe place to be until Yashar's friends go and talk to that factor who's trying to get more money out of them. They headed out right after we talked to them."

"I'll bet they did." Brax replied in a dry voice.

"Yup, so everything's sorted out, just like I promised." Hovering backward before them about two inches off the ground, Hisar cast them a shrewd look. "So, what were you two doing? You were talking about me. I could feel it."

Spar shrugged. "About the cistern mostly. Sorting out how to deal with Your spirits."

"And?"

"And we can get in."

"When?"

As a new rumble of thunder sounded in the distance, Spar glared up at the sky. "When it stops raining. I don't wanna get drowned in an underground tunnel if it starts flooding out."

Hisar followed his gaze with a reluctant expression. "It's gonna rain all day," He said, matching Spar's accent and adding a sullen note of His own.

"Then we wait all day."

"I hate waiting."

"I know. So do I. Too bad." Pulling his cloak more tightly about his shoulders, Spar headed in the direction of Estavia-Sarayi without another word.

Brax and Jaq squelched resignedly after him.

Hisar watched them go, with an annoyed expression. He hated waiting, but He was starting to think He hated Spar's habit of stomping away even more. They next time he did it, Hisar decided, He was going to fly right over his head and land directly in front of him. He was tired of people leaving Him, and it was going to stop. But for now, He would go back to His temple site. Maybe the youth He had spoken to would be there and maybe they would talk and maybe she would give her oaths. Maybe.

Changing to Its dragonfly-seeming, It shot into the air, resisting the urge to knock Spar's hair into his eyes as It flew past him.

11

The Dark Place

THE STORMS CONTINUED ALL week, growing steadily worse. A heavy fog sweeping down from the Bogazi-Isik Strait settled over Anavatan, bringing the water trades to a standstill and turning the city skyline into an ocean, turrets and minarets thrusting upward like islands in the waves. In the streets, trade stumbled along blindly but doggedly. People still had to eat and most maintained a strained good humor, believing that even if they couldn't see to walk, at least their enemies couldn't see to attack. As the rain continued to fall, turning puddles into ponds, flooding wells and fountains, and creeping into homes and businesses, the civic beys finally called for the overflow tunnels under the Temple Precinct to be opened.

Standing on Estavia-Sarayi's easternmost battlements, soaked despite a heavy, waterproof cloak, Spar listened to the water spewing from the overflow pipe below, wondering if it came only from the temple cistern or from the main cistern as well.

He glanced at Hisar standing beside him, annoyingly dry despite the weather.

"Are there spirits pouring out of that?" he asked.

The young God just shrugged. "I can't tell in all this fog. But it doesn't matter. It'll only catch up the surface spirits; the lower ones'll go deep like fish in a storm. I can feel it." His golden brows drew down in a scowl very similar to Spar's own. "I hate fog," He complained. "I hate that I can't see through it."

"Me, too," Spar agreed distractedly. Leaning his elbows on the dark, wet stone, he peered over the battlements. Although it was only just past midday, it might as well be midnight for all the distance he could see.

To the north, the signal fires atop Gerek and Dovek-Hisar—transforming the two structures from watchtowers to lighthouses—glowed sullenly as if they could sense that their precious cache of oil had been lit unnecessarily. No vessels dared to navigate the strait in this weather even with their lights to guide them. That should have made Spar feel more secure, but it didn't. Their enemies were creeping closer on every front and it was only a matter of time; days, maybe hours, before they attacked.

And he wasn't ready, he brooded. He was never ready. The continued flooding made entering the cistern to deal with Hisar's water-spirits an impossibility and as for Graize, Brax sent word from the aqueduct every morning: nothing to report; and Spar returned from vision every evening with nothing to add. Every day the urge to press Hisar into rooting out his rival grew stronger, and every day he managed to resist it. But it was getting harder. If the fog didn't lift soon, they were going to have to change their tactics and go out physically to find him because Spar wasn't fooling himself into thinking that Graize had halted his journey. Like the rest, he was creeping closer using the storms to hide his movements.

Beside him, Hisar mimed throwing His own elbows onto the battlements. "Do you suppose the *older* Gods can see through this?" He demanded, breaking into the youth's thoughts.

Spar just shrugged.

"I should be able to," Hisar continued. "It's only physical and I'm more than just physical."

Spar snorted. "You're *other* than just physical," he allowed. "You can't affect the physical. That's not *more*."

The young God rose a few feet into the air. "This is more," He insisted.

"No it's not. I can do that; I just come down sooner."

Hisar sniffed at him, then, with a restless gesture, flung Itself into the air in Its dragonfly-seeming and, whipping Its tail about to knock Spar's sopping wet hair into his eyes, shot off across the temple rooftops.

Spar pressed his chin down onto his arms. "Show-off," he muttered.

He scowled into the fog. Sable Company had finally seen the sailing of the Skirosian and Volinski fleets. Word from Anahtar-Hisar was that a sudden storm had swept across the Deniz-Hadi, causing their southern enemies some delay, but there was no further sign of their northern. Spar figured it was too much to hope that a sudden storm on the Deniz-Siya had sent them all to the bottom of the sea.

To the west, Sable Company had detected activity on the grasslands. Marshal Brayazi had sent reinforcements to the garrisons at Orzin- and Alev-Hisar and they'd easily repelled a series of minor assaults against Kepek- and Ekmir-Koy by Petchan raiders. Then word had come from Yildiz-Koy that a small force of Yuruk had attacked the village livestock pens, but they, too, had been driven back without casualties or losses by the warrior-backed militia. Although everyone knew these attacks were nothing more than their enemies probing, searching for weakness, finally being called to arms had lifted everyone's spirits.

As the small bell atop the seer's shrine began to toll, calling Sable Company back into vision, Spar grimaced in annoyance. He was tired of sitting in a cold, stone chamber without Jaq to keep him warm, surrounded by people whose seeking kept interfering with his own. He was not a Warrior of Estavia; he was not a Battle-Seer of Sable Company, and their enemies were not his concern right now. Spar was only interested in one enemy and he could make as much use of a concealing fog as anyone. His first prophecies had been made so that his small family of lifters—Cindar and Brax—could ply their trade on the streets of Anavatan in all kinds of weather. Spar knew fog, and he knew how to use it.

Crossing the battlements, he joined Jaq, crouched in a nearby sentry box out of the rain, and pressing his back against the back wall, wrapped one arm around the dog's neck. As Jaq made himself comfortable across his legs, Spar stepped into the dark place where he did his own private seeking. He was tired of letting his rival build up the advantage. It was going to stop. Now.

✦

The fog followed him in, weaving about his feet like strands of fine silk, refusing to be banished. Rather than fight it, he allowed it to build and, in moments, it had blanketed the black sand beach and blotted out the moon. Crouching by the water's edge, he emptied his net and laid it to one side. Then waited. There was more than one way to set a trap. The best way was to lie in wait and let the mark approach as if unseen, then spring. It took skill and patience, but Spar had both. Behind him, he felt Hisar's dark tower-seeming rise up from the sand in response to his actions, but ignored It. The young God would know what he was doing soon enough. The gentle lapping of the ocean waves grew quiet, and when he finally stood in total, silent, and all-encompassing prophetic darkness, he called up a wind to sweep the fog away.

The tableau cleared at once and Graize stood before him, one arm upraised in threat, a knife clenched in his fist. The aqueduct loomed behind him, strong and physical. As the tower-seeming leaped forward, Spar shot one arm out to block It and, using all his strength, drove his other fist into his adversary's defenses.

"Gotcha!"

✦

To the north, Graize jerked backward with a surprised shout as the image of a black sand beach and a dark, fathomless ocean suddenly smacked into his mind. For a single heartbeat, a blond-haired youth outlined in gold, loomed over him, feet planted in the soil of an alien prophecy, fists raised in menace, and a vast tower rising above them both. Then his head hit the ground with a crack and his own vision swept over him through the breach in his focus.

✦

The air grew heavy and portentous, smelling of blood and salt. The sun, unseen for days now, leaped at him like a giant fiery insect, its regard dripping with malice and a vicious, angry triumph. The sound of water raging through a cavernous darkness echoed all around him, and he fell into its churning depths with swarms of waterlogged spirits sweeping over him, tearing at his hands and face. As his lungs filled with prophecy, he grabbed for the protective cloak he'd built among the Petchans and threw it across his mind.

And fell into a total, silent, and all-encompassing darkness. The blond-haired youth and the rising tower appeared before his eyes once more, and as he fought to keep his head above water, the youth came into focus.

Spar, but not as Graize had known him. Spar grown with eyes as black as pitch and the power of prophecy swirling about him in the shape of a wide, black net.

Graize spat a curse at him, but his rival just made a casual gesture and the water closed over his head once again, the weed-choked confusion of the distant past entangling his arms and legs. He saw a mist-covered doorway and a dark-haired boy with a prophetic line of red across his cheek beckoning him toward warmth and safety, but before he could take his hand, a future filled with blood and gold swept them apart. He saw the dark-haired boy—he saw Brax—give his promise of warmth and safety to another—to Spar—and the pain of his betrayal twisted under Graize's feet to become a vast and empty landscape of madness and loss. Brax became a man and Graize fought him in the fields before Serin-Koy and then on the grasslands before the Gurney-Dag foothills. When he raised his arm to strike him down, his Godling screamed Its denial, and he plunged under the churning waters once again.

"*Kardos!*"

A single word shot toward him through the maelstrom, and he struggled to catch hold of it, but the water was filled with choking weeds once more, the past became a future of madness and death dragging him under again. Far in the distance, he thought he saw Brax, outlined in silver, standing on a snow-capped mountain ridge, beckoning as he had before, but then the path split, and Brax struck him a blow that hit him like a lead ball, throwing him backward.

A sharp pain blossomed in his chest, and the water filled with blood. It swirled about him, driving the spirits around him mad with hunger. He fought them as savagely as he'd fought them years before, but the blood leeching into the water was his own and he found himself slowly weakening. The mountainside exploded in crimson fire, and the past reared up, writhing like weeds in a storm, seeking to ensnare him and Brax together. Darkness rushed toward them, Spar in its center. His rival watched them struggle, his face twisted in uncertainty, and then as the spirits rushed forward in a swarm of hunger, he stepped aside as Hisar suddenly slammed into the water above them.

"*NO! MINE!*"

The young God slapped the spirits away with a single smack of Its hand, then knocked Graize from the water with an equally violent gesture. Spar jerked Brax to safety and Graize felt arms, both strong and physical, catch him up and jerk him out of prophecy.

"Kardos!"

He opened his eyes.

Danjel's smooth features swam before him, the Yuruk's own eyes wide with concern. For a moment, he thought Danjel had fallen into the water beside him, then he tasted blood where his teeth had scored his lips. The physical and the prophetic struggled for supremacy; with his head swimming with vertigo, he caught hold of the Yuruk's hand to steady himself and slowly the physical won through.

Danjel's eyes cleared.

"Are you back?"

Graize coughed weakly. "Almost . . . back," he gasped as the whisper of prophetic pain echoed across his ribs, then faded. "Where?"

Danjel smiled in relief. "In my arms, in the mud, outside a shearing shed, on the north bank of the Halic, beneath the aqueduct, a mile or so from Anavatan's Northern Trisect. We were just about to make camp when you collapsed." Lifting him into a sitting position, Danjel swept a lock of rain-soaked hair from Graize's face with one hand while maintaining a comforting grip around his chest with the other. "Did you have a vision?"

"An attack."

"You had an attack?"

A dozen cryptic answers came and went, each one choked with weeds, and with a burst of unusual impatience, he snarled at them to get back into vision where they belonged. "No," he answered harshly. "Got . . . attacked."

Danjel's eyes widened again. "By?"

"Doesn't matter. Over now. I won."

"NO! MINE!"

The echo of Hisar's presence thrummed against the lien, and Graize stared blearily past Danjel's face, expecting to see the Godling vibrating the air above them, but Hisar was nowhere to be seen. As his head finally cleared completely, he saw the huge pillars of the aqueduct disappearing into the fog, heard the sound of running water high above his head, smelled the faint odors of dung and hay from the fields all around them, and heard the distant bleating of sheep and the lowing of cattle. The sun of his prophecy disappeared behind a blanket of purely physical rain, and he remembered where he was.

He and his small party had parted ways with Rayne, leaving their ponies in her charge and crossing the Halic just hours before this latest round of storms had spun the waters into an impassable maelstrom.

Always wary of boats, Danjel had argued against any crossing at all, but standing staring at the gathering storm clouds, Graize had cut the argument short with unusual bluntness.

✦

"We can't infiltrate the Western Trisect as a group without notice. The God-Wall's too high to climb, and its gates are guarded by Estavia's Sworn. We have to enter through the Northern Trisect where the wall is purely physical and guarded with less attention.

"Besides, you remember the lovely jagged rock formations and piles of broken blocks and rubble gathered around the aqueduct that we navigated last time we boated down the Halic, Kardos," he continued in a sweeter tone. *"The waters swirl and churn on the quietest of days, throwing up eddies and whirlpools that spin around the great pillars, ever searching for an imprudent little wild-lands swallow to . . ."* he chuckled. *"To swallow,"* he finished. *"Look into your prophecy and tell me what these storms have wrought on such a landscape."*

✦

Danjel had glared at him but remained silent, and so, led by the more experienced Skirosians, they'd made the crossing with a northern hills fishing party who neither knew nor cared about their conflict with the shining city to the south. They'd traveled on foot through increasingly savage weather until they'd finally fetched up beside the aqueduct's more northerly expanse, making good time under its partial protection. Until now.

Graize reached up to touch the blood-smeared lump spreading across the back of his skull. "The others?" he rasped.

"Are inside in the dry where we should be. Can you stand?"

"Yes."

Danjel helped him up, then catching him around the waist, half supported, half carried him into the shearing shed as the skies opened up with still more driving rain.

✦

Warmth and the comfortingly muted silence of stone and thatch surrounded them at once as Danjel kicked the door closed behind them. The Skirosian entourage had already stowed their gear and gotten a fire going in the hearth, Yal and Hares were pulling food from their packs, and Panos was standing by the largest of the empty stalls, staring up at a complex spider's web in the corner as Graize headed for the fire. She glanced over at him as he sank onto the hearthstone with an inaudible sigh.

"We are discovered?" she asked in a tone of simple curiosity.

Graize just shrugged.

"By Spar," Danjel answered, merging swiftly to the female form. Pulling out a pouch of herbs from her own pack, she handed them to Yal. "Can you make a poultice from these?"

The Petchan woman nodded. "I'll need to boil some water first. How long have we got?"

"Long enough," Graize answered, his voice growing stronger as he soaked in the fire's comforting warmth. "He's seen us by the aqueduct, but the aqueduct's long. As long as a snake swimming through the water," he added in his more usual singsong manner. "A grass snake maybe, swimming in the weed-choked water? No, it had better be a water snake, hadn't it? But he doesn't know what part of the water snake's body we're swimming beside and he can't send any snake catchers against us in this weather, so we have time to build a rat trap."

Yal raised one eyebrow at him. "Well, it's nice to see your fall hasn't addled your wits any," she said in a dry voice. "I'll just see to your poultice, then."

As Graize pressed a hand against his chest, feeling the last of Hisar's presence whisper along the lien, he nodded. "A poultice," he echoed, "to staunch the flow of prophecy into the world before it builds itself into a snow-capped mountain ridge."

"Would that be such a bad thing?" Danjel asked, gently removing Graize's jacket and tunic.

Graize's right pupil contracted until it almost disappeared. "Yes."

"Why?"

Feeling the metaphysical bruise along his ribs, Graize bared his teeth. "Because I don't want to climb it." Accepting the dry cloak the wyrdin held out to him, he wrapped it about his shoulders and refused to say more. As thunder rumbled in the distance, he thrust aside the last vestige of the black beach and its accompanying future streams.

✦

Far to the south, in the dark place, Spar and Hisar—still in Its tower-seeming—stood regarding each other with equally dark expressions.

The young God was the first to break the silence.

"You stopped me," It accused, Its voice echoing across the now-empty beach.

"You were interfering with the vision," Spar retorted. "We needed to see where it would lead."

"Into the future? Into that future?"

"Maybe. Into a future we can use, anyway."

"No. I don't like it. It's too confusing. His present is all muddied up with his past, and it looks like there might be two separate futures branching out with the same strength: the mountainside one where Brax and Graize stand together, and one where Graize gets injured, maybe even killed. By Brax. And then they both fall." The tower bared a sudden set of teeth. *"I don't want that,"* It snarled. *"I won't have that. I saw one path, not two. I won't have two."*

Spar raised an eyebrow at It. "Then don't have two. At the end of the vision you intervened to save Graize. Intervene in the future."

"I intervened to save Graize in the dark place," Hisar corrected stiffly. *"It's not the same thing."*

"So, make it the same thing."

"How?"

"I don't know yet. You saw us all together with the spirits of the cistern. That has to be where we'll make our stand. Do it there."

"There." Hisar sniffed dismissively. *"Your great trap isn't there,"* It reminded Its First Priest. *"It's on the* other *side of the Halic."*

"Then we have to get there."

"How?" Hisar demanded again, changing from tower-seeming to golden-seeming in an agitated spray of light. *"The rain and the fog have driven every boat and barge off the water. You can't cross."*

The sudden shrieking of a lake gull spun Him about to stare, wide-eyed at the symbol of Incasa perched on a dark rock at the water's edge. The waves lapped gently against the bird's feet, keeping the fog at bay with their gentle motion. The bird stared steadily back at Him and Hisar's eyes narrowed in reluctant understanding.

"I . . . could go for help," He said slowly.

Spar's own eyes widened in surprise. "From who?"

The young God just shrugged. *"I dunno,"* He hedged, continuing to stare at the gull. *"But on the grasslands Kemal said it was all right to ask for help, remember? And Yashar said it only just this morning. Besides, you got help from First Oracle Bessic once."*

"Just once, and I'm still not sure it wasn't a mistake."

"It wasn't."

"You've *seen* that?"

Hisar frowned at him. *"No, but it worked out, didn't it? Bessic helped us, and . . . Incasa helped us,"* He added with renewed reluctance. *"On the grasslands."*

"Yes, they did," Spar admitted just as reluctantly. "But I don't think they can help us now. They have bigger things to worry about. Besides," he added. "Graize is our problem. He always was."

"Brax said that."

"Yes."

"He's wrong."

"Oh?"

"You're all three tied up in a prophecy that affects everyone. First Oracle Freyiz saw that right from the beginning."

"How do you know what First Oracle Freyiz saw?"

Hisar kicked at the sand beneath his feet. *"Incasa hurt me once,"* He said quietly.

"He hurt you?"

"He caught me, and He threw me at Freyiz. She saw right inside me and I saw inside her. I saw her visions. I didn't understand them until now. She saw the past: four figures fighting on the streets of Anavatan. One died; the spirits killed him."

"If the figures were us, that that would be Drove."

"One became silver."

"Brax."

"One ended up in Brax's arms; that was you. But the other got taken by the spirits of the Berbat-Dunya."

"Graize."

Hisar nodded. *"They would have destroyed him, but Incasa intervened and instead of killing him, the spirits became Me. That's how I was born."* He stared out across the waves. *"Freyiz had another vision about me later, just before she died,"* He continued in a quieter voice. *"I was a shimmering tower, blazing as brightly as the noonday sun, first gold, then silver, then gold again. Back and forth and back and forth,"* he whispered. *"Three figures stood before my gate; the first was wrapped in a silver light."*

"Brax again."

"The second was holding darkness like a shield."

"Me, I'd guess."

"And the third one wore a cloak of gray mist."

"Graize."

"We all stood before a range of mountains burning with a crimson light that looked to set the whole world on fire. If we don't come together, it just might. That's what Freyiz saw. That's what she showed Bessic just before she died."

"And he knew that when we talked," Spar mused. "That's why he helped."

"Probably. So, he can help again. They both can, him and Incasa."

"I dunno, Hisar. Gods are big, and they'll do you if you let Them, remember?"

"So don't let Them," Hisar snapped impatiently. *"Make Them help us instead. We can't sort this out all on our own, not this time. It's what They're for. It's what . . . WE'RE for."*

Spar noted how the young God's voice resonated across the beach, and his expression grew serious. "Yeah, It's what You're for," he allowed, "but how do we make Them help?"

Hisar's gray eyes narrowed in thought. *"You send Bessic my dice; he'll know what they mean. And I'll go and . . . poke him."*

"Poke him?"

The young God shrugged impatiently. *"Incasa won't let me poke Him; I've tried. So, I'll poke His First Priest, and he'll poke Incasa for me, and Incasa will help us."*

"Brilliant thinking."

Hisar glared at Spar. *"It'll work,"* He growled. *"You'll see."*

Spar raised his hands in a gesture of mock acquiescence. "I'm not saying it won't; you always get your own way when you poke me. But you can't just go around poking Gods or Their priests for help without knowing exactly what kind of help you need." He gave the young God a warning look. "You can't leave it up to Them. Ever. It's not safe. They'll do you, even if They don't mean to. They're just too big."

"Yashar said . . ."

"I know what Yashar said, but this is different."

"*So, what kind of help do we need, exactly?*"

"We need to cross the Halic, so the Halic has to be calm enough to cross." He turned. "You're right, Hisar, we need help, just like on the grasslands, but this time we need Havo's help."

"*Havo?*" The young God stirred uncertainly. "*How do we get Havo's help?*"

"Same way as last time, through First Oracle Bessic." Spar gestured at the seagull. "'Cause it's his God's bird that's invaded my dark place, so it's his God that's gonna do the asking. You go to Incasa-Sarayi and poke Bessic, then go to Brax and warn him that Graize is close."

Hisar gave him a penetrating look. "*Graize saw us in vision just like we saw him,*" He reminded him. "*And he saw the trap. What if he breaks off his attack because of it?*"

Spar snorted. "Do you honestly think he will? At this stage? For any reason?"

Hisar met his gaze. "*No,*" he answered after a long moment. His brows drew down. "*And Brax promised he'd give me the chance to talk to Graize,*" He said, "*but Graize didn't promise anything. What if he goes after Brax right away?*"

The ghostly image of Graize, arm upraised in threat, rose up from the dark water before them.

"*Brax'll have to defend himself,*" Hisar continued.

Another image, this time of blood leaching into the water as Graize sank beneath the waves, appeared.

Spar's brows drew down thoughtfully. "We have to keep them apart, at least at first."

"*But they need to come together,*" Hisar repeated, more to himself than to Spar. "*And they have to be kept apart. Together and apart. Together . . .*"

"Stop it."

Startled by the vehemence in Spar's voice, Hisar just blinked at him.

"You sounded like Graize," the youth explained with a scowl.

"*Oh.*" The young God's seeming wavered for a brief moment, His hair moving from golden to light brown, then snapped back as He turned to stare at the gull still perched on its rock by the water's edge. "*Sounded . . .*" His eyes widened. "*I know how to bring them together and keep them apart,*" He said suddenly.

When He continued to stare at the gull as if mesmerized by it, Spar raised an expectant eyebrow. "How?"

"*What?*"

"How?"

Hisar shook Himself. "I can't tell you exactly. I can't even think it through completely yet or Graize will figure it out. But it will work. I know it will. You just have to trust me."

Spar chewed at his cheek for a moment, then nodded. "All right, then. Let's get to work. You go to Incasa-Sarayi and get First Oracle Bessic on board. I'll go to Chamberlain Tanay and see if she can find me a boat-master willing to brave the crossing, and then I have to talk to Kaptin Liel."

Snapping into Its dragonfly-seeming immediately, Hisar flung Itself from the dark place with another spray of metallic light. Spar watched It go, then turned to regard the gull with a jaundiced eye. "Don't you have someplace else to be, too?" he demanded. "Go on. Piss off."

The bird stared back at him for a deliberately long time, before it also took flight in a spray of light. Once he was alone, Spar pulled Hisar's wooden dice from the pouch at his side. Here, in the dark place, they gave off an opalescent glow that reminded him of Incasa's own tools of prophecy, and he closed his fist over them, refusing to even glance at the numbers they revealed. Shoving them back into his pouch, he, too, left the dark place, his expression thoughtful. Then, with Jaq at his side, he headed swiftly into the temple proper as the rain began to drive against the battlements with increased fury, Hisar's plan burning brightly in his mind.

✦

A short distance away, in the central arzhane chamber at Incasa-Sarayi, First Oracle Bessic felt a buzz of wings across his mind as Hisar whirred over the temple rooftops. The young God left a flaming trail of multiple possibilities behind It, fracturing the more established streams in Its wake, and Bessic took the opportunity to shift his weight a little as they settled. He'd been in vision for most of the day, and his legs felt like blocks of wood.

"Blocks of wood left on a cold, damp floor to grow soggy and covered in moss," he muttered to himself.

The delinkos supporting his back stirred. "Sayin?"

He shook his head, but the damage was done. All around him, he could feel the rest of Incasa's seers drawn up—almost too eagerly—from vision by the sound of his voice and realized that he had spoken aloud on purpose. With a sigh, he opened his eyes, allowing each physical sensation to return to his consciousness, one by one.

The room swam into focus: light-and-sound-muffling stone covered in dark wood paneling, with four wall lamps providing just enough dim light to see by, and four iron incense burners filling the air with the heavy, prophetic odors of acacia, marigold, and wormwood. The polished walnut floor was covered in a heavy woolen carpet and dozens of soft cushions to keep out the damp, but even so, the faint taste of wet stone, cold earth, and salt coated his lips. Two dozen expectant pairs of mist-covered eyes met his. Someone at the back of the room coughed almost apologetically. The buzz of Hisar's wings vibrated through his mind again, beating at his focus the way a bird's wings might beat against a window.

"*Yes, I can feel you,*" he told It sternly. "*Just a moment.*"

"We'll pause for a time," he said out loud, keeping the weariness he felt from entering his voice. "Walk about and take some refreshments while you can."

The gathered seer-priests did their best to maintain their dignity as they left the arzhane, but even so they reminded Bessic of a crowd of delon released from lessons. At the First Oracle's signal, his delinkos helped him to his feet. Feeling eighty-four rather than forty-four, he stifled a grunt as a rush of painful tingling swept up his legs.

"Tea, Kassim. Then go and eat as well."

"Will you be joining us, Sayin, or shall I bring you something back?" his delinkos asked, pouring him a small porcelain cup of rize chai laced with raki from the small pot to one side.

"Bring me a warm mutton kebob and a cold bowl of asure."

"Yes, Sayin."

Handing him the cup, Kassim followed the others from the room. Once he was alone, Bessic sipped at the lukewarm liquid with one hand while working the stiffness from his neck and back with the other.

With the looming threat of invasion imminent, Incasa's seer-priests had maintained a constant Seeking throughout the Spring, searching for even the tiniest signal that their enemies were closing in. In the last week, pressure from Incasa Himself had kept them on high alert, ready to throw their strength behind their God at a moment's notice. Their enemies were close. Bessic could feel it although Incasa had yet to point them out in vision, but they were so very close.

The restless beating of Hisar's metaphysical wings thrummed across his consciousness for the third time, and he resisted the sudden urge to shout shoo at It. He had enough to worry about without a half-grown God-delos flitting about his minarets.

A throbbing headache began to travel across his left temple and he rubbed at it irritably as he considered the problem of Hisar. He needed to keep the ever-shifting streams of possibility from tangling together, and Hisar did more than tangle them, It tied them into knots. The sooner Its stubborn little delos-priest got It into Gol-Beyaz the better.

With his mind's attention now turned toward the young God, an image flowed unbidden into his thoughts: a simple request for help from Spar.

Bessic's eyes widened in surprise. Spar had made a single overture to Incasa-Sarayi last year, but since then it had become blatantly obvious that he was not meant for the Prophecy God's temple; that stream had gone dry. Spar was Hisar's First Priest, and as subtle and slippery a First Priest as any who'd ever carried the title. He'd be difficult to deal with. However, despite his considerable talents, he was still very, very young. Bessic could work with that.

He grimaced as the request blossomed in his mind, revealing further details like a flower opening its petals: help with Graize. His grimace deepened. Little save what Freyiz had managed to impart to him on her death was known about Hisar's abayos. Little save that he was important enough for Incasa Himself to rescue above the wild lands years ago.

A cool caress, like a sprinkling of snow across his mind, smoothed his headache away as Incasa responded to his thoughts and Bessic opened his mind to Him with a grateful sigh. The God of Prophecy caught him up—much as He'd done when he'd been a small delos—and accepting the request from his mind, laid him gently into a new stream of possibility. Buoyed up by the waves, Bessic watched it grow, studying each aspect and element involved with a thoughtful expression. The young God and Its delos-First Priest had enacted an ambitious, if somewhat untenable plan of attack. They would indeed need help if they were to win through, and there was so little time left. He would have to move swiftly.

As if to confirm the thought, a fleet of brown-sailed ships suddenly winked into being on the horizon of his prophecy, jerking him out of vision in surprise. Opening his eyes, he found Kassim standing respectfully in the doorway with his kebob and his asure on a small, silver plate in one hand and a pair of stained wooden soldier's dice in the other.

"Pardon the interruption, Sayin, but these just arrived from Estavia-Sarayi," his delinkos said almost apologetically. "There was no message attached."

"Of course there wasn't," Bessic snorted. Suddenly ravenously hungry, he accepted the food at once. "Send a message to Havo-Sarayi asking First Cultivar Adrian to convene Havo's priests for a most unseasonal working," he said, stripping off the first piece of mutton from the kebob with his teeth. "They need to ask the God of Seasonal Storms to calm the Halic."

His delinkos blinked. "Calm the Halic, Sayin?"

Bessic held one hand out for the dice. "Not its entire length, just a five-foot-wide trough at its mouth stretching from Estavia-Sarayi to the Northern Trisect should be fine."

Kassim handed the dice over. "Yes, Sayin."

"And summon the others. I've seen the enemy approaching from the north."

"At once, Sayin!"

As his delinkos withdrew at a run, Bessic drained the bowl of asure in a single swallow. With Incasa's Luck, that would keep the streams untangled. Whether it kept Hisar and Its very inexperienced two priests out of harm's reach, however, remained to be seen, but the possibility had been created; now it was up to them. Jiggling the dice in his palm, he watched the numbers merge and shift, then closed his fist over them much as he sensed Spar had done earlier. "With Incasa's Luck," he repeated.

Reaching out, he laid one mental hand across Hisar's intent, calming the young God as best he could.

"Don't be afraid, Delin," he said, speaking through Incasa's lien and knowing that the God of Prophecy would relay his words to Hisar. *"We're coming as quickly as we can."*

12

Gerek-Hisar

PERCHED ON INCASA-SARAYI'S HIGHEST minaret, Hisar accepted Bessic's assurances with relief. Then, stretching Its translucent wings as far as they could reach, It leaped into the air and, swooping past Incasa-Sarayi's main gate, headed across the city. Reaching out with suddenly clawed feet, It grasped the air around the flagpole atop Gerek-Hisar and spun around to face the shrouded strait.

Far to the north, It could feel Illan's approaching fleet as a great flock of brown birds beating against Its immature abilities, and shook off the sudden sense of foreboding that followed in its wake. The defense of Anavatan was not Its concern right now. That was for the older Gods and their established temples to worry about. Its concern was to save Graize and probably Brax, too.

And it could be done, It thought with a sudden burst of excitement. It could bring Brax and Graize together and keep them apart at the same time. It had a plan.

But first It had to find Brax.

Twisting Its head to what would have been an impossible angle had It been a fully physical being, the young God bared Its teeth at the sky. The rain and the fog were too thick to see through, but there were other ways of finding someone other than by looking. Reaching out along the lien It shared with Spar, It traveled down the bond of trust and memories the youth shared with no one except his older kardos and found Its answer. Brax was in the courtyard below. Resisting the urge to laugh out loud, the young God tucked Its wings tightly against Its body and dropped.

As It plummeted downward, the flock of brown birds took wing across Its mind, and once again It shook off the accompanying sense of foreboding, ordering them away with an imperious shake of Its head. Obedient to Its command, the birds wheeled about and headed across the water, becoming a fleet of ships, before disappearing up the strait.

✦

Far to the north, the Volinski fleet lay quietly off the headlands of the Bogazi-Isik, shielded from sight by the fog and guided by the royal weather sorcerers. Dressed in leather boots, breeches, and a heavy woolen kaftan to ward off the rain, Prince Illan stood on the flagship sterncastle, staring into the distance.

They'd made an auspicious crossing, losing only two ships, when a sudden squall had come upon them in the night. Now they anchored in a shallow bay on the eastern shore, putting the heavier galleys to the seaward side to protect the lighter. To either side, blue-gray cliffs disappeared into the fog like vast, natural battlements, hiding any possible sentry post as effectively as it hid the fleet.

A cold breeze whistled past his face and behind him, Vyns stirred restlessly.

"I always heard the lands in the south were warm," the sergeant-at-arms noted in a sour voice.

"Warmer," Illan corrected absently before turning to the senior water sorcerer standing a respectful distance from the prince and his man. "What does the strait speak of, Nadiev?" he asked.

Removing her hood, the old woman bent to sight along the length of the water. "It's difficult to interpret, Highness," she answered, pushing a lock of fine, gray hair back from her face. "It speaks in a foreign, southern tongue, but I can sense both crosscurrents and undercurrents of great strength in the distance, each one speaking its own language."

"That would be the fabled God-waters of Gol-Beyaz," he noted.

"Yes, Highness." She straightened. "Within its own depths, the strait speaks of its resident fish remaining deep with no encroachment by foreigners and a few squabbles over shelter. This suggests lasting bad weather with little or no respite in the near future. It does not speak of the break of our oars upon the water, nor of any enemy oars approaching us. I would hazard that we are still undiscovered from the waterside."

And to the landward?"

She stared up at the mist-covered cliffs towering above them. "We approached a heavily wooden landscape in a driving rain with a deeply enveloping fog. It would stand to reason that we remain hidden from any posted sentries, but their Majesties' land sorcerers could address that more accurately than I, Highness. We should ask them when they return."

As one, they glanced over to where a number of small boats were making for the thin strip of pebbled beach.

"There's a strong wind coming in from the north," she continued. "At home this would herald a freezing rain, maybe even hail, but here . . . more rain at the very least, I would think. A hard-driving and cold rain from the smell of it. It may sweep away the fog."

Her voice held a touch of anxiety that hinted at more than just concern about the weather, and Illan nodded. No one in the fleet would speak of the last time a Volinski duc had ordered an invasion of Anavatan, but it would be foremost in their minds. There had been no fog when Duc Leold had sent his people against the Gods of Gol-Beyaz and lost a fleet, the throne, and his life. No one wanted to see the ghosts of ancient shipwrecks in their visions.

"Lovely," Vyns snorted.

"Yes," Nadiev continued, retreating back into the depths of her hood as the rain began to fall with greater force. "It would be better if our land sorcerers didn't linger. The rain will make their return difficult."

Illan inclined his head in agreement. "Let's hope their prophecy warns them of that in time, then," he said in a dry voice.

Nadiev glanced over at him, gauging his mood. "What does your own prophecy tell you, Highness?"

Illan returned his gaze to the cliffs. "That we're in a desolate place where even a gull cannot see far, but that it won't last." His brows drew down in a thoughtful frown as he studied the clouds above. "There was a pinprick of light to the southwest earlier," he noted. "And a corresponding spark of clarity in my vision. It may have been enough for the Anavatanon seers to gain some small sense of our proximity."

"They know we're coming, Highness?"

Anxiety colored the water sorcerer's tone again, and Illan raised an eyebrow at her. "They've known we're coming for some months, Nadiev," he chided. "Just not exactly when. Aided by their Gods, they'll

know that soon enough. Maintaining surprise was never our intention."
He returned his attention to the clouds. "However, we should not linger
too long seeking signs of prophecy in the rocks and trees so far from our
real objective," he added.

"When they finally do discover when, we'll have the advantage of
many heavier and stronger galleys," Vyns offered with a hint of pride
in his voice. "Dromons with mounted catapults and archers of consum-
mate skill. All they have are lake pentenconters," he sneered.

"True. And they will be beset by our allies on every shore." Illan
raised his face to the wind, seeking for the fine thread of memory that
led him to Panos. "Some more hidden than others," he added as he
found it. Their thoughts caressed for a brief moment, warming his
spirit, before the fog swept them apart once more.

He turned. "We should not linger," he repeated. "Vyns."

"My lord?"

"Inform Prince Pieter that I advise all possible speed. If he can order
the fleet to move in this weather, he should do so. The fog is our ally, but
it's a fickle friend, and wilts before the onslaught of a cold wind. He has
perhaps . . ." Illan stared up at the sky, trying to gauge the time through
the clouds. ". . . three hours until nightfall. Do you concur, Nadiev?"

"I do, Highness."

"Then tell him that he would do well to make use of it."

Vyns bowed. "Yes, my lord."

The sound of boats scraping against rocks told them that the land
sorcerers had finally reached the shore, and Illan made for his cabin
with an impatient snort. Reading omens on the cliffs and beaches of
the Bogazi would do them little good. They needed to reach Anavatan
before the fog lifted.

A silken thread of ancient prophecy whispered past him, and he
raised one hand to sweep it away before it tainted his own vision. He had
no time for the ghosts of long-past shipwrecks or of the battles fought
seven centuries ago. He had time only for the present and for the future
he'd devised. He would make it happen no matter what.

✦

The thread of prophecy spun away on the wind, traveling south until it
finally came to rest in Panos' open palm. She regarded it for a moment,

her black eyes filled with unshed tears, then sent it off in a new direction with a single breath. A distant breeze caught it, and it vanished into the past once again.

✦

Fog.

From within the confines of his helmet, he frowned. Fog was the bane of sentries and not just because it limited sight. It also distorted sound, made it louder, and threw it around so that one never knew just where it was coming from.

Standing on the top of Estavia-Sarayi's new armory tower as Kaptin Haldin once again, he closed his eyes, straining to make sense of the mishmash of noise that filtered up to him. The crash of waves coming from inland, birdsong coming from below, muffled ships' bells ringing beside him, people talking as if they stood directly in front of him, and the single note of Havo's priests beginning the Evening Invocations seemingly everywhere at once. Sounds that were both frustrating and confusing, but not precisely heralds of approaching danger.

He opened his eyes.

Anavatan stretched out below him, half hidden by the fog, but shining like a silver beacon in his mind; the City of the Gods; completed now down to the last municipal dovecote; its God-Wall strong and its markets filled to bursting. The chain that protected the western docks was ready to be stretched across the mouth of the Halic-Salmanak, and Estavia's fleet was ready to embark at the first sign of danger. And there was no sign of danger. Not yet. None save the fog . . .

Removing the helmet, he wiped the mist from his face with a grimace, smearing the painted symbol of the God-Wall on his cheek. He was a Warrior, a Champion, famed for his coolness in the face of the enemy and his prowess in battle.

But you couldn't fight what you couldn't see, and things you couldn't see could make use of an enveloping fog to creep close enough to attack. And an attack was imminent, whatever the signs. He could feel it, just as Estavia could feel it. As he stared across the city, an errant breeze swept the fog aside for a single moment, and the God of Battles stood at his side, staring as he did, across the city, staring at the Wall gleaming with a brilliant, indigo light in the setting sun.

The nearness of Her presence bathed him in shimmering warmth, and he closed his eyes, feeling himself uplifted by the force of Her love.

A thread of prophecy carrying a woman's golden voice whispered across his mind.

"The Wall will not stand."

"He'll crumble under the weight of it."

His eyes snapped open. Who will crumble? he demanded.

✦

The thread vanished. Standing in Gerek-Hisar's central pavilion, Brax shook his head in a frustrated gesture. Around him, a group of militia delinkon waited respectfully for him to return his attention to their training and, moving to one side, he signaled for them to continue.

He'd had this third vision two days ago and, with Spar spending so much time in the seer's shrine with Sable Company, he'd braved the rain, the fog—and his old teacher's delighted laughter at this unprecedented second visit in as many days—to seek Ihsan out at the Bibliotheca.

After wiping his eyes on his sleeve, the priest of Ystazia had leaned back with an attempt at a more serious expression.

✦

"Very little is know about Estavia's first favorite," he observed. "Beyond the myths, of course, which may have elevated his status beyond his actual deeds."

Brax frowned. "How do you mean?"

"I mean he may not even have existed at all, but been created by the heroic deeds of many others brought together under a single name. Well, consider it," he continued after noting Brax's shocked expression. "The ultimate hero? Already a kaptin and a beloved Champion of Estavia before the stories about him even begin? How did he rise to such a status without notice? Where did he come from? When was he born? We know only that he helped to build Anavatan and that he defended the City of the Gods against its enemies for season after season until the stories about him just cease. No one knows how or when he died. Like the origin of the Gods themselves, Kaptin Haldin's final days have been lost. Shrouded on purpose perhaps, or . . ." Ihsan raised an ink-stained finger in dramatic emphasis. "He might never have died because he might never have lived. Not as a single man at any rate."

"But I've been having visions of his life," Brax insisted. "Feeling what he felt and seeing what he saw."

"What you've been told he felt and saw," Ihsan corrected. "From what I understand, prophecy is more like a banquet of symbols rather than a single, physical loaf of bread, yes?"

As Brax's stomach growled, he glared at his old teacher. "You're just trying to distract me with the mention of food because you don't know the answer to my questions," he accused.

Ihsan just laughed. "Of course," he admitted, then leaned forward. "As pleased as I am to have your company, Braxin-Delin, you need to speak to a seer, not a scholar. Go and see your Kaptin Liel if you need answers about prophecy. Or speak to your own kardos. I understand that Spar has excellent instincts regarding interpretation."

"I've talked to Spar once already," Brax admitted.

"And?"

"He thinks I see myself as Kaptin Haldin, the Protector of Anavatan."

"That's nothing new, is it?"

"No, but these visions are."

"Then perhaps your understanding of what it means to be Kaptin Haldin has changed, and your visions are trying to—what's the phrase seers use—navigate you into the right stream?"

"Then they should find me a boat instead of just throwing me at the water," Brax groused, running a hand through his hair in annoyance. "And I don't trust this voice that keeps warning me about the Wall either. I swore to Estavia that I would defend the Wall. If it's in real danger, I need to know how to protect it, and if it's a trick, I need to know how to avoid it. Panos of Amatus is an ally of Graize's. Nothing good can come from her sending me warnings. It can only mean that she wants me heading into the wrong stream. I just don't know what the right stream is."

Pressing his fingertips to the bridge of his nose, Ihsan nodded thoughtfully. "It's a confusing image, I agree," he allowed. "The Wall is strongly made and ably defended. Perhaps, like Kaptin Haldin, the Wall is meant to symbolize something else, some particular protection that you feel is under threat." He pointed at the painted ward on Brax's wrist. "You draw its symbol on your body every morning, just one of the many things you love and swear to protect anew each day. Perhaps in this instance the Wall symbolizes that protection." At Brax's mystified expression, he sighed. "Perhaps you are the Wall, Ghazi-Delin," he expanded.

"That doesn't make me feel any better, Ihsan-Sayin," Brax retorted. "She keeps saying the Wall will not stand."

"Perhaps it's not as ably defended as it might be. You do have a habit of trying to fight your battles alone. Add some sentries to your battlements. You'll feel better."

Brax frowned at him, but nodded. "Ask for help," he said ruefully."

"Exactly."

"Spar's already done that."

"Very wise. Enlist the aid of others, and I think you'll find the Wall ably protected once again."

✦

In the pavilion, Brax scratched at the dried ink on his wrist, then frowned as the familiar buzz of Hisar's approach interrupted his thoughts. Rather than talk to the young God with a dozen curious delinkon watching, he called an end to their training, waiting until they gratefully dispersed into the tower keep before leaning against the pavilion's vine-wrapped entrance. When Hisar materialized in front of him in His golden-seeming, Brax cocked his head to one side.

"How's your new worshiper?" he asked in a conversational tone.

Hisar just shook His head at him, His hair slapping against His cheeks with the movement. "Not now. *He's* coming," He said without preamble. "We saw him, Spar and me. Graize is coming."

"When?" he asked, keeping his voice as carefully neutral as possible. "Soon."

"Be warned and be ready," Brax murmured.

"Are you ready?"

He wiped a new line of mist from his face with a grimace. "I will be."

The young God leaned against the opposite side of the entranceway, mirroring Brax's stance with eerie precision. "You said you'd give me a chance to talk to Graize," He reminded him. "You promised."

"I remember. Have You?"

"Not yet. I will. Soon, but not yet. It isn't time yet." His expression frustrated, Hisar ran a hand through His hair in a gesture that Brax recognized immediately. "Everything's always . . . what was it you said, absolutely and maybe?"

"Hurry up and wait," Brax agreed.

"And now and later." Hisar finished in a petulant tone. "I feel all itchy and tense, like there's a storm coming. I wish Graize would just arrive already. I hate waiting."

"Maybe it is just a storm coming," Brax suggested. "Another storm," he amended, glancing back at the wispy lines of fog crisscrossing the floor of the pavilion.

"I don't think so," Hisar replied tersely. "It feels more like a storm on the inside. But there will be another storm on the outside soon," He added. "The northern fleet's coming, too. I've seen it and I'll bet Incasa has, too. They're headed for the strait."

Brax nodded. "They'll attack Gerek-Hisar first," he noted.

"You think so?"

"It's what I'd do, establish a secure base on the Northern Trisect that keeps us from using the sea chain, then cross the unprotected Halic and attack Anavatan from behind the temple walls. That's where we're the most vulnerable."

Hisar chewed at His upper lip in a very physical gesture of concern. "My temple site's right beside the sea chain's Western Trisect bollard," He noted. "And it's vulnerable, too. I don't want them there. They'll . . . break things."

Brax made himself smile reassuringly. "Don't fret. We have six Gods and a fleet of our own, remember? They'll never get that far. Besides . . ." Even though he knew he couldn't see past the watchtower's high walls, he still glanced in the direction of the strait. "If they were that close, the alarm would have sounded already. We have time."

"Not much time."

"No."

"It's not our problem anyway," Hisar stated, His voice matching Brax's exactly in pitch and timber. "As you said before, Graize is our problem. He always has been." Stepping out into the rain, the young God turned. "Be warned and be ready," He said. "They're both coming." Changing fluidly to Its dragonfly-seeming, It shot into the air, the metallic spray of light shimmering off Its wings swallowed up by the fog almost at once.

Brax watched It go with a frown, then headed for the tower keep in search of his troop. If the northern fleet really were coming that soon, they needed to be in place on the aqueduct before they got drawn into the defense of Gerek-Hisar because, as Hisar had said, Graize was their problem. He always had been.

✦

To the north, a streak of lightning lit up the sky as Graize and his party left the thin cattle track that wound along beneath the aqueduct to join with the main trade road. A single ox-drawn cart splashed its way past, its driver so deeply huddled in cloak and hat that they remained unnoticed. In the distance they could just see the signal fire atop Gerek-Hisar glowing faintly through the fog.

A rumble of thunder sounded overhead, and Hares pushed his hood back, his eyes narrowed in concentration. "From what I remember of this Trisect's topography, I'd estimate we were no more than a mile away from the North-Cattle gate," he stated, then glanced over at Graize. "Now what?"

Graize closed his eyes, feeling the present rush past his prophecy with all the strength of a swollen river. "The baby-seer and his guard dog will expect me to slink over the wall nearest the aqueduct like a rat entering a storage bin," he mused, more to himself than to Hares. "It's what they would have done in the past; sly little lifters hiding in the shadows, waiting for the sharp-eyed garrison guards to pass them by." He tipped his head up to scrutinize the sky with a thoughtful expression. "And it's what I might have done in the past as well," he allowed. "But we aren't sly little lifters anymore and we don't hide in the shadows; we hide in plain view," he continued, gesturing at the Anavatanon style clothing they'd all donned. He glanced over at the Skirosian mapmaker. "We wait," he stated.

"For?"

"For a flock of brown birds to sweep down the strait and fill the road."

"With?"

"Frightened farmers and herders running for the safety of the North-Cattle gate."

"Ah." Hares nodded his understanding. "And we run along in their midst?"

"Yes."

"Soon?" Yal asked plaintively. "Before we drown on land?"

From within the confines of her own hood, Panos nodded. "Soon," she answered for Graize. "The Volinski fleet is near." She reached out to catch a raindrop on one fingertip. "It won't be long." She glanced at Graize. "The fog remains heavy," she noted.

He met her gaze with a blank expression of his own. "Yes."

"It will grow even heavier before it clears," she continued. "Like soup. As long as it remains heavy in the pot and not in the bowl, all will be well. The bowl needs to maintain some clarity inside its own mind as it gets closer to the pot that birthed it."

He shrugged. "Outside, inside, inside-out," he answered in his familiar singsong voice. "It doesn't matter, the game is begun, the shine isn't soup, and the pot has a crack in it."

"The die is cast, then?"

"The die was cast years ago."

"Can we get closer to the city without being discovered?" Hares asked in an impatient voice.

Graize nodded. "The fog will cover our movements and shield our identities. We can get all the way to the north wall."

"Then let's do it," Danjel said, stepping onto the road at once. "We need to be in place when the time comes." She glanced up at the sky in disgust. "The wall should grant some small cover from the rain. I hope."

One by one, they followed her. Graize held back for a moment as a faint sense of impatience and anticipation fluttered past his thoughts. He studied them, but then, as nothing more than the echo of a bird's wings made itself known, he turned onto the road also, ignoring the lines of fog which swirled about his feet and puddled at the edge of his thoughts. Soup, he thought, was always better in the bowl than out, however heavy it might be.

✦

High above, in the guise of a hunting hawk, Hisar struggled to keep Its own thoughts hidden. Graize wasn't to notice It, not yet. Its immature lien buzzed anxiously as It watched until he disappeared around a bend.

Soon, It told Itself sternly. As Brax had noted, the alarm hadn't sounded yet; like Graize, Hisar had to wait for the alarm.

Running over Its plan for the hundredth time, It caught an updraft and followed behind Its abayos on silent wings, noting how much heavier the fog had become as Panos had noted, and how heavy it seemed to be becoming within Graize as she'd warned.

✦

They reached the Northern Trisect's stone wall by dusk. As the long, undulating notes of the Evening Invocation filtered out to them, Danjel glanced over at Graize, but when he returned her questioning expression with a stony look of his own, she continued to make camp with the others.

Night fell. Graize stood staring up at the cloudy sky for a long time, feeling the fog within his mind growing ever thicker. The lien he shared with Hisar burned low in his chest like a hearth full of banked coals. It had increased, bit by bit, the closer he came to Anavatan, but the sky remained clear of the Godling's presence. Resisting the sudden, almost painful urge to press a hand against his chest, he shoved the sensation to the far recesses of his thoughts. He would not call to It, no matter how painful it became and no matter how clouded his mind became without It. Spinning about, he headed into the tent he shared with Danjel and Yal.

✦

Beyond the northern wall, Anavatan's Trisects settled into an uneasy sleep. At Incasa-Sarayi, the Prophecy God's seer-priests maintained a constant seeking, ready to throw their considerable powers behind their God at a moment's notice, while at Estavia-Sarayi, Sable Company stood ready to send their own God whatever power She required. The guards on the walls patrolled with increased vigilance, their spirits warmed by the presence of Estavia Herself, who stood poised at the headlands of Gol-Beyaz. Her twin swords spun in a constant circle above Her head, lighting up the shoreline with an eerie silver glow, but there was no sign of the enemy, physical or prophetic, throughout the long, stormy night.

✦

The next morning, as the rain continued to drive against the city, Incasa arose from the depths to begin His orchestration of the defense of Anavatan. The vision of a tiny boat filled with prophecy formed in His palm and he set it gently in the waves, watching as the tide caught it up and carried it across the water.

On Estavia-Sarayi's kitchen wharf, Chamberlain Tanay threw a waterproof cloak over Spar's shoulders and then caught hold of Jaq's collar, preventing the dog from following as the youth stepped into the small boat she'd managed to commission for him despite the weather.

As he took his place, he stared up at her, the misty-eyed gaze of a senior seer belying the youthfulness of his features.

"You'll give Kemal and Yashar my message?" he asked, his voice falling flat in the fog.

She nodded. "They'll be in place by the time you need them. And so will I, Delin," she added, "in case you need me."

He ducked his head, suddenly embarrassed by the warm sensation her words invoked. As the first note of the Morning Invocations sounded from Havo-Sarayi, he turned his attention to the open water to see the God of Seasonal Storms rise silently from the waves, with skin, hair, and eyes echoing the stormy gray of the cloud-filled sky above. Their eyes met, Spar dipped his head stiffly in thanks, and the boat-master pushed off into the churning waters as Havo breathed onto the waves, causing a thin channel of calm to stretch out before them.

They followed it up the Halic, hugging the western shore until just before the aqueduct, then made the crossing to the Northern Trisect. As the last note of Havo's Invocation faded and the first note of Oristo's began, Spar stepped ashore.

One by one, new visions formed in the God of Prophecy's palm, each one being set upon the waves in turn.

In the Hearth God's temple, First Abayos-Priest Neclan breathed in the scent of baking bread as she and Oristo passed images of the supplies Anavatan required to withstand an attack by sea to each and every temple chamberlain and cami priest across the city.

In the Tannery Precinct, a youth left her share of a stolen loaf of bread to be divvied up by her crew, including Zeno, then headed out into the rain with a small piece of tile clutched in her fist.

Incasa watched these visions bob up and down in the waves like a line of tiny penteconters, then added new ones to their midst.

Oristo's priests fell silent while in Anavatan's hospitals and infirmaries Usara's physicians and orderlies stood by the bedsides of the sick and began their song of healing and respite. Usara sang with them, holding His handful of medicinal herbs out to Incasa with an expectant expression.

Incasa nodded. Healing and respite began with care and nurture; from the first vision of Hisar's birth that had heralded every event that had followed, care and nurture had begun with two ghazi-priests of Estavia.

And at Estavia-Sarayi, Chamberlain Tanay stared thoughtfully at her larder, the faintest line of white mist crossing in front of her vision. Then, after curtly telling Jaq to stop his pacing, she crossed the kitchen to a small nook holding Usara's statue and began to fill a wicker basket with medical supplies.

✦

At Estavia-Sarayi, Kemal and Yashar made their way to the temple's central shrine. Rarely visited by anyone except Brax, it was quiet and dark and smelled of wood polish, stale incense, and stone. Only the wall sconce by the door was lit. As Yashar moved around the room, lighting the rest, Kemal set their supplies to one side and then felt his way to the far end. The six-foot-tall onyx statue of Estavia seemed to watch him advance, Her ruby eyes glittering in the flickering lamplight.

Pulling his sword, he kissed the blade, then laid it across the altar and stepped back, one hand pressed against his chest where Her lien glowed as warmly as a hearth of banked coals.

Yashar lit the mangel in the corner, and once it was sending out a comforting amount of heat, he joined Kemal at the altar. After laying his sword beside the other man's, he glanced over at the polished, black marble slab that covered Kaptin Haldin's tomb.

"The last time we came here together it was to tuck Brax and Spar out of harm's reach five years ago," he observed. "Do you remember?"

Kemal nodded.

"You don't suppose that Spar's just done the same to us, do you?"

The younger man chuckled. "It had occurred to me," he admitted.

"Hm." Crossing his arms, Yashar planted his feet more comfortably on the stone floor. "So, what do we do now?" he asked.

"We practice patience as you once told me to do, and we wait."

"For?"

"Some signal from Spar, or from Estavia."

"We should stay vigilant, then?"

"Yes."

"So, no chance of sex, then?"

Kemal laughed. "Later, when we're off duty."

Dropping into parade rest, he closed his eyes. Once his mind and body were equally still, he reached out along his lien to Estavia. Beside him, he felt Yashar do the same, while in Her temple, and in every Estavia-Cami, watchtower, and village courtyard, on the decks of every fighting ship, and braced on the stone trough of the great aqueduct, every Warrior, militia, and delinkos sworn to Estavia stood to attention waiting for their marshal to begin the Battle God's Invocation.

✦

To the south, at Incasa-Sarayi, First Oracle Bessic felt Estavia's rise as a maddening scratch across his prophecy. He and his senior oracles had been sequestered in the central arzhane chamber all night, tracking the progress of their enemies in vision and following Incasa's movements as He cast His dice into the waves, forming, destroying, and re-forming stream after stream in His own vision questing.

Now, banishing the Battle God's distraction as well as the fleeting wish for hot water and cool sheets, Bessic sank back into prophecy waiting for his turn to Invoke his own God.

In the silver lake, Incasa sent a loving caress along the lien He shared with His First Oracle as Ystazia rose from the waves beside Him in response to Her own Invocation. Weaving and spinning in time with the music that swelled from every home, workshop, and studio along the shores of Gol-Beyaz, the God of Arts and Dancing cast handfuls of rainbows into the air, laughing with delight despite the gravity of the situation as they sparkled in the rain all around Her.

The spray of multicolored light reflected in Incasa's ice-white gaze, warming it for the briefest of moments. He studied the patterns they made as they fell; then, dipping one hand into their midst, He brought a palmful to His lips. More than any other, the power of Ystazia tasted of Creation and Destruction and, as He wove it into His plans for Hisar, Incasa felt the young God's future grow both stronger and brighter with their addition.

Then, accepting the Art God's outstretched hand, Incasa joined in Her dance, allowing Himself a moment's respite within the circle of Her arms until Her song faded and His own began. Then, with the added power gleaned from the worship of every priest and follower with even the slightest gift for Prophecy, He sent His First Oracle the clear-cut image of a fleet of warships.

Moments later, the bronze bell atop Incasa-Sarayi's highest tower rang out.

Estavia-Sarayi's bell tolled next, then Oristo's, Ystazia's, Usara's, and Havo's, followed by the bells of Gerek, Dovek, and Lazim-Hisar. Finally, the great bell atop the Derneke-Mahalle Citadel, which rang only in times of the greatest danger, began to sound. People streamed into the streets, making for any ground high enough to see the Bogazi-Isik and the Gods arose to stand on Their temple battlements, each one mirroring the position of Their guardian statues. The ships of Volinsk fleet had been sighted in the strait. The invasion of Anavatan had begun.

13

The Northern Market

IN THE CENTER OF the Northern Trisect marketplace, Hisar
stood under a wine merchant's awning, listening to the sound of alarm
bells ringing as much inside His head as outside it. All around Him,
people spilled into the rain, most of them heading for the strong walls
of Gerek-Hisar. He could feel their panic scrabbling at His juvenile
sensibilities, calling up His own need to respond, but their ties of worship and obligation were not to Him, so he was able, with some effort,
to set them aside.

The approach of Illan's fleet of brown bird-ships beat against His
prophecy in a rush of wings, and deep within Himself, He could feel
Anavatan's priests in the temple shrines offering up the power their
Gods required to defend the city. He could feel the Gods' response as a
dark and feral hunger, greedy for all that power. He could feel His own
hunger rising and again, with some effort, forced it aside as well. If he
was going to have all that power, He was going to have to bring more
than just Brax and Graize together; He was going to have to bring His
only two priests, Spar and Graize, together at a temple. At His temple.

The yellow-green tunic He'd wrapped about His golden-seeming
today remained untouched by the driving rain as He stepped into the
street. If He'd had a real physical body, He knew His heart would have
been pounding against His chest like a hammer. As it was, He could feel
a growing anxiety sizzling through Him like lightning.

As if on cue, the sky lit up as a bolt hit the top of Gerek-Hisar with a
crack of fire. The need to follow it back into the clouds traveled up and
along His back and shoulders in a stretching of unformed wings, and He
shook Himself with a grimace of irritation. There was power in light-

ning, but that was not the kind of power He wanted. When the accompanying roll of thunder signaled that His chance had come and gone, He laid a hand against His chest as He'd seen Brax do so many times before, then reached out ever so gently along the lien, to find Graize.

✦

The faint smell of burning followed the lightning strike to the south, and Graize resisted the urge to press himself against the wall of a nearby cattle pen. He'd never liked lightning. The power it threw around muddied his sight, and right now he needed as much clarity as possible. Just setting foot on Anavatanon soil again had been enough to send a spray of unhappy memories splattering across his stability; memories of hunger and of loss. The last thing he needed was to allow memories of pain and fear to follow in their wake. The spirits of the wild lands that had gained access to the city in such a storm; the spirits that had killed Drove and flung Graize far from his home in their attempt to destroy him had met their destruction at his hands instead. He'd spent the last six years reminding himself of that. He would not allow a little rain and wind to undermine what should be a memory of victory and triumph. With a savage gesture, he thrust all memories—whatever their kind—aside and bore down upon the present.

His small party of Yuruk and Skirosians had gained access through the North-Cattle gate as easily as he'd predicted once the alarm bells had begun to toll. Skirting the rows of animal pens and granaries that made up this corner of the marketplace, they'd joined the crowds of people streaming into the streets. No one looked twice at them; they were just another clump of people trying to find safety.

Now they bunched up behind him as he paused.

Beside him, Danjel made an inquiring noise. The Yuruk wyrdin had held the male form since early that morning and already a fine speckling of black whiskers, sparkling with raindrops, graced the length of his jaw. Graize stared at him, using his face as a focus, before giving a sharp gesture with his chin in reply.

"For now we go southeast until we reach the shore wall northeast of Gerek-Hisar. That's where Illan will stage his first attack," he said with unusual simplicity.

"Not at the sea chain's housing?"

"The sea chain'll be protected by the Anavatanon fleet. He'll attack the most vulnerable spot first; the merchants and farmers of the Northern Trisect. That'll create panic and draw most of the militia away from Gerek-Hisar. After that, he'll go for the sea chain."

Danjel nodded. Gesturing for the others to move out, he glanced back at his kardos as a faint thrill of unusual anxiety caused Graize to remain where he stood.

"Something?" he asked.

His eyes narrowed, Graize scanned the nearby row of stalls and barrows, then shook his head slowly. "No," he answered. "Just memories trying to chase down my attention."

"Bad memories?"

"There was little else here."

"Then we should quicken our pace and outdistance them."

"Yes."

As Danjel splashed his way through a line of puddles growing ever wider in the hoof-rutted ground, Graize glanced about once more, his expression wary, then reluctantly allowed himself to be drawn after him.

✦

Peering around a stack of crates and barrels, Hisar carefully withdrew His presence from the lien. He hadn't realized that Graize would be that sensitive to His touch. He'd have to be careful. But, He amended, He'd also have to be quick. Graize was headed in exactly the wrong direction. Hisar needed him heading northwest toward Brax not southeast toward Illan.

Scanning the rest of Graize's party, the young God sized them up as they passed. The Petchan woman, Yal, and Panos' Skirosian bodyguards could safely be ignored; they were all too busy gawking at the unfamiliar sights and sounds around them, and Hares had his hands full trying to keep them all together. Panos carried herself stiffly as if she walked in a dream, or more likely in a vision that was consuming her attention. It was Danjel that He'd have to be wary of. Despite the crowds pressing in on them from all sides, the Yuruk wyrdin kept his attention fixed on Graize. If His plan was to succeed, Hisar would first have to get His abayos away from Danjel.

Imitating the deep breath He'd seen both Brax and Spar take before beginning an enterprise, Hisar darkened His hair and His eyes, changed His yellow-green tunic to one of blue and added a black leather cuirass with Estavia's eyes gleaming with crimson fire in the center. As He stepped out into the crowd, He sent the tiniest seed of power pulsing down the lien.

Graize's head snapped around at once, but before they could make eye contact Hisar jerked back behind a cart piled high with citrus fruits.

He waited, slowly counting to ten to steady the renewed sense of anxiety traveling through Him, then peered out again. Danjel was leaning close to Graize, speaking in his ear; one hand raised, poised to catch hold of him if necessary, the other gripping the pommel of his dagger. The young God bared his teeth at him. Changing to the seeming of the youth who'd spoken to him at His temple site, He moved off in a tight circle to come upon them, unregarded, from the opposite flank.

✦

"What is it, Kardos, memories again?"

Danjel's jade-green eyes peered into his as Graize shook his head, his expression distant.

"Memories," he echoed in a singsong whisper. "Memories flitting about like tiny white moths around a lamp flame." He found himself tapping the fingers of his left hand against his thigh—a habit he hadn't fallen into for years—and, with a grimace, thrust his hand through his belt to stop it. "Unwanted memories are like unwanted moths," he chided in a stronger voice more to himself than to Danjel. "An irritant, nothing more."

He jerked his head to the east. "The fish market in this part of the Northern Trisect offers small, local catches of fresh crabs, scallops, and whelks," he continued, forcing himself back to clarity. "The shore wall's at its lowest there, and it's pockmarked with gates and wharfs to allow the fishmongers easy passage. We should reach it soon."

He headed off at once, trusting Danjel and the others to follow him. The crowds here seemed to press in on him even more tightly and he shook off the growing need to fight his way through them. A thin whisper of sea air, smelling of clean water and seaweed, flitted through his hair, tempting him to move even faster, and he deliberately slowed his pace. All his life he'd been driven by his own prophetic abilities;

he would not now be driven by anxiety or fear on the eve of achieving his goals. Focusing his gaze on a gap between a table piled high with cucumbers and aubergines and a barrel of pickled herring, he moved forward.

And saw Drove.

✦

Hisar felt Graize's reaction shoot up the lien and caught Himself before He could instinctively send a pulse of comfort back to him. He watched as His abayos jerked to a halt, a white mist filling his gray eyes until he stood frozen, staring at nothing. Ahead of him, Danjel had yet to notice and the young God made a swift decision. Snapping back into His Brax seeming, He stepped into Graize's line of sight.

His abayos' eyes cleared.

✦

Drove became Brax. The dark eyes of his old enemy widened in recognition, then he turned and vanished into the crowd.

Graize leaped forward at once ignoring Danjel's shout of alarm.

A few of the merchants had hung covered oil lanterns within the recesses of their stalls to try and chase away the gloom, but it only added a new sense of shadowy oppression as a strong wind began to pick up, blowing down from the strait. The line between the physical and the prophetic grew faint, then began to merge as a troop of militia passed by. For a moment, Graize thought he saw the distinctive cuirass of the Warriors of Estavia among them, but the crowd, now wavelike and indistinct, parted, then re-formed too swiftly for him to be sure.

A protectorate of Oristo, arms laden with bundles, turned to stare at him. The bundles became a map of Anavatan which tore down the middle and then mended itself again before the man moved on.

Two boys, one slight, the other heavyset, stole a purse right in front of him. As he watched, the former vanished into the rain, leaving the latter to stare deliberately back at him before he disappeared as well.

Far away, he thought he heard Danjel call his name, but ignored it as the air above his head crackled with power. A streak of lightning hit a nearby minaret, sending a flock of storks flapping into the air. They filled his mind with the sound of rushing alarm bells in the form of wings. His nostrils filled with the smell of burning. Everything felt heavy and portentous, and for just an instant, he tasted blood and salt upon his lips.

✦

Hisar could feel Graize's sudden descent into prophecy and, sending a hard pulse of power snapping down the lien, jerked him back to the present, then spun out of sight again.

✦

Graize felt the pulse like a hard slap against his mind, but before he could identify where it came from, a flash of black hair disappearing behind a whelkmonger's barrow caught and held his attention. He threw his abilities out like a net, seeking any sense that it might be his quarry.

And the past rolled over him like a dense fog.

✦

Hisar narrowed His eyes in frustration as Graize's mind slipped away from Him again. He sent another pulse of power down the lien, but as He prepared to show Himself, Drove stepped between them, made so real by the power of Graize's abilities that Hisar could see the dirt under his fingernails.

✦

Drove appeared again, but this time Graize shook his head with a savage gesture. Snapping his fingers in front of his face to force himself to focus, he gained just enough clarity to banish the ghost of his fellow lifter—he would not be driven by guilt any more than by anxiety or fear. The fog began to lift from his mind, but in its place the black sand beach, dark tower, and blond-haired youth of his earlier vision rose up before him.

He snarled at it, refusing to be distracted by someone else's prophecy either; using Drove as an anchor, he caught hold of another memory: a warm and peaceful autumn afternoon at Havo-Cami in the Northern Trisect.

The image held for a single moment, then twisted under his control to become water raging through a cavernous darkness, swarms of spirits tearing at his hands and face. He fought them off, forcing the cavern to become a cool, dark place smelling of damp rock and lamp oil and a Petchan Sayer wearing the muting effect of the Gurney-Dag Mountains like a cloak.

But all too soon, the air grew heavy and portentous once again. The scents of blood and salt filled his nostrils while above him, the dawn sun peeked above the wild lands like a great, fiery insect. As he struggled to free himself from its regard, he sensed a familiar presence hovering in the distance.

He reached for it.

✦

Standing so close He could have laid a hand on Graize's shoulder if He'd wanted to, Hisar threw caution to the wind and, reaching out along the lien, jerked His abayos' attention forward again. Again Graize's eyes cleared.

✦

And Brax stood directly in front of him, one hand reaching forward, the other hidden from view.

Graize reacted at once. Pulling his knife, he lunged toward his long-time enemy with a half-muffled scream. Brax stumbled backward as the blade passed within an inch of his face, then he turned and ran.

Graize gave chase.

✦

Hisar zigzagged through the crowds as fast as He could run, dodging stalls, carts, and people, trying to keep them between Graize and Himself while still remaining in sight. Graize stayed right on His heels, coming on so quickly that Hisar was afraid He might have to take to the air just to keep him from catching up. They raced through the fruit and bread markets and finally broke free of the crowds as the cheese and milk markets gave way once again to the cattle pens built up against the north wall. Hisar spun left, pelting toward the aqueduct now towering above them, Graize still in hot pursuit. As they reached the wall that separated the grounds of Havo-Cami from the marketplace, Hisar sent a pulse down a very different lien.

✦

Spar's head jerked up as a frantic plea hit him in the chest like a blow. He, too, had been struggling to make his way to Havo-Cami through panicking crowds and driving rain. Now, with the strength of Hisar's own panic making him gasp for breath, he shoved himself up against a vintner's stall and sent a stream of reassuring power back to the young God. The panic gutted out like a candle flame and after a moment, he pushed himself up and pressed on again with a greater sense of urgency, reaching the cami's grounds a few moments later.

✦

The added strength calmed Hisar at once. Putting on a renewed burst of speed, he vaulted the north garden wall and took flight in a blur of invisible wings, heading straight for the aqueduct.

Just before It reached the top, It saw Spar.

✦

High above, Brax pressed against the cami wall, out of the worst of the storm. From this distance, he couldn't have seen the strait on a clear day, but he still stared into the rain, feeling Estavia's restless patrol as a throbbing tension that made his sword arm ache. Flexing his fingers to work the stiffness out, he nearly fell off the sentinel platform in surprise as Hisar rocketed past him in a spray of metallic fire.

Throwing one hand out to brace himself, he shot the young God an angry glare.

"What!" he demanded.

✦

Below, Graize vaulted the north garden wall after his enemy, intent on keeping him in view, but when he landed in the soft, moss-covered earth of the cami's rose garden, Brax was nowhere to be seen. Quickly, he scanned the wet earth around him for footprints, but found none. He dropped into a crouch, pulling his knife, and spun about, but there was nowhere Brax could be hiding either beside him or behind him.

His eyes narrowed. He'd seen his quarry leap over the wall. He had to be here.

A shadowy figure, nearly invisible in the mist and the rain, emerged from a stand of cypress trees near the cami and beckoned to him. Recognizing Drove from the breadth of his shoulders, Graize set off at once. Brax was here somewhere and his fellow lifter was going to show him where.

✦

Hisar buffeted Brax with Its wings, sending a plume of water from the trough at his feet shooting up into the air. Gripping the iron ring with one hand, Brax made a grab for the young God with the other, but It leaped back out of reach, before returning to buzz about his head once again. Jaw set, Brax made another grab for It, his hand passing right through Its body.

"Get a grip on yourself, you jackass!" he shouted. "And tell me what's wrong?"

Taking on Its Graize-seeming, Hisar manifested before him immediately.

"HE'S COMING!" It panted, making no attempt to dampen the resonance that caused It voice to reverberate in the air between them. "GRAIZE IS COMING, AND SPAR'S IN THE GARDEN! THEY'LL MEET ANY MOMENT NOW!"

Brax's expression hardened. "Get to Spar," he growled. "Warn him."

"THERE'S NO TIME!"

"Then get me down there."

Hisar's eyes widened, then sucking as much power as It could manage through both liens—so much power that down in the gardens, both Spar and Graize stumbled and almost fell—It caught Brax around the chest, and hurled Itself from the aqueduct.

They hit the ground hard enough to knock the wind from Brax's lungs. As he struggled to his feet, Graize rounded the corner and saw Spar.

✦

The scream of rage caught Spar completely by surprise. Intent on reaching the cami's kitchen door, he never saw Graize until he was upon him. The world took on the misty quality of the past, the rain became hail, and the grounds of Havo-Cami became the rain-slicked cobblestones of Liman Caddesi six years before.

Brax tried to dive between the two of them only to see Drove, made physical by the strength of both Graize and Spar's abilities, leap toward him, knife in hand. As the ghostly lifter attacked, Brax instinctively rolled to one side, then came up with his own knife at the ready, the strength of the past driving away any thought of the sword at his side. Swinging the blade in a tight arc to keep Drove at bay, he worked his way toward Spar.

His kardos, meanwhile, had recovered quickly enough to aim a vicious kick at his old rival, catching Graize in the chest and knocking him backward. But Graize righted himself at once. As lightning skipped across the sky above them, he shifted his own blade from hand to hand, then lunged at Spar again, only to come face-to-face with Brax, who'd finally managed to get between them.

As they'd done six years ago, Graize showed his teeth at him while Drove inched forward. Brax swung his head from side to side, keeping them both in view as Spar drew his own knife and moved to stand beside him.

"The baby rat-seer's finally grown up enough to quit hidin' behind you, yeah?" Graize sneered, his eyes glittering with madness. "But this time it won't help you. Look up, Brax. The past is here, and I'm going to use it to strip your God's protection away from you just like I did on the grasslands a year ago!"

A scattering of hail scored across Brax's cheek. As he flinched back instinctively, Drove attacked. But this time, when Drove moved under Brax's guard to slice at him, Brax brought his own blade up, cutting through the apparition's jacket to draw a line of white across his arm.

"No, you won't!" he shouted back.

Meanwhile, beside him, Spar fell back before the ferocity of Graize's assault. Ducking a wild flurry of blows, he dropped to the ground, then came up with a rock clenched in one fist. Rather than throw it at his old adversary, he waited for Graize to lunge forward again, then dodged to one side and hit him as hard as he could in the right temple. Graize's head snapped sideways, and behind them, they heard Hisar gasp in pain.

Weakened by His attempt at a physical manifestation, the young God had been able to do little more than watch His two priests fight, but now, as blood began to pour down Graize's face, He felt the past surround him in layers of freezing cold mist. They tore at His human-seeming, causing Him to waver in and out of focus, then finally, with a cry of distress, His seeming shattered to become a spinning vortex of wraithlike creatures of hunger and need.

They fell on Drove at once and, with all the grace of a pair of ghostly dancers, they replayed the terrible events of six years ago. Drove turned. The creatures caught him up. Leaping upon his back and neck, they sucked greedily at his image until he was little more than a series of fine white lines, then flung him into the street. As the other three combatants watched in horror, the creatures rose into the air, mist-covered claws outstretched toward them.

Graize stumbled back against Spar, his blood-covered face pale with shock. He turned to grab him as he had six years before, but as his hand caught hold of the other's shoulder, Brax leaped forward. His knife streaked out in a deadly arc, but suddenly the creatures vanished and Hisar appeared between them, His golden-seeming snapping back and forth as He struggled to keep a physical form. The young God cried out again and, remembering his promise, Brax jerked his hand back just in time. The blade scraped against Graize's tunic, slicing through the cloth and leaving little more than a thin line of red across his chest, then he jerked his arm up and hit his old enemy a vicious crack across his injured temple with his elbow.

Graize collapsed like an unstrung puppet, Hisar falling to the ground beside him, almost as insensible as His abayos. As the world around them returned to the present, Spar and Brax stood over them, expressions of weary uncertainty on their faces.

✦

Deep within his mind, darkness crashed over Graize with all the fury of an ocean storm. He stood braced against it for a single moment, but when a swarm of sharp-clawed spirits, clad in the tattered remnants of the past, hurled over the crest directly toward him, his mind broke and ran.

✦

To the south, Panos stopped so suddenly that Yal nearly trod on her heels. They'd been searching the marketplace for Graize ever since he'd suddenly disappeared. Now the Skirosian oracle raised one hand to forestall any questions before taking a deep breath through her nose. She let it out slowly and carefully, then pursed her lips.

"Acacia, wormwood, and marigold; the signature odors of Incasa's hand at work," she observed, tapping one fingernail against her teeth. "But old and just a bit stale. His hand at work years ago, not now. I see." She nodded to herself. "A future that that should have been, waylaid by a God's design, re-forming now, and three figures poised to choose if they will follow a mountain path reopening before them, a path that may just lead them to a silver tower. All by the God's design again."

She scanned the crowd once more as if to satisfy herself that what she was sensing was fully accurate, then turned to Danjel and Hares.

"Graize has returned to a path he's both run from and run to for so very long," she said. "He doesn't need us now."

Hares nodded at once. "The Volinski fleet will be sailing down the strait," he agreed. "We should carry on to the eastern shore as planned."

Danjel's eyes narrowed. "Wait. He doesn't *need* us?" he echoed in an incredulous voice. "Since when?"

Panos' expression remained even. "Since now." She reached out to catch a raindrop on her fingertip, staring at it with an expression of deep sadness. "Would you prefer me to say that we cannot help him?" she asked.

"Not really."

"Does your prophecy say any different?"

As Danjel made no reply, she shrugged eloquently. "Then as hard as it may be to accept, it is what it is. You are not his destiny; nor am I. We walked beside him for a time; sometimes we even carried him," she added acknowledging his sour expression with an indulgent one of her own. "But now he stands before a choice and we cannot help him make it. That's up to the ones who were waylaid along with him."

"Spar and Brax?"

"None other."

Danjel shook his head. "Do you really think they'll help him? They're more likely to try and kill him."

"Perhaps at first, but don't forget, there's a tower standing beside them, and it's still a golden one. It may make them see sense before It changes color."

"Is it going to change color?"

Panos shrugged. "I don't know. Clearly, It has a choice to make as well."

Danjel's expression showed his opinion of Hisar's ability in that regard and Panos waved a weary hand at him. "Whatever may come to pass, Graize's old adversaries cannot make their choices without him any more than he can make his choice without them. The mountain path has manifested before them. There are only the two ways left to go: up . . ." she raised a hand into the air, " . . . or down." She dropped it. "Future or past."

"And you don't care which one they choose?" Danjel pressed.

"Grow up," she snapped, an uncharacteristically angry note in her voice. "My caring has nothing to do with it, nor does yours. We all walk our own paths. Sometimes they cross and we're able to walk together for a while, but in the end everyone walks alone." She wrapped her cloak more tightly around her shoulders. "Now, my path leads me south. Throw grasses in the air or sing to the spirits of the storm if you cannot proceed without direction, Wyrdin, but move shortly or you may drown in war." Without waiting for a reply, she spun on her heel and disappeared into the crowds, her retinue struggling to fall into line behind her.

Danjel remained where he stood, his smooth brow furrowed with indecision, until Yal slipped a hand in his.

"What did your prophecy tell you before, my love," she asked gently, nudging him until his features flowed to her preferred female form.

Danjel frowned. "That our path lay with Graize."

"And now?"

"Now?" Danjel glanced up at the sky. "I don't know. The world is covered in mist and rain and surrounded by stone walls and tall buildings. I can't see anything clearly."

"Then choose without seeing like the rest of us have to. We have three paths before us: we can go home, we can continue to search for Graize, or we can follow Panos. Which path calls to you the strongest?"

The Yuruk gave a soft bark of laughter. "Home. Always home."

"Without Graize?"

Danjel hesitated. "It would have to be," she said after a moment.

"Can it be?"

"I don't know." Danjel squared her shoulders. "But I do know that our path doesn't follow Panos."

"So we don't go south."

"No." The Yuruk glanced up at the sky with a sour expression. "And we can't wander the marketplace hoping to trip over Graize either." She grew thoughtful. "We can't get home without mounts, and Rayne has our mounts. She'll be joining the attack on Bahce-Koy, and that's west across the Halic and through the mainland Trisect of Anavatan. So we go west."

"During an attack?"

"It's good cover. No one's going to notice us in these clothes if they're busy staring at a northern attack fleet."

"That's true. All right, my love, we choose to go west. We will walk our paths together." Tucking her arm in Danjel's, Yal grinned up at her. "Was that so hard?"

"I suppose not."

"Then come on."

Rejoining the crowds, they headed west toward the Halic-Salmanak.

✦

Far to the southwest, with the warning bells of Anavatan ringing in her ears, Rayne brought her band of Yuruk raiders in line with those of her kin moving against Bahce-Koy. It was an ambitious plan and one so absurd that their leaders had reckoned that even if Sable Company did see them in the midst of all the other looming dangers, they'd never take them seriously. Historically, Bahce-Koy was exempt from most of the Yuruk raids. The garden village was built right up against Anavatan itself in a small hollow and shared the highest point in the God-Wall with the city. They had no flocks and little else in the way of livestock; instead, they tended to vast fields of flowers grown to grace the tables and altars of Anavatan's many temples and camis. The Yuruk had no interest in flowers, and so Bahce-Koy had grown lax and complacent. Their western gate was old and in need of repair and, unlike the other villages along Gol-Beyaz, it had done little to prepare itself for the attacks they all knew were coming. This would be a raid more to cause mischief and panic than for spoils, but that suited Rayne just fine. She liked both mischief and panic.

As her teyos, Ozan, raised his red yak's tail standard, she followed suit and with an undulating cry that was echoed by her people, urged her pony into a gallop.

✦

To the south, the Petchan hill fighters swept toward the villages of Kepek and Kinor-Koy, casting the muting effect before them like a cloak. The militia met them at the edge of the grasslands. Reinforced by two troops of Verdant Company archers and a full circle of Sable Company seers to combat the muting effect, they dug in and held their ground against a foe that blinked in and out of their line of sight like hundreds of guttering candle flames.

Meanwhile, to the south, word came down from Anahtar-Hisar that enemy ships had been sighted in the southern strait, their sails stowed for battle. New bells began to toll, and in moments, a full complement of warriors and militia lined the shore while eight of Estavia's penteconters moved into position across the narrow waters. Smaller than the Skirosian vessels, they were counting on their greater maneuverability to cut off any of King Pyrros' heavy ramming ships that might break through their defenses. The archers crouched at their stations, oars drawn in, bows at the ready, and the signalers raised their trumpets as the kaptins stood on the prows above each great painted oculus, waiting for the bell atop Anahtar-Hisar to toll again. As the Skirosian fleet appeared, it sounded three times, its ringing tones echoing across the water. The archers stood, weapons raised, and Estavia's lien thrumming down their bowstrings to spark against the arrowheads.

To the north, the red-sailed ships of Volinsk swept down the Bogazi-Isik Strait, and Gerek-Hisar's heavy militia-barge began the laborious task of dragging the sea chain across the Halic as the bulk of Anavatan's fleet went out to meet the enemy in the driving rain. A Sable Company seer stood on every prow and, as a single trumpet sounded from the battlements of Estavia-Sarayi, they began to sing their invitation to the God of Battles to join them on the line.

14

The Crossing

THE SPIRITS WERE NEARLY upon him, there was no clear path to safety, and he couldn't run any longer. Lost in prophecy, Graize stumbled to his knees, feeling the first of them score a line of fire across his back. With a surge of rage, he spun about and struck out at them with every ounce of strength and hate he still possessed. They would not steal his life away, not again.

◆

In the cami garden, Brax was the first to shake off the effects of the past. Blinking the rain from his eyes, he stared down at Graize for a long moment, wondering why, after six long years of dreaming about this moment, it felt so hollow. Maybe because his enemy lay so pale and still on the sodden ground. Maybe because Hisar, barely able to drag Himself forward and catch Graize up in His arms, looked so distraught. Maybe because Brax's own confused sensibilities kept insisting that this was a tragedy rather than a triumph. He glanced over at Spar.

His kardos sat beside them, heedless of the mud, hands in his lap, blue eyes flickering from white to black to white again. Blood, trickling from his right nostril, struggled to make headway down his upper lip before being washed away by the rain. A dispassionate part of Brax's mind noted that it was the same color as the blood washing down Graize's temple. Feeling as if his body were acting of its own accord, he watched his hands cut a strip of cloth from the bottom of his cloak and bind it around the other man's head. Then he turned.

"Spar."

His kardos ignored him.

"Spar."

"What?"

Brax paused, unsure of what to say now that he had some small amount of the other's attention.

"You're bleeding."

Spar's hand came up, smeared a line of red across his cheek, then he shrugged as the rain washed it away. "Hisar needed power," he said distantly, dropping his hand back into his lap. "It took me by surprise."

Brax gave a soft bark of laughter. "That wasn't the only thing, yeah?"

Spar glanced up, his gaze still misted by prophecy. "What do you mean?"

"All of this." Brax gestured. "You didn't see it. Graize didn't see it. That's . . . pretty amazing for two such powerful seers, don't you think?"

Spar's eyes cleared slightly as Brax's half-amused, half-accusing tone of voice cut through his reverie as little else could have. He scowled. "I knew Hisar had a plan, but I don't think even He knew all the details. That's the trick to blinding seers; you make decisions at the last moment. You know that."

"Hm." Brax looked unconvinced but dropped the subject. "So now what?" he asked, wiping his hands ineffectively on his cuirass.

His expression wan, Spar just shrugged. "I don't know. Ask Hisar. Like I said, it was His plan."

Brax turned. "Hisar."

The young God blinked rapidly, His seeming fading to a pale, nearly translucent gold. For a moment, Brax could almost see the cami wall right through Him.

"It hurt," the young God whimpered. "It hurt so much. I was whole and then I was shattered into bits." As He continued to fade, Graize began to slide from His arms, and with a concerted effort, He forced His physical seeming to steady.

Beside them, Spar closed his eyes briefly, his face paling to a sickly gray.

"And then I attacked him," Hisar continued so softly that they could barely hear Him. "Why did I do that, Spar?"

"I don't know," the youth answered wearily. "I didn't know you could do that."

"It felt like I was being torn into a million tiny pieces and the only thing those pieces could feel was hunger." The young God swallowed reflexively, His seeming growing gaunt and thin with the motion. "I was so hungry and so angry. I just wanted to feed and it felt like he could feed me, but he wouldn't and so I attacked him.

"And now I can't feel him on the inside at all," He added, His voice young and frightened and muted by the sound of the rain pelting against the garden all around them. "Did I lose him, Spar? Did I lose his oaths when I attacked him?"

His voice was close to panic and, with a slight groan, Spar forced himself to straighten. Closing his eyes, he pressed his hand against his chest, and Hisar shuddered as a renewed trickle of power passed between them.

"I can feel our lien," the youth answered. "And far away, I can feel his." He opened his eyes. "Just barely."

"So he's not . . . dead?"

"No."

"And his oaths are still there?"

"Reach for them Yourself. You'll see that they are."

"He feels so cold." Hisar blinked rapidly again as if trying to hold back tears. "He feels . . ." He glanced down suddenly, His expression confused. "How can I feel him physically, on the outside?" He asked, staring, wide-eyed, at the red bead hanging from Spar's neck. "How can I do that?"

"Because You're pulling power to stay in the physical," Spar answered weakly. "A lot of power," he added.

"I could never do that before."

"Yeah, well, I guess you never really needed to before."

"But I can't feel it. How can I pull power if I can't feel it? If I can't feel him?"

"Because You're pulling it from me, not from him."

"Oh."

Reaching over, Spar pried Graize's left eyelid up. "He's pretty far away," he noted. "His eyes have gone all white. That's probably why You can't feel him." He straightened. "He's run into prophecy."

"But where into prophecy?" Hisar insisted. "He hasn't got a dark place like you have."

"I dunno, then. Someplace safe, I guess." Spar sat back with a squelch of mud. "Did he ever have a safe place?"

"Like the shed on my site?"

"Yeah, like that."

Hisar shrugged. "He had lots of safe places. On the plains, at Cvet Tower, even in the wild lands. He was only ever not safe here where he was born."

"I mean, did he ever have a safe place in prophecy?" Spar expanded, ignoring the revelation. "Maybe not as fully made as my dark place, but like it?"

"I dunno." The young God's expression grew sad, then hardened as his gray eyes cleared. "Wait. He had that place in the Gurney-Dag Mountains where he built a kind of a cloak-net thing to fight the muting effect. That cave with the Petchan seer, Dar-Sayer. I couldn't get to him there." His shoulders slumped. "I guess he could have used the cloak and gone there. Maybe." A thread of pain feathered across His face. "He said he wouldn't be gone from Me, but he went where I couldn't reach him. Has he gone there again, Spar? Back to where I can't go? Why would he go there again? Why would he be gone from Me *again?*"

His voice sounded so hurt that Spar instinctively placed a hand on His shoulder. Hisar's seeming grew immediately stronger while Spar's features paled and, his own expression alarmed, Brax drew them apart as gently as he could. His lien with Estavia tingled against Spar's arm, and both he and Hisar blinked up at him as if they'd forgotten he was there.

"Because he's scared," Brax answered with as much sympathy in his voice as he could manage. "Because everyone runs when they're scared."

"You don't," Hisar replied.

"Only because I was trained not to. It doesn't mean I don't want to."

"Oh." The young God pulled Graize tighter into His arms. "What was he scared of, Brax?" He asked quietly. "Me?"

Brax searched Hisar's face for a long moment, then shrugged. "Probably," he answered. "You were pretty scary."

"I didn't mean to be."

"You should tell him that."

"How? He's gone from Me. And he won't listen to me anyway," He said sadly.

"So, go find him and make him listen." Brax swiped at his face with an impatient grimace. "But not here," he added. "It's pouring rain and we're about to be attacked by Volinsk. We need to get Graize under cover and see to his wounds." He craned his neck around. "The cami's the closest," he suggested. "Feridun'll be down here any moment. He can help us get him inside."

Spar shook his head. "It won't do. We need somewhere quiet where we can try to reach his mind and bring it back to his body."

"A cami's not quiet?"

The youth frowned. "I meant quiet of any God noise. It's a Havo-Cami. Graize'll feel the Hearth God and his mind won't come back there. It won't feel safe enough. We need someplace safe; someplace that doesn't have any God noise in it."

"Gerek-Hisar?

"Too many people."

"A hostel?"

"Again, too many people."

Hisar looked up. "We need My temple," He stated.

Brax's brows drew down. "Your temple's a hole in the ground," he reminded Him, but when Hisar threw him a scowl equal in strength to Spar's infamous dockside glare, he threw up his hands. "All right, we need Your temple." Straightening, he glanced over at Spar. "It'll be tricky," he observed. "It's a long way to carry a body . . . an unconscious, injured body . . ." he amended as Hisar's scowl deepened, ". . . in the rain, through a marketplace filled with panicking people."

"And across the Halic," Spar agreed. "Even if we could hire a boat, the whole area may be closed off by now. Are you *absolutely* sure that no place else will do, Hisar?"

The young God nodded vehemently, His expression growing more confident. "I don't have enough strength here. There's no tower symbols here or anything. I need to be at My own site. There're symbols there and offerings. Not from sworn people, maybe, but they're still offerings. And the people who made them are still . . . mine. They've made a connection with Me, a link. They'll bring Me strength. I can reach him if I have enough strength. I can feel it." He chewed at His lip in a very human gesture. "If we had to, we could ask Incasa or Havo for help again, I guess. Maybe. They might help us again. If we asked," He added in an uncertain tone.

"They might," Spar agreed with equal reluctance.

"Then it's settled," Brax interjected. "Whatever else we do when we get there, we make for the Halic." Reaching down, he lifted Graize from Hisar's arms. A faint moan escaped from the other man's lips as he hoisted him over one shoulder. "If nothing else, we can bind his wounds properly in a taproom and wait until the rain lets up before we head across. There'll be little enough God noise there."

He turned as Feridun emerged from the kitchen at a run. "We're done here, Ghazi. Take the troop and reinforce Gerek-Hisar."

His eyes wide, the older man looked about to protest, then jerked his head silently. As he returned inside, Brax headed for the gate.

Spar and Hisar were left sitting in the rain staring uncertainly at nothing until finally, the young God glanced over at the youth with a bleak expression.

"Should I stop being physical now so I stop pulling power from you?" He asked in a hesitant tone.

Spar regarded Hisar thoughtfully, sensing another question behind His words. "Are you scared of not being physical?" he asked after a moment.

Hisar looked away. "If I stop being physical, I might . . ." He swallowed again. "Shatter again," He whispered. "Do you think I might?"

"I don't know. I guess You better keep pulling power from me for a little while longer, at least until we get to Your temple site and all those tower symbols, yeah?"

"Will you be all right if I do?"

"All right?"

"I mean, you won't run from me, too, will you?"

Spar gave a weak snort. "No. *I'm* not scared of you."

Hisar's eyes narrowed with reluctant pique. "You didn't think I was scary?" He demanded, His voice less of a whisper now. "Even Brax thought I was scary."

"I'm your First Priest. You've never been scary to me." Spar rose with visible effort and tugged Hisar to His feet. "So, C'mon. We make for the Halic like Brax said."

"But . . ."

"Just follow Brax and it'll be all right, Hisar, really. Things are always all right when we follow Brax, Yeah?"

The image of two young lifters pelting down Liman Caddesi swirled about him as Spar tucked Hisar's shoulder under one arm, and he ignored it with a determined expression. He was nearly an adult now. The past didn't scare him any more than Hisar did, and neither one of them was going to control his actions. Slowly, he led Hisar toward the garden gate.

✦

Brax had made it to the far edge of the marketplace by the time they caught up with him, the sight of his sword and leather cuirass opening a path through the crowds and keeping the curious at bay. When they reached the Halic, they found the boat-master who'd brought Spar across the water huddled beneath a nearby wharf, trying to keep a clay pipe alight.

"Incasa," she said sourly in answer to the youth's questioning expression. Tapping the pipe bowl empty, she emerged with a grimace, one eyebrow raised at the sight of Brax's burden. "He dead?" she asked.

Brax shook his head. "Just hurt." As Graize began to twitch and shudder in his arms, he shifted him with a grunt. "And heavy."

"What about Him?" she added, gesturing at Hisar who all but hung off Spar's arm.

"Hurting."

"And also heavy," Spar added in a tired voice.

Tucking the pipe away safely, she gestured with her chin. "Get 'em both aboard as quick as you can, then you can help me cast off. Keep 'em toward the middle," she added as Brax set Graize into the boat as gently as he was able. He shifted slightly as Spar helped Hisar take His place behind them, and she nodded. "Take hold of that line there, Delin, and pull it free when I say. You got it?"

Spar nodded.

"Good. Then let's get going. I'd like to get home some time today."

"Me, too," Brax muttered.

They cast off into the waves.

✦

Once again, the spirits snatched Graize into the air, their desperate shrieking tearing at his mind as sharply as their claws tore at his body. He felt the icy blast of power that had protected him in the past hovering in the wings, but older now, he recognized its source as Incasa and, with a snarl, he knocked it aside. He would not be some God's pawn. He controlled his own destiny.

Once again he fought the spirits of the wild lands, but without the added strength offered by Incasa, he found himself weakening under their onslaught. Bleeding power from a dozen wounds at once, he fell out of prophecy and into the swirling maelstrom of the past.

✦

Havo's channel of calm was still in place, but it had narrowed dramatically, making this crossing much more difficult. The waves were high, slapping across the barge and threatening to flip it over, and the rain, which had begun to drive down like a thousand needles, scored their hands and faces. As they passed the heavy barge that labored to pull the sea chain across the Halic before the enemy fleet arrived, Spar glanced over at Hisar.

The young God sat huddled behind Graize, impotently clenching and unclenching one fist into the back of his abayos' jacket as Graize struggled in the throes of some inner conflict. Finally, Spar gently untangled Hisar's hand, laying it in His lap and covering it with his own. The memory of a mass of spirits swarmed across his mind when they touched, and he banished it with a scowl.

"Quit it!" he snarled and, responding instinctively to the command in his voice, Hisar relaxed a little.

In front of him, Spar watched Brax move to better support his old enemy, one arm across his back, the other across his chest, and the ghost of another memory swirled across Spar's mind: a confectionary shop wall, an angry, drunken man, and the feel of Brax's arms holding him secure. It left a trail of disquiet rather than comfort in its wake and he shivered, recognizing its meaning: the past was going to play itself out on this gray, stormy day, whether he liked it or not. It had already begun in the gardens of Havo-Cami with their fight on Liman Caddesi, and Graize looked like he was reliving the attack that had sent him hurling into the wild lands.

Except that things were different now, he considered. This wasn't the past. Hisar was a God now, nearly as powerful as the rest of Them, and Graize was one of His sworn. They were bound together by oaths of power and obligation, oaths that demanded a response when he was in danger or in pain. No wonder Hisar was so upset. His lien with Graize must be constantly pulling at Him to run to the rescue, but Graize himself was blocking Him.

Laying his hand against his chest, Spar felt his own lien with Hisar tingle against his fingertips. As much as he'd fought against giving oaths of any kind to any God, now, only nine months after giving them to Hisar, he was finding it hard to remember living without them. He wondered how Graize could have spent those same nine months ignoring his.

✦

The boat fetched up on the opposite shore as the alarm bell atop Lazim-Hisar changed from alarm tones just long enough to toll noon. As Brax hoisted Graize back onto his shoulder, Spar helped Hisar from the boat. Once the young God's feet touched the pebbled beach of His temple site, He grew visibly more substantial. A rumble of thunder sounded overhead, and He straightened, casting a nervous glance up the strait.

The boat-master chuckled. "You couldn't see that far even in good weather, Hisarin-Delin," she noted. "Don't fret. Our fleet will soon put paid to those filthy invaders long before they get this far."

The young God ducked His head in embarrassment. "I just like to see things for myself, that's all," He muttered.

Despite his burden, Brax gave an amused snort. "Typical seer."

Hisar frowned at him. "I'm not a seer," He retorted, indignation bringing his voice renewed strength.

Brax just shrugged. "You can see the future, can't you?"

"Sometimes."

"Then you're a seer."

"Maybe. But I'm *not* typical."

Brax rolled his eyes. "You're right; you're not typical. You're a God." He headed up the slope. As Spar made to follow, Hisar turned back to the boat-master.

"Um. Thank you," He said awkwardly.

She inclined her head. "You're welcome, Young One." She eyed Him critically. "Accept the strength of Your people to bring You success, and their weakness to bring you wisdom."

Hisar blinked at her unfamiliar phrasing. "How will weakness bring Me wisdom?" He asked with a confused air.

She chuckled again. "Other people's actions are like maps showing the placement of hidden shoals, Hisarin-Delin. They show you where not to sail as much as they show you where to sail. Now, help me cast off, will you? There's a woman with a hot cup of raki and a warm fire waiting for me and I want to slip past the chain-barge before it cuts me off from her."

With His newfound physical ability, Hisar helped push the boat back into deeper water, shuddering as the God-waters of Gol-Beyaz, even this close to the Halic, snapped at His feet with a buzz of unwelcoming disaffection. Quickly returning to shore, He watched as she fought the waves up the Halic, then turned and followed Brax and Spar to His temple site with a thoughtful expression.

✦

They surprised a figure sitting on a pile of marble at the near end of the foundation pit. She jumped up as they approached and Hisar recognized the youth He'd spoken to a few days before.

He gaped at her in surprise, then shifted to Her Rayne-seeming at once. "Did something else happen at the safe?" She asked anxiously.

The youth paused in mid flight, then shook her head, water droplets flying everywhere with the movement. "No. I just came for a quiet . . . think," she explained defensively, purposely not looking at the piece of tile lying by her foot. As Lazim-Hisar's alarm bells began again, almost directly overhead, they all winced.

"In the rain?" Spar asked.

The youth scowled at him. "Best time not to get interrupted. Usually."

Her gaze moved past Hisar to Brax. "He dead?"

"No. Just heavy." Carefully maneuvering Graize off his shoulder, Brax took the place she'd vacated with a sigh.

"You Spar?" she asked, turning her head just enough to keep them both in view.

He nodded wearily. "You're . . . ?"

"Kez."

"The one Hisar's been talking to."

"Yeah." She tipped her head to one side. "What're *you* doin" here . . . in the rain?"

Spar gestured at Graize with his chin. "Hisar says She needs Her temple site to make him better."

Kez raised one quizzical eyebrow. "Her temple site's a hole in the ground," she pointed out.

Spar raised a hand before Hisar could answer. "We know."

"Well, I'd say you need a warm, dry place more'n that or he's gonna die. I've seen that look before."

Brax glanced down. Graize's face was deathly pale. Pressing one hand against the other's chest, he felt the faintest trickle of warmth through the damp cloth of his jacket and, pulling off his cloak, wrapped it around Graize's shoulders before giving a sharp nod.

"So have I," he agreed. "She's right, Hisar. Since we've already decided not to let him die, we need to get him under cover." He glanced up. "Lazim-Hisar's the closest," he suggested without much expectation.

Her seeming flickering in and out of focus with the return of uncertainty, Hisar chewed at Her lower lip again. "No, It can't be there. I can't reach him there," She said, her voice tinged with panic. "And if I can't reach him, he'll still die. We have to be here on the grounds of My temple site. I can feel it. Could we get into the shed? He's injured, so by the rules, he's allowed, yeah?"

Kez frowned at Her. "Yeah, by the rules, sure, but it's not warm and it's not dry neither, the roof leaks in a dozen places."

"And there's no cover anywhere else here," Brax added gently.

Kez gave a snort worthy of Spar. "There's cover nearby. Why don't You just make your grounds big enough to include it," she said in a caustic voice. "That'd solve Your problem, wouldn't it?"

All three turned to stare at her.

"What?" she demanded. "All the other temples have way more land than this. And the city camis take extra land whenever they want it. It's not like anyone's livin" around here. You need a bigger site what includes a warm, dry building, just take it."

"How?" Hisar demanded.

"I dunno, just say it's Yours. Or have your priest there say it." She thrust a thumb at Spar.

"He can't just say Lazim-Hisar's mine," Hisar sneered. "It's too . . ." She struggled to put the half-formed explanation into words. "Big. I haven't got the power to hold onto something that big."

"I didn't say take Lazim-Hisar. Take another shed or a warehouse or . . ."

"The cistern."

They turned as Spar spoke.

"We've been trying to get there for days now," he added. "You said You saw us in the cistern, so that's where we have to go."

"Into the water in darkness," Hisar answered. A martial light lit up Her eyes. "Where the spirits are that tried to catch Me in My vision."

"And where You ate them," Spar added. He peered into the rain. "Ihsan said there was an entrance close to here."

"There is," Kez confirmed. "Just fifty yards north."

"Is fifty yards close enough?"

Hisar nodded. "It should be if I take the land in between, too—there's at least a dozen tower symbols in between I can draw on—but the cistern's even bigger than Lazim-Hisar. How'm I supposed to hold that with only two people sworn to me?"

"We don't take the entire cistern," Spar answered. "We just take the entrance. You have enough power for that, yeah?"

Hisar's countenance brightened at once. "Yeah."

Brax's brows drew down. "Won't the cistern be flooded out? You've seen the city fountains. They're spewing water like they were built in the middle of the Halic. How's that going to provide warm and dry?"

"There's laborer's alcoves that are protected from the floodwaters," Spar explained. "There should be one at every entrance."

Hisar nodded eagerly. "That's right. That's what I saw. I saw us in an alcove."

Kez glanced at Graize with a doubtful frown. "He's gonna need more than just crouching in some damp alcove. He's gonna need dry clothes and real bandages; that one's soaked through already. And food, maybe even medicine." She turned to Spar. "You got any money?"

He shook his head. "Go to Estavia-Sarayi. Tell Chamberlain Tanay what happened. She'll give you what you need."

Kez looked skeptical. "She'll trust me? Just like that?"

"On my word she will. But if you're worried, tell her Jaq can come back with you." His lips quirked up. "As a guard."

"Jaq?"

"My dog."

"Right." Once decided, Kez headed across the site at once and, a moment later they saw her scale the south wall and disappear into the rain.

Spar turned back to Brax. "C'mon, then. Let's get him under cover."

Brax nodded wearily. Rising, he lifted Graize up for the third time and, with Spar and Hisar in tow, headed for the cistern.

✦

Graize could not have said how long he fell before he hit the ground. A silvery flash of pain burst before his eyes, blinding him, and then there was nothing but icy cold, empty and echoing darkness. A pale, silver light shone at the end of a fine thread of power, but he turned his head away. He would not reach out for it. He would not ask any God for help; no matter who It was. Black water shimmered above his head, and he kicked out, heading for the surface, using his own dwindling strength with a harsh expression on his face. He would not ask any God for help; not even his own.

✦

The cistern's entrance was a small, nondescript set of iron railings built against the side of a nearby shipping warehouse with a flight of stone steps leading down to a stout wooden door. As Spar bent to study the brass keyhole with a professional air, Hisar shifted back to His golden-seeming, peering over his shoulder with an impatient expression.

"Is it locked?" He demanded, running His fingers absently over two tower symbols drawn on the railing.

Both Brax and Spar gave equally dismissive snorts, and the young God frowned at them, sensing that He was being made fun of. "What?" He demanded.

"We were raised to be lifters," Brax explained. "There isn't a civic lock in Anavatan we can't open."

"Maybe in the past, but you haven't been lifters for a long time."

"Once in, never kept out," Spar muttered. "One, two, done." The door swung open.

✦

Cold, damp air enveloped them as soon they stepped inside. The sound of rushing water echoed all around, blocking out the alarm bells. For a moment they feared the water would sweep them up, but the high wall that separated the entrance from the cistern proper protected them. Leaving the door ajar to provide some light, they made their way to a laborer's alcove off to one side. The young God moved toward the wall at once only to be brought up short by a loud cough.

He turned to see Brax gesture at Graize with his chin.

"Save first, fight later, yeah?"

Hisar nodded reluctantly. "Yeah."

Motioning Him to sit with His back against the wall, Brax laid Graize down gently, cushioning his head in the young God's lap. Laying his cloak over him, he crouched down and gently undid his makeshift bandage. "His head wound looks pretty bad, but now that he's out of the wet, it might have a chance to clot." Glancing down, he cut a slightly dryer piece of cloth from his tunic and rebound the wound. Then, moving cloak and jacket aside, he lifted Graize's shirt to study the pale flesh underneath. "There's only a little blood on his chest. That's good. I don't think I caught him all that hard, but I can't see if there's any bruising or swelling in this light. I guess we'll have to wait until Kez gets back." He covered Graize up again and, unbuckling his sword belt, set it to one side as he sat down beside him. "I hope Tanay thinks to send a lantern."

"She will. In the meantime . . ." Spar joined him. "Hisar needs to take the entrance as part of His temple site . . ." He paused as he felt the young God's lien draw another gout of power, then widen as he felt His influence extend to the laborer's alcove from His temple site. "And then we need to find Graize," he added weakly, once it was over.

"How?" Brax demanded.

"We start in the dark place."

"Good. Go. I'll stand watch."

Spar shook his head. "It's gonna take all of us."

"Why all of us?"

"Because Hisar saw all of us and because it started with all of us. Together."

"It?"

"Hisar's birthing into the world. Everything that's come since, the fight on Liman Caddesi, Graize going one way and us another, came out of that."

"I thought it started with Freyiz's prophecy and that was only about Hisar," Brax pointed out. "You know, It drawing strength from the unsworn on Havo's Dance and all?"

"With the twin dogs of creation and destruction crouching at Its feet."

"So?"

"So, that's probably you and Graize. Creation," Spar stabbed a finger at Brax, "and destruction." He pointed at Graize. "You know how prophecy loves symbolism. But even if it doesn't," he added before Brax could voice another protest, "Freyiz's vision wasn't the first one about Hisar. Elif had a vision before she came to Estavia-Sarayi. She told it to me on her deathbed." He drew himself up. "*A child, armed and armored, and a shimmering tower standing before a snow-clad mountain covered in a crimson mist.*" His voice echoed across the walls, temporarily blocking out the sounds of rushing water. "And Graize's earliest vision saw the two of you standing on that very same mountain. So, all of us. It's time we brought both those visions into being.

"Now, Graize has been thrown back into his fight with the spirits of the wild lands."

"Me," Hisar said in a painful whisper, clutching Graize to His chest in renewed distress.

"No, not You, a bunch of mindless spirits no different than the ones You defeat in Your vision." Spar jerked his thumb at the water behind the wall. "You're the God of Creation and Destruction. You gonna let a bunch of mindless spirits attack one of Your sworn, one of Your *priests?*"

Hisar glared at him. "No," He shot back.

"Then let's go save him."

"And we fight these spirits after?"

"We fight them after."

"'Cause I'm hungry, Spar." The young God's eyes glittered red in the faint light from the doorway. "And they're singing at Me. They want Me to come to them 'cause they think they can eat Me, but I'm gonna eat them, just like I saw in my vision."

"We fight them after."

"Sounds great," Brax interrupted. "But in the meantime, you two can get into this dark place of yours with no problem, but how am I supposed to get there?"

"It's a place of prophecy," Spar answered. "Of images and symbols. Hisar usually goes in wearing His tower symbol, you go in wearing your symbol."

"My . . . symbol?"

"You're the Champion of Estavia, aren't you?" Spar retorted, his voice dripping with sarcasm. "Her very most favorite ever since Kaptin Haldin, yeah? You've been having visions of him, so you go in through those visions as him."

"But I'm not a trained seer. I can't just call up a vision of Kaptin Haldin and step into it."

"Yes, you can."

"How?"

Spar rolled his eyes. "Don't be so thick," he snapped. "It's your vision. Take control of it like you would any other weapon. Practice stillness like Kaptin Liel tried to teach you last year, then pull it out of its scabbard and wave it around till you hit something with it."

Brax glared back at him. "Fine," he grated. "And assuming that works, how am I supposed to find this dark place of yours afterward?"

"Follow our lien." At Brax's mystified expression, Spar just shook his head. "People make liens with other people just like they do with Gods. Follow *our* lien, yours and mine; the one we made when Cindar handed me over to you and told you to take care of me." He gave a soft bark of laughter. "Are you trying to tell me that that wasn't the first oath you ever swore," he asked. "Protector of sickly, crippled little seer-lifters, protector of Anavatan, there's no difference." Loosening his shoulders, he closed his eyes. "We'll meet you on the beach."

Hisar caught Brax's gaze, His olive-skinned features so like Brax's own, glowing with a pale golden light.

"You'll need to take Graize," He noted.

"Take?"

A brief flash of irritation crossed the young God's face. "Spar goes in with his mind," He explained. "I go in as Me. As all of Me. He'll fall."

"Oh. Right." Shifting until his back pressed against the wall of the cistern, he accepted Graize into his arms. He draped his cloak over both of them, then blinked in surprise as Hisar abruptly vanished. Beside them, Spar also seemed to almost disappear into himself, leaving Brax feeling as if he and Graize were alone in the alcove.

He breathed out a long, doubtful sigh. "Right. Stillness. Kaptin Haldin. Sure."

Glancing about for a moment, he nudged his sword a little closer, then closed his eyes. Focusing on the feel of the consecrated weapon tingling against his leg, he remembered everything it meant to him since the day Kemal had gifted it to him, the day he swore his oaths to Estavia, then reached out along his oaths to the God of Battles, for his visions of Kaptin Haldin.

✦

And stood on a rocky promontory overlooking the City of Anavatan. Fountains sparkled in every marketplace, green-leafed plane and cinar trees shaded every courtyard. The sound of flute music issuing from a dozen inns and cafes mingled with the spicy aromas of fruit and fish and baking bread. To the north, the vast sweeping arches of the aqueduct brought a steady stream of fresh, clean, controlled water splashing into the reservoir. To the south, the six huge temple statues stood poised above the sparkling waters of Gol-Beyaz where the Gods reposed in the cool, silvery depths.

All was quiet, and prosperous, and safe.

But to the west, past the Gods' great Wall of stone and power, he could just make out a mass of storm clouds hovering above the wild lands, and beyond that, a black sand beach stretching out along a cold, churning ocean. Spar's dark place. Beyond that, a double flock of birds, one white, the other brown, wheeled about in the sky, getting closer at every turn. As the sound of hooves pounding across plains and grasslands shook the ground beneath his feet, an unwelcome voice whispered in his ear.

"The Wall will not stand."

He shook his head impatiently.

"Not now."

"He's already crumbling under the weight of it."

"I said. Not. Now."

Drawing the bejeweled weapon that Estavia Herself had gifted him with on the night he'd sworn his oaths to Her, he stepped forward into prophecy.

✦

And onto a cold, dark beach of black sand and jagged rocks. A dark-cowled figure and a tower made of smooth obsidian speckled with gold stood by the water's edge. As Brax moved to stand beside them, the waves crashed against the beach, splattering them all with surf until the figure raised one hand and the tower rose up to block the bulk of the water's fury. The cold, white moon shone just above its top battlements, causing a silver glow to dance across its surface.

The figure turned.

"Now, Hisar. Take the entrance in prophecy as well as in the world."

A shudder traveled up the tower's length as, very slowly, the moon's silver glow began to spread until it covered the entire beach. Beyond the dark place, Brax could almost see the city streets sparkling with the power of hundreds of tower symbols all leading to a small, nondescript set of iron railings built against the side of a shipping warehouse with a flight of stone steps leading down to a stout wooden door. It touched each one of them, absorbed the power of Spar's oaths, and then Graize's, then lapped against his lien with Estavia, testing it for a single moment, before ebbing back as Her Presence turned toward it, crimson eyes narrowed in warning.

Sheathing Kaptin Haldin's sword, Brax glanced over at the cowled figure.

"So, the three of us are here," he said, his voice sounding strangely disembodied in this place. "Now what?"

Spar wordlessly lifted his black net, and Brax raised one eyebrow in sudden amusement. "You're going fishing for Graize?"

Dropping the cowl onto his shoulders, his kardos shook his hair from its confines before shooting Brax one of his familiar dockside glares. "Just shut up and stay alert," he grated. Shaking out the net, he cast it into the water, watching as it slowly sank out of sight. He waited a moment, face tight with concentration, than began to slowly haul it back up from the depths.

Beside them, the tower seemed to shift its base more securely in the sand, then Hisar's voice, made much more resonant in this place, echoed across his mind.

"BE READY."

"For what?"

"FOR BATTLE."

"With who?"

"WITH GRAIZE. HE'S COMING."

15

The Cistern

*T*HE FIRST SENSATION THAT *reached Graize as his mind kicked upward out of prophecy was the sound of dripping water. He scrabbled through his memories, trying to identify its source. At first he thought he might be back in Dar-Sayer's cavern in the Petchan Mountains, the crippled oracle's soft, intrusive voice dredging up things that were best left forgotten. But there were no accompanying odors of damp clay and lamp oil. He was not in Dar-Sayer's cavern.*

The dripping water became the rhythmic pounding of waves against rocks and again he struggled to identify the source. The waves of the northern sea had beat against the rocks of Volinsk. But there was no accompanying sound of crackling fire and low, murmured conversation between Illan and Panos. He was not at Cvet Tower either.

Nor was he lying among the Yuruk listening to the waves splash against the shores of Gol-Bardak, or huddled together with Danjel and Yal as the rain beat against the sides of their sheep's hide tent in the midst of the wild lands. He was in no safe place of quiet respite.

As the pounding of waves became the crashing of surf, he opened his eyes and saw a black sand beach with a cold, white moon in the sky. With a scream, he flung his mind backward out of prophecy.

✦

"Watch it!"

In the dark place, Brax leaped forward as the net tore from Spar's hands, shredding under the force of Graize's reaction. The water at their feet exploded in a gout of spray, and as Brax jerked his kardos from harm's reach, it slammed into the beach, then sucked back to become a churning maelstrom of waves and power. Deep within its center, Graize rose on a column of gray smoke, his eyes blazing as white as Spar's were black.

Spar's power hit him in midair.

The force of their meeting sent violent shock waves pulsing out in every direction. Brax went flying as if he were still wearing a physical body, and Hisar rocked backward, as a slap of heat and steam followed in Its wake. The dark place buckled, split, then, as a huge rent tore across the beach, Graize punched a hole through into the physical world, reconnecting with his own body with a speed that made him gasp.

The pain of his injuries slammed into him, causing his body to jackknife in reaction. He felt arms around him, and for a single instant he almost gave in to the safety of their physical embrace, yet as he recognized who held him, he tore his mind away. But the damage was done. With his focus split, he lost control of the maelstrom. Waves of prophecy crashed over him, and he was swept under once again.

In the dark place, Graize disappeared under the waves. Hisar leaped forward, the tower seemingly disintegrating under the young God's distress.

"SPAR!"

"I see him!"

The remnants of his black net arched across the water, then fell, descending faster and faster through the waves until it found its target.

The net caught him up, entangling his arms and legs. He fought against it with every ounce of strength and ability he still possessed but, half in and half out of the physical world, he quickly began to weaken. The cold white moon of Spar's prophecy became the dawn sun of his own, but then he saw water sparkling in a cavernous darkness and, with a sudden shout of triumph, twisted his mind from the black net's grip and plunged into the spirit-filled waters of the great cistern.

The shock hit him like a blast of frozen air. A swirl of silver rushed toward him, and he stared, mesmerized, as it quickly coalesced into a swarm of surface spirits, razor-sharp claws outstretched toward him. He waited until they almost touched his cheek. Then, taking a great breath, he sucked them into himself,

using their tiny allotments of power to rebuild his focus. Revitalized, he hurled
them at the dark place with a wild shout of laughter.

✦

A huge flock of spirits came streaming through the rent, and Hisar reacted at once. Screaming in outrage at this invasion of Its territory, the
young God exploded into the air, taking the form of a vast and turbulent
electrical storm. The sky filled with black, pendulous clouds, lightning
streaking from one to another. Thunder crashed and the skies opened,
rain and hail poured down, shredding the lead spirits into a fine spray of
silver light, and driving the rest back through the rent.

✦

The spirits tumbled back, torn almost beyond recognition, but Graize was wait-
ing for them. Once more he caught them up, and sucking their power and their
prophecy into his own, he flung them at the rent again.

✦

Another swarm of spirits boiled through, and now it was Spar and Brax
who reacted. Catching up a handful of black sand, Spar hurled it at the
waves. The sand became a force of defending militia. With Brax in the
lead, they slammed into the invading creatures, and once again the spirits were driven back.

Only this time Hisar followed them through the rent like a bolt of
avenging lightning.

✦

The young God hit the waters of the cistern in a great spout of steam and
spray. Enraged from Its battle in the dark place, It thrashed about like an
angry whale, churning the water into a silvery froth, destroying what spirits It did not consume and hurling the fragments of their prophecy against
the walls without bothering to heed what they foretold. In the streets
above, water exploded from fountains and wells all over the city, flooding
into homes and shops alike while within, Graize's mind was snapped back
into his body with a force that nearly tore him from Brax's arms.

✦

Darkness rushed over Graize, gutting out all sensations save a great roaring in his ears that threatened to drown what remained of his sanity. He struggled to catch hold of any sight or sound that might anchor his mind, and very slowly the sound of dripping water came to him once again. He focused on the echo of each individual droplet until they became a single, golden light shining in the distant past. He fled toward the light, and the roaring grew fainter and fainter until it disappeared from his perception altogether.

✦

"He's gone limp!"

Shouting to make himself heard over the roar of Hisar's anger, Brax struggled to his feet on the black sand beach, his eyes half closed against the wind that howled from the rent. "I can feel it in the alcove! Do you think it's killed him?"

"No! He's gone to ground again," Spar shouted back.

"So, how're we supposed to get him again? I thought Hisar was supposed to reach him from His temple site?"

Spar gave his familiar one-shouldered shrug as the roaring changed pitch to become an undulating screaming, much like a battling tomcat might sound. "That was the plan!" he replied with heavy sarcasm.

"So what do we do now? Go fishing for him again?"

Wordlessly, Spar held up the tattered remains of his net. "You'll have to go after him!"

"Me? Why me?"

"Because he saw you!"

"He saw me *here!*"

"And he saw you in a doorway and he saw you on a mountain ridge! All his life he's been seeing you, but he's never been able to bring his visions into being! It's just about driven him mad! You have to go after him, find him, take him to that mountain—drag him if you have to—and make his vision come into being!"

"How? I don't even know where he's gone?"

"Start in the doorway!"

Brax shook his head in frustration. "You know I don't remember that!"

"You will when you go looking for it!" Spar's upper lip pulled up in a half-sneer, half-snarl. "And before you ask me how; you know how!

238 ◆ FIONA PATTON

Practice stillness, concentrate on one image, and grab the answer like a weapon! Simple!"

"Right, simple."

"Go back to the alcove!" Spar continued. "It'll be easier if you aren't trying to do two things at once! You share a prophetic link with Graize; it'll be stronger if you can feel him in your arms! Once you get hold of the link, just follow it right to him!"

"What will you be doing?"

Spar winced as the young God's screaming became shrieking and then roaring once again. "Bringing Hisar!" he shouted, clamping his hands to his ears with an impatient expression.

"Right." Brax glanced down at the rent boiling along the waterline with a tense expression. "Any other way to get back into the alcove?" he asked. "Other than going through that?"

"That's how Graize came in! That's how you go out!"

"Great."

"Just go!"

"Right." Stepping into the surf, Brax resisted the urge to shiver. The black water was just as cold and wet as he'd expected, even though a small part of his mind noted that neither the waves nor his body were actually physical so it shouldn't be either.

"Right," he muttered for the third time as the water reached to midthigh. "And I won't actually drown either when my head goes underwater."

Through the lien with his kardos—a lien he'd always felt but had never consciously thought about until now—he sensed Spar's disdainful amusement and, recognizing his own distraction, he shook it off with a disciplined gesture. He was going into battle now, however strangely he might be entering the field; now was not the time to be focusing on anything except duty.

Estavia's lien glowed warm and familiar inside him as the thoughts of battle aroused Her interest as always. It steadied his mind, and as the lien with Spar faded back to where it belonged, he returned his attention to pushing through the water. The waves reached his chest, his throat, his mouth. He forced himself to take one more step then, as they closed over his head, he threw the image of a ship's line out toward his physical body, following his oaths back to the real world as quickly as he was able.

✦

The sound of Hisar's roaring grew louder and more substantial as, one by one, each physical sensation returned to him. He tasted salt on his lips and smelled the odors of damp brick and stone in his nostrils. His hands and feet felt numb at first. Then, as a sharp biting tingling shot up his arms and legs, he jerked convulsively, almost dumping Graize off his lap. He caught him just in time. As the other man gave a faint moan at the movement, Brax peered down at him in the murky darkness.

Graize's face was almost translucently pale, his cheeks spotted with sweat and dried blood. He was shaking despite the cloak wrapped about him. Through his clothes, Brax could feel an unnatural warmth growing in his body. He shook his head. He'd seen enough battlefield injuries to know that Graize was slowly going into shock. If they didn't get him out of here soon, it would be too late.

He glanced over at Spar. His kardos sat peacefully, eyes closed, back against the wall, hands clasped loosely in his lap, maybe the faintest tracery of silver lights traveling across his features as if the spirits in this place were slowly building a caul about him . . .

A new tingling traveled up Brax's spine, and he shook the feeling off abruptly.

"Get a grip on yourself," he snapped, starting as his voice echoed across the alcove. "You're not a delos anymore and neither is Spar. He's sworn and just as capable of defeating these buggering creatures as Hisar is."

Behind him, the roaring in the cistern grew louder and he resisted the urge to crane his neck over the wall. Hisar was Spar's problem, not his. His was finding Graize.

Taking a deep breath, he tried to still his mind, concentrating on a single image: a doorway in the mist; a doorway he didn't remember, but had to remember, and slowly his limbs grew numb once again. As he reentered the black waters of Spar's prophecy, the roaring in his ears grew distant then finally faded away altogether. He sank quickly, a line of past experiences whispering along his face and through his hair like a trail of bubbles. He studied them carefully as they passed.

The earliest memories he'd ever been able to recall were those of rats scurrying about in the walls above his cot and the odors of raki and the damp, half-cured wool of a threadbare blanket that had never seemed to keep him warm enough. Although he would soon shove both memories into the farthest corner of his mind, he would never develop a taste for raki, and the sound of rats would always make him feel cold and anxious.

He followed these memories, ignoring the growing undertow that tugged against his legs, feeling the faintest understanding of another's presence laying beside him in the cot; smaller and warmer than he was. Too much smaller and too much warmer. He'd known that even then, although he'd welcomed the extra warmth.

The other had cried a lot. It had stirred something deep inside him that made him want to comfort and protect it; to drive away whatever was making it cry so that it could sleep in peace and safety. So they both could. But then the other had stopped crying, its presence had faded from his understanding, and he'd shoved its memory to the same far corner with the rats and the raki. So far that even when he'd had a second smaller and warmer presence to comfort and protect—Spar—he hadn't really remembered the first one. He'd just remembered being cold and anxious and failing someone and feeling them die.

He'd tried to comfort and protect every other presence that had come into his life since then. Sometimes he'd succeeded and sometimes he'd failed.

Newer memories bubbled past him. A dim and grimy room smelling of mold and blood. Their abayos, Cindar, standing over Spar; the man drunk and desperate, the boy feverish and in pain. Brax stood between them, fists raised, feet planted on the grimy floor like a shield wall made of strength and anger, the first hint that his lien to Estavia was both natural and almost predestined, blazing from his eyes.

Cindar had backed down, and Spar had recovered. Brax had won that fight.

Another memory: a bright and crowded street. Hiding behind the wall of a confectioner's shop, holding Spar, one arm across his chest, while Cindar, drunk and belligerent, faced down an abayos-priest and a troop of garrison guards. His choice loomed before him: if they moved now—right now—they could still get Cindar out of there, but it might put them—put Spar—in danger. His disgust at Cindar's drunkenness and his fear of Estavia's guards made a bitter taste in his mouth, but the fierce protectiveness that drove nearly every decision he'd ever made held sway. As Spar tried to dart around him to help the only abayos they'd ever known, he made his choice: he pulled the younger boy back and let Cindar die to protect Spar.

The undertow grew more insistent, and he let this trail of bubbles pass; they were not the memories he was searching for. Farther down lay the cold and frightening night he needed to remember. With a deep breath, he reached out for the latent tie that bound his destiny to Graize and followed it into the depths.

And found himself frightened and alone. The air was full of rushing wind and spattering rain, and the streets were covered in a gathering mist that harbored creatures of hate and hunger. They swirled along the cobblestones seeking the unwary with teeth and claws outstretched like knives.

At age four, Brax already knew how to keep the creatures in the mist from getting him. You never went outside at night during Havo's Dance. And if you were caught outside one night when your abayos, drunk and raving, had sent you out for more raki, you ran until you got inside again. You ran and you didn't look back and you didn't look down. You never looked down. If you looked down, you would see them and they would see you, and that was how they got you. That was how they killed you.

So he'd run for a rag-and-bone shop he'd known was never locked. The owner was a drunkard like Cindar and never remembered to close his door properly. A man had seen him running, an abayos-priest of Oristo, protected from the creatures in the mist by his oaths to the Hearth God and driven into the storm by another God, Incasa. Brax's twenty-one-year-old eyes could see that plainly now, and far away, he felt Spar's recognition as well. But then he was swept back into the past. The priest had called out and given chase, but taught to fear Oristo's people even more than the creatures in the mist, Brax had kept on running.

He'd felt another child's presence in the doorway before he'd seen him, felt his desperation and his fear and the stirrings of an unnatural and familiar warmth growing in his body. Brax had nearly run right into him. But then he was past, the door was open, and safety beckoned. He'd turned to drag the other child inside, but then the priest had been upon them. The boys' eyes had locked together, the image of two figures standing on a snow-clad mountain ridge had flashed between them and then the other child was swept away and Brax had slammed the door and bolted it, safe for another night.

✦

The memory had sunk down to the same corner with the rats and the raki, its effects trickling into his actions like a line of bubbles unregarded in the darkness.

Brax stared into its midst, locking it in his adult memory, then deliberately turned and walked out the door again. He was not a delos anymore, he repeated to himself. He was a man, a warrior, sworn to the God of Battles and like Spar, fully capable of defeating the spirits that lay harbored in the gathering darkness. Most especially the spirits of memory.

Pulling his sword, he felt Estavia's lien shoot down his arm and streak along the consecrated weapon like a bolt of fire. It leaped almost joyously from the blade and smacked into the mist, vaporizing the spirits hidden within it in a hiss of steam. Then, holding it before him like a lantern, Brax stepped out into the storm, following the trail of prophetic bubbles left by the abayos-priest and his three-year-old burden, moving toward a single, golden light that shone from the depths of Graize's past now instead of from his own.

✦

Deep in the darkness, Graize fought his own battle with the spirits of memory.

He'd been cold and hungry and desperately afraid. He'd been outside, and it wasn't safe to be outside. The sun had been going down and the wind had been coming up and the rain had driven against his face until he couldn't see where he was going. He'd stumbled into a doorway, crouching there until the dark-haired boy had come, leading the man in yellow who'd carried him away. He'd been too cold to struggle, too frightened to cry out, but he'd reached for the boy with his mind and his latent abilities had forged a link with him before the iron gates of the Tannery Precinct's Oristo Cami had blocked his view of the first person who'd ever tried to protect him.

But he'd never forgotten him. He reached out for him in the darkness, year after year, feeling the other's growing strength and taking comfort from it. It was only after he'd found him protecting another boy on the Western Dockside streets that he'd turned away from that strength to face a cold and echoing emptiness alone.

But that was not this memory, and his mind rejected it out of hand. In this memory he dozed in a corner of the cami's shabby central chapel; five years old and charged with the evening duty of tending the few candles the priests were willing to burn after dark during the three stormy nights of Havo's Dance. Unlike the rest of the orphans under their care, Graize had schooled himself to deny the urge to crouch beneath the candles while the rain battered against the shutters and the winds howled about outside, tearing tiles off the roofs and hurling them into the gardens beyond. He never clung to the false security their flickering lights afforded. He knew the spirits pooling outside the cami walls couldn't get him here, and so he knew there was no real danger hidden in the chapel shadows just as he knew that some day he would have to face those spirits and defeat them. His growing prophetic abilities had told him that, but they'd also told him that he would not be facing them alone. The dark-haired boy would be facing them with him.

In the alcove, Graize's body twitched violently as this realization flooded back into his mind.

And, standing beside him in the memory, Brax watched him remember. Five-year-old Graize's fingers twitched in the throes of some prophetic dream, tapping a steady rhythm against his thigh, but he otherwise remained absolutely still and quiet. As gently as he was able, Brax reached out along their link to touch his sleeping mind. The scents of incense and mildewing wood filled his thoughts, but behind them, he saw himself as Graize was seeing him: as a dark-haired boy, armed with a sturdy wooden sword and shield. He watched himself draw the other boy to his feet and guide him toward the future up a narrow minaret staircase. Brax followed them and found Graize's one safe place of prophecy that Spar had spoken of.

Watching the two boys leaning over the edge of the minaret, Brax nodded his understanding. No wonder Hisar had been unable to feel Graize in this place. This memory had been created long before Graize had screamed his oaths of possession and jealousy into the wind; long before he'd fashioned a God-child from the spirits of the wild lands, and long before those spirits had attacked four unsworn delon beneath a wharf on Liman Caddesi. If Hisar was going to reach him, Brax was going to have to draw Graize out to a place where his relationship with the young God already existed. But a place without the memory of a ten-year-old Graize coming upon his dark-haired protector standing by the side of another boy that should have been him and wasn't. Otherwise, they'd just have to start all over again.

Far away in the alcove, he felt Graize shudder through their link and eased back carefully.

"Two figures standing on a snow-clad mountain ridge."

Spar's voice echoed down their lien, and Brax grimaced at it.

"I know," he muttered back at it.

"A child armed and armored, and a shimmering tower strong and defensible, standing before a snow-clad mountain."

"Like I said, I know. Piss off. We'll be there. You just make sure you bring Hisar."

Closing his eyes, he stepped forward into Graize's image of the dark-haired boy, feeling a strength and a confidence that he himself had never possessed at that age. With a sweep of his wooden sword, he laid out the vision they'd shared in the cold waters of Gol-Beyaz the day Hisar had taken His first steps into the physical world; the vision Graize himself had denied until today. It streamed out between them with an eerie double-visioned quality as both of them relived the memory for the first time together, seeing it through the clarity of their childish eyes, untainted by the rivalry that was to come.

The enemies of Anavatan rose up before them, and Brax saw himself a man, armed and armored, taking the field against them.

The enemies of Anavatan rose up, and Graize saw the dark-haired boy, armed and armored, taking the field against them.

Brax saw a figure on a white pony raise his hand in battle and knew it to be Graize, but Graize as he'd never seen him before, clear-eyed and armed with steel and stone.

Graize saw himself on a white pony raise his hand in battle, but himself as he'd never been before, clear-eyed and armed with steel and stone.

The vision steadied to become a snow-capped mountain ridge overlooking two fleets of ships while a man in a red tower moved wooden figurines on a painted board of mahogany and mist and a woman with golden hair danced in the surf below.

Graize's later memories bubbled up around them, drawn forward by the instability and anger of his adulthood, intent on filling in the preceding years. Brax felt his grip on the vision slipping as he scanned the mountainsides for any sign of Spar and Hisar, but the horizon remained dark and empty. As the vision began to fail, Graize's later prophecies forced their way to the surface. The ridge disappeared behind a crimson mist, the air felt heavy and portentous, smelling of blood and salt as the dawn sun rose above them like a fiery insect, revealing its true prophecy: the discovery of their plans by Prince Illan of Volinsk.

Brax pointed his small, wooden sword at the image as steadily as he could manage and behind it, he saw the future—saw the present—the faintest image of a child with hair the color of ripening wheat and a shimmering tower battling an army of spirits in a cavernous darkness. Alone.

Brax threw his hand to them at once, but before he could reach them, the spirits rose up, a terrible roaring filled his ears, and the image winked out of sight. The mountains disappeared into an enveloping fog, alarm bells sounded, a woman's warning echoed in his ears, a man with eyes as fathomless as the sea moved flocks of birds upon a painted table while a white-clad king sailed ever closer to four figures surrounded by water sparkling in a cavernous darkness. As the roaring became screaming, the fog became a rain-splattered doorway, and he and Graize clutched at each other as they might have done years before. The sound of wings became the snap of sails against the wind and both boys pressed their hands against their ears to keep out the present as much as the past.

✦

A mile away out on the water, Illan stood on the forecastle of the Volinski flagship, a faint smile playing across his lips. Behind him, the blue-gray cliffs of the Bogazi-Isik Strait fell away while before him, the fog lifted slightly to reveal the watchtower of Gerek-Hisar at the southernmost tip of the Northern Trisect. One third of the fleet broke formation at once, heading in that direction, while the rest carried on south. As the sound of alarm bells echoed across the water, he could just make out the distinctive forms of Anavatanon penteconters moving to intercept them.

Seconds later, a scout in the flagship's fighting top sang out a warning that was quickly taken up by the rest of the fleet. Archers hurried past him into position on the forecastle as their bow officer made for the fire urn, a pot of glowing coals held protectively in his hands. On the sterncastle, the fleet's commander, Prince Pieter of Rostov, stood surrounded by court sorcerers, listening with his head cocked to one side as they spoke their prophecy for the coming battle, the pilot and captain awaiting his word.

Illan gave a soft snort before calling up the image of his atlas table, the silver-and-blue-painted Gol-Beyaz situated in the exact center now that they were across the sea. Under his control, the pieces began to move in the complicated dance of present and future possibilities, each one taking on a more appropriate symbolic form than the carved wooden tokens that represented them in the physical world.

The bronze-cast dromon galleys of Volinsk moved into position in a double wedge of power, while the polished white marble Skirosian triremes spread north, their beaklike rams glittering just below the waterline. Caught between them, the shallow-drafted, onyx-carved penteconters of Estavia struggled to hold two lines of defense at once. Meanwhile, hundreds of tiny horse-backed figures made of twisted grass thundered down upon a force of mounted warriors on wooden horses and stone-carved militia stretched too thin along the western shoreline.

And from one end of Gol-Beyaz to the other, the six silver figures of Anavatan's Gods winked in and out, Their strength divided, as Their followers called to Them from every front to help defend their homes and lands. Just as Illan had predicted, he thought with a chuckle, the might of the Gods negated by Their own followers.

With one last glance to ensure himself that the God of Battles in particular had been called away from the northern strait by the danger to the south, he set this prophecy aside, and called up the image of a fog-enshrouded cavern, ringed by mountains. Four pieces moved across the board in their own, prophetic dance. But no less predictably, he noted as he studied them, his upper lip curling in disdain.

The golden tower had taken its turn prematurely and, unseasoned and immature, the youngest member of Anavatan's pantheon had swiftly found Itself surrounded by enemies. It would soon fall and Its unrealized potential would wash into Gol-Beyaz to be consumed by Its own kind.

With one motion, Illan knocked the tower on its side.

Its black-clad champion would fare no better, he mused. Heedless of anything save his own prophetic strength, Spar had failed to recognize the thread of weakness in his past—a thread Illan himself had exploited years ago—his terror born on the mist-covered cobblestones of Liman Caddesi. All spirits, be they storm-formed creatures of the wild lands or lake-fed Gods retaining thousands of worshipers, recognized this kind of weakness and preyed upon it.

It would be no different this time.

The black-clad piece was knocked down in its turn.

On the mountain ridge, Hisar's silver champion sworn to another God had already fallen, unable to master the skills needed to fight in a prophetic war. Only one move would save him as it had in the past, but Brax was afraid to make it, afraid to call on Estavia for fear his own weakness would turn Her gaze away from him.

The silver piece joined the others on its side.

That left only Graize.

Illan chuckled to himself. The hidden element that was only hidden from itself and the piece on which every other outcome hung. Illan's final move.

Graize's madness blazed like a beacon in the night, warping his prophecy and hiding all but the single path that led to retribution. If the golden, black, and silver pieces did not defeat themselves, the gray piece would be brought in to finish the endgame. It hardly mattered that it would destroy the gray piece as well. All that mattered was the destruction of Anavatan's power base.

Illan turned and, as the flagship's bow officer gave the order to fire, he swept the image of the atlas table away and concentrated on the coming battle. All was as it should be. The endgame would be no different. He had seen it all.

16

The Mountain Ridge

IN THE CISTERN, IN the seeming of a huge, golden shark, Hisar thrashed the waters into a churning froth as Its frustration grew. The upper sprits had fallen so easily; all It'd had to do was suck them up in much the same way as It had the spirits in the aqueduct trough above Havo Cami. But, where those spirits had fed Its hunger with a bright, sparkling power that made It want to soar into the clouds, these spirits just made It feel bloated and sluggish; as waterlogged as they were. The more It ate, the emptier It felt, and the angrier It became. It was not supposed to be this way; Its vision had showed It eating them; It was *supposed* to eat them. Slapping Its tail back and forth across the surface of the water, It flung a new spray of upper spirits against the walls, all the while roaring in increasingly impotent hunger.

Below, the under spirits began to rise in response to the violence above them. Sucking up the shattered bits of their lighter kindred, they used the extra power to move silently toward the young God, their fine claws outstretched and their mouths agape to reveal rows and rows of glittering teeth. Coming together into one vast school, they picked up speed, then attacked.

Hisar caught sight of them at the last moment, Its golden eyes silvering in surprise, but before It could react, the swarm was upon It. A dozen struck Its face while the rest rushed toward Its body, striking here and there, then breaking off—trailing long, thin lines of the young God's power in their wake—before regrouping to strike again.

Enraged, Hisar spun about in the water, Its seeming changing to that of a huge water snake. Sucking up a great mouthful of spirits as Graize had taught It, It drove Its teeth into their ethereal bodies, then snapped Its head back, spitting their allotments of prophecy out in a spray of silver light.

Some of the under spirits followed the line of carnage, but hundreds more swarmed up to take their place and Hisar felt Its seeming warp under the pressure of their assault. It resisted, fighting the almost overwhelming urge to take on the same shape as Its attackers, until a sharp pain snapped Its attention down to a tiny spirit—all teeth and shimmering copper claws—with its head buried in Its flank like a leach. Hisar tore it away, watching in growing horror as a fine, twisted tendril of gold-and-copper droplets trailed off behind its shattered body.

The under spirits fell on it at once, tearing it into the finest shreds in their frenzy to lap up this bright, new power, then spun about, seeking their copper-speckled kindred and driving them toward the young God in a single, solid mass.

Hisar jerked back in fear. Its rising panic caused Its seeming to warp still further and, as Its physical manifestation began to come apart, Its mind shot from the cistern, separate for the very first time and desperately seeking help.

✦

In the dark place, Spar was knocked to the ground as a tower of golden fire exploded into the air, painting the sky with a blast of crimson flame and fusing the black sand beach into a mass of onyx glass. Struggling to his feet, he gathered up his power and flung it down the lien toward Hisar, then followed, diving headfirst into the boiling surf.

And plunged into a frigid world of froth and violence. Silver-and-copper lights swirled all around him, teeth and claws flickering in and out of their midst too fast for him to focus on. He saw Hisar enveloped in a cloud of spirits and, as he reached for Him, the nearest turned toward him, their silvery gaze awash in feral hunger. For an instant they hung frozen in the grip of Spar's prophetic ability, then, as Hisar's need shot down the lien, they followed it.

Spar went down under their onslaught and, as the first of the spirits tore into his mind, he fled down his original lien with Brax.

✦

They collided with a force that flung Brax off his feet with a cry of pain. As Spar and Hisar's combined peril caused an involuntary pulse of red-and-orange power to shoot from his chest and down the lien, his grip on Graize's prophecy snapped. Graize was thrown down one side of the mountain path to slam into a future of fog and rain, while Brax was catapulted backward down the other side to land, sprawled and insensible, on a night of violence and death, four figures struggling on the storm-lashed cobblestones of Liman Caddesi.

In the alcove, Brax's physical body jerked in reaction, a fine welling of blood rising between his lips to spill out and down his chin, and as he slumped, Graize's eyes snapped open, the left significantly more dilated than the right.

✦

Graize's vision swam in sickening circles as his mind fought to maintain a single time frame. One moment he was three, crouched in a doorway with the dark-haired boy in a memory that had never been, then five, standing beside him on Oristo-Cami's single minaret in a memory that had.

He was fifteen, being dragged from the waters of Gol-Beyaz by Panos of Amatus Then he was ten, watching Brax put his arm around Spar's shoulders on the western docks.

He was nineteen, raving and screaming in the wild lands.

He was thirteen, ignoring Drove who glanced nervously up at a sky filled with dark and ragged storm clouds.

In the alcove, His twenty-year-old body shook with a combination of shock and damp, his head injury throbbing up his temple, while on the streets of memory, a three year old's terror caused his heart to pound painfully in his chest.

The years piled onto each other, then pulled apart like twists of wool, the earliest entangling in the later, but throughout, a roaring, scream of pain and need hammered at his mind. He followed it to a place of power and obligation, created on the plains of the Berbat-Dunya, and stumbled back onto the mountain ridge before a shimmering tower that shifted from gold to silver to gold again.

He shouted Its name into the rising wind.

"HISAR!"

The word echoed all around him, throwing up a host of memories to spin around him in a swirling maelstrom of images and feelings and, as he sucked them back into his mind, he felt them reattach themselves in proper order.

Riding behind Kursk, gathering up the flock of lights that had followed him from the wild lands; weaving and binding each tiny spark of consciousness together under the pressure of their guidance until he'd fashioned them into a crude, human-seeming.

The bargain he'd struck with that seeming, pointing to the wavering image of a child of unformed potential hovering behind a dark-haired man surrounded by a host of silver swords, and speaking his first words to It: "That one, give me that one." And feeling Its ready and eager compliance.

Standing before Danjel and a host of Yuruk youth, answering the demand: "What can you do?" with "I can make a God," while above him the human-seeming made of lights grew brighter and brighter with his promise of strength and power.

Standing in the saddle on the blood-soaked ground before Serin-Koy, summoning a Godling, formed and ready to go into battle for the first time. Watching It streak from the clouds with all the speed and power of a blazing comet, feeling It flowing around him and through him, and watching It envelop his enemy in a mass of teeth and claws.

And orchestrating the final, violent stage of Its birthing on the battlements of Estavia-Sarayi.

Throughout, his and Hisar's lighter moments together wove through each memory like golden threads in a tapestry.

Climbing the rocks before Cvet Tower with the Godling draped about his neck, and running his fingers along Its shimmering flank to feel It rumble back at him in sleepy contentment.

Watching It cavort across a rainbow and spin lazily about a tent pole in the Gurney Dag Mountains, and flying with their minds as one, above the sparkling indigo length of the Terv River at sunset.

The darker moments wove throughout these memories as well.

Crouching in the rain and mud at Chalash with the Godling shrieking and shuddering in his arms and rocking It back and forth, keeping up a constant flow of comforting words and snatches of half-remembered lullabies until It calmed.

Catching It just before Its immature body disintegrated at the entrance to Dar-Sayer's cavern and cradling It in his arms again, his new protective cloak wrapped about It like a balm.

Seeing It take the seeming of his oldest enemy, staring up at him in mute entreaty with Brax's wide, dark eyes dull with the memory of pain.

Having that enemy helpless before him, raising his knife, and having the Godling leap between them, screaming out the possession It had carved without him.

"*Mine!* Mine, Mine, MINE, MINE, *MINE!*"

On the mountain ridge, the echo of Its words rose to a shrieking crescendo, flooding his mind and body with another memory, the memory of the Godling's pain the day that Spar's sudden oaths had forced It to manifest in the physical world before It was truly ready. The Godling had slammed into Graize with a force that had knocked them both to the ground, and as the memory played out once more, Hisar's voice thundered across the mountains.

"*IT HURTS! MAKE IT STOP! YOU PROMISED YOU'D NEVER BE GONE FROM ME AGAIN! MAKE IT STOP!*"

And the words he'd screamed as the image of Spar's oaths had swept over him ricocheted across the mountainsides.

"*No! He can't have you! He won't have you! You're mine! Only Mine! My God!*"

The sky above him caught fire as his earlier vision swept over him again. The air grew heavy and portentous as the dawn sun prepared to soar over the horizon. Far away water sparkled in a cavernous darkness, and in that darkness Hisar screamed in pain and fear. The lien they'd forged on the grasslands burned with a silver fire that tore through Graize's body like lightning, and through it all Hisar's voice hammered against his mind like a battering ram.

"*IT HURTS! MAKE IT STOP! MAKE IT STOP! HELP ME! HELP ME! HELP ME!*"

"YOU PROMISED YOU'D NEVER BE GONE FROM ME AGAIN!"

In the alcove, Graize's body spasmed from the force of Hisar's cry, while on the mountain path, he was thrown to the ground. He scrabbled about, frantically searching for anything that might regain his control, and suddenly his physical hands found Brax's body lying slumped against the cistern wall.

His mind slid easily down the all-but-forgotten link they'd forged sixteen years before. As the innate strength of the other man—the strength that had reached out to Graize all his life in the seeming of the dark-haired boy—flowed between them, the deepest part of Graize's mind, empty for so long, suddenly filled and calmed. The chaos of his inner thoughts stilled, fashioning a path of stability and sanity that began in a mist-enshrouded doorway and snaked along a snow-clad mountain ridge and off into the future. The path winked in and out of focus as anger and desire in equal measure battled for Graize's decision. Then, with a scream of his own to match Hisar's, he tore Brax from the past and, throwing his protective cloak over them, hurled both their minds off the mountain ridge and into the frigid darkness of Anavatan's cistern.

✦

They hit the water with an explosion of power that sent another gout of spray and spirits shooting from the city's fountains to flood across the streets in a purely physical reaction.

Graize's mind was the first to recover. With his eyes as wild as the mass of creatures around him, he shot to the surface, taking in the tableaus before him in a single instant.

To one side, the mist-covered streets of Liman Caddesi undulated in the water, its hold over their memories giving it added solidity in this place of power. Beneath the wharf, Spar struggled to keep his footing, while hundreds of spirits, in the guise of their stronger wild land cousins, swarmed about him like a mass of angry bees.

For a single heartbeat, Graize considered leaving him to his fate, but with Brax's strength still coursing down their mended lien, he saw the future stream created by such a decision stretched out before him with almost painful clarity.

And he saw who it would benefit most, a man in a red tower moving wooden figurines on a painted board of mahogany and mist.

Illan of Volinsk.

The memory of his time with the northern sorcerer played out before him just as swiftly. Illan had instructed him in the ways of his people's prophecy, but always with an agenda. Graize had known that, but with an agenda of his own driving him, he'd accepted it; he controlled the game and the game's outcome had always been to defeat Brax and Spar.

But he'd also known that had never been the outcome of Illan's game. As the atlas table wavered in the waters before him, he watched the ghostly figurines of armies, navies, and Gods move to the pattern set out by the prince's ambitions alone. And he saw the pattern set out by the four figures that represented himself and the others. Illan's outcome had always been the defeat of Anavatan, but hidden within that outcome was the single move that would see it done: the defeat of Hisar by using Graize as a pawn, his single-minded drive to hurt Brax at all cost blinding him to every other possibility.

In the farthest corner of his mind, he heard Panos' voice.

"It's said among the Skirosian oracles that prophecy is like a broken mirror, showing everything there is to see except oneself.

"The element which hangs in the balance is not shrouded at all, beautiful one. It's you. How easily swept aside do you think it is now?"

"Not swept aside at all, Panos," he acknowledged. "But taken up and wielded like a weapon. But you're right. The mirror needs to be mended first. And then looked into with every ounce of prophetic strength available."

He returned his attention to the atlas table, watching four familiar figures moving in obedience to Illan's prophecy and falling, one by one, to the floor. A hitherto unseen future stream hovered in the background and, buoyed up by the power of Brax's strength still flowing along their lien, he reached for it.

✦

And smelled the pungent aroma of wet clay as he found himself in Dar-Sayer's cave in the Gurney-Dag Mountains. The Petchan sayer had also instructed Graize in the ways of his people's prophecy, but his agenda had been no more than a simple bond of obligation and the curiosity to see what his words would draw forth.

"You pass from moment to moment, ally to ally, cause to cause. What is it that you truly want; what motivates your blood to stir in your veins?"

In the cool, mental silence caused by the mountain's muting effect, Graize had paused to consider the question seriously. What did he want? The answer, however unwelcome, had been simple enough. He'd wanted Brax. Then and now. Boy and Man. But whether he wanted him alive or dead was still uncertain, now as then.

THE SHINING CITY ✦ 255

Graize studied the memory with a frown, his new stability causing him more confusion than clarity. When had it become uncertain, he wondered?

His own words came back to him.

"When are you gonna walk away from that fat piss-pot and the little cripple and make some real shine?

"I've seen it. A long time ago in a dream. I saw the two of us ruling the streets together.

"So, don't go too far. I'll only have to come and find you."

And on the cobblestones of Liman Caddesi—the same street that wavered in and out of the waters now—he'd almost screamed at Brax to run, to save himself for the future he was certain they shared.

That he was *still* certain they shared. But to remain focused, to remain strong, he'd driven every other possibility from his mind the night he'd been snatched away by the spirits of the wild lands.

As the mental chaos struggled to return, he shook his head impatiently. No wonder Panos had seen it so clearly; no wonder Illan had believed he could manipulate it so easily. The way to blind a seer was to act unpredictably, and he had been about as predictable as the dawn.

Time to change that. As the sun of his vision began to force its way into the cistern with his revelation, Graize dragged Brax to the surface, one hand bunched in the front of his tunic and hit him a blow across the face that snapped his head back. As an ethereal line of blood welled up from his cheek, Graize bared his teeth at it, daring it to distract him. He raised his fist to strike again, and Brax's eyes fluttered open. The other man squinted at him groggily as the years flipped back and forth between them, then Graize spun him about and hurled him toward Spar.

The two collided with a crash, sending the spirits about the youth flying in every direction, but they quickly regrouped and attacked again, filling the ethereal streets of memory with a broiling, blood-flecked mist.

As Spar snapped into a fetal position, arms wrapped about his head to protect his face, Graize felt the youth's own memory of that night, a memory he'd never shared with anyone, not even with his kardos, sweep down the link they now shared with Brax.

✦

He was cold and he was frightened. All his short life he'd known which way to turn, but with Cindar's death, there was nothing but darkness and danger all around him, so he'd blindly followed Brax as they'd run for the uncertain safety of an unturned fishing boat under a wharf on Liman Caddesi.

He should have seen Graize and Drove before they practically crashed into them. He should have seen the spirits amassing in the shadows. He should have seen Drove flung about like a rag doll, the deadly shroud of spirits latched onto his body like misty lampreys. He should have seen Graize catch him by the back of the jacket and spin him into the street. He should have seen it. He should have stopped it. But he hadn't.

He hadn't seen Brax lift Graize into the air with a strength born of desperation and hurl him into the midst of the attacking spirits. But he had heard Graize's scream.

He still heard it in his dreams to this day.

He hadn't seen the midnight silhouette of the ruby-eyed figure wavering in and out of the darkness. Or seen the future stream appear as the figure reached for Brax and he'd reached for It. But he had felt Brax's arms wrap about him as the older boy had tried to protect him from the spirits with his own body. And he had heard Brax cry out the words that had summoned a God, "Help us!"

He still heard that in his dreams as well.

But in this place and in this time there was no midnight silhouette and no summoning words to drive the spirits away; there was only the darkness and the danger that had surrounded him before.

His prophetic ability darted back and forth, desperately seeking a clear stream to navigate into until the strangest thread of power he'd ever felt trickled through his mind along a link he'd never expected it to come from, a thread of bronze-cast bells and marbled prophecy. It drew up another thread that tasted of gilded feathers and honey-sweet intrigue and, on that thread he found the stream of memory he'd been seeking.

"Who will you bring to stand against the white king and the fathomless prince?"

He bared his teeth triumphantly, recognizing the memory.

"I will bring my family."

As the laughter became light, he followed it to a familiar chapel in the heart of Estavia-Sarayi and remembered.

He hadn't seen Kemal and Yashar in the seer's shrine the night that he and Brax had fought the spirits on Liman Caddesi either. But he had heard the story from every one of his self-styled abayon in Cyan Company. How they'd dropped to their knees, weapons across their palms, offering their worship and their service through Kemal to the God of Battles. How the bells from Anahtar to Lazim-Hisar had tolled, calling on the rest of Her Warriors to join with them, and how She'd responded even before the Invocation was complete, knocking Kemal off his feet and sending sprays of power shooting through the shrine like a thousand wicked little knives. How, with blood pouring from a dozen tiny cuts across his face and neck, he'd scrambled to find his sword, and how Yashar had retrieved it for him, wrapping his arms about his arkados and hauling him to his feet, the strength of his arms and the strength of his love flowing into the other man almost as heatedly as the strength of Estavia Herself. And how, together, they had called the God of Battles to a full physical manifestation on the streets of Anavatan.

Spar had counted on that strength just as he'd counted on Brax's ever since; holding on to it with an absolute, unshakable certainty that they would always stand beside him.

Always.

Taking a deep breath to more fully focus his intent, Spar shot down the lien toward the two men waiting in the central shrine.

✦

Kemal was the first to react. Shouting in surprise he nearly fell over backward as Spar's need slammed into his mind. His hand flew out, catching Yashar by the shoulder and, as the older man's steadying influence shot down their own lien, he righted himself.

"Spar!" he gasped.

Yashar's hand clamped down on his arm. "How do we help him?"

"I think I . . . we . . ." Gripping the altar edge until his knuckles grew white, Kemal struggled to understand the barrage of emotions flooding into his mind. "I think we just remember."

"Remember what?"

"Him. Us. Brax. Our family."

"Right." Straightening, Yashar slapped his other hand down on the altar top, using the cold, hard marble as a focus. "I remember . . ." He scowled as his mind drew a blank, then his expression softened. "I remember they were so young when they first came to us. So young, but so ferocious, both of them. So certain. Facing off against the whole command council, demanding they take them in, insisting that it was Her will. Remember?"

"I remember."

"Spar hardly said a word in those early years. It was so hard to get close to him. Only Jaq could manage it at first."

Kemal nodded. "And Brax. He worked himself into exhaustion trying to live up to Her expectations until he finally understood that asking for help didn't make you weak, it made you strong."

"You told him that here. He always came here."

"And Spar always went high, to a wall or a rooftop."

"Not now."

"No."

"We should have gone with them."

Kemal closed his eyes, feeling the lien with both their delon stretch past the walls of Estavia-Sarayi to the small alcove beyond Lazim-Hisar. "We are with them."

"Will it be enough?"

Kemal nodded. "Yeah. It'll be enough."

✦

On the streets of memory, Spar felt the strength of his abayon flowing into him, and used it to force himself to rise to his knees. The nearest spirits fell back in confusion, but dozens more pressed forward. Ignoring them all, Spar scrambled about in the murky darkness until he found Brax lying, insensible, beside him. He caught him up and, holding him as tightly as Brax had once held him, sent his own power flowing down to him on the wings of a memory that had begun years ago as words from a powerful enemy lurking on the edge of his still-latent abilities.

"The Wall will not hold."

Brax stiffened with a gasp and Spar bore down, keeping their attention locked on the memory of his response.

"The Wall has always held."

"No, it hasn't and you know it."

The anger he'd felt as a delos lit up the waters with a gout of red flame as he spat out his answer in tandem with the memory.

"Brax'll be her Champion; the greatest ever since Kaptin Haldin, and he'll keep your stupid Wall from falling, you'll see!"

The certainty of his nine year old's belief merged with his fifteen year old's and within the circle of his arms, Brax opened his eyes. The twin liens to both Spar and Graize made him see double, but then, as they also merged, the image of an atlas table swam before him. The silver-cast figurine stood frozen in place, but as he watched, a stream of possibility begun on a cold, moonlit night at Serin-Koy and traveling along the strength of a family's welcome, opened up at its feet.

He followed it and Gol-Beyaz stretched out before him, its surface as calm as a sheet of clear glass. Before him, Estavia's crimson gaze bored into his, and he heard his own words spoken with an equal measure of supplication and bravado.

"*I need your help.*"

And Her response.

"*I WILL GIVE YOU WHAT YOU NEED TO BE MY CHAMPION. IN RETURN YOU WILL GIVE ME YOUR LIFE, YOUR WORSHIP, AND YOUR LAST DROP OF BLOOD TO DEFEND MY BARRIER.*"

The power of Her lien, sharp with gluttonous possession, blazed across his wrist where She'd carved the symbol of the God-Wall. It slapped across his mind with a crack of impatient reproach and he felt the warmth of understanding finally sizzle through his veins. He had not pledged his strength to Her that night, or his ability to fight, only his worship.

And his worship was everything to the Gods.

Within the circle of Spar's arms, Brax raised his hand and, as he'd done that night, dropped all pretense of strength and courage, and allowed the frightening overpowering need he'd always kept hidden fill his gaze, then shouted two words into the spirit-filled waters of Anavatan's great cistern.

"*HELP ME!*"

✦

His words shot down his lien, and in the midst of Her Bronze Company cavalry in the fields before Yildiz-Koy, Estavia snapped Her head about. Her crimson gaze tracked north, then, with a single gesture, She hurled a bolt of pure power toward Anavatan. It shot down Her liens with Kemal and Yashar hard enough to knock them both off their feet, blazed along their lien with their delon, splattering against Spar and Graize—covering them both in a thick patina of silver power—before hitting Brax full force in the chest. It flung him to his feet and, armed and armored in the seeming of Kaptin Haldin, and surrounded in a nimbus of silver light so brilliant that it almost blinded him, he threw himself at the enemy without a second's hesitation.

✦

And stood on the featureless plain of his dream five years before. The spirits came at him in twos and threes and tens and hundreds, and he slaughtered each one. As power slammed down his arm and into the gem-encrusted sword She'd given him, he laughed out loud at the strength of it. He was her Champion; Kaptin of Her Warriors, builder of her temple and Protector of her city. Beloved and favored, he could fight forever with Her power burning through his veins like fire. And he would do.

As he screamed out Her battle cry, the atlas table shattered into a thousand pieces.

✦

On the Volinski flagship deck, Illan jerked backward in surprise, his teeth snapping against his tongue. The fine spattering of blood that erupted from between his lips lit up the shattered atlas table with a new spray of possibilities that writhed out from its destruction like a nest of snakes.

Vyns stepped forward at once, but Illan snarled at him to keep back. Righting himself, he forced the image together, scrabbling through the wreckage to discover just what had occurred, and found a fine prophetic thread made of bronze-cast bells and gilded feathers leading his enemies toward a future he'd been certain they would never see.

A soft voice, thick with sadness, filled his ears.

"Missed opportunities taste like dust and the bitter, inner peel of citrus fruit, my love, and the blind ambition of kings and princes might as well be etched in stone."

✦

In the cistern, his eyes blazing as hotly as Brax's, Graize howled in triumph, before turning on the spirits attacking Hisar.

Close to the bottom of the cistern now, the Young God continued to strike out at Its enemies, screaming in both fear and anger, but Its movements were growing noticeably weaker as the spirits spun about It furiously, churning the water into a silvery froth that flashed with gold and copper power.

"Blood and gold!" Graize shouted as the water began to warp under the force of his prophetic ability, "Feed the people! Not the spirits!"

Taking hold of the dawn sun, he squeezed it until it gutted out, then spun its ashes into the vision of a darkened sky, bloated with storm clouds. Below, the waters of Gol-Bardak Lake glimmered in the dim light, casting a faint glow over the tiny Yuruk encampment on its southern shore. As sheaves of rain began to course across his face, he threw his arms wide and leaped into the memory.

Lightning flashed continuously, sending out a dozen streaks of energy at a time to scatter across the rumbling clouds. As each one touched the air, it changed the spirits of the cistern to the tiny, newborn creatures Hisar had fed upon in Its infancy. Opening his mind as wide as he'd done in the past, Graize sucked them in, feeling them fill him up with the power he'd once feared might tear him into pieces. But he was not a delos this time, battered and raw from his encounter above the wild lands; this time he was a man, a prophet, a leader, and a priest sworn to the God of Creation and Destruction. Gathering the power inside him until he was almost blinded by the copper light pouring into his eyes, he turned and spewed it down the lien toward Hisar.

It hit the young God with an impact so hard it flung It from the cistern altogether, rending the surrounding spirits into a thousand glittering shards and scattering them like glass. Drawing these pieces into his body as well, Graize spewed them down the lien toward Hisar as the young God shot into the sky above Anavatan.

As the waters of the cistern grew still, Graize then turned his attention to Brax and Spar.

With their own battle over, the two of them stared back at him, the lien they shared with each other and the lien he'd forged with Brax so many years before undulating in the waters between them. The mist-covered cobblestones of Liman Caddesi disappeared to become a snow-clad mountain ridge and, as the three of them set foot upon the path, a dense fog rose up, coiling around Graize's arms and legs until they covered him in a mantle of gray mist. The darkness behind them split apart, allowing a single tendril from Spar's own place of power to clothe him all in black, while beside them, Brax's oaths to Estavia surrounded him in a blinding silver light.

As the Gray, Black, and Silver Champions stood together for the first time in prophecy, a future stream appeared, becoming a mountain path that led to an ethereal tower flowing from golden to silver to gold again.

Graize moved toward it at once, only to lurch to a halt as a sharp pain scored his temple. He began to shake, the smell of chill, damp air assailed his nostrils, and a creeping cold began to worm its way up his limbs and pool inside his chest. He fell, to be caught in Brax's arms and in the distance, he heard shouting and the sound of frantic barking.

Spar was the first to react. Eyes as black as the midnight sky, he turned and jerking his head at Brax, he disappeared back to the physical world. Brax nodded, then catching Graize around the chest, yanked them both off the mountain path and back into the alcove.

Physical sensation returned in a painful rush, making Graize gasp out loud. His eyes snapped open, and he found himself entangled in Brax's arms. Beside him, Spar sat with his back against the wall, his own arms wrapped about the neck of a large, red dog his face pressed into its fur, while before them, a hooded youth pulled medical supplies from a wicker basket. He tried to rise, then fell back, fighting a wave of nausea as his injuries swept over him. His lien with Brax sent a fine tendril of strength to calm his mind, but in this world, his arms and legs trembled with fatigue and his head throbbed with pain as his own power continued to pour down his lien with Hisar as the young God began to manifest above the towers and minarets of Anavatan.

17

The God of Creation and Destruction

SNAPPING FROM SEEMING TO seeming, Hisar ricocheted across the clouds, then froze as a bolt of lightning hit a minaret directly in front of It. The flash of orange fire lit up Its face as It changed to Its golden-seeming, Spar's blond hair sticking up in all directions and Graize's gray eyes wide in Brax's face. He spun slowly in midair, growing larger with every turn until His feet finally hit the ground, one landing on the roof of the cistern entrance, the other planted on His temple site, His head and shoulders a full ten feet above the tallest of the city's minarets.

His expression suffused with hunger, He bent and drove His hand through the cistern roof, drawing up the last handful of spirits from the depths and pouring them into His mouth until they spilled down his chin and chest in rivulets of silver-and-copper light.

This time they fed him as they should, and sated for the moment, He turned to stare about Him with wondering eyes as the events taking place across the length of Gol-Beyaz came to Him in near painful clarity as if played out directly in front of Him.

Above, the sky rumbled with continuous thunder. Rain scored against His skin, sending burning trails of power along his legs to pool about His feet. Below, the alarm bells continued to toll as, in the strait, Illan's brown-winged bird-ships spat flaming arrows at the pentecont-ers of Anavatan, setting their decks alight, and far to the south, the white bird-ships of King Pyrros came in close to make the most of their bronze-cast rams, while on the western lands, the horses made of mist and grass engaged the militia and Warriors of Estavia.

Throughout, the Gods of Anavatan fought beside Their people, each one granting them the power of His other domain.

The God of Art and Music, Her silken gown whirling about Her like a multicolored maelstrom, sang one continuous note into the air, amplifying the Invocations of Her priests until their combined voices battered against the clouds in a thunderous call to arms.

The God of Seasonal Bounty, sides rippling with green and brown power, stalked the village pasturelands, drawing up the slender grasses to catch at the hooves of the Petchan and Yuruk ponies and snatch their riders from their backs.

The God of Healing darted here and there, pouring a power as blue as a summer sky into His physicians as they tended to the wounded on every battlefield, while the Hearth God raced from rooftop to rooftop, putting out the enemy fire with great gouts of water drawn up from Gol-Beyaz.

And through it all, the God of Battle's spinning blades scythed a path of destruction through the enemy, north to south.

But the enemies were many, and, moment by moment, the fleets pushed farther into the silver lake and the charging horses drew closer to the God-Wall of stone and power.

Hisar's golden brows pulled down into a deep vee as He swept His gaze from side to side and finally lit upon a single, ice-pale figure standing in the very center of Gol-Beyaz. Incasa.

The God of Prophecy stood immobile, a hundred feet above the glittering surface, His long white hair spread across His shoulders like a cloak, and His opalescent dice were held high in one fine-boned hand. Eddies of power swirled about His feet, like drifts of snow in a winter storm, and as He turned His frosted gaze upon Hisar, the young God felt a gust of frigid air puff across His cheek.

They stared at each other for what seemed like an eternity. The God of Prophecy's expression remained impassive even as a catapulted shot from the midst of the Volinski rearguard fleet hit the watch fire atop Gerek-Hisar, showering the roof of the nearby Incasa-Cami with a spray of flaming coals.

Hisar reared back, His golden eyes blazing.

"DO SOMETHING," He shouted, using the power of the spirits that still flowed through His seeming to launch His voice across the water.

Incasa jiggled the dice in His palm with deliberate care, then arched one pale eyebrow in the young God's direction.

"YOU DO SOMETHING," He countered.

"WHAT?!"

The older God's expression grew bored, and He turned His head to watch, with apparent engrossed interest, the battle going on in the waters before Satos-Koy.

King Pyrros' first line of triremes had come in hard in line ahead, counting on their superior size to drive a hole in the defensive force of lighter penteconters. A rain of arrow fire peppered them from Anahtar-Hisar, but then the lead trireme had rammed its counterpart and back oared to disengage. Its complement of hoplites had hurled their javelins into the defending oarsmen and then, with chaos erupting on the Anav-atanon ship, the trireme had shot past toward the shore.

Hisar bared His teeth at Incasa in frustration, then swung His gaze down as the Volinski vanguard fleet, whistled orders flying thick and fast, sailed into the mouth of Gol-Beyaz. To Hisar's left, the barge pulling the sea chain across the Halic hadn't quite made it two thirds across, and as He watched, the Volinski catapults now turned its way.

Hisar took a step into the surf beyond His temple site, then jerked back as the sudden half-physical, half-ethereal shock of the Gods' unwelcomingly cold water slapped against His calf.

The whistled order came again, the catapults were loaded, and Hisar snapped His head back and forth, unsure of what to do. His first instinct was to change seemings and flee down to the alcove and demand advice from Spar, or even Brax, but with the spirits of the cistern spent, and only two priests wholly sworn to send Him strength, He was afraid He'd never be able to manifest this powerfully again.

His gaze flickered to Incasa once more, but the older God was now watching the battle going on in the fields before Bahce-Koy, and did not return His gaze. Balling His hands into fists, Hisar stepped back into the water and, ignoring the freezing-then-burning sensations that traveled up His legs, He waded into Gol-Beyaz.

The Anavatanon penteconters were between Him and the Volinski dromon galleys, but as His eyes darted back and forth, He caught a glimmer of stone shining beneath the waves at His feet. Reaching down, He drew up a fist-sized chunk of blue-tinged yellow marble, the silver power of the Gods etched like a patina across its surface. Its weight felt heavy against His palm, and it took all His concentrated focus to hold it in midair. As the first of the catapults shot their payload at the barge, He almost dropped it, but the cries of alarm from the nearby pentecenters steadied Him. Screwing up his face in concentration, He leaned back, then hurled the marble with all His might at the Volinski fleet.

It hit one of the lead ships with a crash, smashing into the steering oar mounted beneath the sterncastle.

Hisar showed His teeth in feral pleasure as the cries of alarm turned to cheers. Twisting His body, He reached out and, with as much care as possible, took hold of the barge pulling the sea chain and drew it forward until He beached it on the shore before the iron bollard. Then he reeled backward as the strength He'd used to accomplish both in the physical world left Him in a rush. His need for power shot down His lien with Spar, pulling as much as He dared from His First Priest as He staggered back out of the water, nearly spent. With His golden-seeming flickering dangerously, He reached out again, this time traveling down a familiar lien. Graize accepted His Presence with only the slightest hesitation and, with a grateful cry, Hisar caught his abayos' injured mind up in His own and hurled them both into the clouds.

In the alcove, Graize collapsed like an unstrung puppet.

✦

Out on the Volinski flagship, Illan snarled silently as Hisar's latest move threatened to shatter his atlas table once again. The game was far from over, whatever the young God and Its champions might believe, he growled as he struggled to keep the pieces fused together. Panos' interference had provided them with a few extra moves, but nothing more than that.

The thought of his lover's betrayal caused the pieces to slide away from each other once again and, with a sharp gesture, he jerked them back into position. Whatever her reasons—and he would discover them soon enough—they would not change the endgame. That had been determined years ago. Volinsk would defeat Anavatan and the ghost of Duc Leold's failure would forever be forgotten in the wake of Prince Illan's victory.

Slamming the four pieces back onto the board, he scrutinized their new positions, then motioned Vyns to his side.

"My lord?"

"Inform Prince Pieter that prophecy has thrown up a new target, rich in possibilities, and that he should bring the van's weapons to bear against it with all possible speed."

"And the target, my lord?"

"I will direct him to it if he will attend me on the forecastle."

"At once, my lord."

After a swift consultation, the whistled orders went out again, and the main bulk of the Volinski vanguard fleet suddenly turned hard to stern, heading straight for the tip of the Western Trisect in line abreast. The weapons crews scrambled to load their catapults and, when the order was given, fired a full volley at a small area just north of Lazim-Hisar.

✦

In the alcove, Kez spun about as a series of heavy explosions rocked the walls of the cistern. A line of dust and grit pattered down on them and Brax swiftly covered Graize's face with his cloak.

"What was that?" she demanded.

Spar turned, his eyes as white as Incasa's own. "Illan of Volinsk," he answered, his voice hollow. When she continued to stare at him, he shook his head to clear it. "A really powerful seer . . ."

"And a really personal enemy," Brax added.

"From the beginning," Spar agreed weakly. "He's seen us in prophecy. He's directed the attack . . . against us." His head fell back against his arm.

"From the *strait*?"

Kez's voice was incredulous and Brax shook his head. "From Gol-Beyaz by the sound of it. Ship-borne catapults couldn't reach this far from the strait."

"What about Estavia's fleet? Why aren't they stopping them?"

"They must have fallen back or been taken by surprise." Brax placed his hand on his chest and closed his eyes. The God's Presence buzzed against his fingertips and, in the far recesses of his mind, he saw the southern tower of Alev-Hisar. "The Skirosian fleet has broken through the line and is heading for the Ekmir-Koy. The Battle God's joined the fighting there."

"Wonderful," Kez sneered. "Gods. There's never one around when you need one."

Brax opened his eyes as Spar made a faint noise.

"You all right?"

His kardos reached out blindly and, catching Jaq by the collar, used the dog's stability to pull his head upright. "There is," he slurred, his face paling almost as white as his eyes. ". . . a God here. Hisar's here. Drawin" power. Needs power . . ." his voice trailed off.

"Hisar?"

"Fightin' the Volinski fleet. He . . . we . . . need to help him."

"We need to get out of here, is what we need to do," Kez snapped as a second series of explosions sounded even closer than the last. As another rain of dust and grit spattered over them, she ran to the entrance and peered out cautiously. "Can we get out of range?" she asked, glancing back at Brax with a strained expression.

"They can't get up the Halic if the sea chain's in place," he answered. "Is it?"

Spar nodded groggily. "He doesn' know th' streets," he slurred. "Illan. His prophecy won' find us in th' streets. Too narrow . . . too many people pressin' in on th' future streams. Need to get lost in . . ." He blinked rapidly as his eyes went from white to black in an instant. "Dockside."

Brax gave him a worried look. "Can *you* make it to Dockside."

"Yeah. With help."

"Right." He stood. "Kez and Jaq'll help you. I'll help Graize." Stooping, he lifted the other man up and over one shoulder. "Come on, let's get out of here before they have time to reload."

He straightened with a grunt, heading out the door and up the stairs at once. Spar followed, one hand on Kez's arm and the other still clutching Jaq's collar. As they emerged onto the rain-splattered streets, both kardon glanced back to see Hisar, swaying a hundred feet into the air, eyes half closed, arms spread wide, seeming flickering from gold to silver to gold again.

"Move now, stare later!" Kez snarled, pulling their attention back to earth. But as they plunged down a narrow close, both risked another backward glance.

✦

Wrapped in the young God's mind, Graize felt his grip on his own body fade. They seemed to go on forever, growing larger and larger until their heads touched the clouds. Beneath their feet, he could see the temples, homes, and warehouses of Anavatan laid out like little boxes, the cobblestone streets weaving between them like lengths of twine. Thunder rumbled in the distance, a streak of lightning lit up the sky, illuminating the God-Wall glowing with its customary afternoon blue and inlaid with streaks of silver that shone to Graize's God-enhanced vision.

He laughed out loud. He felt bloated with power and potential. And yet, on the very edge of being, he felt strained and stretched to the breaking point. He ignored it. Far to the south, he felt a stirring of alarm and then a sudden tugging in his groin. He looked down.

A copper thread of power, little more than a breath of possibility and fine as a strand of spider webbing, stretched between him and a tiny figure fighting on horseback in the fields of Bahce-Koy. It held his attention as nothing else had and, little by little, he felt it drawing him back to himself.

He disengaged from Hisar so fast that the young God staggered backward and, in the streets, both he and Spar cried out as the bulk of Hisar's power drain transferred from one to the other.

Spar stumbled and would have fallen if Jaq hadn't shoved himself in front of him.

Kez pulled him back upright. "How far?" she shouted.

Brax just shook his head. Behind them, he heard the sound of another volley hitting the area around the cistern's entrance and turned suddenly to stumble down an alleyway behind two warehouses.

"The way to blind a seer . . ." Brax panted. "Is to act unpredictably."

"For how long?!"

"For as long as we can."

"That's not gonna be much longer," she groused as she shifted Spar's weight across her shoulders. "He's gettin' heavier."

✦

Above the city, Hisar turned blazing eyes on the Volinski fleet. His merging with Graize's abilities had given him the understanding of Illan's purpose, and He would not suffer it to be. He only had two sworn and he would not allow the foreign seer to threaten them.

Growling low in his throat, He stepped back into the waters of Gol-Beyaz.

✦

On the streets, Brax turned and caught Spar under the arm with his free hand as they emerged from the alleyway and onto a wider, cobblestone street. It marched due north to open up on the sandy shore of the Halic Salmanak and, as they hurried along it, Brax glanced about him with a frown of recognition. But it was only when they reached the dilapidated wharf that he rocked to a halt.

Kez glared at him. "What? Why are we stopping? Are we resting?"

He narrowed his eyes. The upturned fishing boat was long since gone, but the wharf on Liman Caddesi looked much the same as it had six years ago. He nodded with a resigned expression.

"I guess we weren't so unpredictable after all," he noted.

"What?"

"Nothing. Yeah, we're resting."

Laying Graize down as gently as he could, he covered him with his cloak, then assisted Kez in setting Spar down beside him. Jaq immediately took up position beside the youth, and as the dog pressed against his side, Spar's arm snaked out to wrap around his neck. He opened his eyes.

"Hisar needs power," he whispered.

Brax crouched down beside him. "You said that before," he answered, moving a lock of plastered hair from his kardos' face. "Looks like He's already taking more than His fair share."

"He needs more."

"There's no more to be had. Graize is unconscious and you're close to it."

"He's going after Illan through Gol-Beyaz."

"Then He'll get power from Gol-Beyaz."

Spar shook his head. "He can't. He's not . . ." He struggled to find the right words, then just slumped.

"He's not a real God yet?" Brax hazarded.

"No."

"So, how do we make him a real God?"

"You Invoke Him."

They both turned to glance at Kez who glared at them.

"What? That's what you do for Gods, isn't it? That's what the priests at Dockside's Oristo-Cami say. When the Gods need power Their priests call for an Invocation an' Their worshipers send Them what They need to manifest."

Spar waved a weak hand in Graize's direction. "We're Hisar's only priests and He hasn't got any worshipers."

"Horseshit. He has dozens of worshipers. He has had for weeks." Turning, she pulled her knife and drove the tip into the wharf, scratching out the four lines that made up the simplest of the tower symbols. "Just because we haven't sworn officially doesn't mean we aren't worshipers. Besides, He saved Zeno. Everybody knows that. We owe Him."

She sheathed the knife with a snap. "You call. We'll answer."

Straightening painfully, Spar draw Jaq closer to his side. "All right," he panted. "But if I'm gonna . . . do this I can't do it . . . by myself. I'm gonna need Graize's help." He gave a cynical snort that took years off his age. "Ever think you'd hear me say that?" he asked Brax.

The older man just gave a snort of his own. "Can you get him woken up or do you need my help?"

"I need your help."

"How?"

"You need to go back to the mountain ridge."

Brax sighed. "Figures. I was kinda hoping you just needed me to slap him."

"No such luck."

"Right." Sitting down with his back against the bank, Brax pulled his own, larger, heavier knife from his belt. "Keep an eye out," he said, handing it to Kez. "We won't be able to defend ourselves if anyone comes on us."

"Who'd *come on* us," she demanded in a sarcastic voice. "You're wearing Estavia's leather cuirass."

"Better safe than sorry."

"Sure. Whatever." Accepting the weapon, she made herself comfortable where she could see both up the street and along the shore. "Go ahead. I've got your backs."

Nodding, Brax pulled his sword, laid it close beside him, then after lifting Graize until he was tucked under his arm, he closed his eyes, and as he'd done in the alcove, reached out along his oaths to the God of Battles for his visions of Kaptin Haldin. Spar began to sing the single note of Hisar's Invocation, and beside him he felt Graize stiffen and then relax as the music took him.

✦

Far away, Graize floated easily beside the copper thread, unwilling to be drawn away, but slowly, very slowly he heard a single note sung into the distant darkness. It called to him along a path of power and obligation and reluctantly at first, he followed it.

✦

And stepped back onto the snow-clad mountain ridge. Brax, wrapped in silver light and overlaid by the seeming of Graize's dark-haired boy, stood to one side of him. Spar, wearing the midnight robes of a seer over a golden tunic shot with greenish threads stood to the other. Before them, the shimmering tower that was Hisar moved from gold to silver to gold again but then, as Spar pressed his hand against his chest and sang one long clear note into the crimson air, the silver began to overtake the gold.

✦

Wading hip-deep in Gol-Beyaz, Hisar paused as a thread of silver power began to travel up His body.

✦

On the mountain ridge, Graize stared into the sun as a hundred streams appeared before him, drawn to the surface of his prophecy by the sense of urgency in Spar's song. The past, the present, and the future; streams upon streams upon streams, reaching out into the darkness. But one shone brighter than the others. It began in a mist-shrouded doorway and flowed unimpeded to a sea of possibilities. With a sigh of weary acceptance, he reached for it.

"*That one. Give me that one.*"

And, pressing his own hand to his chest, joined his voice to Spar's.

✦

Their song moved out past Liman Caddesi, past Hisar's unfinished temple site, and out across Anavatan. The strength of its call caught the young God up, shifting and merging His seeming until It became a vast tower of gold and silver, standing like a bastion between the Volinski fleet and the people of Anavatan.

And the people responded. Hisar's people. Lifters, beggars, tricksters, students, apprentices, and laborers, the unsworn youth of a dozen precincts, stood by the carved tower offerings that had turned an entire city into a temple and stared up at their young God of Creation and Destruction. One by one, they joined their voices to their two young priests, until finally Kez stood and shouted a simple oath into the wind, echoing the words Graize had shouted on the grasslands nine months before.

"Mine! My God!"

Hisar's tower-seeming exploded in a spray of golden fire, flickering from male to female, to both, and back again, faster and faster, as each one of His young followers added their oaths to their leader's.

"MINE! MY GOD!"

He rose higher and higher, then, twisted about in midair to stare at the six great statues standing guard above the Gods' temples. She gestured and a golden tunic, streaked with threads of green, flowed suddenly about His chest and down Her hips, a red and silver-flecked bead appearing on a hide cord about His neck. Her thick, blonde hair grew longer, spilling down over His shoulders to fall into Her pale gray eyes, the pupil of the right ever so slightly smaller than the left. A scattering of fine copper whiskers spread across His olive cheeks tinged with honey-gold and silver, and down Her arms and legs in a fine down. A pair of military sandals wrapped about His feet, the cords spinning up Her calves as a copper belt wrapped about His waist with a scabarded silver sword on one side and a golden knife on the other. In one hand, She held a pair of wooden soldier's dice and with the other, He reached down to stroke one fingertip along Jaq's forehead and the dog woofed a greeting at Her as She straightened. And stared out across the water, Graize's prophecy blazing in His eyes.

A single future streamed out before Her and, with one move, He stepped over the gathered penteconters. For a single instant, She and Illan stared into each other's eyes, the ghost of Leold Volinsk shimmering in the air between them, then, as His people's Invocation built to a crescendo, She closed Her fist around the dice and drove it through the center of the Volinski flagship. As the atlas table shattered into a thousand pieces, the vessel cracked in half, the sterncastle and forecastle nearly meeting in the middle before being sucked to the bottom by a sudden vortex of silver power.

Hisar stared at the wreckage for half a heartbeat, and then opening Her hand, scooped up half a hundred oarsmen struggling in the water and set them gently on the shore by His temple site, then turned Her gaze on His city.

"*THE BOUNTY OF HISARO: CREATION AND DESTRUCTION IN EQUAL MEASURE!*" He shouted, preening as the sound of cheering echoed across the water, then turned again, and dove headfirst into the center of Gol-Beyaz, splattering Incasa in a shower of silver surf.

✦

On the southern shore of the Northern Trisect, Panos swayed, pressing against a wooden pier, her expression grieving. Beside her, Hares touched her shoulder gently but said nothing.

"I saw it," she said, her usually musical voice thick with unshed tears. "Towers. Rigidity and the blind ambitions of kings and princes."

They stood together for a long time, watching as both the dromon galleys and the pentecenters moved in to gather up the survivors from the flagship, then the artist stirred.

"What do we do now, Oracle?" he asked quietly.

Panos turned her gaze to the south. "Now?" she echoed, her black eyes shrouded. "Now we go home."

"To Skiros, Oracle?"

Drawing the cloak more tightly about her, she shook her head. "No, Hares. I have done my duty by king and father. He has all he could wish for now. Volinsk and Anavatan are weakened equally and he will soon have his free and open trade and access from the southern sea to the northern. May it give him pleasure," she added bitterly.

"You *have* seen this?" he asked.

"I *have* seen *this*," she answered, setting her usual metaphors aside. "The young God has entered the field of battle and so the Yuruk and Petchan raiders will withdraw. With half the royal family of Rostov and Volinsk drowned, their fleet captains will sue for terms. King Pyrros will row his royal trireme up the singing silver lake to its shining capital, and meet with Anavatan's governing council."

She paused, staring into the distance for a long time. Beside her, Hares waited patiently and eventually she drew herself up with a sigh. "And we, Hares," she continued, "we will go home to the warm, white shores and glittering green-gem waters of Amatus. And there, amidst the scents of olive trees and grapevines, and the cries of sweetmeat sellers and wine merchants, I will find a humble artisan, priest, or poet to fill my heart and warm my bed and lose myself in its mountains and harbors forever. I am done with royal fathers and with royal lovers. They ask too much and they give too little."

She fell silent once again until her retinue began to shiver in the rain, then she stood with a determined expression. "Come, Hares. Let us find a boat to take us across the Halic. I fear I must attend my father once more before I'm finished. We must seek refuge at Incasa-Sarayi while we await his arrival."

"They will grant us access, Oracle?"

"Oh, yes. They have already seen it."

"Yes, Oracle."

As Panos led the way to the water's edge, she deliberately turned her gaze from the five small figures crouched wearily beneath a wharf on the opposite shore.

✦

Finally the smallest of them stirred.

"Come on," Kez said in an authorative tone. "We still have to get this one somewhere warm and dry or he'll die of his injuries." She jerked a thumb at Graize.

Brax shook himself. "Right." Standing, he reached down and drew Graize up on his feet. The other man weaved groggily, then allowed Brax to put a steadying arm around his shoulders with only a faint hesitation. Brax turned to Spar. "Can you walk?"

His kardos nodded ruefully. "With help." Catching hold of Jaq's collar, he drew one finger along the silver streak emblazed across his forehead with a wondering smile. "Good thing I had all that practice painting that dog symbol on me for all these years," he said in a fond voice.

Jaq woofed at him, then moved forward, drawing the youth up behind him. Spar allowed Kez to throw a hand out to steady him, then together, they left the cobblestone streets of Liman Caddesi behind and made for the warm kitchen fire at Estavia-Sarayi.

Behind them, the youth of Anavatan waited until the sky calmed and the ripples of Hisar's entry into Gol-Beyaz stilled, before returning to their own lives, and Estavia's navy herded the ruins of Illan of Volinsk's invasion fleet into port.

18

Hisaro-Sarayi

BRAX STOOD HIGH ON a rocky promontory above the hospital village of Calmak-Koy watching, as across the strait, the construction of Hisaro-Sarayi came to a close for another day. With the threat of invasion past, the work had progressed quickly; in the last four weeks the foundations had been laid and the walls begun. If he squinted past the late afternoon sun, he could just make out Spar and Hisar standing talking—or rather arguing—with Kez about one or another of the many details.

He chuckled and, standing beside him, Graize turned his own head. "What?"

"Nothing."

Graize glanced away.

The two men had managed an awkward peace as the three fleets anchored in the waters below, but like them, they also had some skillful negotiators at their side. Although Spar had refused to get involved, Hisar had hotly declared that He had no intention of allowing their old rivalry to jeopardize the strength of His new temple and they had better go and have some proper sex right now. And Kez had also declared—no less hotly—that she had better things to do than be a matchmaker, she had a temple to build. But she had spent a fair amount of time hovering about Graize's sickbed anyway, assuring herself that Brax spent at least as much time beside it as she did.

But it wasn't until Kemal and Yashar had taken Brax aside that he'd actually started thinking past the realization that he and Graize no longer wanted to kill each other.

✦

Throwing himself down on a stone bench in the hospice herb garden, Kemal had smiled fondly at his oldest delos. "Did you know that when I first met Yash, I thought he was a bombastic, irresponsible trouble-maker?" he asked with a laugh.

The older man snorted. "And I though he was a stiff-necked, bossy little know-it-all." He dropped down beside the other man, shoving at him until he made room for them both. "Not much has changed, yeah?"

"Yeah."

Brax turned to stare back toward the hospice. "This is a bit different, Aban," he replied.

"Is it?" Yashar demanded.

Kemal cocked his head to one side. "You're not attracted to each other? Hisaro seemed to think you are?"

Brax blinked. He still wasn't used to the young God's new name. To him He would always be just Hisar, a special and private diminutive.

"Hisaro thinks everyone is attracted to everyone," he answered.

"Maybe so." Kemal gave him a pointed look. "But you didn't answer my question."

Brax made a neutral face. "Maybe," he allowed. "But I'm attracted to a lot of people."

"And a lot of people are attracted to you," Yashar noted. "Admitting an attraction to Graize doesn't have to make the two of you exclusive, you know."

"I know."

"Do you not want him?" Kemal pressed.

Brax shrugged. "I don't know. I feel like I might, but . . ."

"But?"

"Maybe, it's too soon. Maybe he doesn't want me."

"Again, Hisaro says he does."

"Hisaro is *five years old*. What does Hisaro know?" He grimaced. "How long did it take you two?"

"To realize it, or to actualize it?" Yashar asked.

Brax blinked.

"To know it or to act on it?" his abayos amended with a sigh.

"Oh. To act on it."

The older man leaned back, running his fingers through the sides of his beard. "Two weeks?" He glanced at his arkados.

Kemal nodded. "Yeah. About two weeks."

"That's not very long," Brax pointed out and Kemal just shrugged.

"Why wait?" He stood. "I'm sorry, but we should get back, Braxin-Delin," he said. "I have to be at Assembly first thing tomorrow morning."

"They're using proxy-beys for the negotiations now?" Brax asked with some surprise.

"No. But the temples expect a show of strength, so the galleries are to be filled. Every day." He sighed. "You'll be expected by week's end, too, you know, you and Graize both, and before I hear any complaints," he added sternly as Brax opened his mouth to protest, "you should know that Spar's been attending every Negotiation Assembly since they began."

Brax waved a dismissive hand at him. "So? He's a First Priest. I'm just a humble Ghazi Ikin-Kaptin."

"You're Estavia's Champion," Yashar replied, "and the Protector of Anavatan. You'll be there."

"Yes, Aba."

"That's better."

They each gave him their own version of a good-bye hug: Yashar's hard enough to squeeze the breath out of him, and Kemal's more gentle. Then, side by side, the two arkadon made their way down to the small wharf below Calmak-Koy.

Brax stood, staring out across the herb garden for the longest time, breathing in the scents of lavender, calendula, and peppermint and debating their words with himself.

"Why wait?" he muttered. "Why? I dunno? Fear, maybe?"

Estavia's presence thrummed against his chest, traveling down until it became an itch between his legs and he nodded in resignation.

"All right," he amended. *"Not fear, anymore."*

Taking a deep breath, he headed back to Graize's sickbed.

✦

That night, after an equally awkward beginning, they finally came together with enough passion to satisfy even Hisaro.

Now they stood, staring out across the strait, listening as the priests of Havo began the first note of the Evening's Invocations.

Graize's lip drew up in a faint sneer. "I always hated doing this at Oristo-Cami," he noted, more to himself than to the other man.

Brax just shrugged. "I never did it at all until I came to Estavia-Sarayi."

"But you did it willingly."

"Yeah. An unwilling follower brings the Gods no strength," he intoned.

"Sure. Tell that to the Abayos-Priests of Oristo."

Both men shared a cynical snort worthy of Spar before returning their attention to the Evening Invocations, watching as first Havo, then Oristo, then Usara rose from the depths of Gol-Beyaz as gracefully as a flock of swans. All the Gods had been manifesting above the walls of their temples every morning and every evening since the invasion fleets had broken off their attacks; another show of strength to press home the point that Anavatan was not, and never would be, defeated. By anyone.

As the God of Healing took His place beside His temple statue, Brax took a step forward. He felt Estavia's presence build inside him even before the singing began and, adding his voice to his fellow priests, he tipped his head back as She filled him from head to foot with a sizzling power so strong it made him shake as if he were having a seizure. She rose from the waters directly in front him, stretching a hundred feet into the air and he threw his arms wide in a greeting no less intimate. He took one step forward, and then another, teetering precariously close to the edge of the promontory. The expression in Estavia's crimson eyes grew feral and hotly possessive. They stood poised together, God and Champion, for the space of a single heartbeat, then She released him. As She turned and stepped onto Her temple battlements, Brax slumped, panting, to the ground.

Graize eyed him with a cold expression. "I think She's trying to make me jealous," he groused.

Brax grinned up at him. "Wait till it's your turn. Hisaro'll be up in a moment."

Across the strait, Ystazia joined Estavia above the city skyline, twirling Her multicolored skirts as fast as the God of Battles twirled Her silver swords. Then the priests of Incasa began their own solemn chanting.

The God of Prophecy rose slowly above the waves of the silver lake without even a ripple to mark His passage, His snow-white hair swirled about His face, then settled across His shoulders as His gaze, both serene and satisfied, swept across Anavatan. He held this pose, as frozen as a statue made of glass, until the last note of His Invocation faded then, with a single, delicate step, He took His place on the top His temple wall.

"Get ready," Brax noted.

"Shut up."

Stepping forward, Graize stared across the water at Spar, standing in the center of Hisar's temple site. As the two of them began to sing the Evening Invocation almost in competition with each other, Brax felt the wind rise up to slap his hair into his face, then, between one heartbeat and the next, the young God of Creation and Destruction exploded from the depths of Gol-Beyaz in a vast spray of silvery water.

Stretching up and up until He towered hundreds of feet above the surface, Hisaro then shot into the sky, throwing His arms wide enough to take in both Graize and Spar, before snapping back and forth from the male form to the female form, to both, to neither and back again. With a great swoop, He made for the Temple Precinct, buzzed the spire atop the Derneke-Mahalle Citadel, then headed back to spin around and around the older Gods until Oristo took an impatient swipe at Him, then landed on the top of Lazim-Hisar with a force hard enough to send a dozen lake gulls squawking and flapping indignantly into the sky.

Beside him, Graize staggered forward. "Show-off," he muttered as Brax threw a hand to catch him.

"Always." Brax cocked his head to one side with a slight frown. "Hisaro hasn't taken the watchtower, has He?"

Graize shook his head. "No, but you know how He . . . She . . . He is—I wish She'd stop doing that—" he growled. "You know how *He* hates for anyone to stand higher than . . . *Her*."

Together, the two men watched as the newest member of Anavatan's pantheon flapped Her arms back at the gulls, then gave a laugh so loud, it ricocheted off the low-lying clouds. Then Brax, Ghazi-Priest of Estavia-Sarayi, and Graize, First Abayos-Priest of Hisaro-Sarayi, turned, and side by side, made their own way down to the small wharf below Calmak-Koy, heading for their respective temples.

Across the water, the storks of the Northern Trisect sat peacefully on their nests and on the shore before Hisaro-Sarayi, a white cat, hunted sand crabs in the surf.